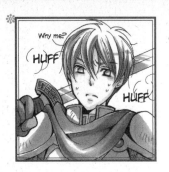

Yuki Kure made her debut in 2000
with the story *Chijo yori Eien ni*
(Forever from the Earth), published
in monthly *LaLa* magazine.
La Corda d' Oro is her first manga
series published. Her hobbies are
watching soccer games and
collecting small goodies.

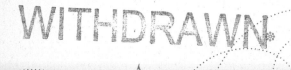

LA CORDA D'ORO
Vol. 14
Shojo Beat Edition

STORY AND ART BY
YUKI KURE
ORIGINAL CONCEPT BY
RUBY PARTY

English Translation & Adaptation/Mai Ihara
Touch-up Art & Lettering/HudsonYards
Design/Amy Martin
Editor/Shaenon K. Garrity

First published in Japan in 2010 by HAKUSENSHA, Inc., Tokyo.
English language translation rights arranged with HAKUSENSHA, Inc., Tokyo.

Printed in Canada

Published by VIZ Media, LLC
P.O. Box 77010
San Francisco, CA 94107

10 9 8 7 6 5 4 3 2 1
First printing, September 2011

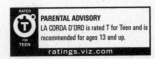

Shojo Beat

La Corda d'Or

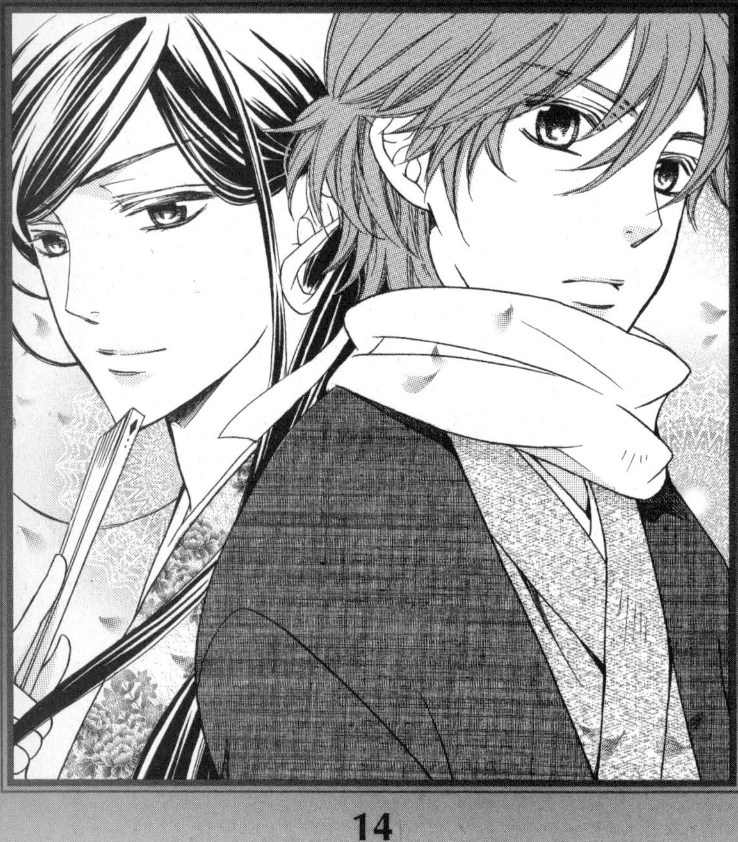

14

Story & Art by Yuki Kure

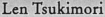

Characters

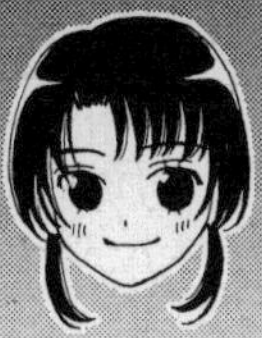

Kahoko Hino
(General Education School, 2nd year)

The heroine. After participating in the school music competition with a magic violin, she discovers a love for music.

Len Tsukimori
(Music School, 2nd year)

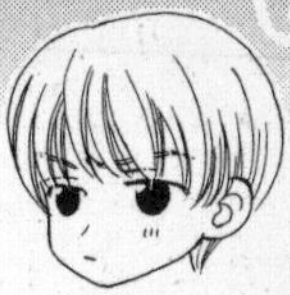

A violin major and a cold perfectionist from a musical family of unquestionable talent.

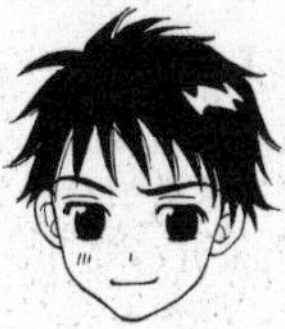

Ryotaro Tsuchiura
(General Education School, 2nd year)

A soccer player and talented pianist who seems to be looking after Kahoko.

Keiichi Shimizu
(Music School, 1st year)

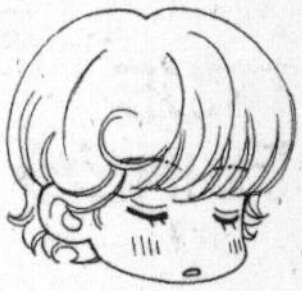

A cello major who walks to the beat of his own drum and is often lost in the world of music. He is also often asleep.

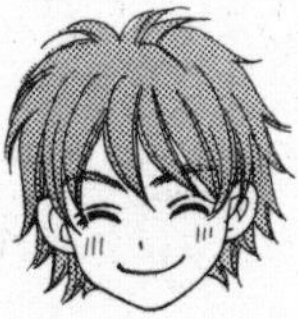

Kazuki Hihara
(Music School, 3rd year)

An energetic and friendly trumpet major and a fan of anything fun.

Azuma Yunoki
(Music School, 3rd year)

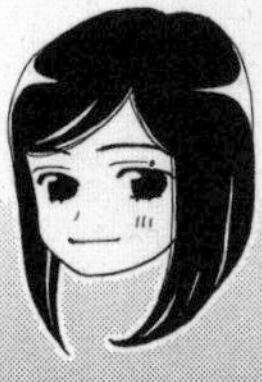

A flute major from an ultra-traditional family who's very popular with girls. Only Kahoko knows that he has a dark side!

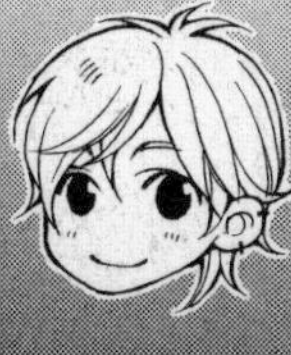

Aoi Kaji
(General Education School, 2nd year)

A handsome guy who just transferred to Seisou. It seems like he's always hanging around Kahoko.

Story

Our story is set at Seisou Academy, which is split into the General Education School and the Music School. Kahoko, a Gen Ed student, encounters a music fairy named Lili who gives her a magic violin that anyone can play. Suddenly Kahoko finds herself in the school's music competition, with good-looking, quirky Music School students as her fellow contestants! At the end of the competition the violin loses its power and disappears, but Kahoko decides to continue studying music.

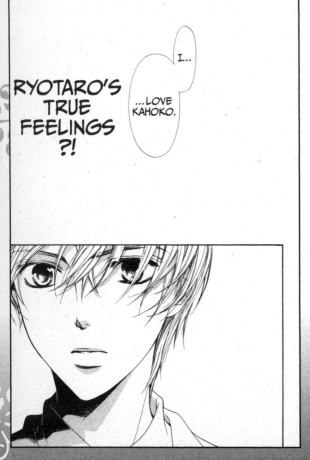

Previously...

Kahoko begins training for a demanding music competition to earn the right to study under the great instructor Mr. Saotome. Meanwhile, new transfer student Aoi has thrown Kahoko's circle of friends into chaos...

I...
...LOVE KAHOKO.
RYOTARO'S TRUE FEELINGS ?!

The music fairly, Lili, who got Kahoko caught up in this affair. ↓

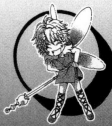

La Corda d'Oro

CONTENTS
Volume 14

Measure 59 7

Sports Festival Special Edition 39

Measure 60 55

Measure 61 87

School Festival Special Edition 119

Measure 62 135

La Corda d'Oro 2
Special Edition 167

Postscript 184

End Notes 187

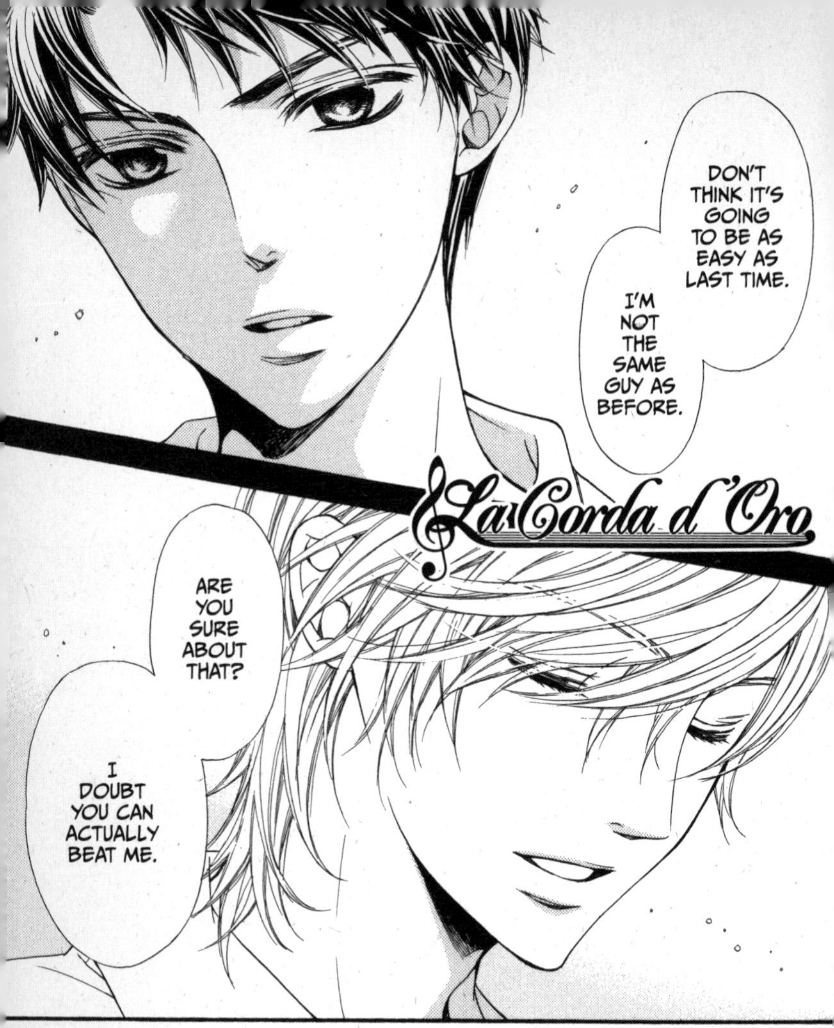
DON'T THINK IT'S GOING TO BE AS EASY AS LAST TIME.
I'M NOT THE SAME GUY AS BEFORE.
La Corda d'Oro
ARE YOU SURE ABOUT THAT?
I DOUBT YOU CAN ACTUALLY BEAT ME.

Daily Happenings 46
Covers...

Often, when I'm shopping for manga, I accidentally buy the same volume twice. Sometimes even three times! This happens even when the cover illustrations are totally different. I hear it's a common problem, so I'm a little worried that people will do this with La Corda. Especially lately, since I've done so many covers with twosomes. This volume, though, is Kazuki's revenge. I know his expression is totally out of character.

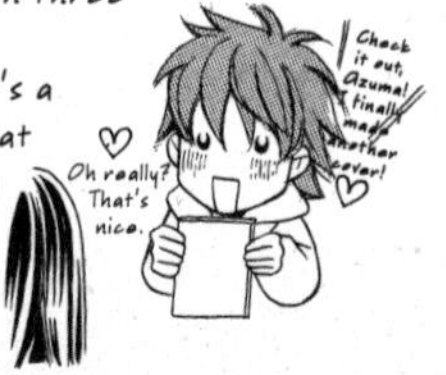
Check it out, Azuma! I finally made another cover!
Oh really? That's nice.

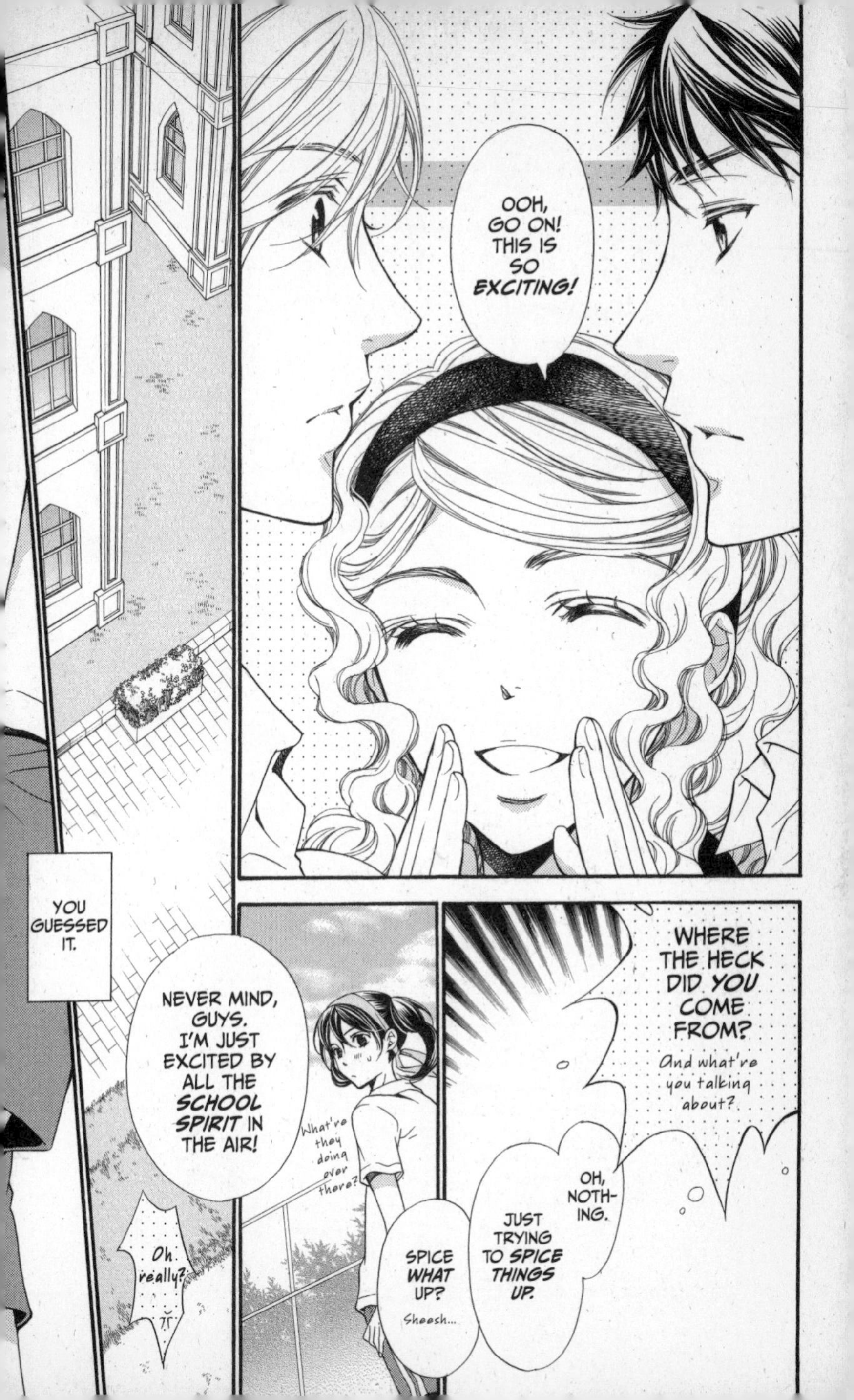
OOH, GO ON! THIS IS SO *EXCITING!*
WHERE THE HECK DID *YOU* COME FROM?
And what're you talking about?
OH, NOTHING.
JUST TRYING TO *SPICE THINGS UP.*
SPICE *WHAT* UP?
Sheesh...
What're they doing over there?
NEVER MIND, GUYS. I'M JUST EXCITED BY ALL THE *SCHOOL SPIRIT* IN THE AIR!
YOU GUESSED IT.
Oh really?

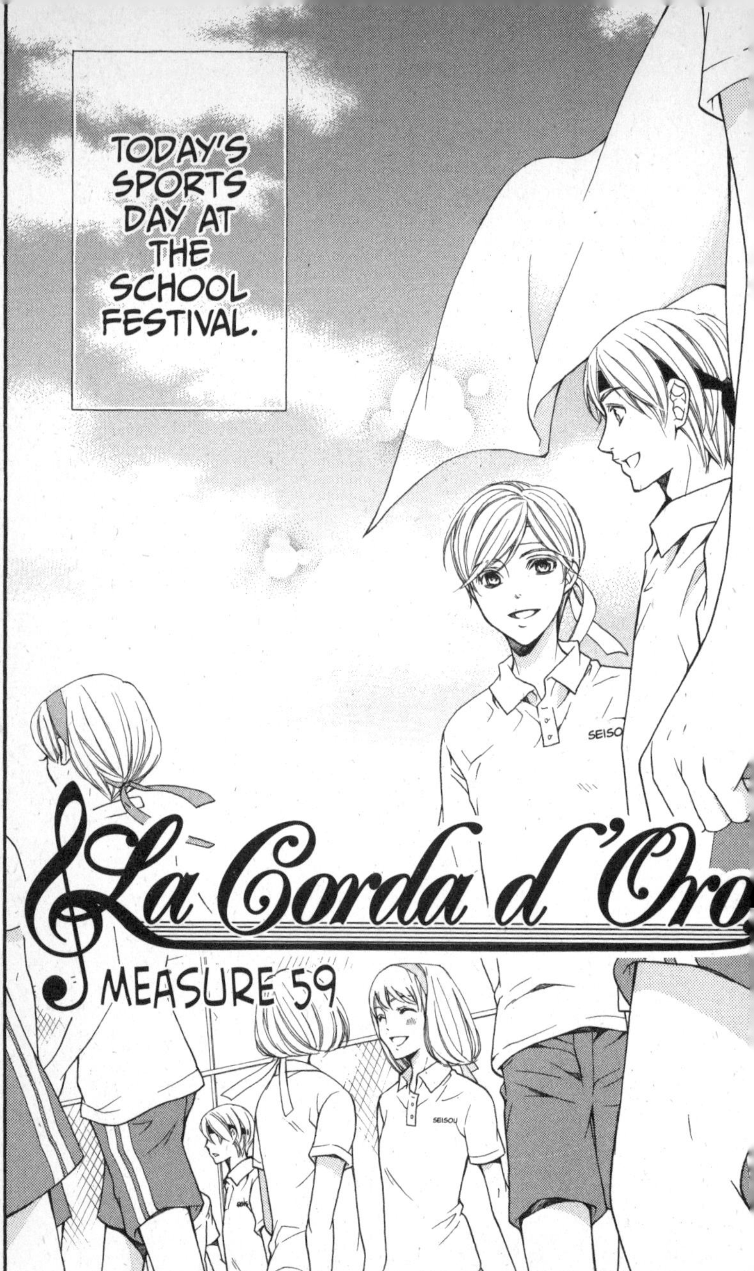
TODAY'S SPORTS DAY AT THE SCHOOL FESTIVAL.
La Corda d'Oro
MEASURE 59
SEISOU
SEISOU

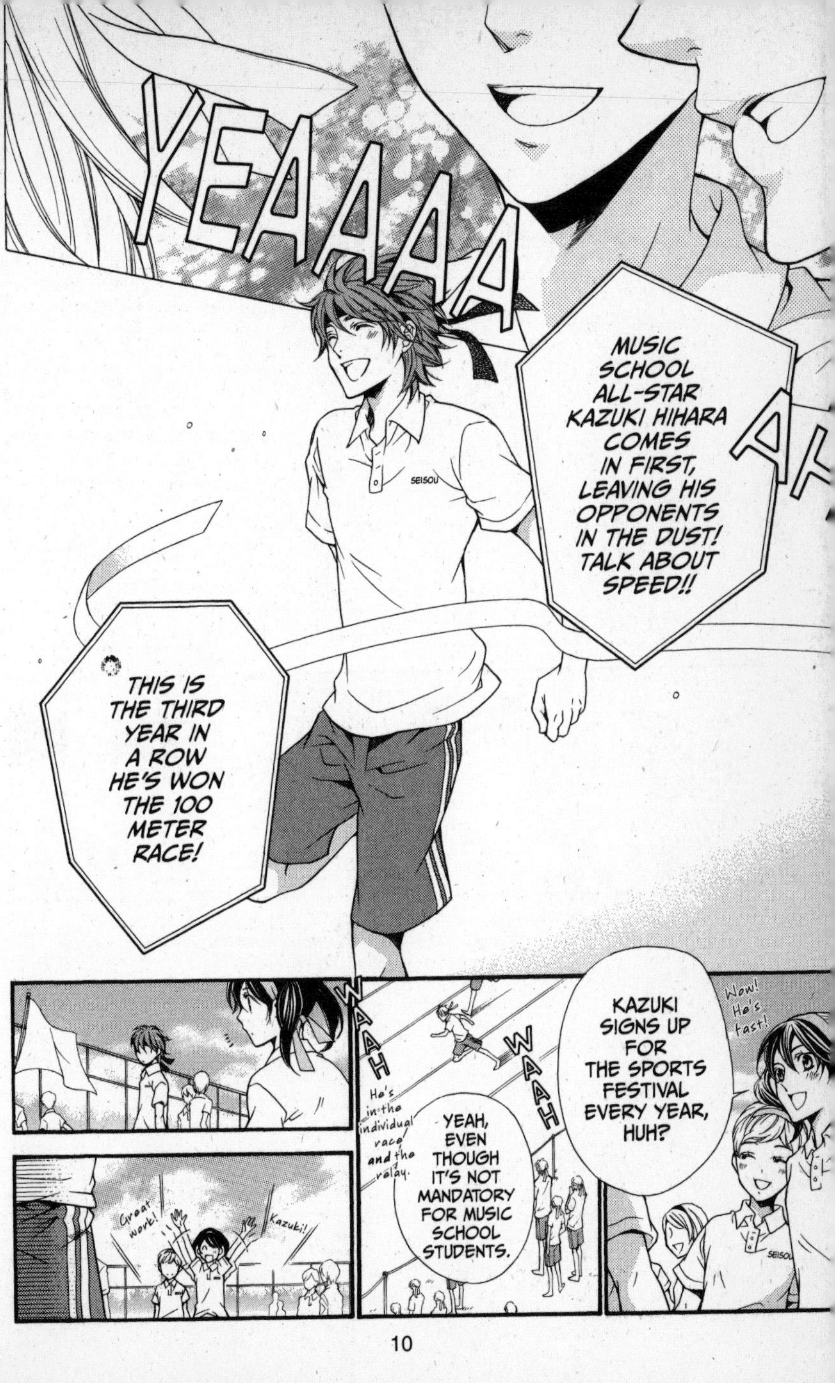
YEAAAAAH
MUSIC SCHOOL ALL-STAR KAZUKI HIHARA COMES IN FIRST, LEAVING HIS OPPONENTS IN THE DUST! TALK ABOUT SPEED!!
THIS IS THE THIRD YEAR IN A ROW HE'S WON THE 100 METER RACE!
SEISOU
Wow! He's fast!
KAZUKI SIGNS UP FOR THE SPORTS FESTIVAL EVERY YEAR, HUH?
SEISOU
WAAH
WAAH
YEAH, EVEN THOUGH IT'S NOT MANDATORY FOR MUSIC SCHOOL STUDENTS.
He's in the individual race and the relay.
Kazuki!
Great work!

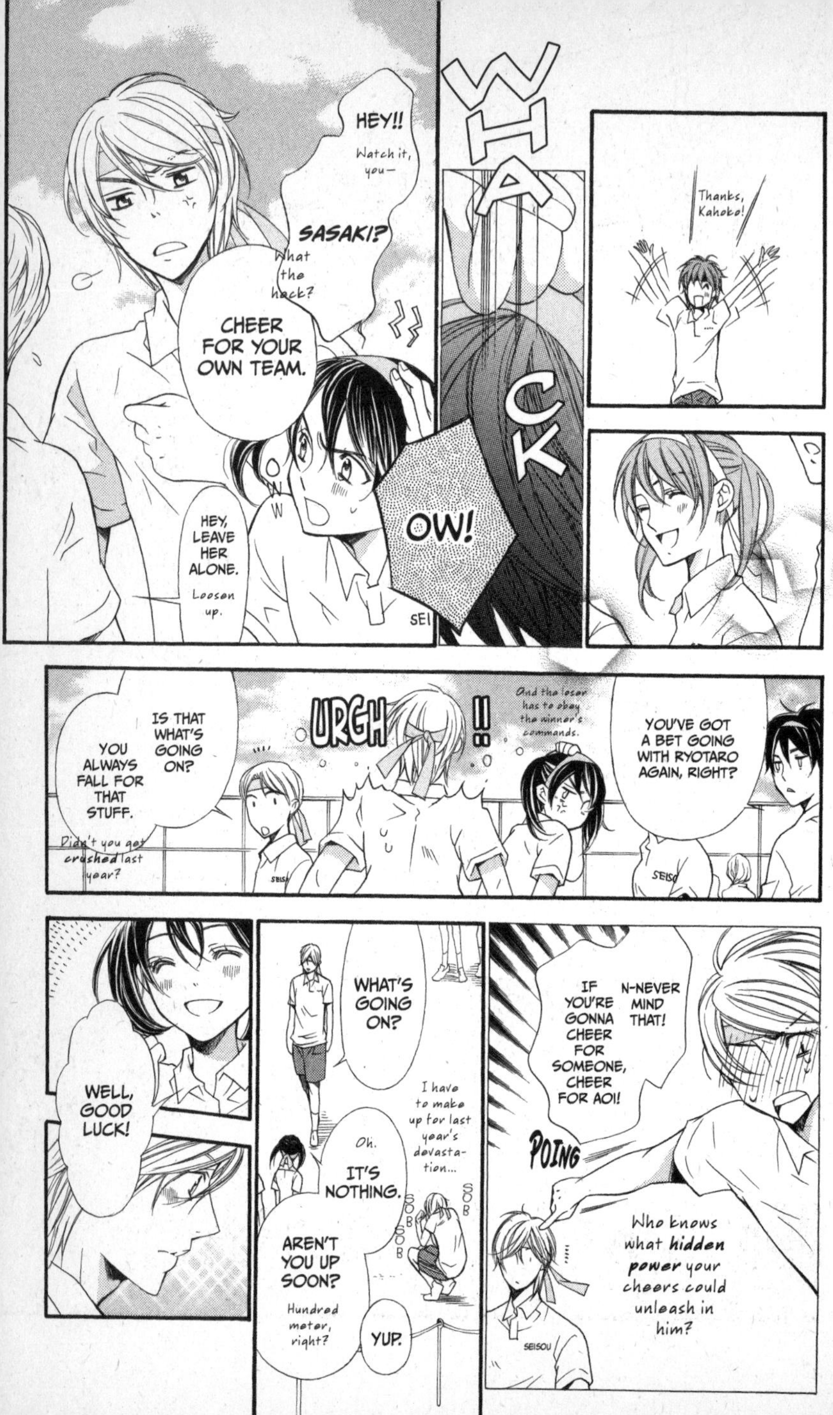
Thanks, Kahoko!
WHACK
OW!
SEI
HEY!!
Watch it, you—
SASAKI!?
What the heck?
CHEER FOR YOUR OWN TEAM.
HEY, LEAVE HER ALONE.
Loosen up.
YOU'VE GOT A BET GOING WITH RYOTARO AGAIN, RIGHT?
And the loser has to obey the winner's commands.
!!
URGH
IS THAT WHAT'S GOING ON?
YOU ALWAYS FALL FOR THAT STUFF.
Didn't you get crushed last year?
SEISO
N-NEVER MIND THAT!
IF YOU'RE GONNA CHEER FOR SOMEONE, CHEER FOR AOI!
POING
Who knows what hidden power your cheers could unleash in him?
SEISOU
WHAT'S GOING ON?
I have to make up for last year's devastation...
Oh.
IT'S NOTHING.
SOB SOB SOB
AREN'T YOU UP SOON?
Hundred meter, right?
YUP.
WELL, GOOD LUCK!

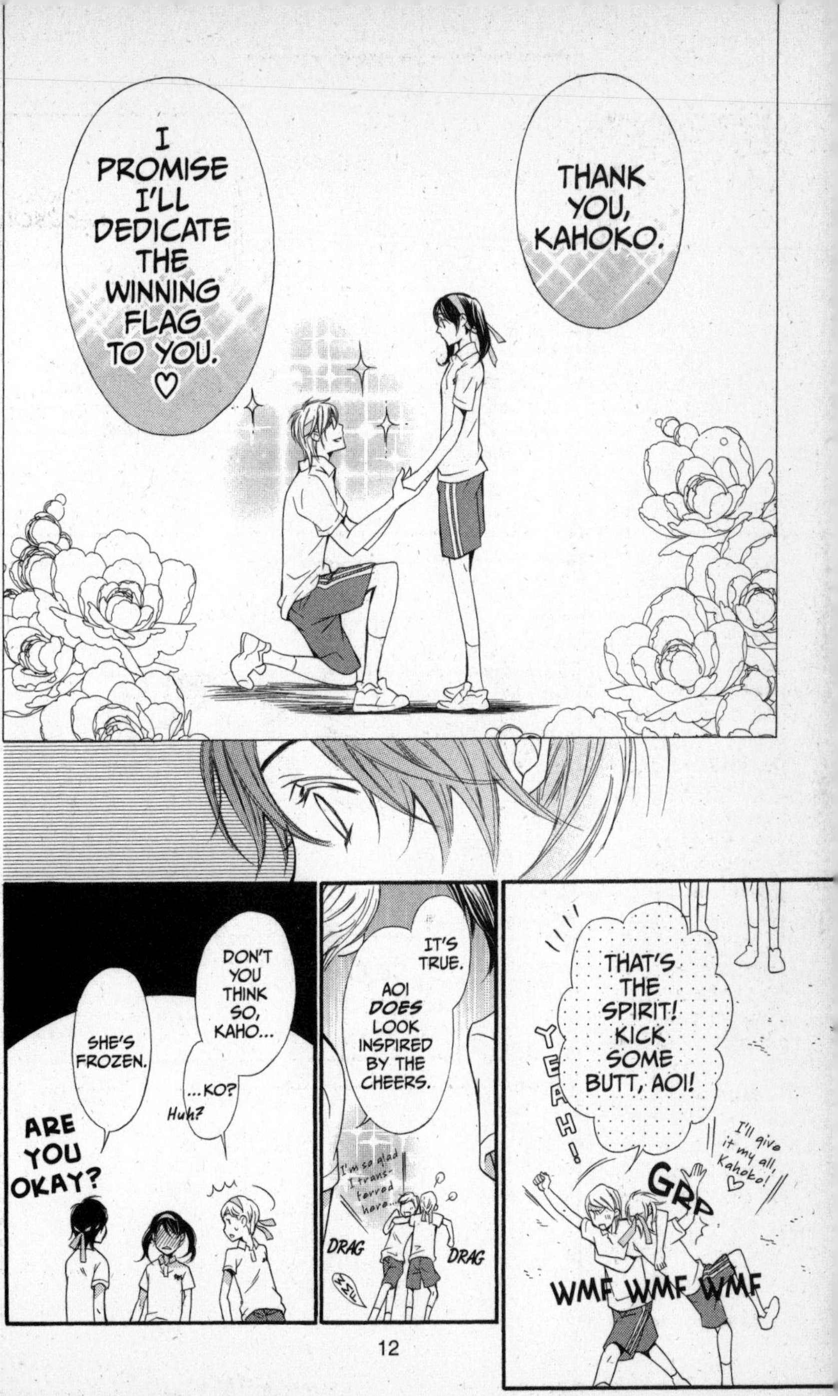
THANK YOU, KAHOKO.
I PROMISE I'LL DEDICATE THE WINNING FLAG TO YOU. ♡
THAT'S THE SPIRIT! KICK SOME BUTT, AOI!
YEAH!
I'll give it my all, Kahoko! ♡
GRP
WMF WMF WMF
IT'S TRUE.
AOI DOES LOOK INSPIRED BY THE CHEERS.
I'm so glad I transferred here...
DRAG
DRAG
DON'T YOU THINK SO, KAHO...
...KO?
Huh?
SHE'S FROZEN.
ARE YOU OKAY?

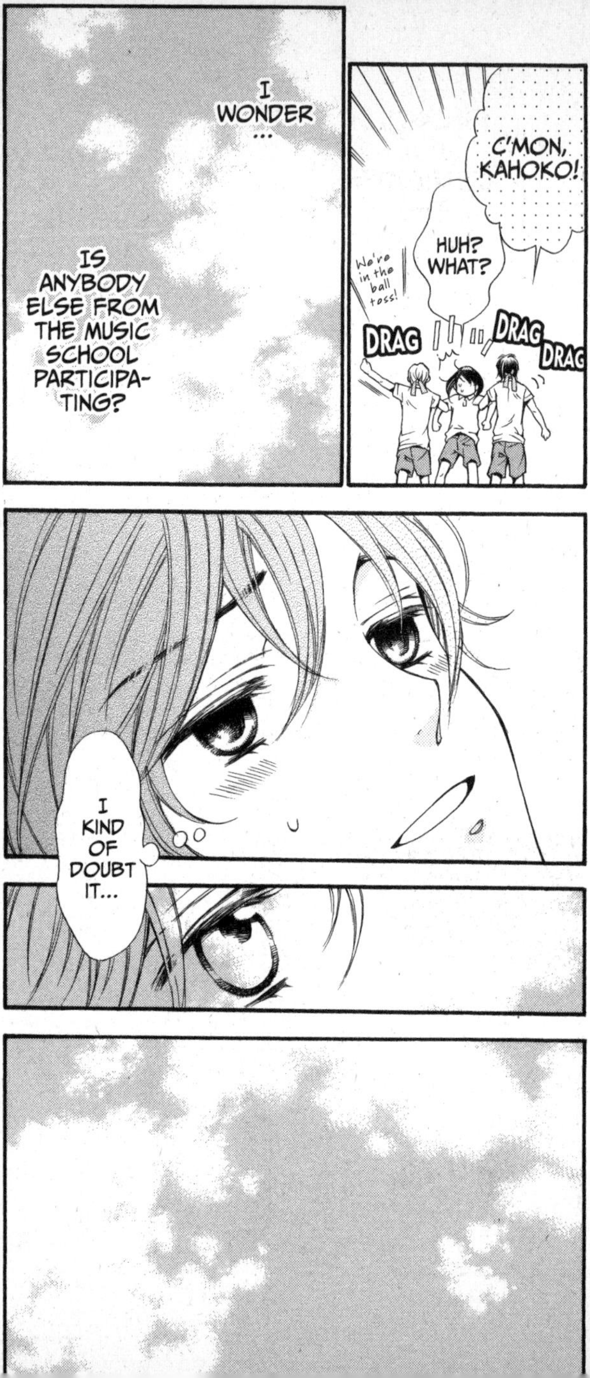
C'MON, KAHOKO!
HUH? WHAT?
We're in the ball toss!
DRAG
DRAG
DRAG
I WONDER...
IS ANYBODY ELSE FROM THE MUSIC SCHOOL PARTICIPA-TING?
I KIND OF DOUBT IT...

Hello! Long time no see. Yuki here!

Thank you so much for picking up *La Corda* volume 14! This volume is full of school events like the Sports Festival.

I remember having to do interpretive dances for my Sports Festival. ***Not*** my favorite memory from high school. My sense of rhythm leaves a lot to be desired...

In any case, I hope you enjoy the manga.

Yuki Kure

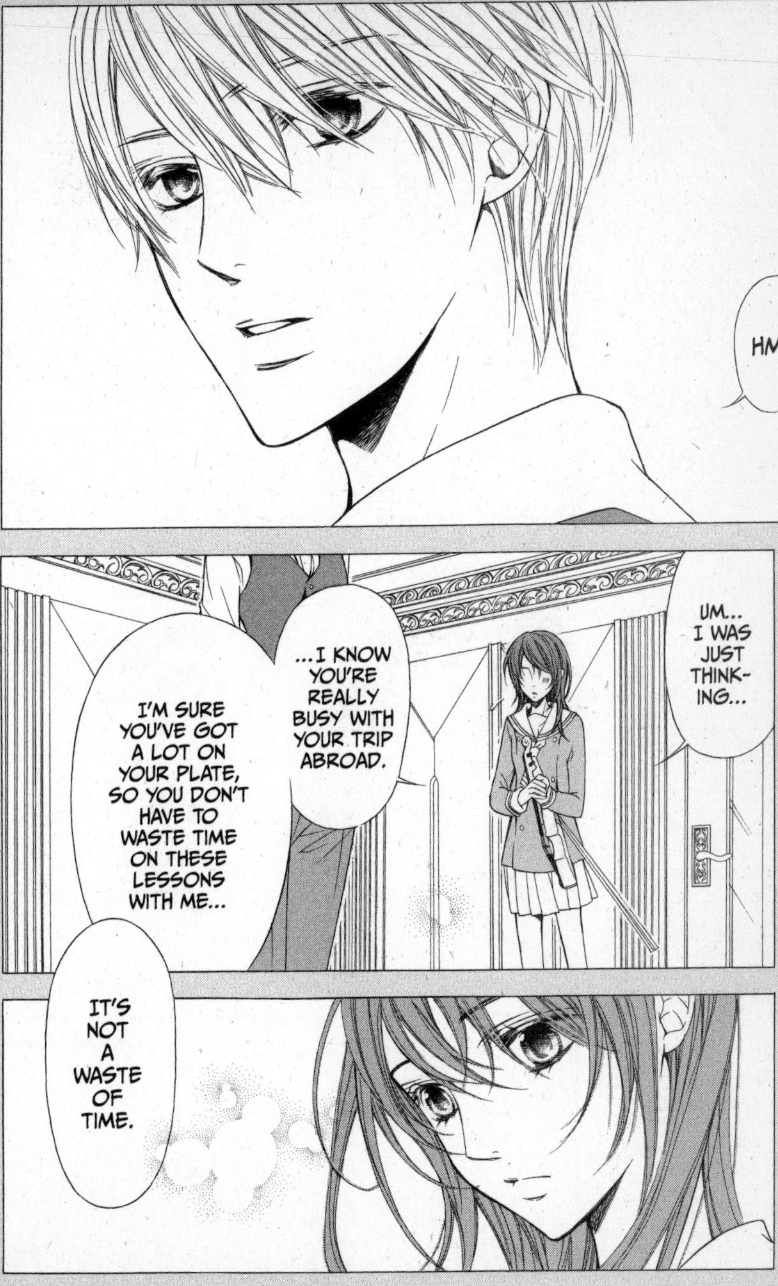
HM?
UM... I WAS JUST THINK-ING...
...I KNOW YOU'RE REALLY BUSY WITH YOUR TRIP ABROAD.
I'M SURE YOU'VE GOT A LOT ON YOUR PLATE, SO YOU DON'T HAVE TO WASTE TIME ON THESE LESSONS WITH ME...
IT'S NOT A WASTE OF TIME.

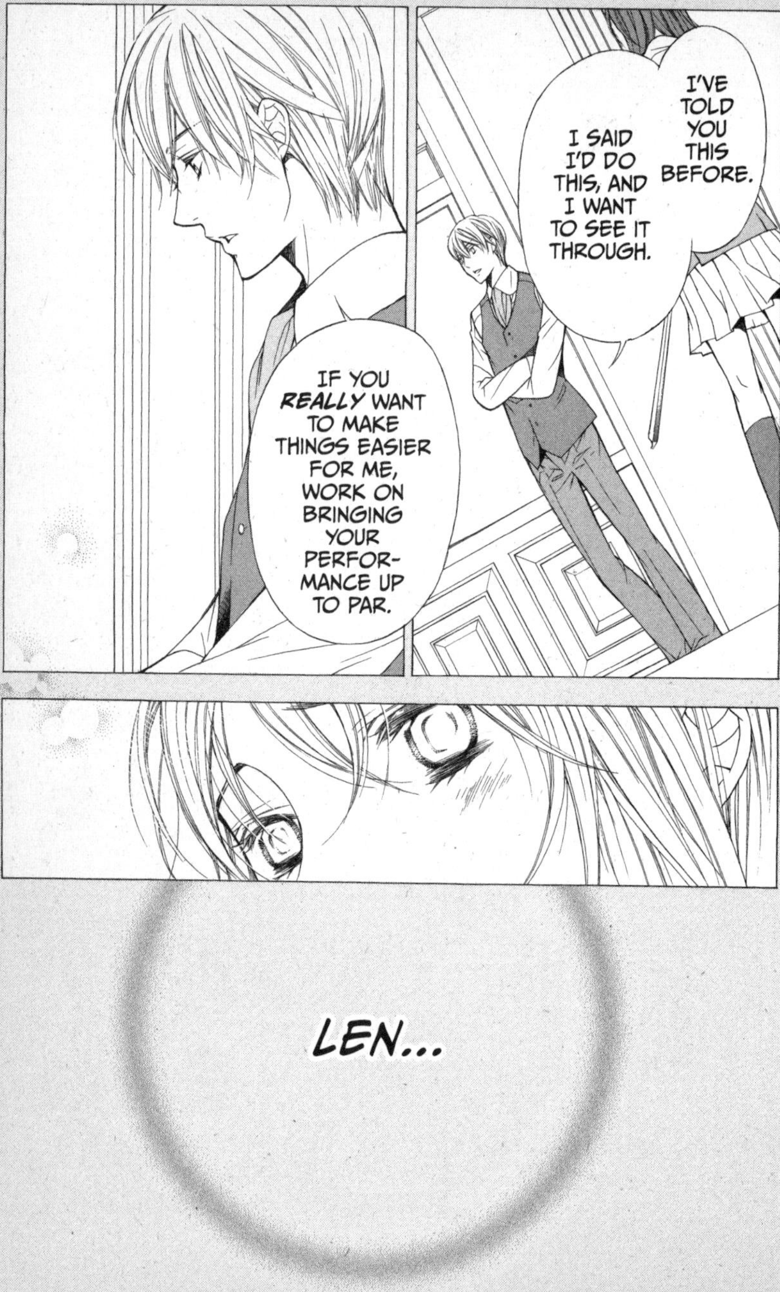
I'VE TOLD YOU THIS BEFORE.
I SAID I'D DO THIS, AND I WANT TO SEE IT THROUGH.
IF YOU *REALLY* WANT TO MAKE THINGS EASIER FOR ME, WORK ON BRINGING YOUR PERFORMANCE UP TO PAR.
LEN...

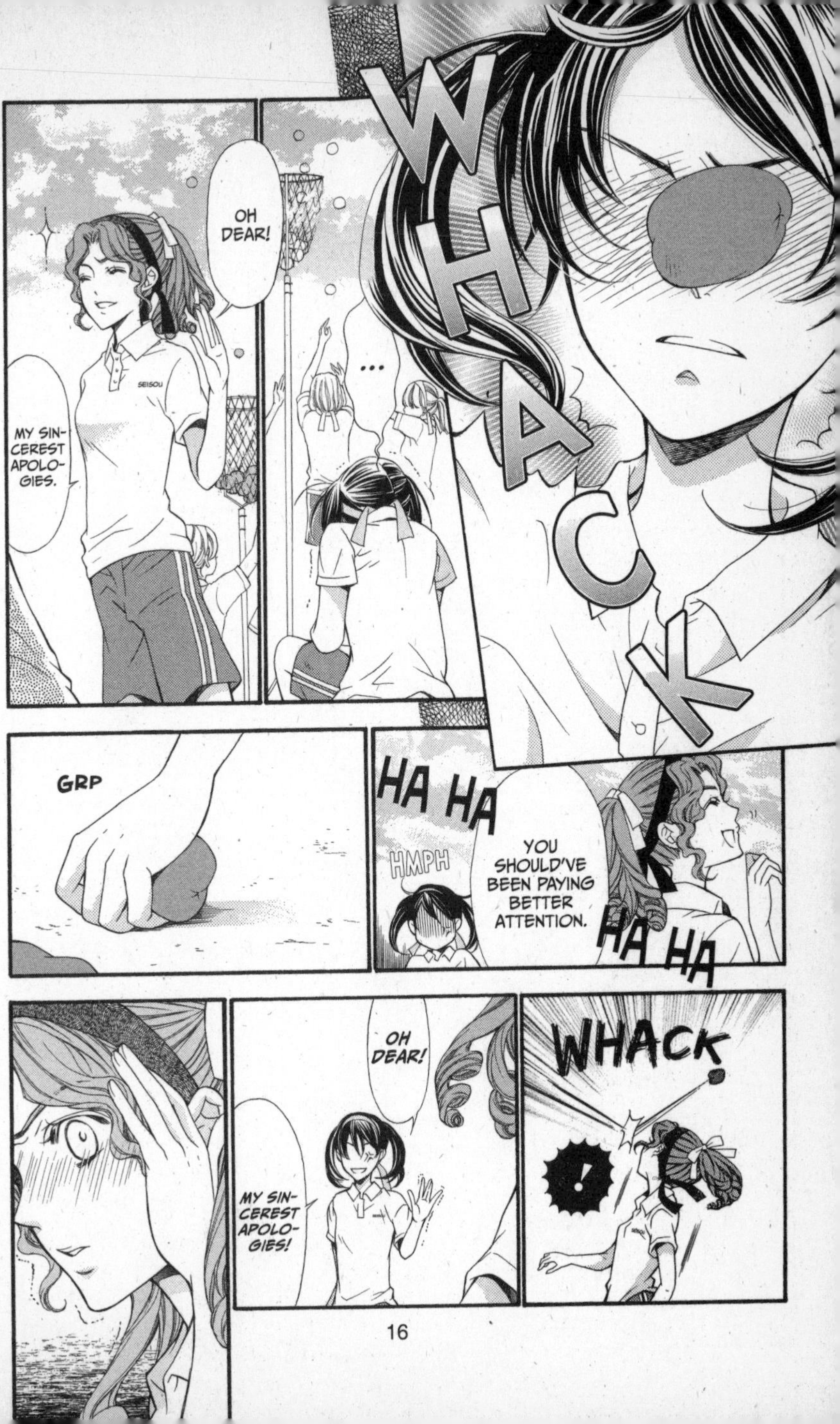
WHACK
...
OH DEAR!
MY SIN-CEREST APOLO-GIES.
HA HA
YOU SHOULD'VE BEEN PAYING BETTER ATTENTION.
HMPH
HA HA
GRP
WHACK
!
OH DEAR!
MY SIN-CEREST APOLO-GIES!

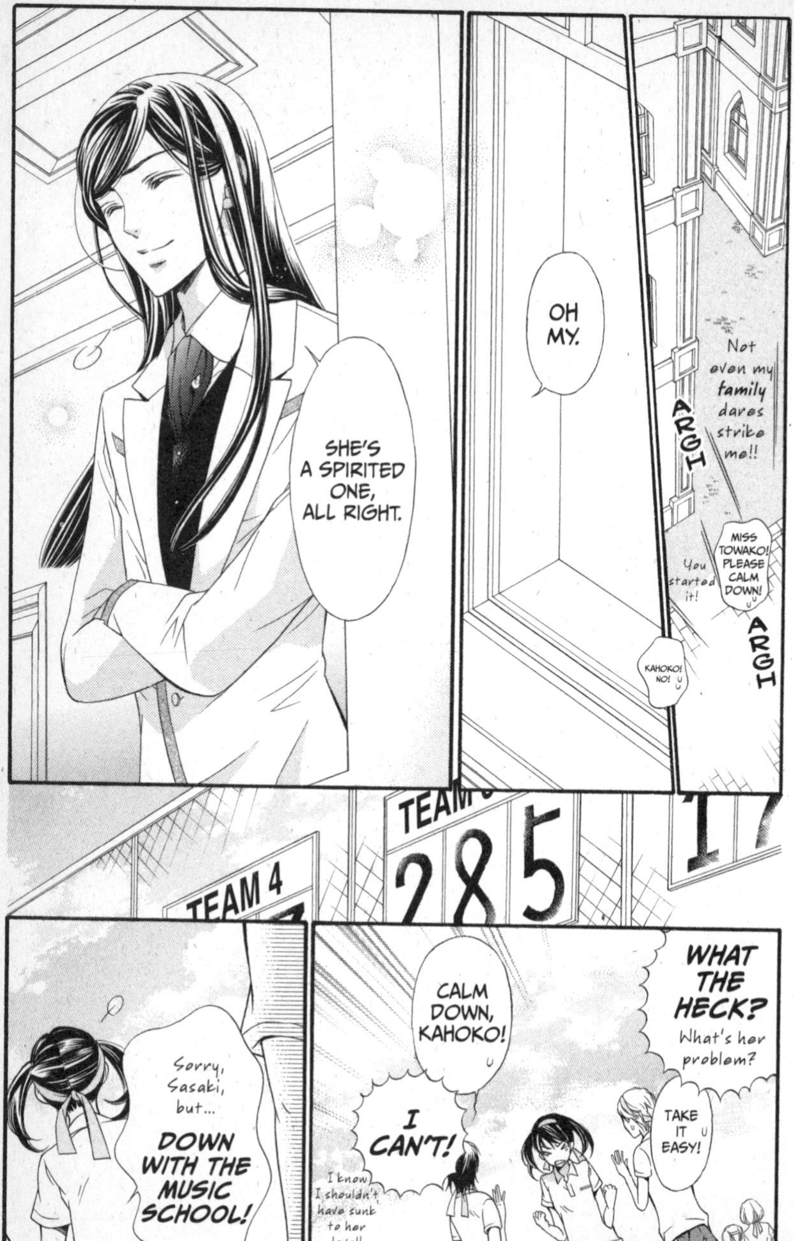
Not even my family dares strike me!!
ARGH
MISS TOWAKO! PLEASE CALM DOWN!
You started it!
ARGH
KAHOKO! NO!
OH MY.
SHE'S A SPIRITED ONE, ALL RIGHT.
TEAM
285
TEAM 4
WHAT THE HECK?
What's her problem?
CALM DOWN, KAHOKO!
TAKE IT EASY!
I CAN'T!
I know. I shouldn't have sunk to her level!
Sorry, Sasaki, but...
DOWN WITH THE MUSIC SCHOOL!

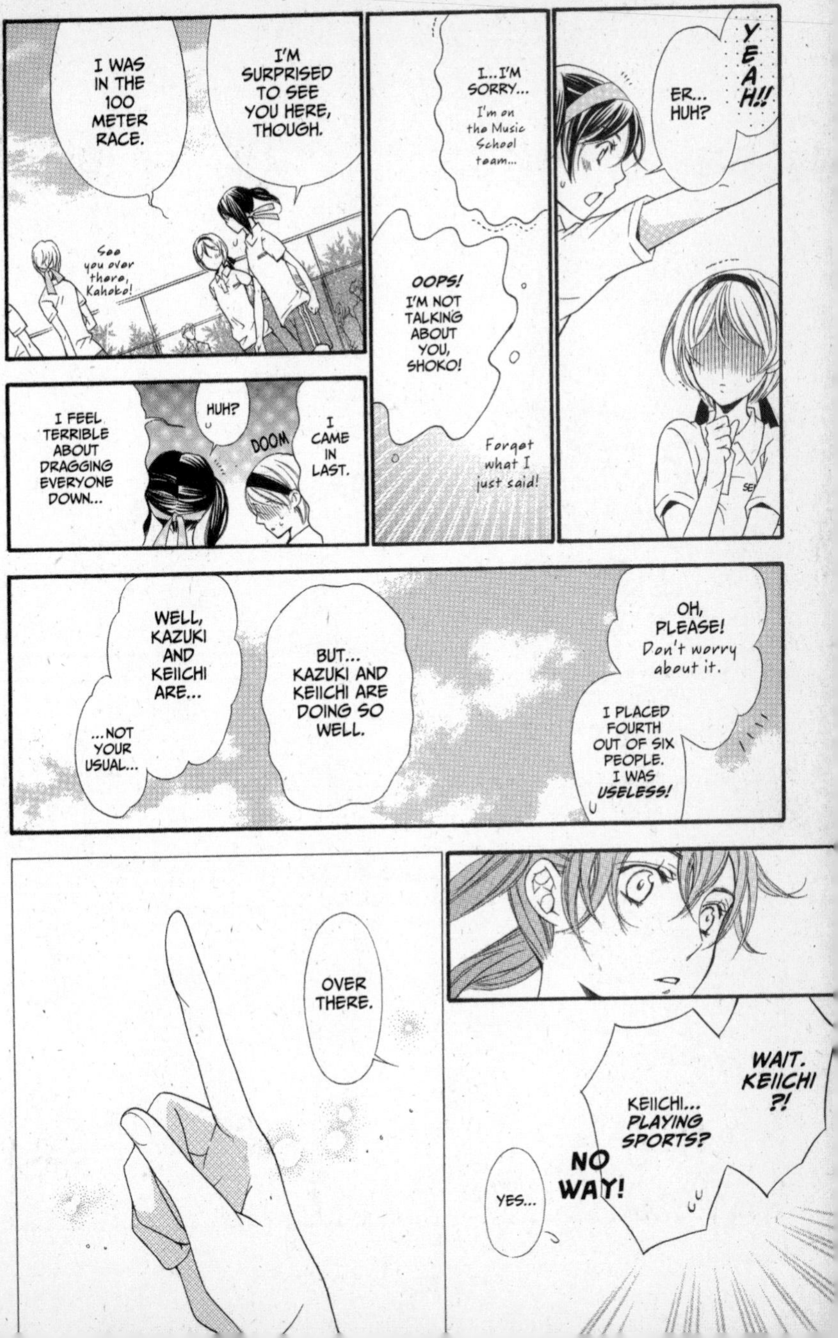
YEAH!!
ER... HUH?
I...I'M SORRY...
I'm on the Music School team...
OOPS! I'M NOT TALKING ABOUT YOU, SHOKO!
Forget what I just said!
I'M SURPRISED TO SEE YOU HERE, THOUGH.
I WAS IN THE 100 METER RACE.
See you over there, Kahoko!
I CAME IN LAST.
DOOM
HUH?
I FEEL TERRIBLE ABOUT DRAGGING EVERYONE DOWN...
OH, PLEASE! Don't worry about it.
I PLACED FOURTH OUT OF SIX PEOPLE. I WAS USELESS!
BUT... KAZUKI AND KEIICHI ARE DOING SO WELL.
WELL, KAZUKI AND KEIICHI ARE...
...NOT YOUR USUAL...
WAIT. KEIICHI ?!
KEIICHI... PLAYING SPORTS?
NO WAY!
YES...
OVER THERE.

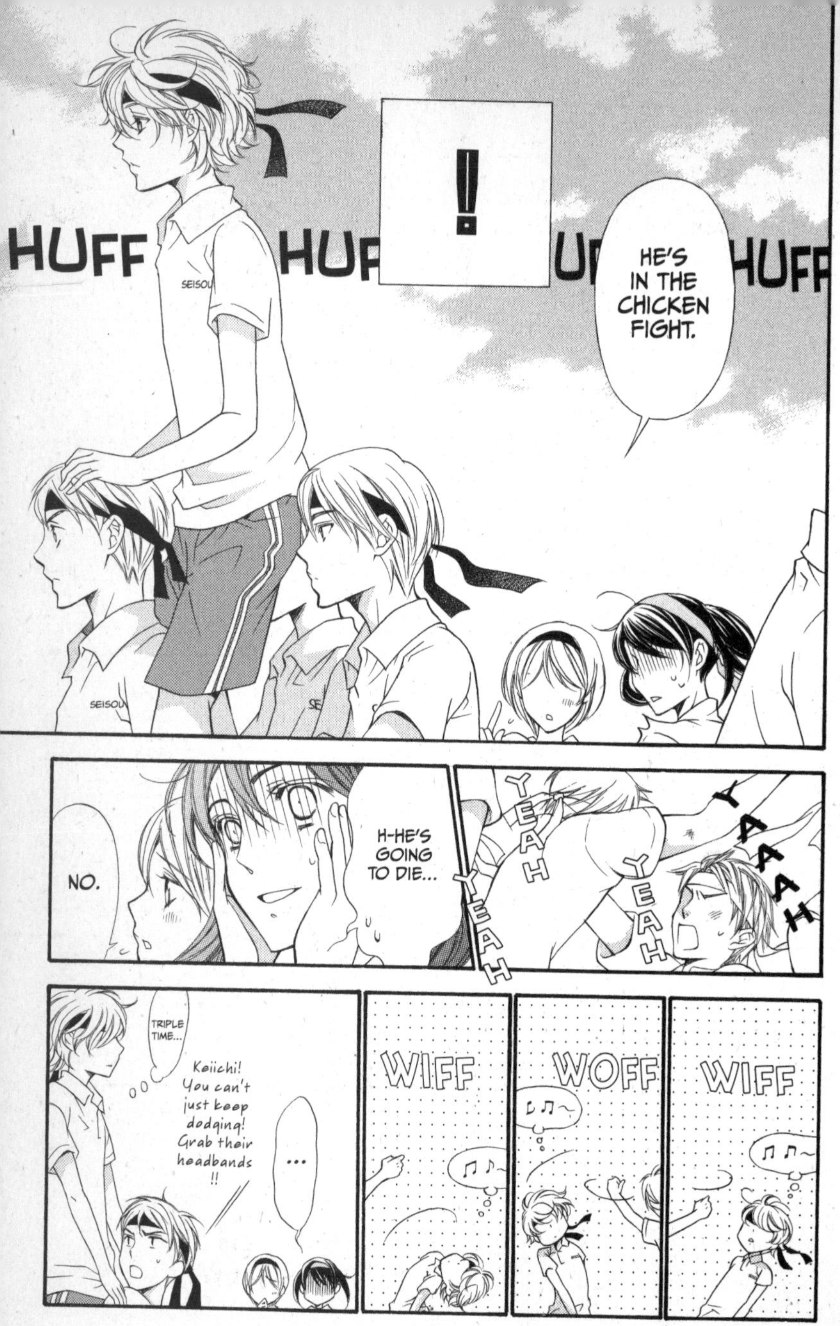
HUFF
HE'S IN THE CHICKEN FIGHT.
UF
!
HUF
HUFF
YAAAH
YEAH
YEAH
YEAH
H-HE'S GOING TO DIE...
NO.
WIFF
♫♪~
WOFF
♪♫~
WIFF
♫♪~
TRIPLE TIME...
Keiichi! You can't just keep dodging! Grab their headbands!!
...

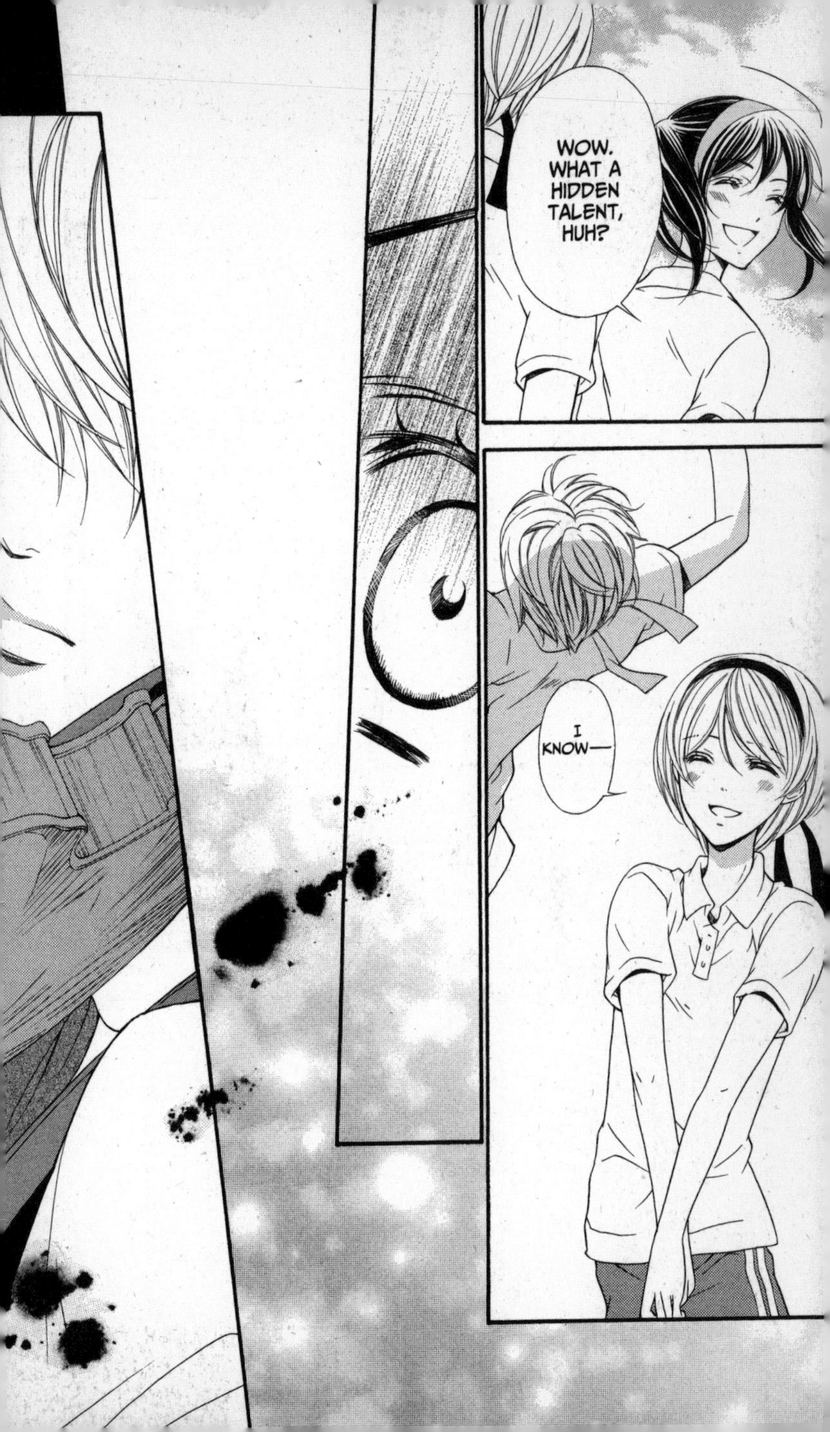
WOW. WHAT A HIDDEN TALENT, HUH?
I KNOW—

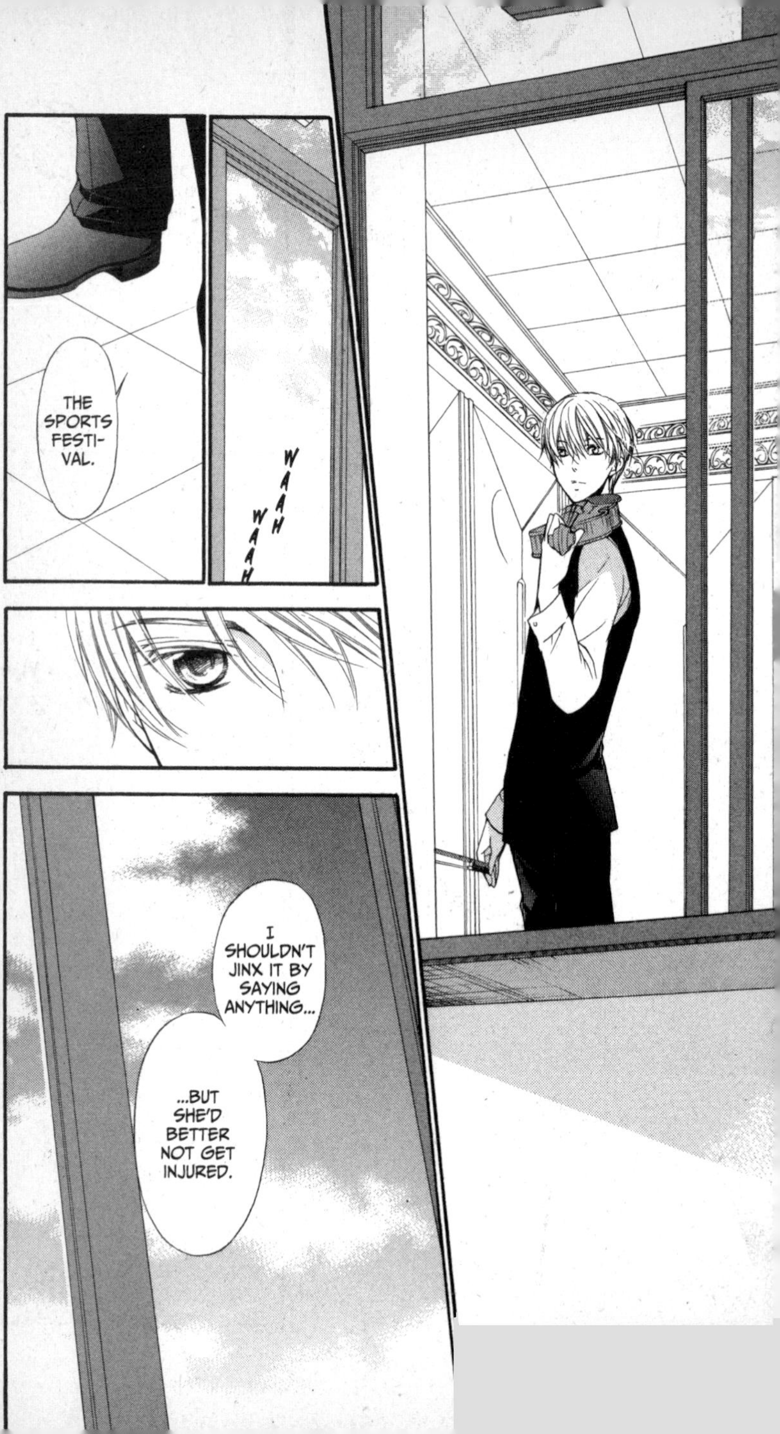
WAAH
WAAH
THE SPORTS FESTIVAL.
I SHOULDN'T JINX IT BY SAYING ANYTHING...
...BUT SHE'D BETTER NOT GET INJURED.

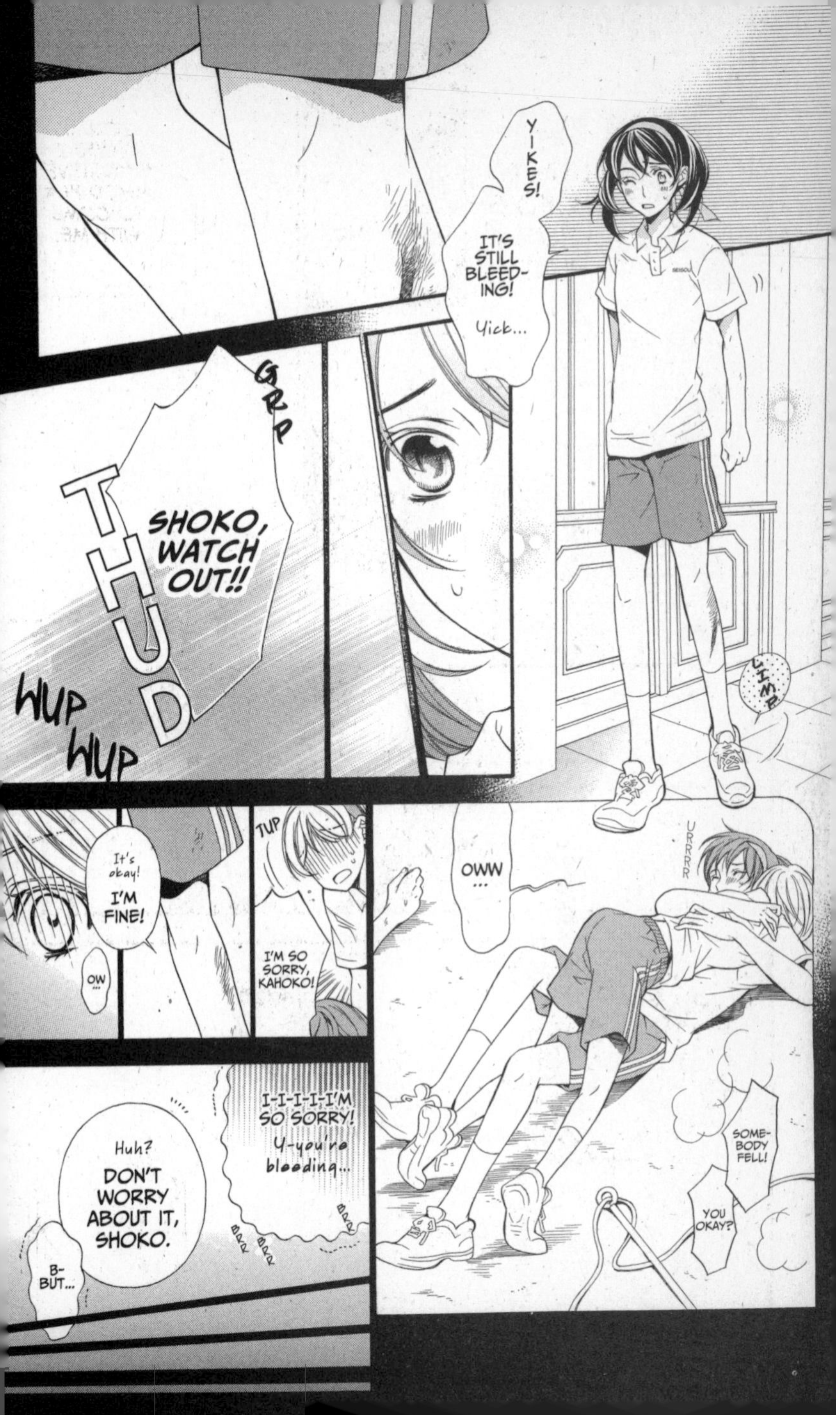
YIKES!
IT'S STILL BLEEDING!
Yick...
LIMP
GRP
SHOKO, WATCH OUT!!
THUD
WUP WUP
URRRR
OWW...
SOMEBODY FELL!
YOU OKAY?
TUP
I'M SO SORRY, KAHOKO!
It's okay! I'M FINE!
OW...
I-I-I-I-I'M SO SORRY!
Y-you're bleeding...
BRR BRR BRR
Huh? DON'T WORRY ABOUT IT, SHOKO.
B-BUT...

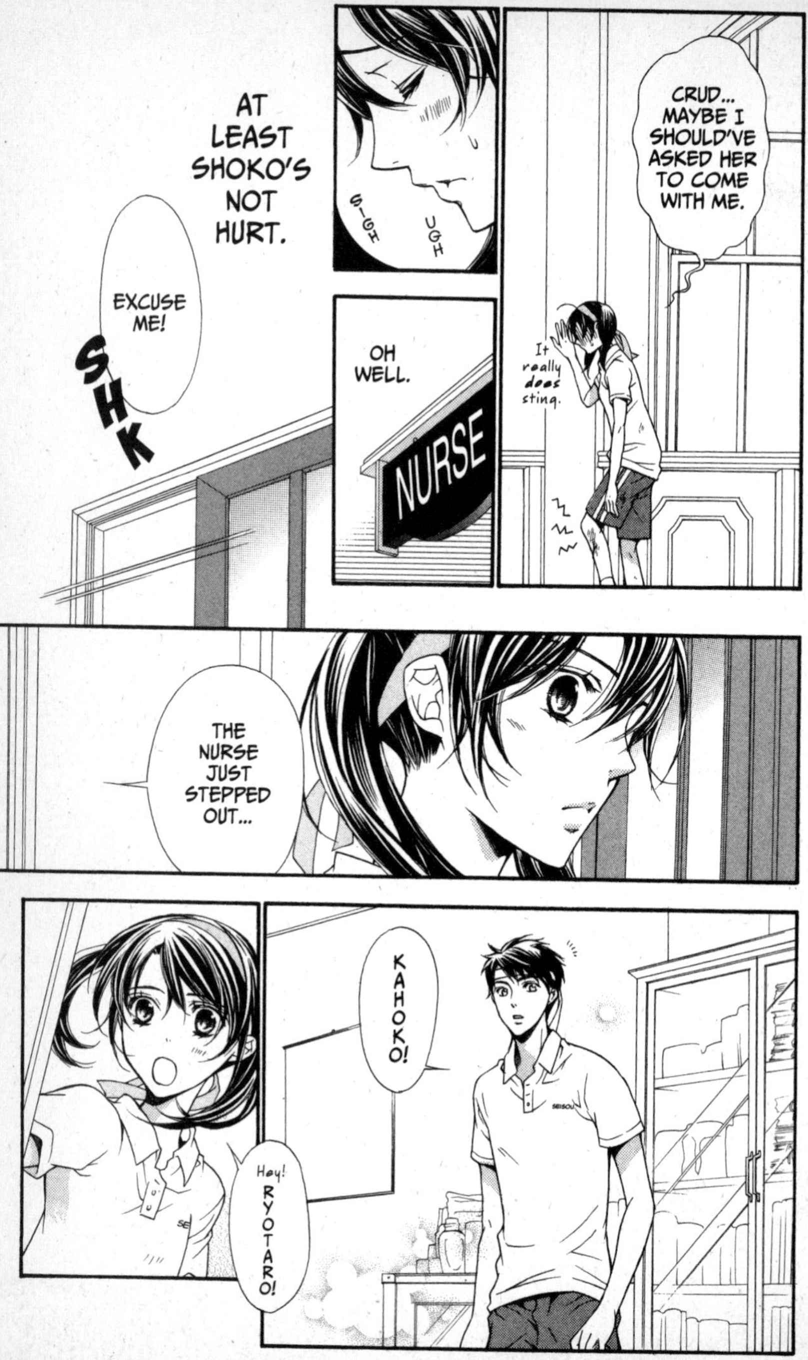
CRUD... MAYBE I SHOULD'VE ASKED HER TO COME WITH ME.
It really does sting.
SIGH
UGH
AT LEAST SHOKO'S NOT HURT.
OH WELL.
NURSE
EXCUSE ME!
SHK
THE NURSE JUST STEPPED OUT...
KAHOKO!
Hey! RYOTARO!

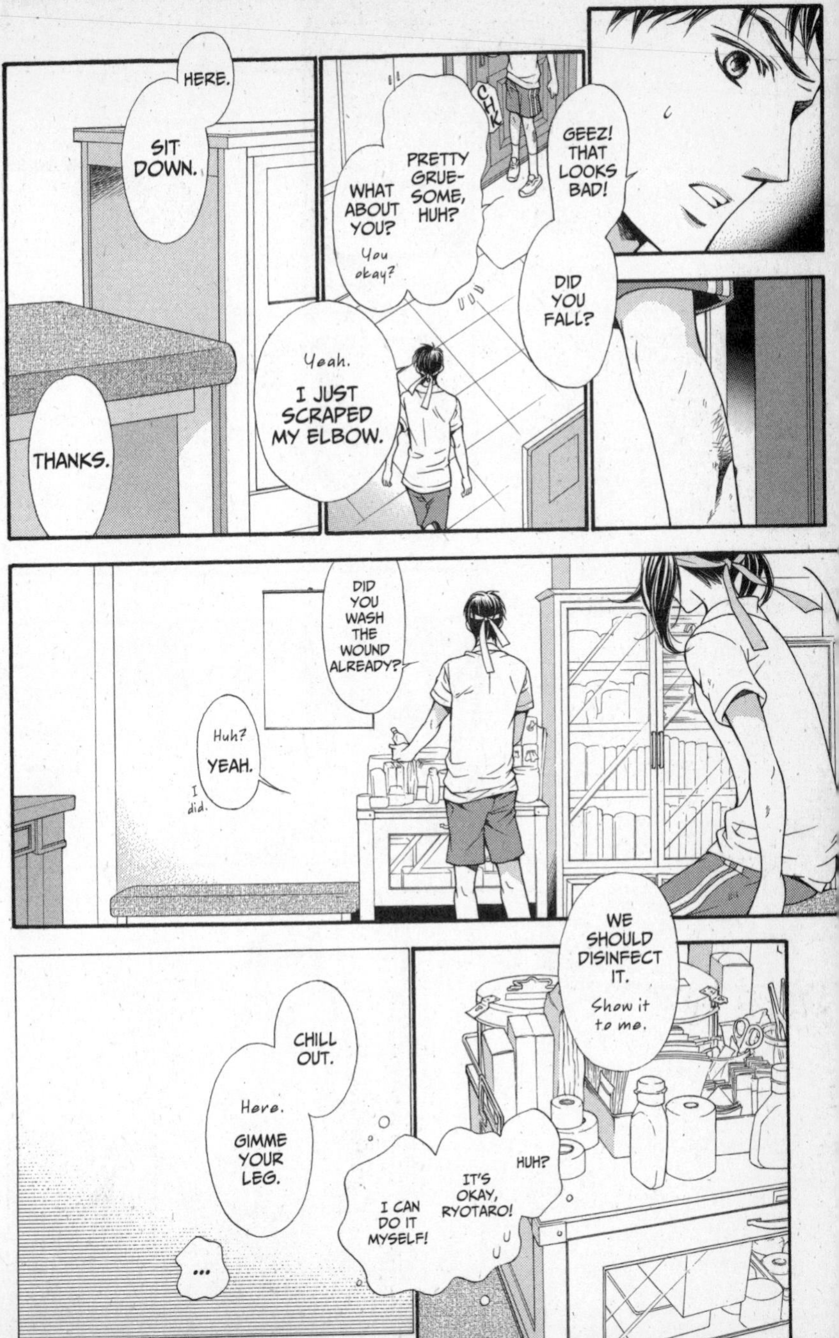
GEEZ! THAT LOOKS BAD!
DID YOU FALL?
CHK
PRETTY GRUE-SOME, HUH?
WHAT ABOUT YOU? You okay?
Yeah. I JUST SCRAPED MY ELBOW.
HERE. SIT DOWN.
THANKS.
DID YOU WASH THE WOUND ALREADY?
Huh? YEAH. I did.
WE SHOULD DISINFECT IT. Show it to me.
HUH? IT'S OKAY, RYOTARO! I CAN DO IT MYSELF!
CHILL OUT. Here. GIMME YOUR LEG.
...

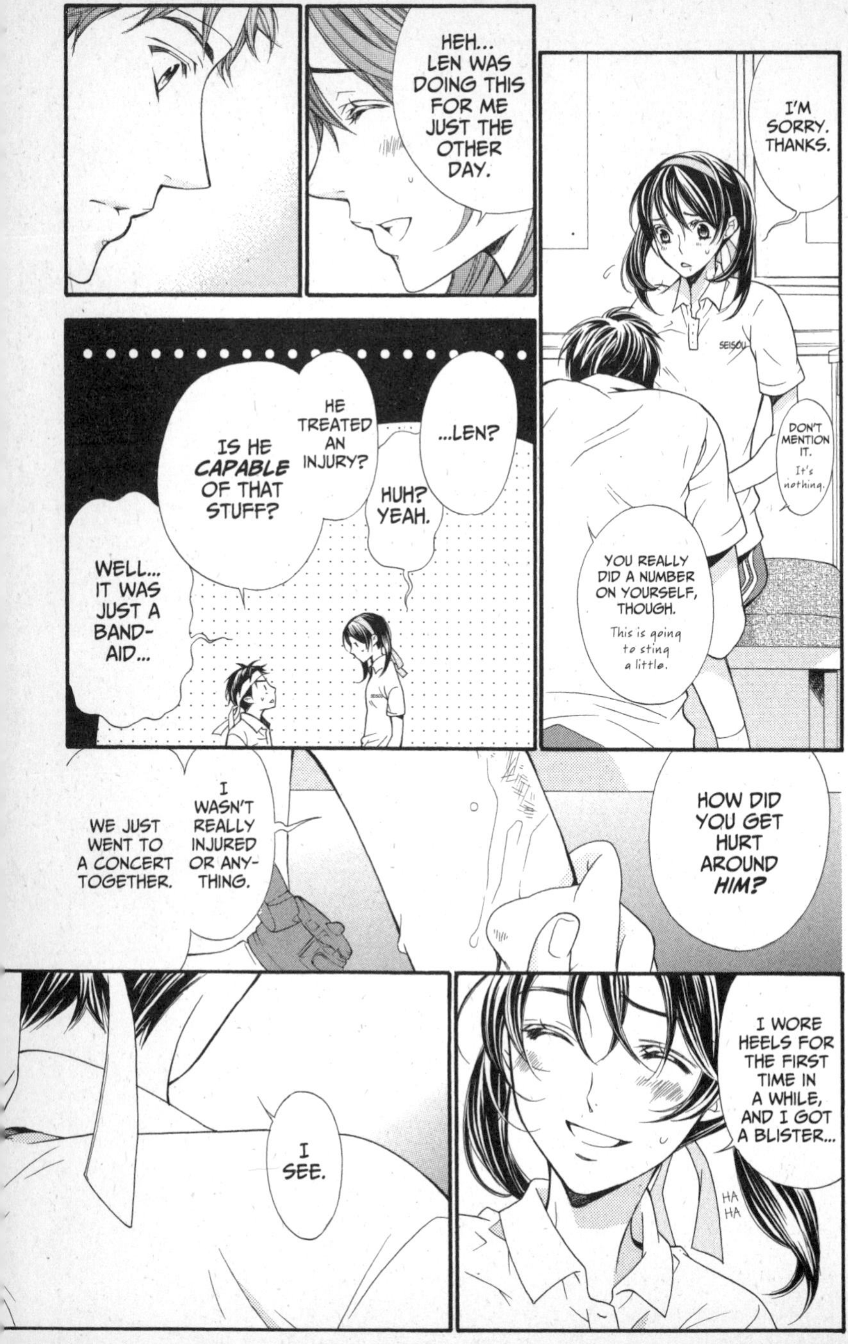
I'M SORRY. THANKS.
DON'T MENTION IT.
It's nothing.
YOU REALLY DID A NUMBER ON YOURSELF, THOUGH.
This is going to sting a little.
SEISOU
HEH... LEN WAS DOING THIS FOR ME JUST THE OTHER DAY.
...LEN?
HE TREATED AN INJURY?
HUH? YEAH.
IS HE *CAPABLE* OF THAT STUFF?
WELL... IT WAS JUST A BAND-AID...
HOW DID YOU GET HURT AROUND *HIM?*
I WASN'T REALLY INJURED OR ANYTHING.
WE JUST WENT TO A CONCERT TOGETHER.
I WORE HEELS FOR THE FIRST TIME IN A WHILE, AND I GOT A BLISTER...
HA HA
I SEE.

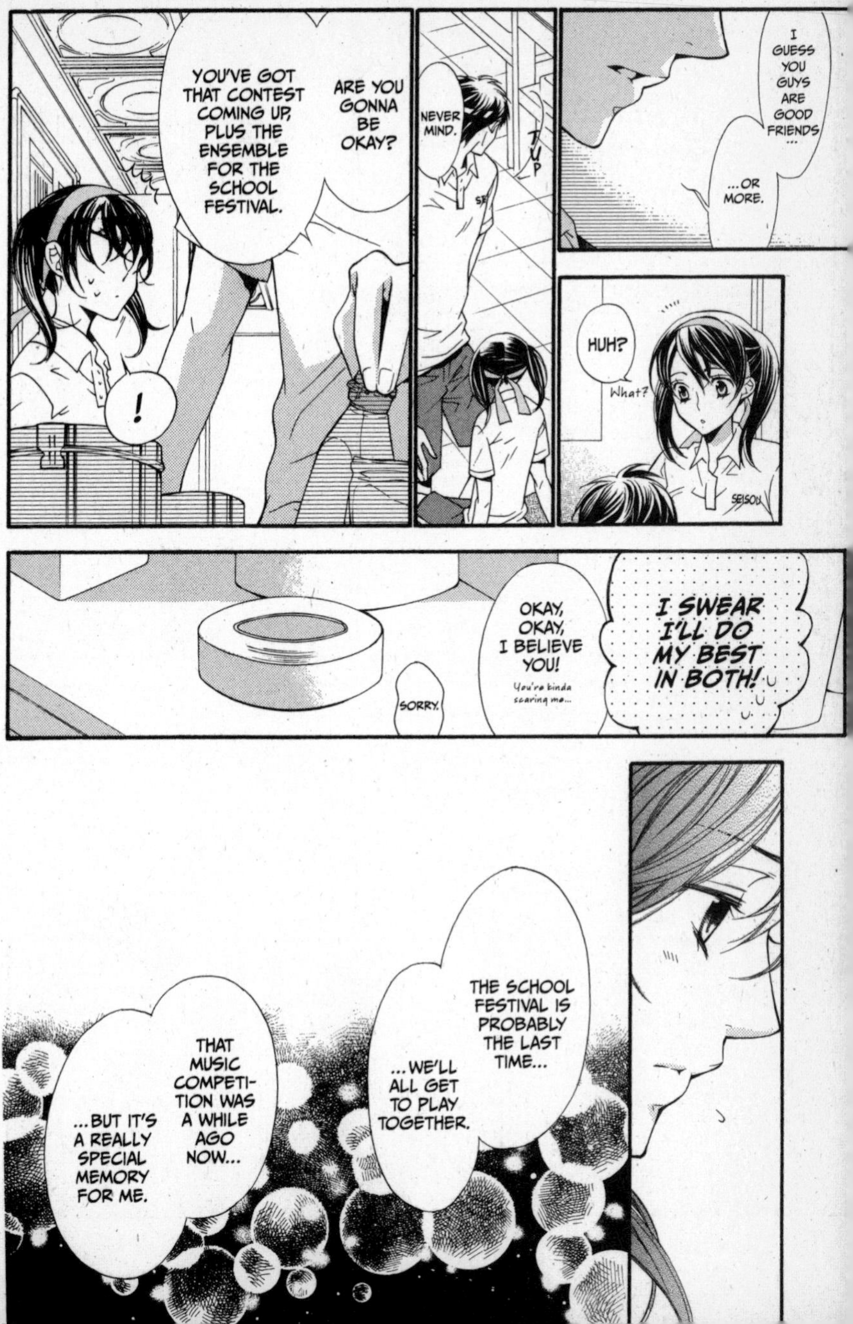
I GUESS YOU GUYS ARE GOOD FRIENDS...
...OR MORE.
HUH?
What?
SEISOU
NEVER MIND.
TUP
ARE YOU GONNA BE OKAY?
YOU'VE GOT THAT CONTEST COMING UP, PLUS THE ENSEMBLE FOR THE SCHOOL FESTIVAL.
!
I SWEAR I'LL DO MY BEST IN BOTH!
OKAY, OKAY, I BELIEVE YOU!
You're kinda scaring me...
SORRY.
THE SCHOOL FESTIVAL IS PROBABLY THE LAST TIME...
...WE'LL ALL GET TO PLAY TOGETHER.
THAT MUSIC COMPETITION WAS A WHILE AGO NOW...
...BUT IT'S A REALLY SPECIAL MEMORY FOR ME.

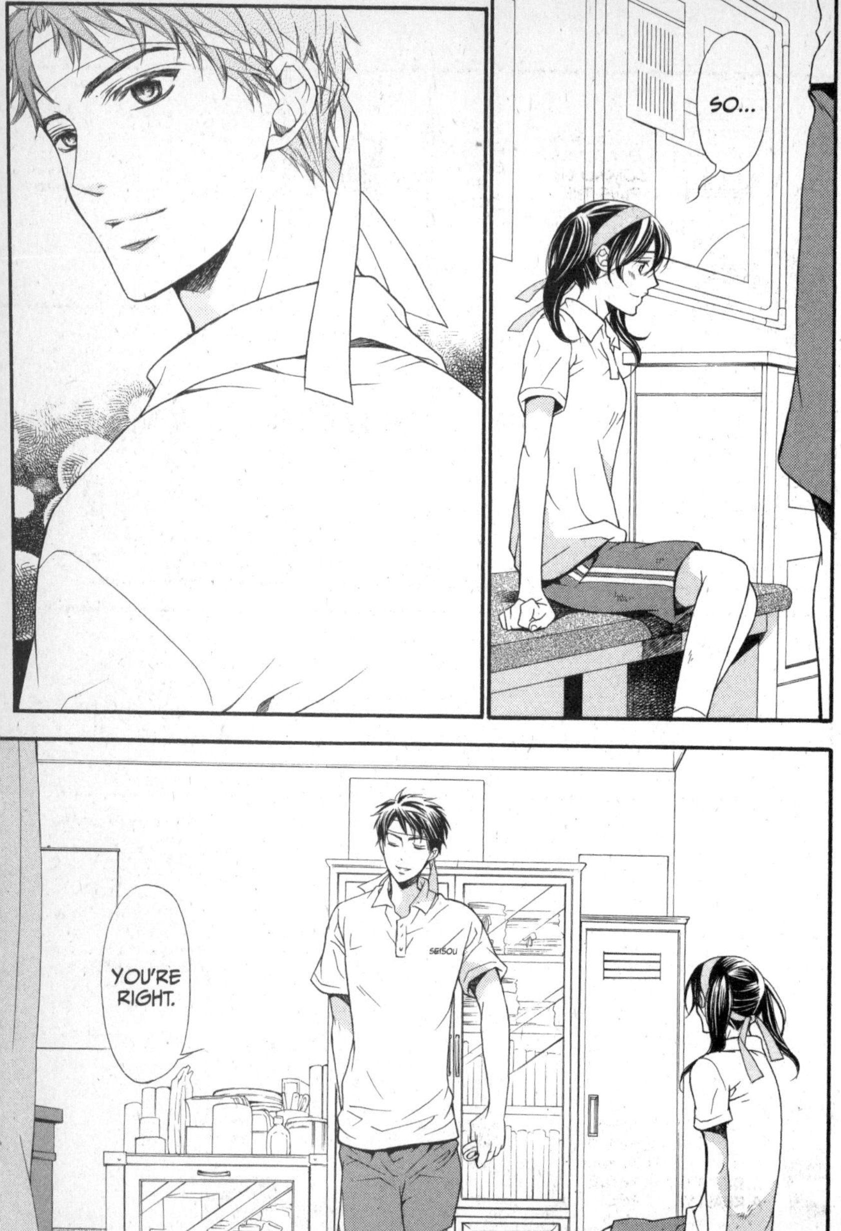
SO...
YOU'RE RIGHT.

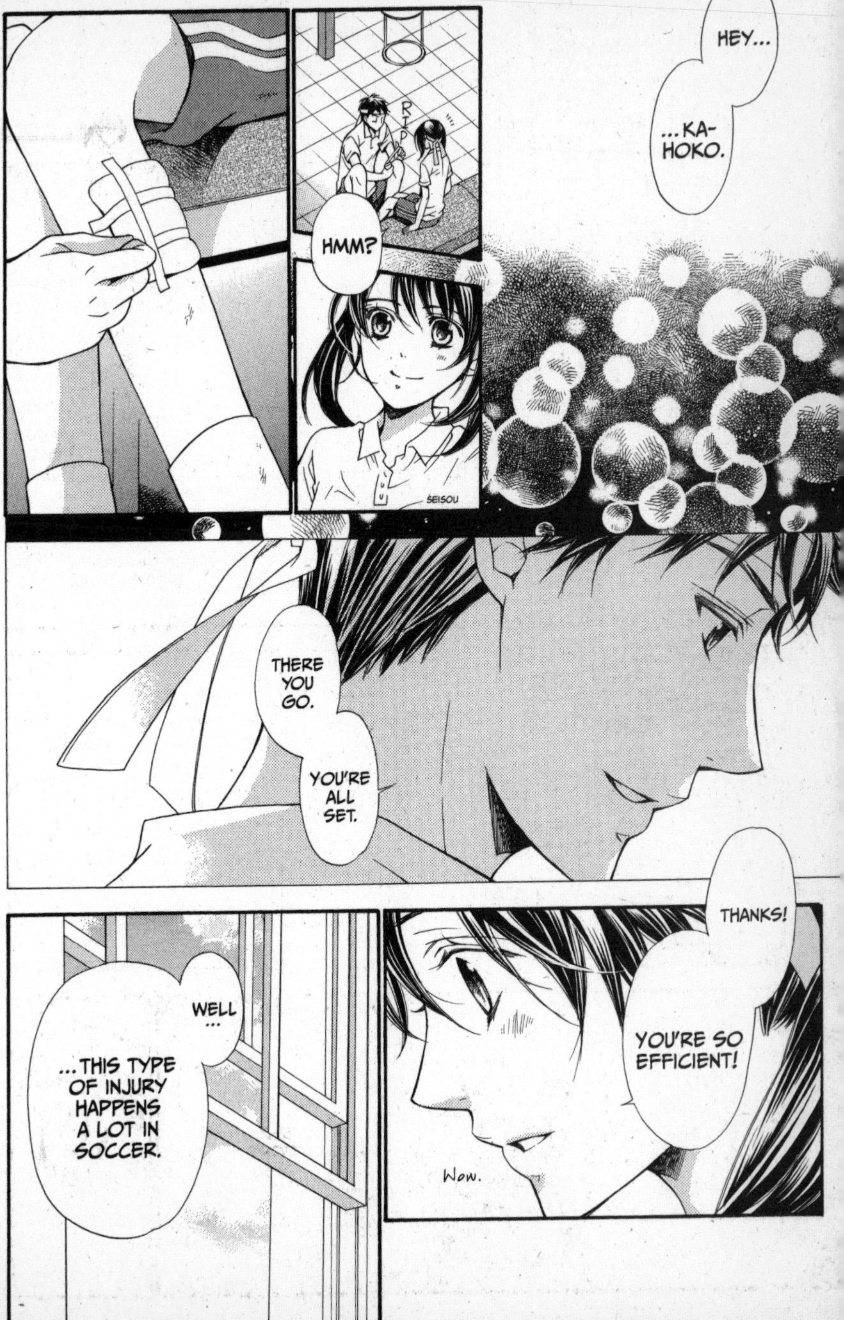
HEY...
...KA-HOKO.
RIP
HMM?
SEISOU
THERE YOU GO.
YOU'RE ALL SET.
THANKS!
YOU'RE SO EFFICIENT!
Wow.
WELL...
...THIS TYPE OF INJURY HAPPENS A LOT IN SOCCER.

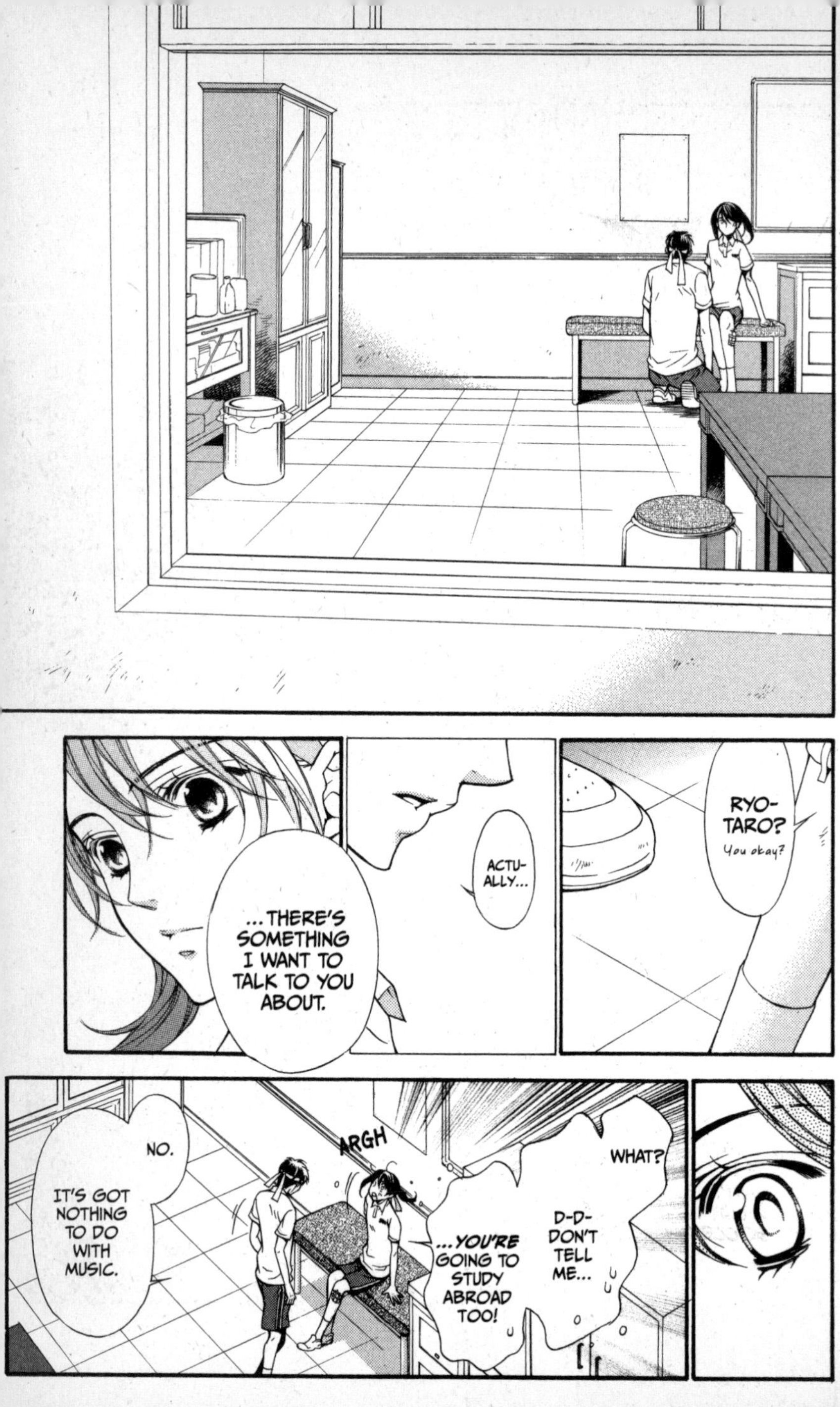
RYO-TARO? You okay?
ACTU-ALLY...
...THERE'S SOMETHING I WANT TO TALK TO YOU ABOUT.
WHAT?
D-D-DON'T TELL ME...
...YOU'RE GOING TO STUDY ABROAD TOO!
ARGH
NO.
IT'S GOT NOTHING TO DO WITH MUSIC.

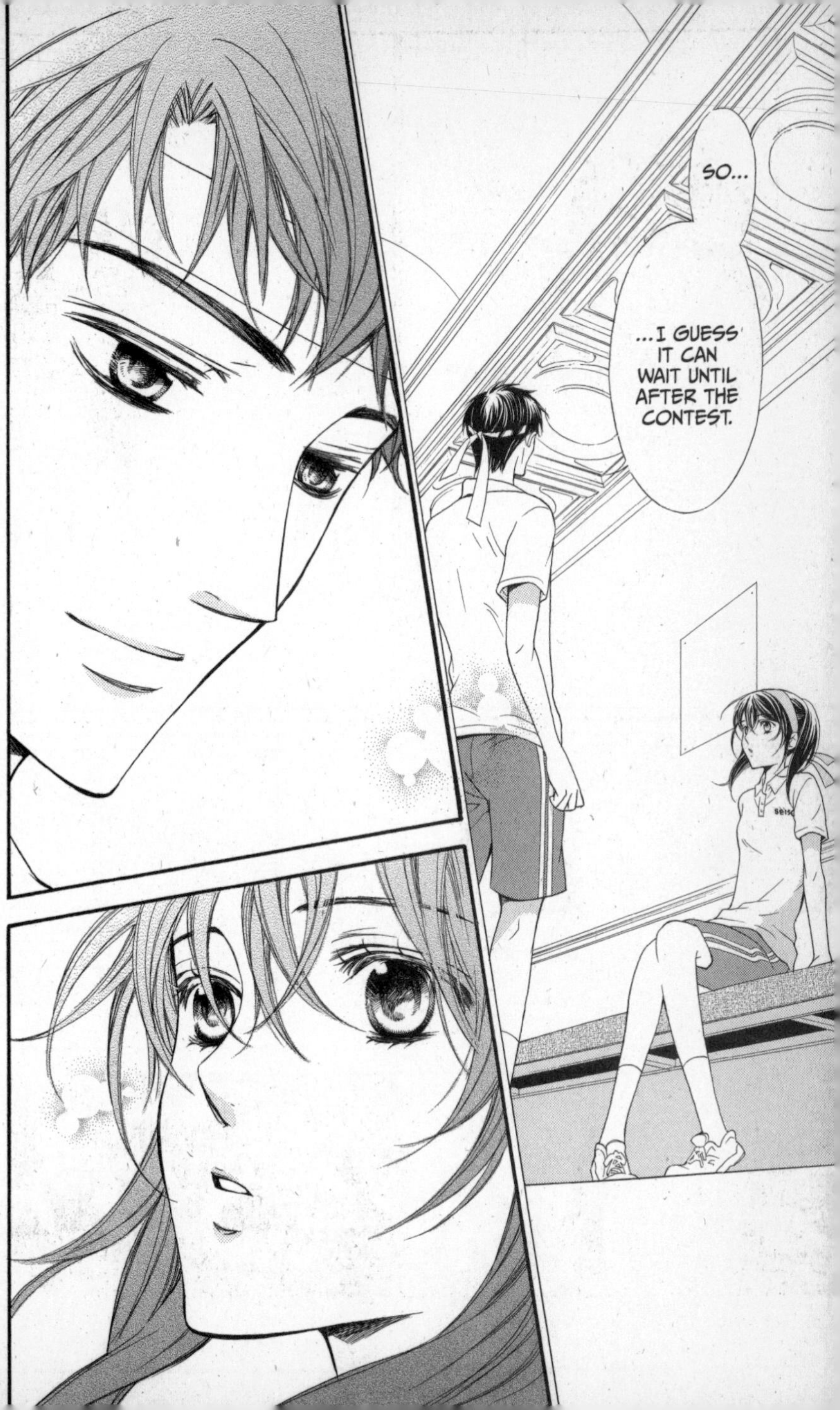
SO...
...I GUESS IT CAN WAIT UNTIL AFTER THE CONTEST.

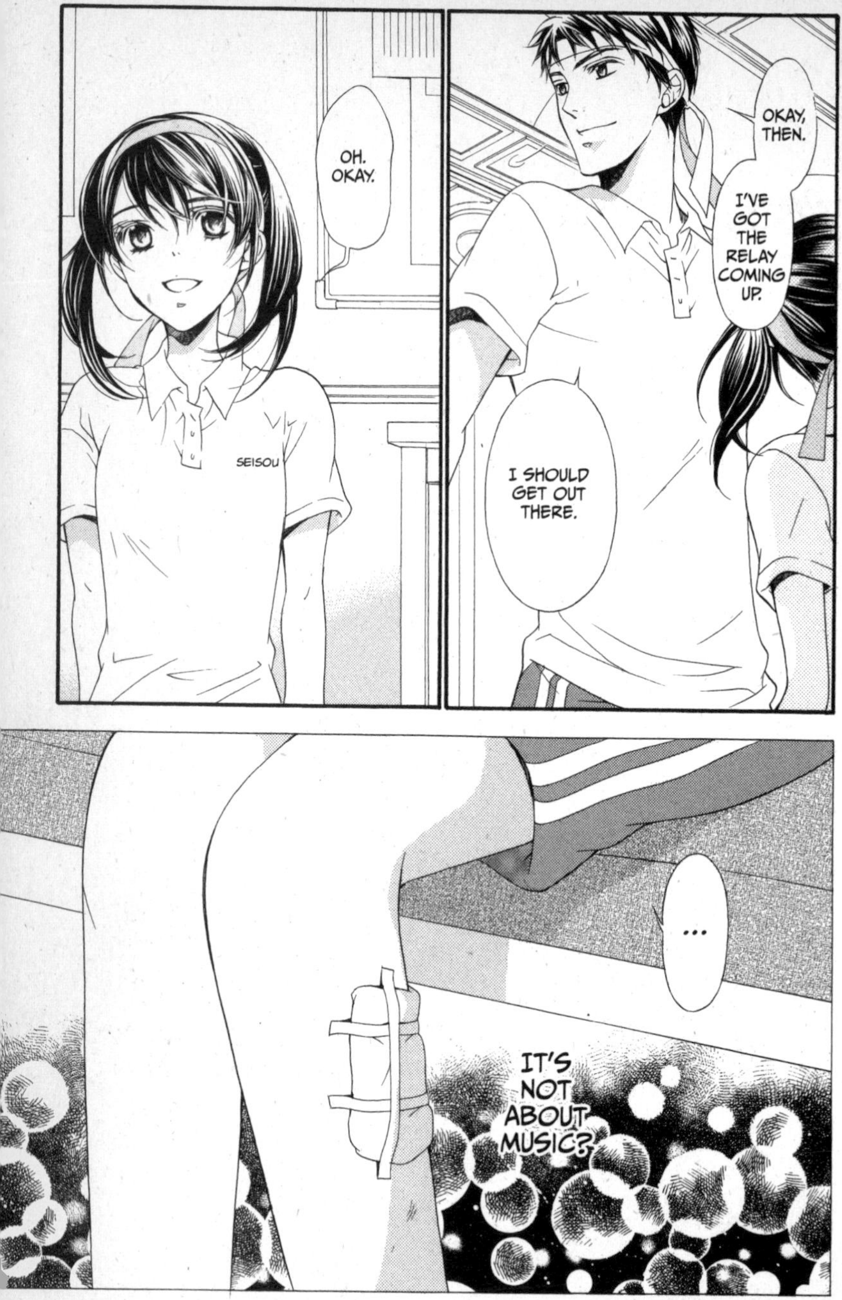
OKAY, THEN.
I'VE GOT THE RELAY COMING UP.
I SHOULD GET OUT THERE.
OH. OKAY.
SEISOU
...
IT'S NOT ABOUT MUSIC?

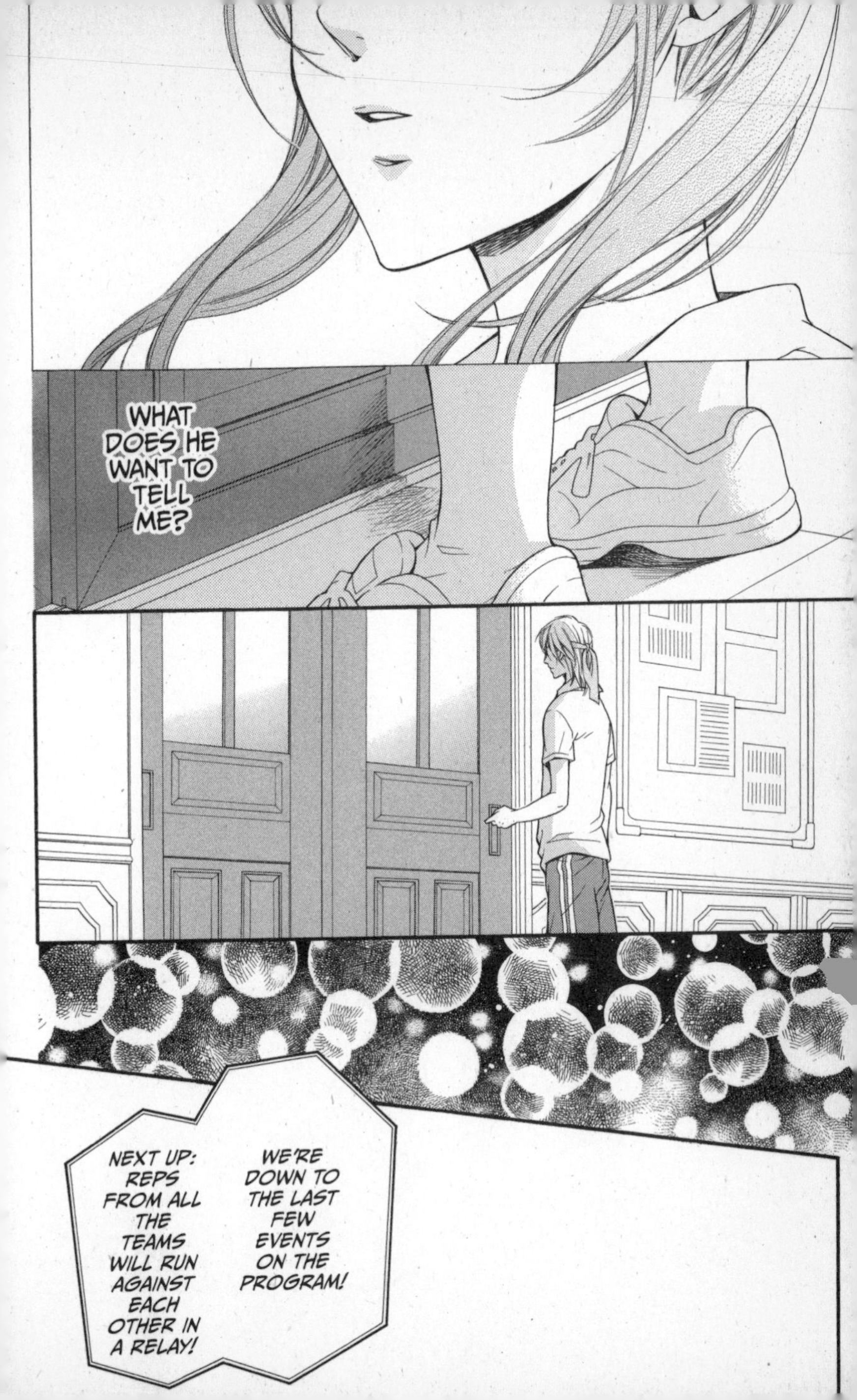
WHAT DOES HE WANT TO TELL ME?
WE'RE DOWN TO THE LAST FEW EVENTS ON THE PROGRAM!
NEXT UP: REPS FROM ALL THE TEAMS WILL RUN AGAINST EACH OTHER IN A RELAY!

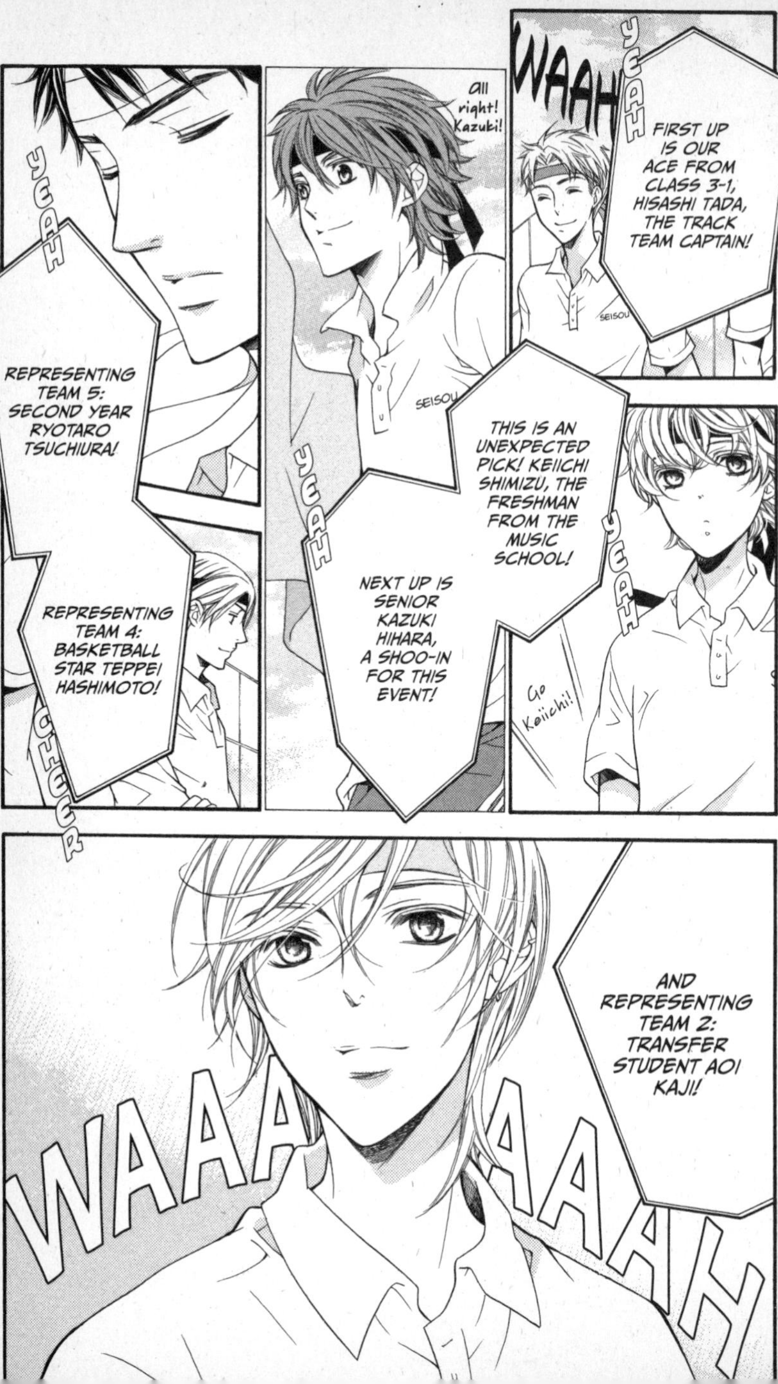
WAAH
YEAH
FIRST UP IS OUR ACE FROM CLASS 3-1, HISASHI TADA, THE TRACK TEAM CAPTAIN!
SEISOU
THIS IS AN UNEXPECTED PICK! KEIICHI SHIMIZU, THE FRESHMAN FROM THE MUSIC SCHOOL!
YEAH
Go Keiichi!
All right! Kazuki!
SEISOU
YEAH
NEXT UP IS SENIOR KAZUKI HIHARA, A SHOO-IN FOR THIS EVENT!
YEAH
REPRESENTING TEAM 5: SECOND YEAR RYOTARO TSUCHIURA!
REPRESENTING TEAM 4: BASKETBALL STAR TEPPEI HASHIMOTO!
CHEER
AND REPRESENTING TEAM 2: TRANSFER STUDENT AOI KAJI!
WAAAAAAAH

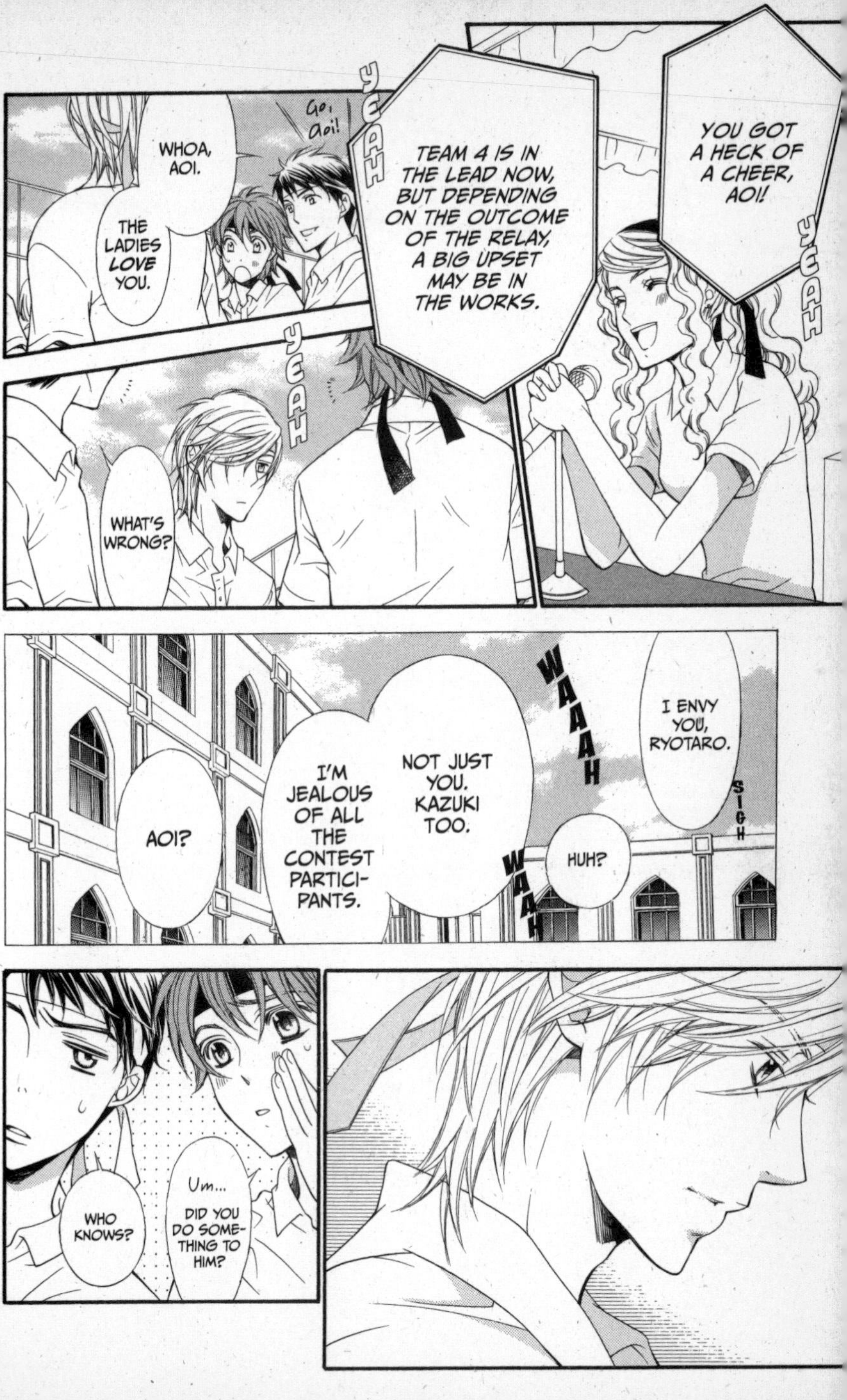
YOU GOT A HECK OF A CHEER, AOI!
YEAH
TEAM 4 IS IN THE LEAD NOW, BUT DEPENDING ON THE OUTCOME OF THE RELAY, A BIG UPSET MAY BE IN THE WORKS.
YEAH
Go, Aoi!
WHOA, AOI.
THE LADIES *LOVE* YOU.
YEAH
WHAT'S WRONG?
I ENVY YOU, RYOTARO.
SIGH
HUH?
WAAAH
NOT JUST YOU. KAZUKI TOO.
I'M JEALOUS OF ALL THE CONTEST PARTICI-PANTS.
WAAAH
AOI?
Um...
DID YOU DO SOME-THING TO HIM?
WHO KNOWS?

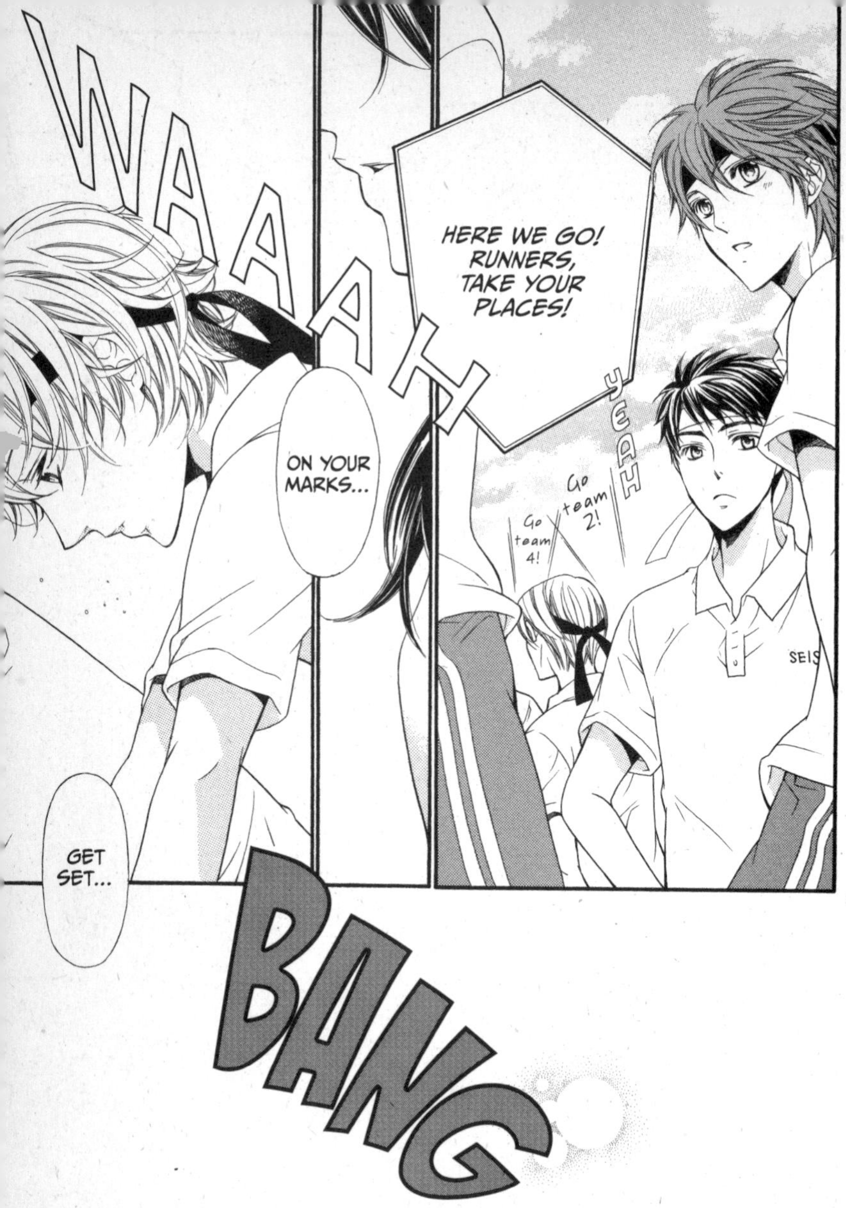
HERE WE GO! RUNNERS, TAKE YOUR PLACES!
YEAH
Go team 2!
Go team 4!
SEIS
WAAAH
ON YOUR MARKS...
GET SET...
BANG

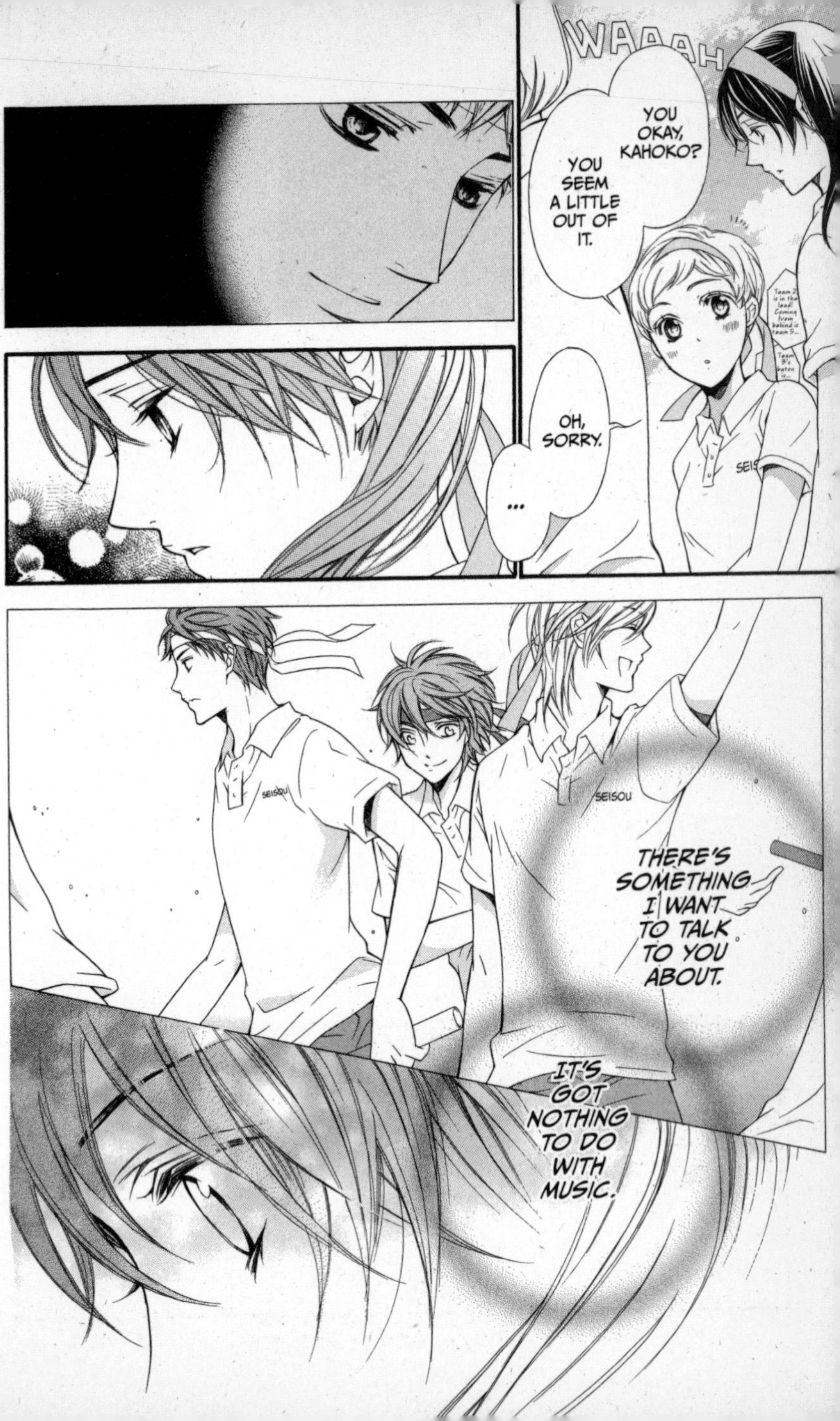
WAAAH
YOU OKAY, KAHOKO?
YOU SEEM A LITTLE OUT OF IT.
Team 2 is in the lead! Coming from behind is team 5...
Team 3's baton is...
OH, SORRY.
...
SEISOU
SEISOU
SEISOU
THERE'S SOMETHING I WANT TO TALK TO YOU ABOUT.
IT'S GOT NOTHING TO DO WITH MUSIC.

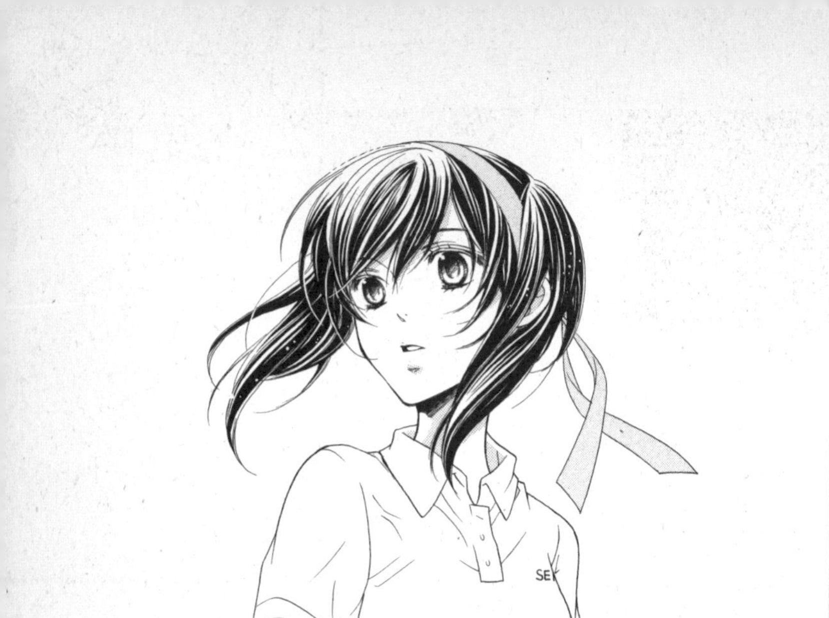
HUH?

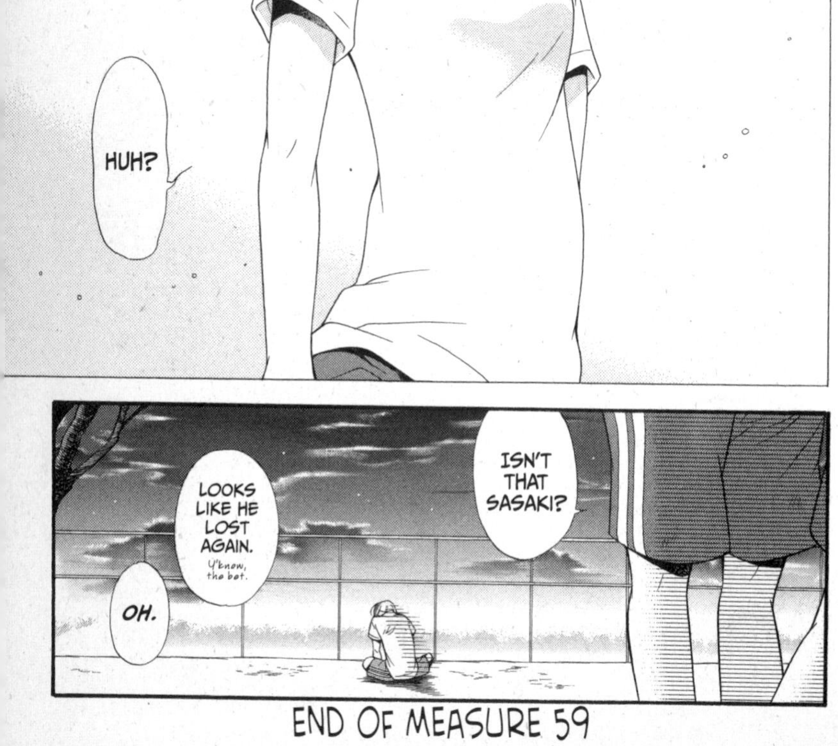
ISN'T THAT SASAKI?
LOOKS LIKE HE LOST AGAIN.
Y'know, the bet.
OH.

END OF MEASURE 59

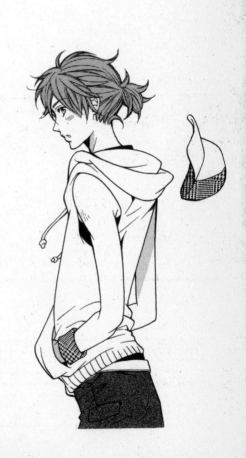

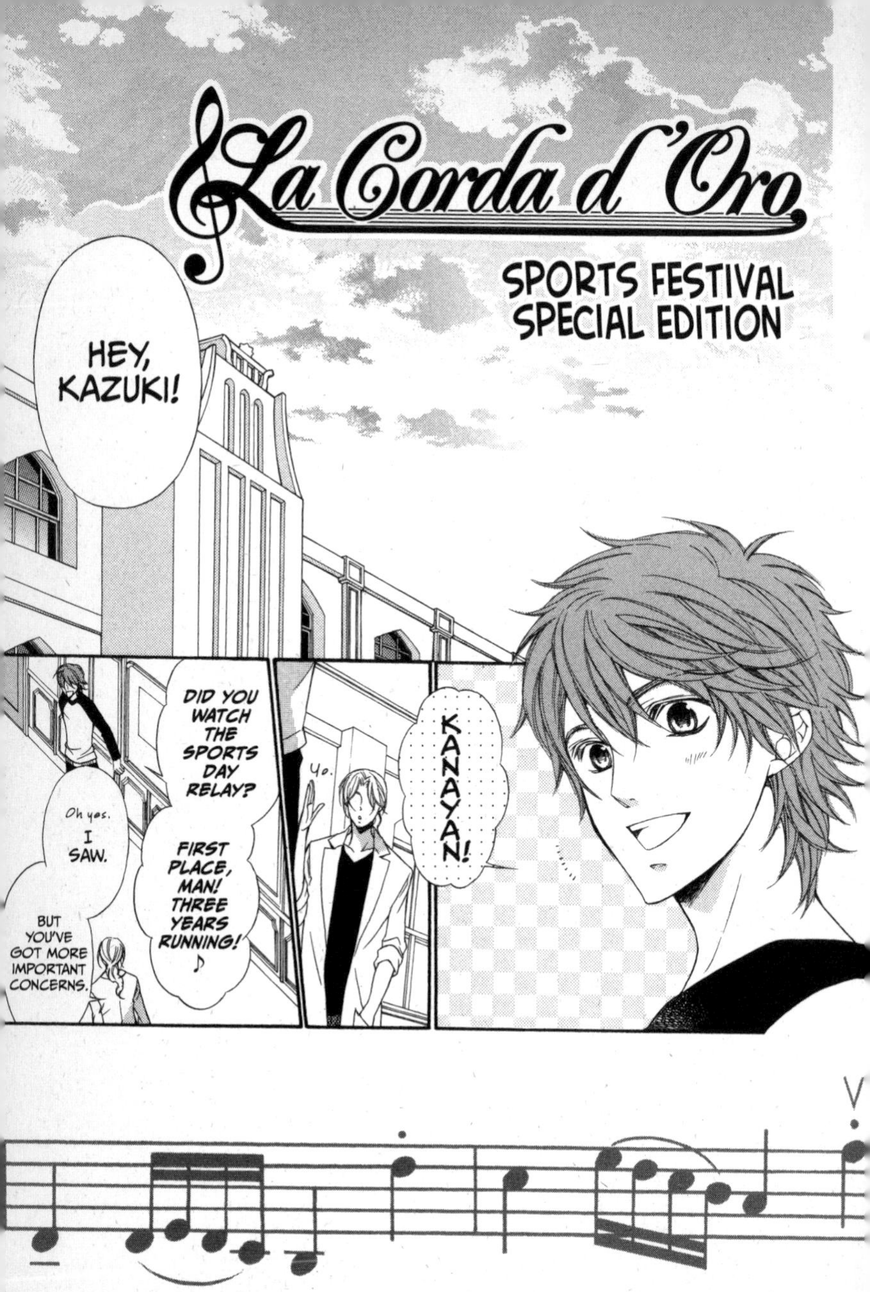
La Corda d'Oro
SPORTS FESTIVAL SPECIAL EDITION
HEY, KAZUKI!
KANAYAN!
Yo.
DID YOU WATCH THE SPORTS DAY RELAY?
FIRST PLACE, MAN! THREE YEARS RUNNING! ♪
Oh yes. I SAW.
BUT YOU'VE GOT MORE IMPORTANT CONCERNS.

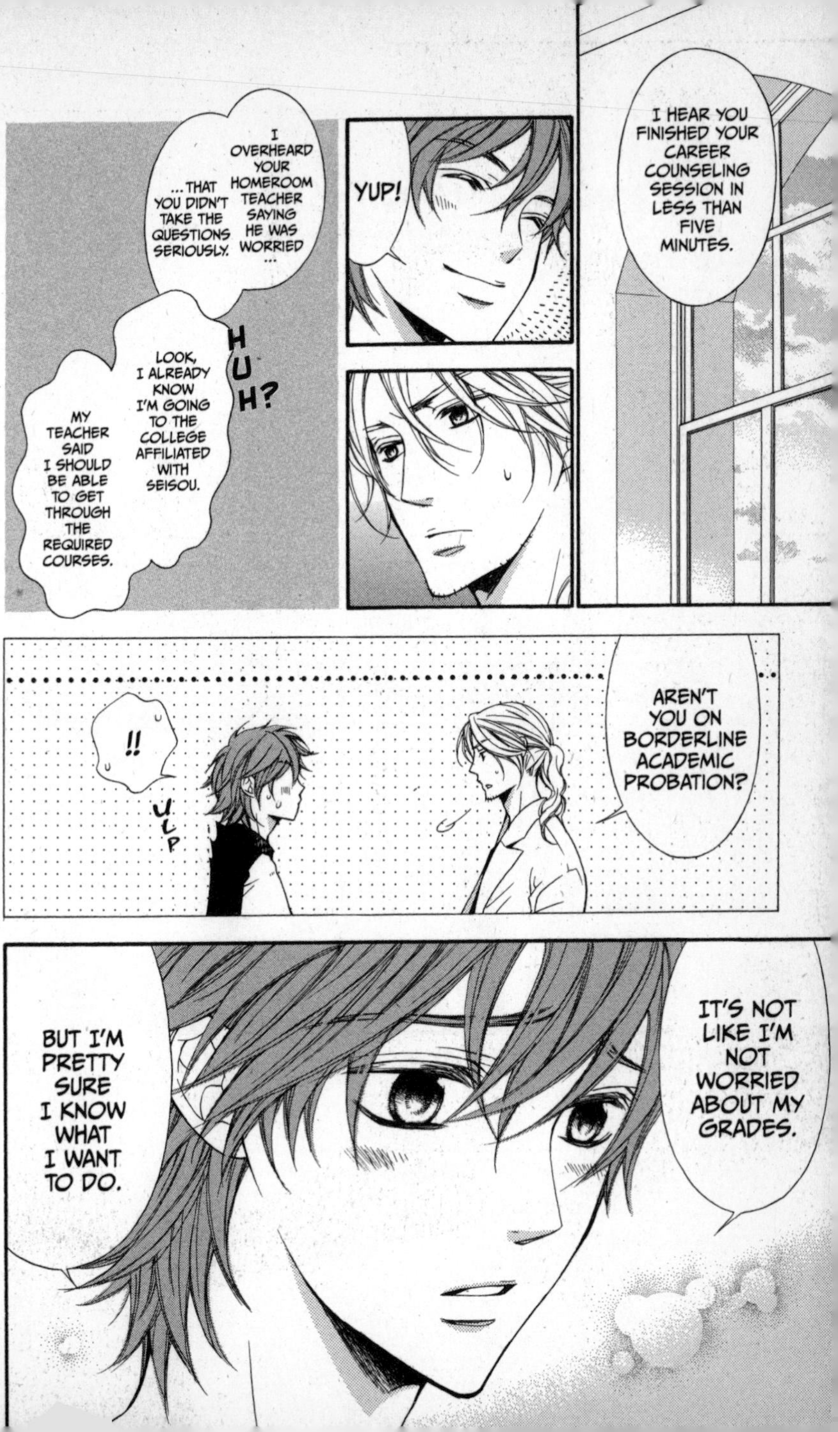
I HEAR YOU FINISHED YOUR CAREER COUNSELING SESSION IN LESS THAN FIVE MINUTES.
YUP!
I OVERHEARD YOUR HOMEROOM TEACHER SAYING HE WAS WORRIED...
...THAT YOU DIDN'T TAKE THE QUESTIONS SERIOUSLY.
HUH?
LOOK, I ALREADY KNOW I'M GOING TO THE COLLEGE AFFILIATED WITH SEISOU.
MY TEACHER SAID I SHOULD BE ABLE TO GET THROUGH THE REQUIRED COURSES.
AREN'T YOU ON BORDERLINE ACADEMIC PROBATION?
!!
ULP
IT'S NOT LIKE I'M NOT WORRIED ABOUT MY GRADES.
BUT I'M PRETTY SURE I KNOW WHAT I WANT TO DO.

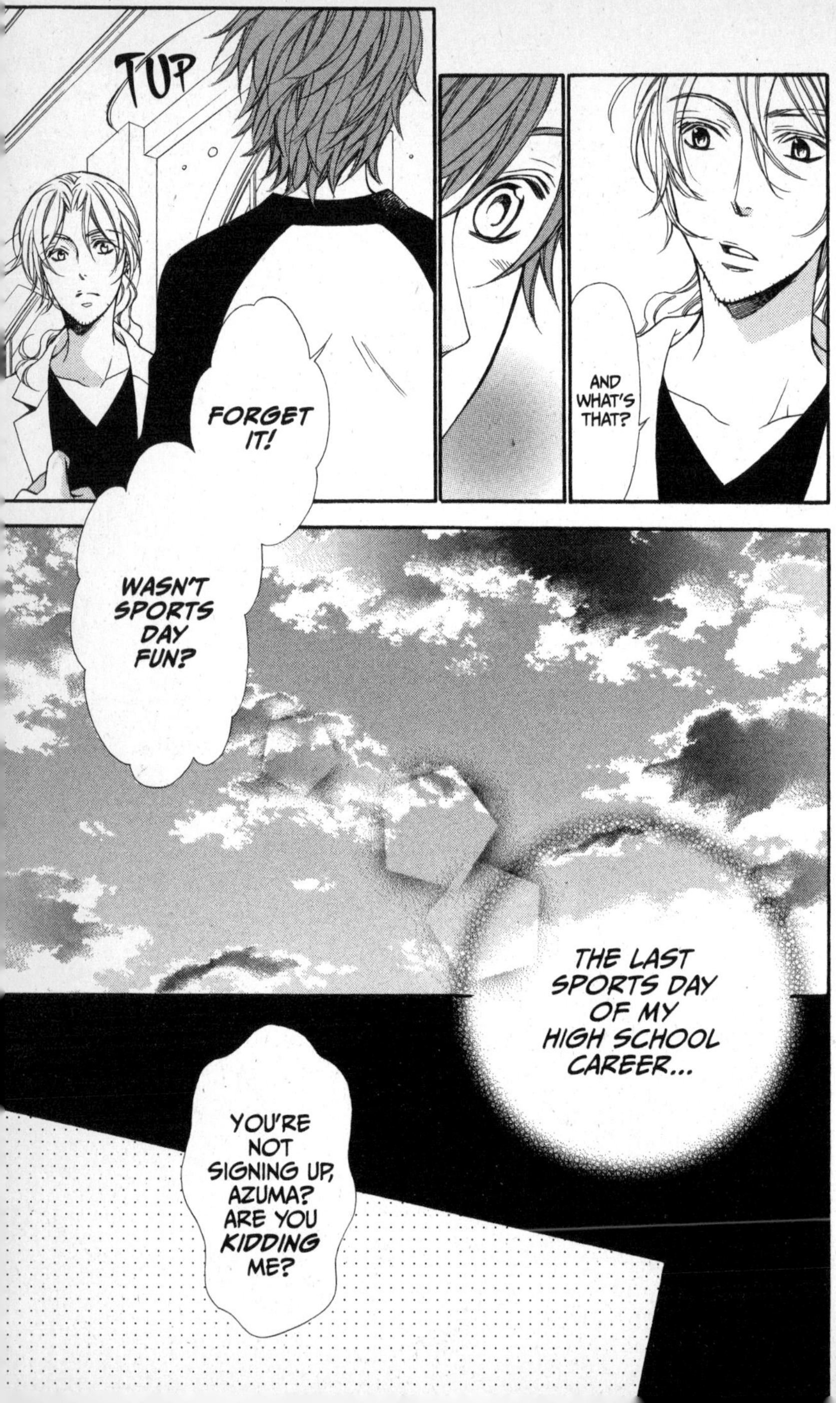
AND WHAT'S THAT?
TUP
FORGET IT!
WASN'T SPORTS DAY FUN?
THE LAST SPORTS DAY OF MY HIGH SCHOOL CAREER...
YOU'RE NOT SIGNING UP, AZUMA? ARE YOU KIDDING ME?

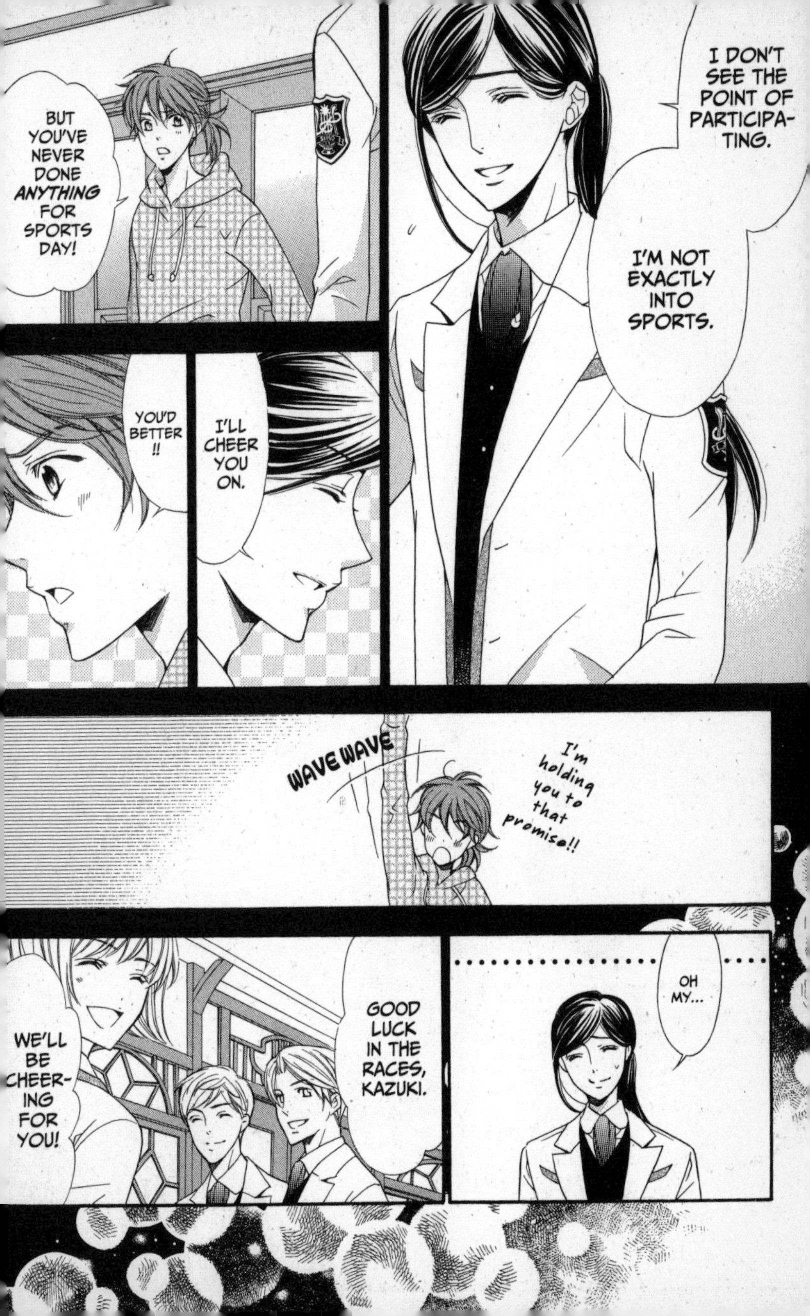
I DON'T SEE THE POINT OF PARTICIPATING.
I'M NOT EXACTLY INTO SPORTS.
BUT YOU'VE NEVER DONE *ANYTHING* FOR SPORTS DAY!
I'LL CHEER YOU ON.
YOU'D BETTER!!
WAVE WAVE
I'm holding you to that promise!!
....
OH MY...
GOOD LUCK IN THE RACES, KAZUKI.
WE'LL BE CHEERING FOR YOU!

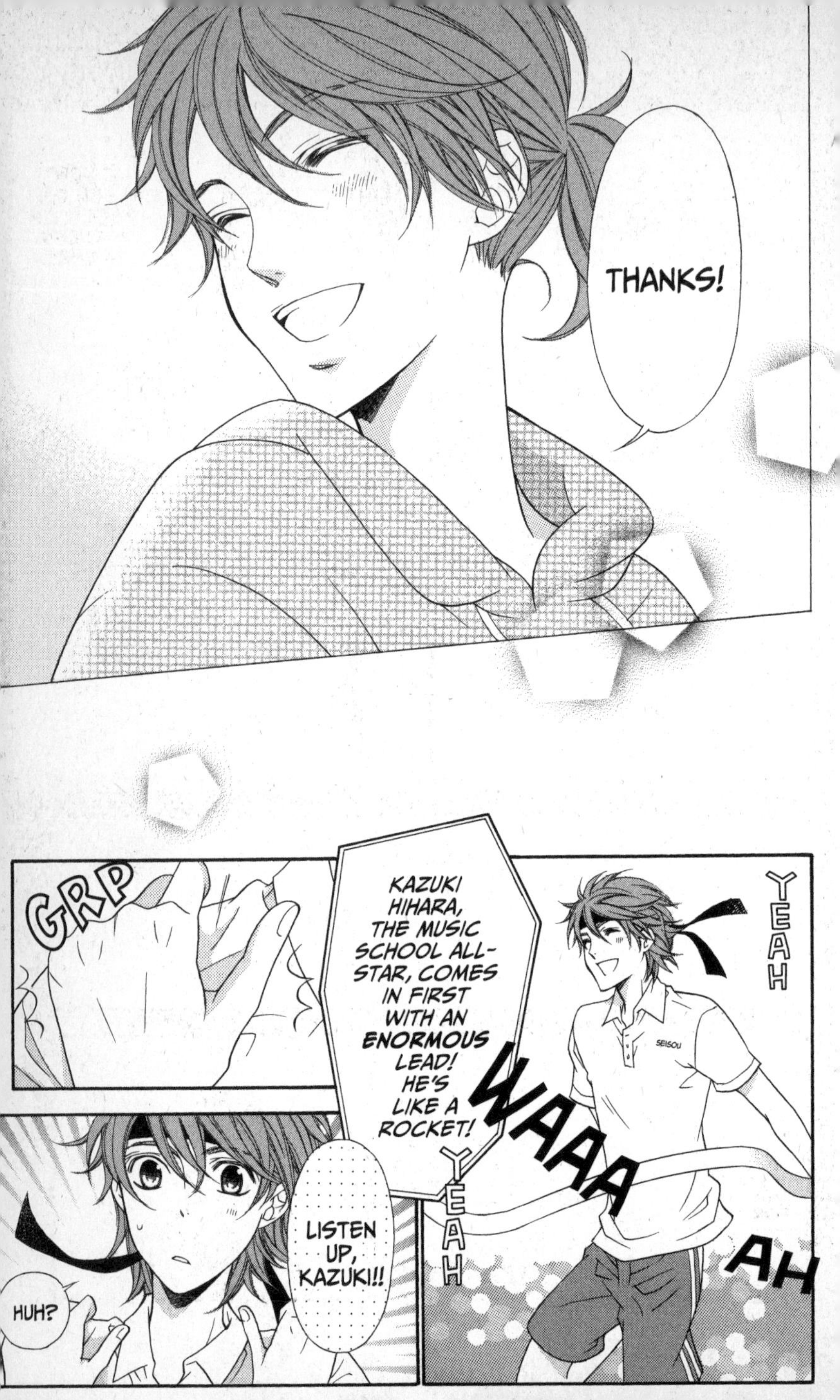
THANKS!
KAZUKI HIHARA, THE MUSIC SCHOOL ALL-STAR, COMES IN FIRST WITH AN ENORMOUS LEAD! HE'S LIKE A ROCKET!
YEAH
SEISOU
WAAA
AH
YEAH
GRP
LISTEN UP, KAZUKI!!!
HUH?

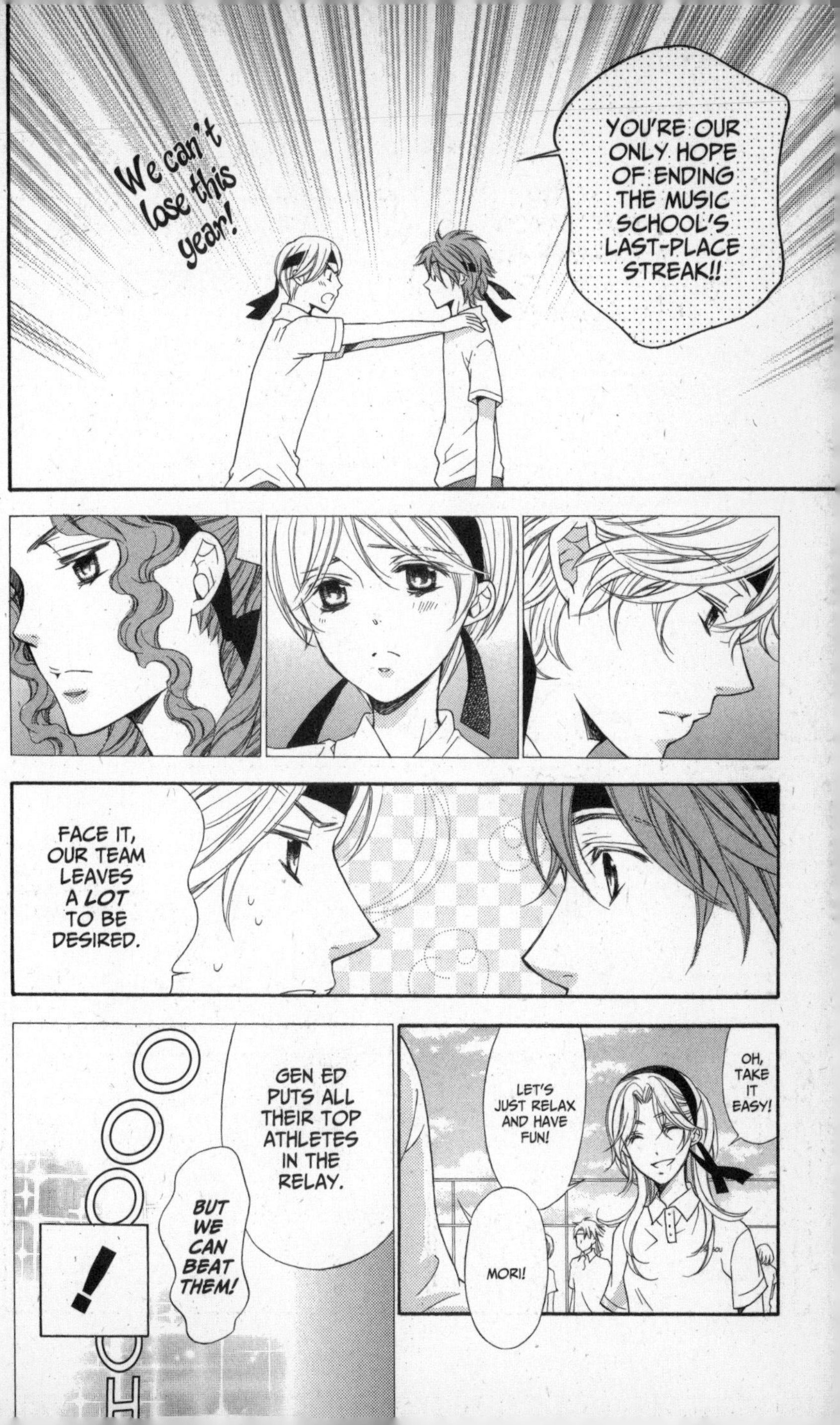
YOU'RE OUR ONLY HOPE OF ENDING THE MUSIC SCHOOL'S LAST-PLACE STREAK!!
We can't lose this year!
FACE IT, OUR TEAM LEAVES A *LOT* TO BE DESIRED.
OH, TAKE IT EASY!
LET'S JUST RELAX AND HAVE FUN!
MORI!
GEN ED PUTS ALL THEIR TOP ATHLETES IN THE RELAY.
BUT WE CAN BEAT THEM!
!

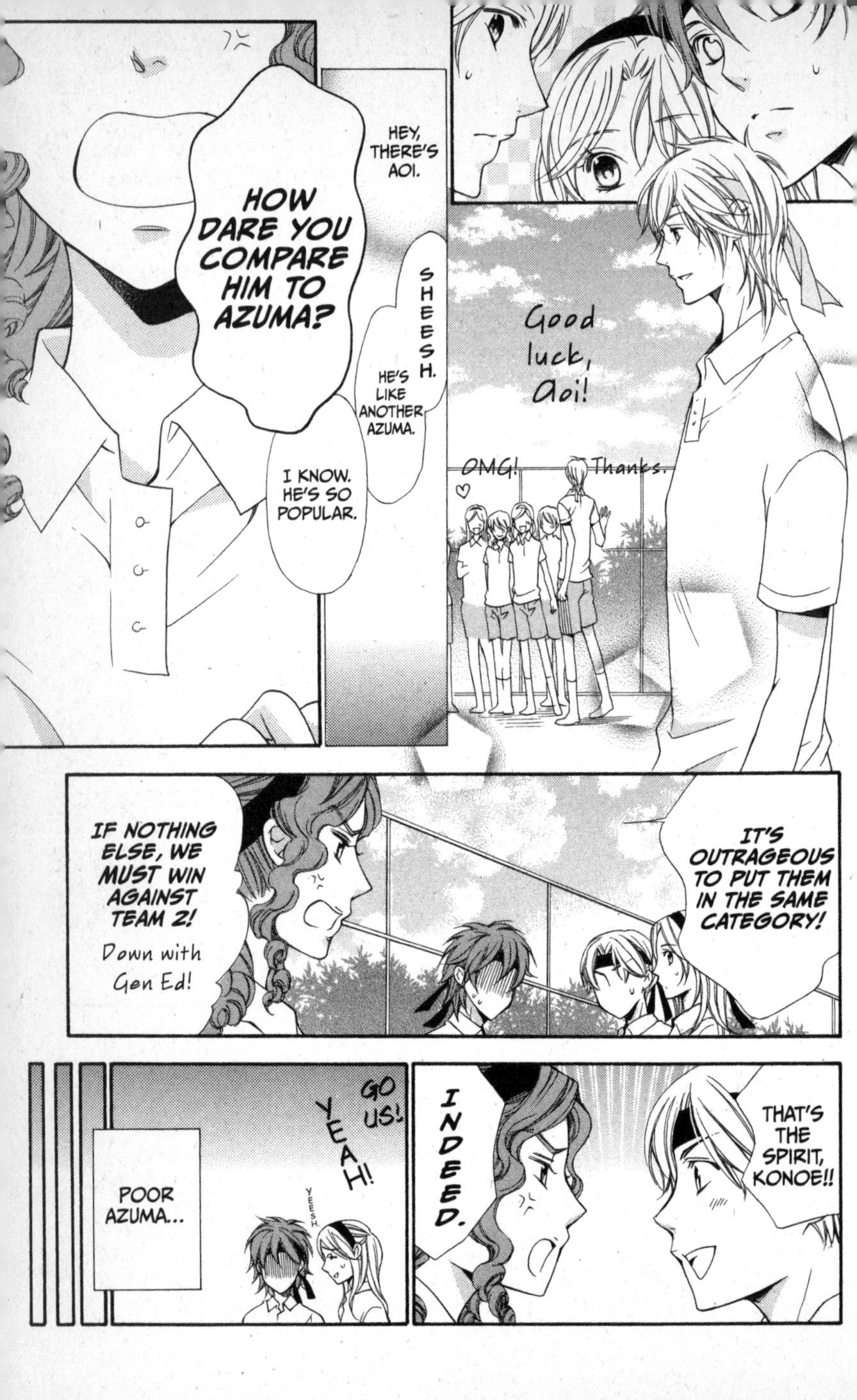
Good luck, Aoi!
OMG!
Thanks.
HEY, THERE'S AOI.
SHEESH.
HE'S LIKE ANOTHER AZUMA.
I KNOW. HE'S SO POPULAR.
HOW DARE YOU COMPARE HIM TO AZUMA?
IT'S OUTRAGEOUS TO PUT THEM IN THE SAME CATEGORY!
IF NOTHING ELSE, WE MUST WIN AGAINST TEAM 2!
Down with Gen Ed!
THAT'S THE SPIRIT, KONOE!!
INDEED.
GO US!
YEAH!
YEESH.
POOR AZUMA...

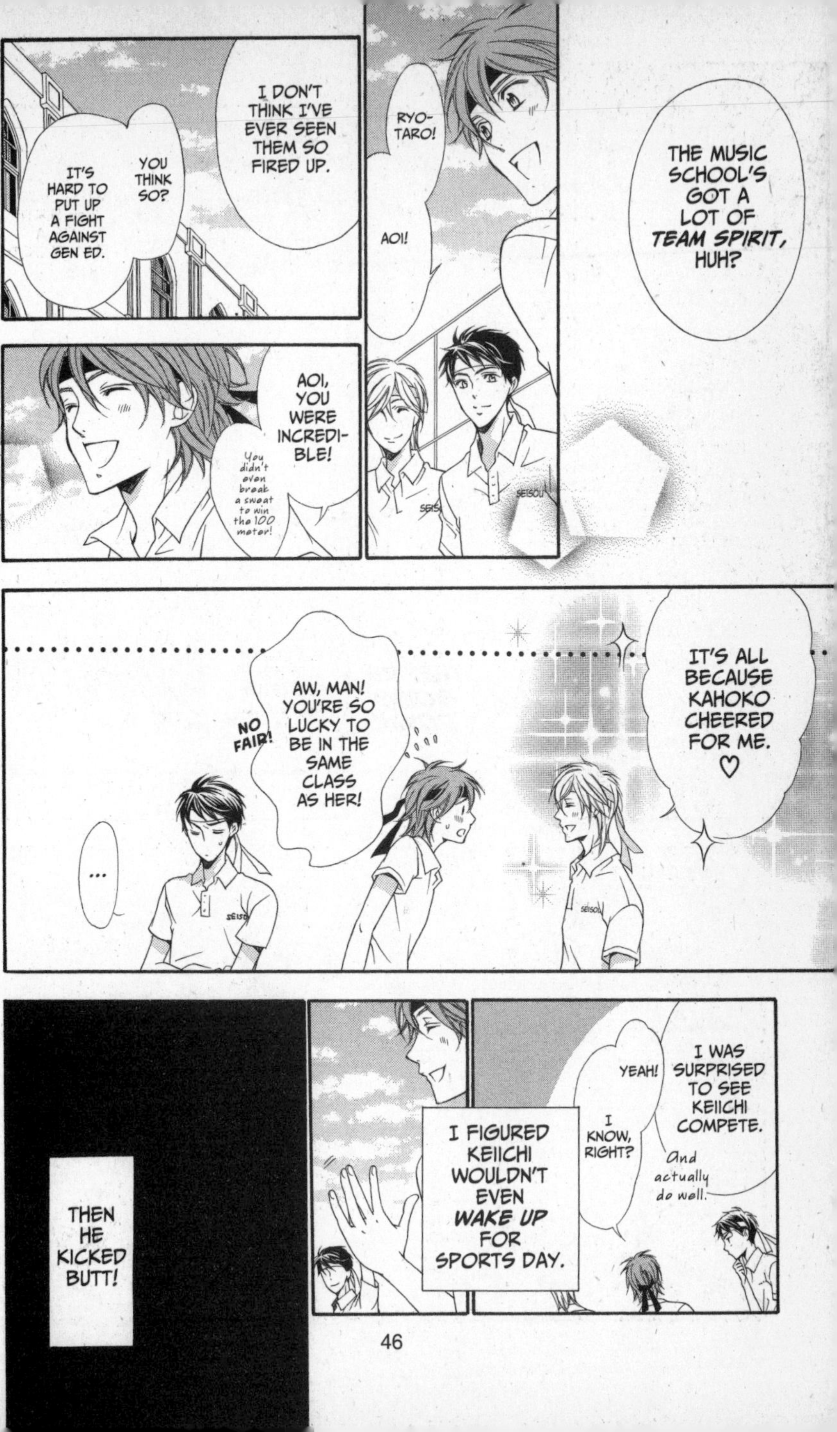

THE MUSIC SCHOOL'S GOT A LOT OF TEAM SPIRIT, HUH?
RYO-TARO!
AOI!
I DON'T THINK I'VE EVER SEEN THEM SO FIRED UP.
YOU THINK SO?
IT'S HARD TO PUT UP A FIGHT AGAINST GEN ED.
AOI, YOU WERE INCREDIBLE!
You didn't even break a sweat to win the 100 meter!
IT'S ALL BECAUSE KAHOKO CHEERED FOR ME. ♡
AW, MAN! YOU'RE SO LUCKY TO BE IN THE SAME CLASS AS HER!
NO FAIR!
...
I WAS SURPRISED TO SEE KEIICHI COMPETE.
And actually do well.
YEAH!
I KNOW, RIGHT?
I FIGURED KEIICHI WOULDN'T EVEN WAKE UP FOR SPORTS DAY.
THEN HE KICKED BUTT!

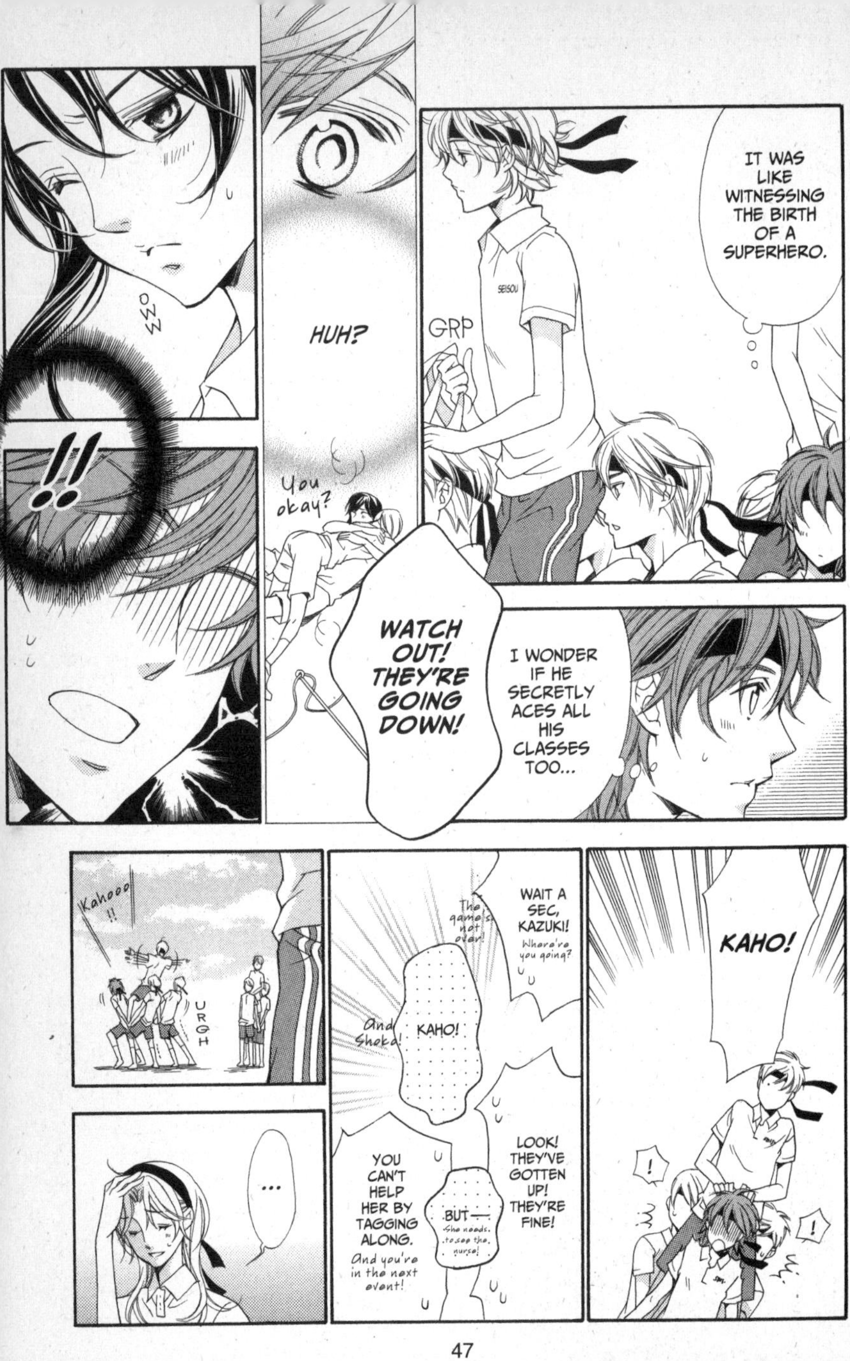

IT WAS LIKE WITNESSING THE BIRTH OF A SUPERHERO.
GRP
SEISOU
I WONDER IF HE SECRETLY ACES ALL HIS CLASSES TOO...
WATCH OUT! THEY'RE GOING DOWN!
HUH?
You okay?
OWW
!!
KAHO!
WAIT A SEC, KAZUKI!
Where're you going?
The game's not over!
And Shoko!
KAHO!
LOOK! THEY'VE GOTTEN UP! THEY'RE FINE!
BUT—
She needs to see the nurse!
YOU CAN'T HELP HER BY TAGGING ALONG.
And you're in the next event!
Kahooo!!
URGH
...

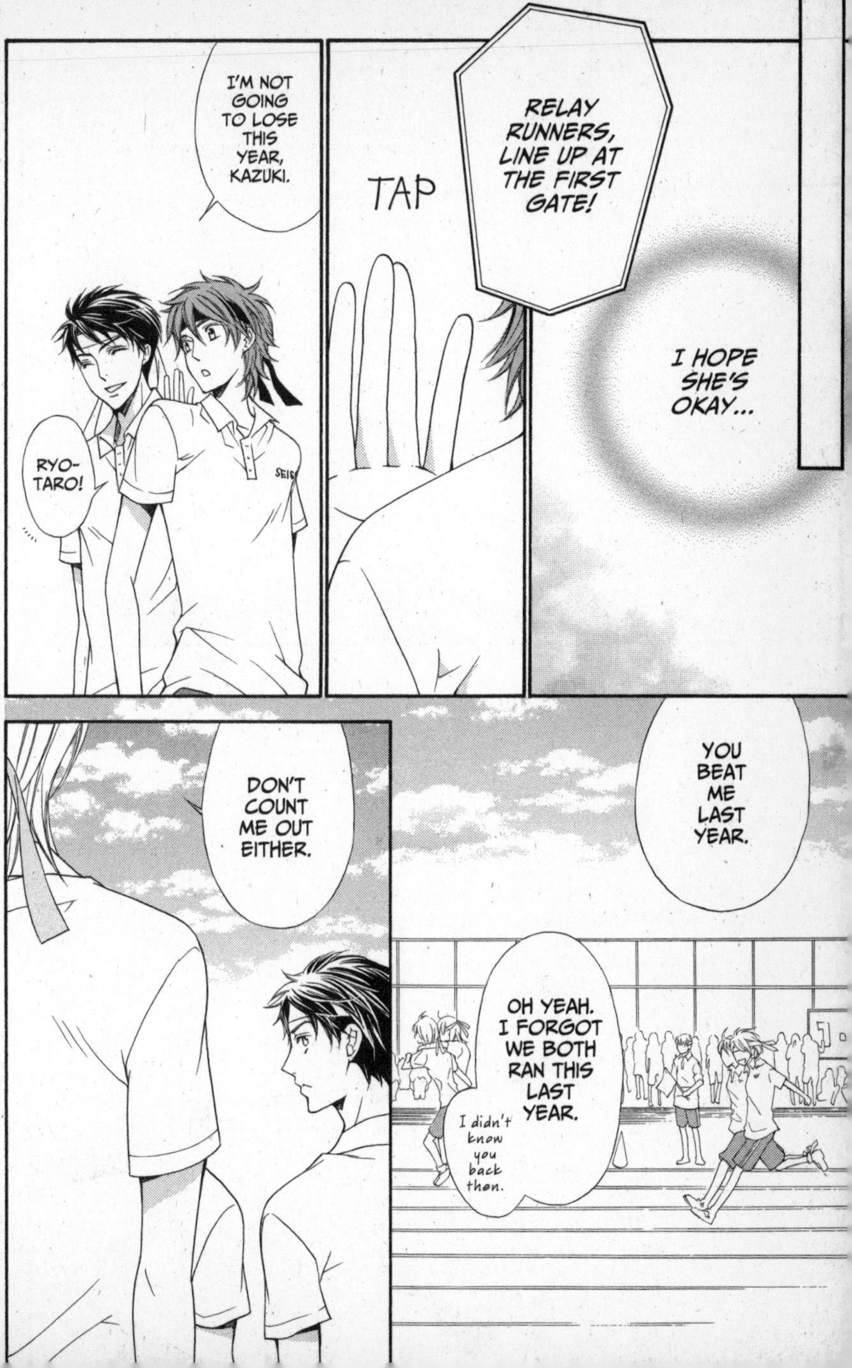
RELAY RUNNERS, LINE UP AT THE FIRST GATE!
I HOPE SHE'S OKAY...
TAP
I'M NOT GOING TO LOSE THIS YEAR, KAZUKI.
RYO-TARO!
SEIS
YOU BEAT ME LAST YEAR.
OH YEAH. I FORGOT WE BOTH RAN THIS LAST YEAR.
I didn't know you back then.
DON'T COUNT ME OUT EITHER.

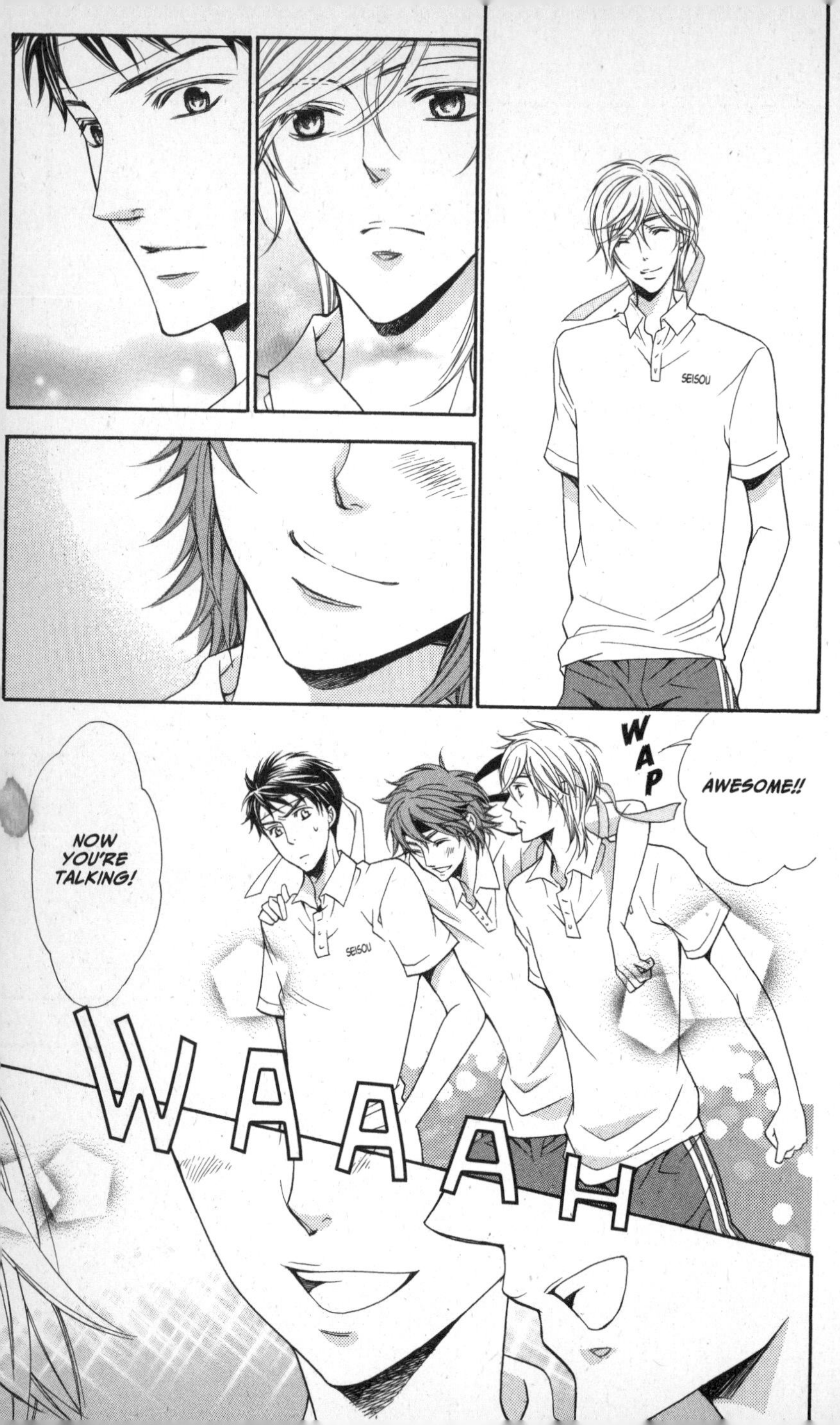
SEISOU
WAP
AWESOME!!
NOW YOU'RE TALKING!
SEISOU
WAAAH

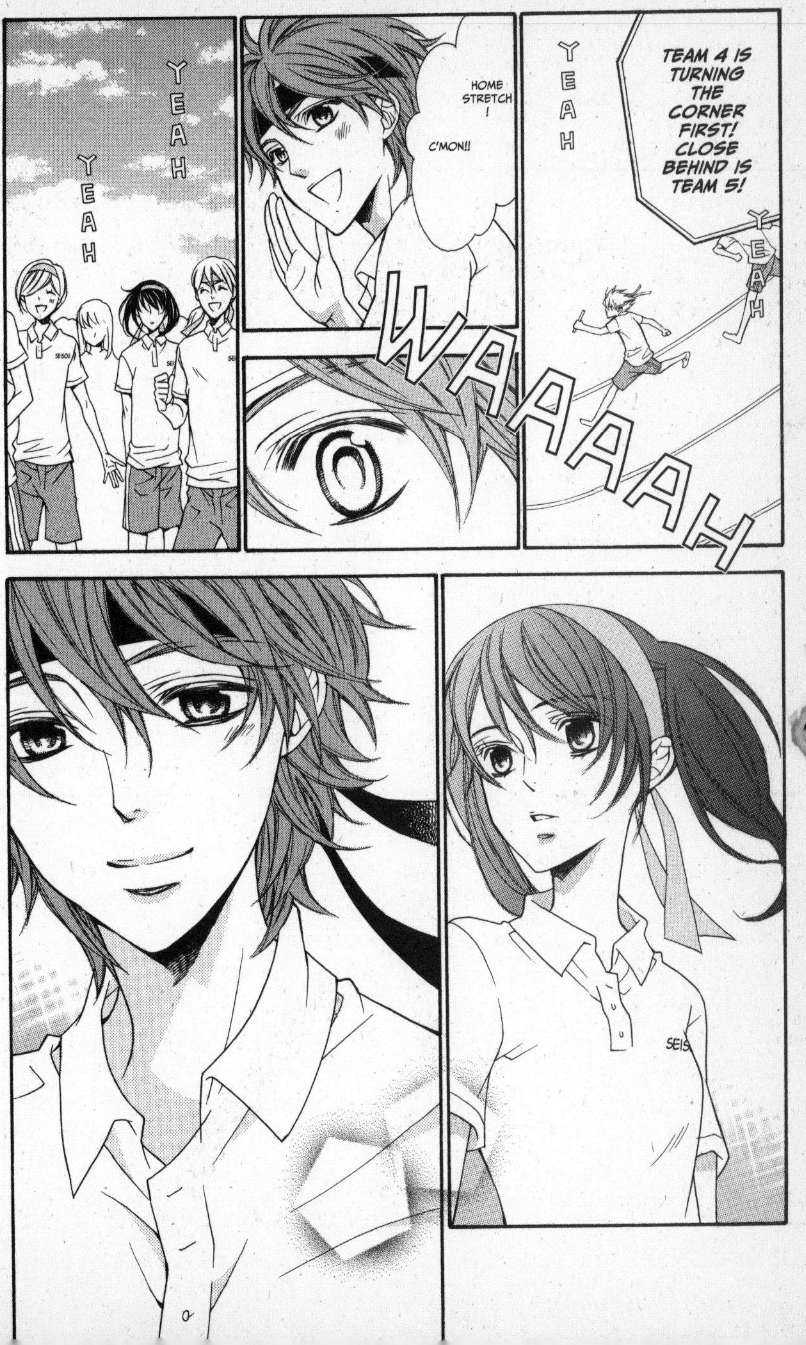
TEAM 4 IS TURNING THE CORNER FIRST! CLOSE BEHIND IS TEAM 5!
YEAH
YEAH
HOME STRETCH!
C'MON!!
WAAAAAH
YEAH
YEAH

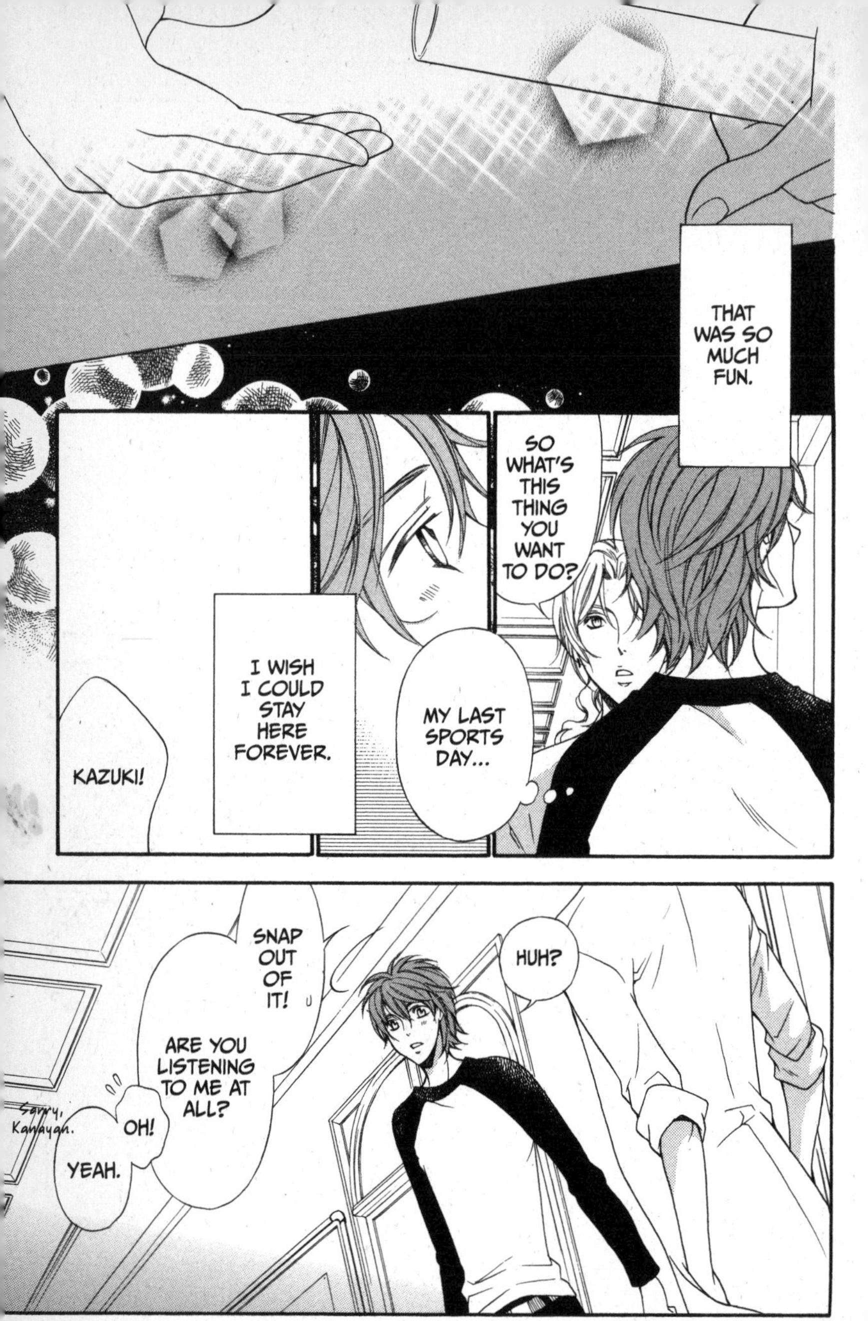
THAT WAS SO MUCH FUN.
SO WHAT'S THIS THING YOU WANT TO DO?
MY LAST SPORTS DAY...
I WISH I COULD STAY HERE FOREVER.
KAZUKI!
HUH?
SNAP OUT OF IT!
ARE YOU LISTENING TO ME AT ALL?
OH!
YEAH.
Sorry, Kanayan.

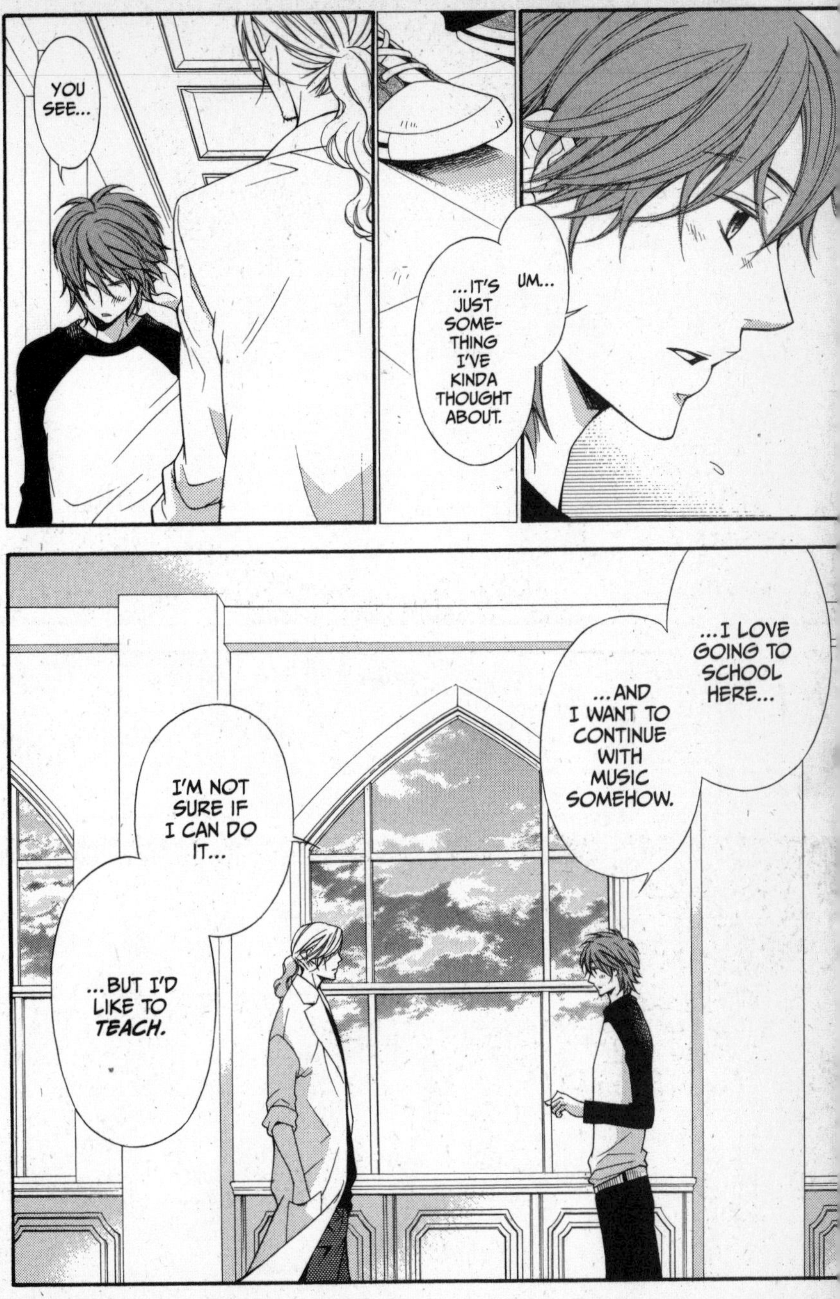
UM...
...IT'S JUST SOMETHING I'VE KINDA THOUGHT ABOUT.
YOU SEE...
...I LOVE GOING TO SCHOOL HERE...
...AND I WANT TO CONTINUE WITH MUSIC SOMEHOW.
I'M NOT SURE IF I CAN DO IT...
...BUT I'D LIKE TO *TEACH.*

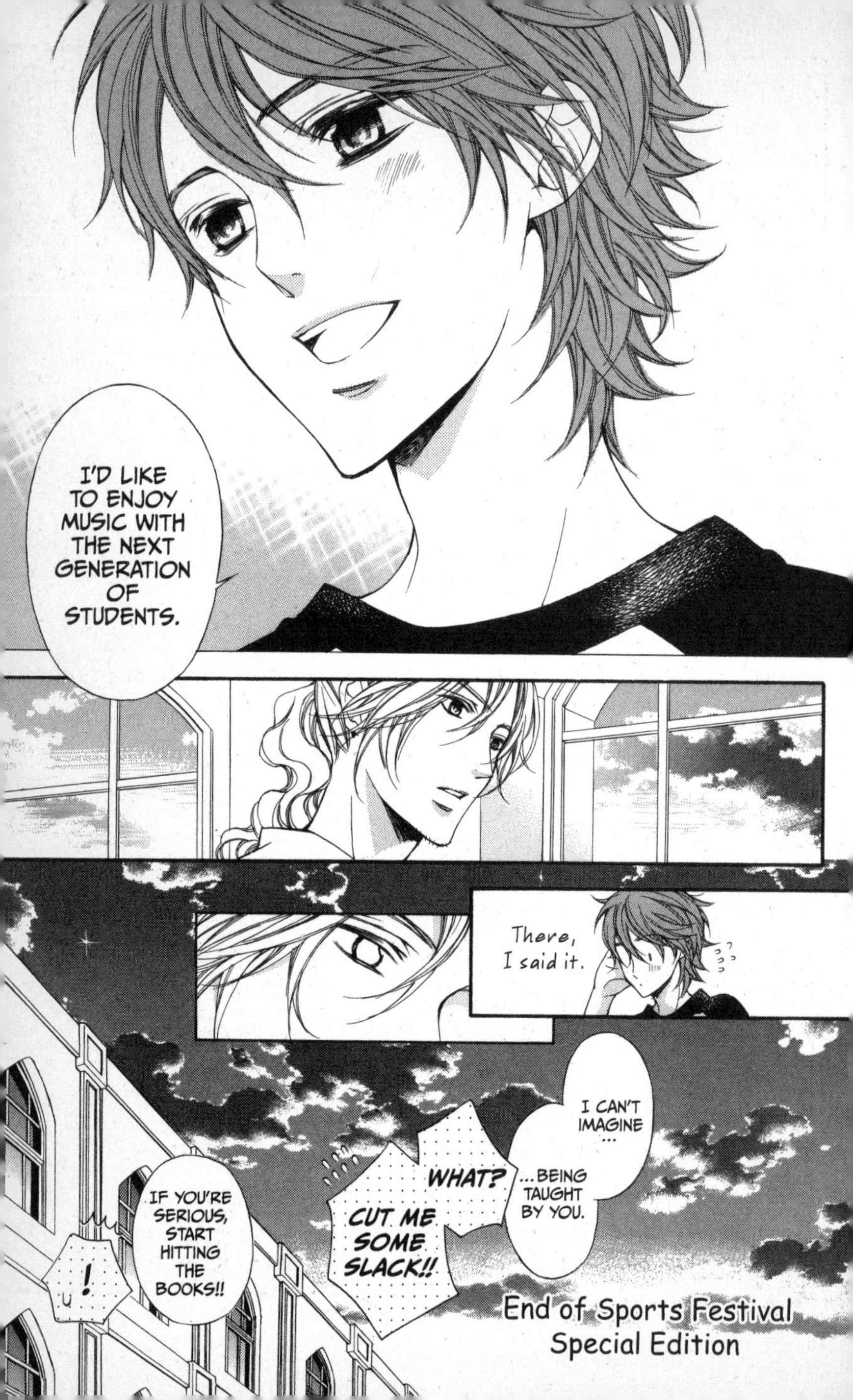
I'D LIKE TO ENJOY MUSIC WITH THE NEXT GENERATION OF STUDENTS.
There, I said it.
I CAN'T IMAGINE...
...BEING TAUGHT BY YOU.
WHAT?
CUT ME SOME SLACK!!
IF YOU'RE SERIOUS, START HITTING THE BOOKS!!
!
End of Sports Festival Special Edition

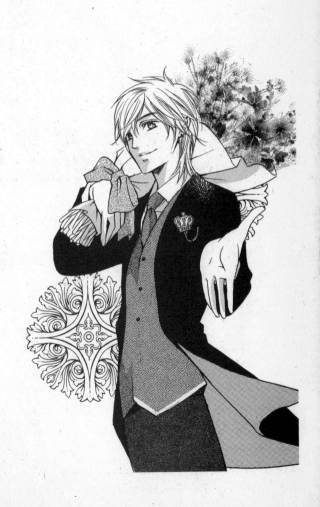

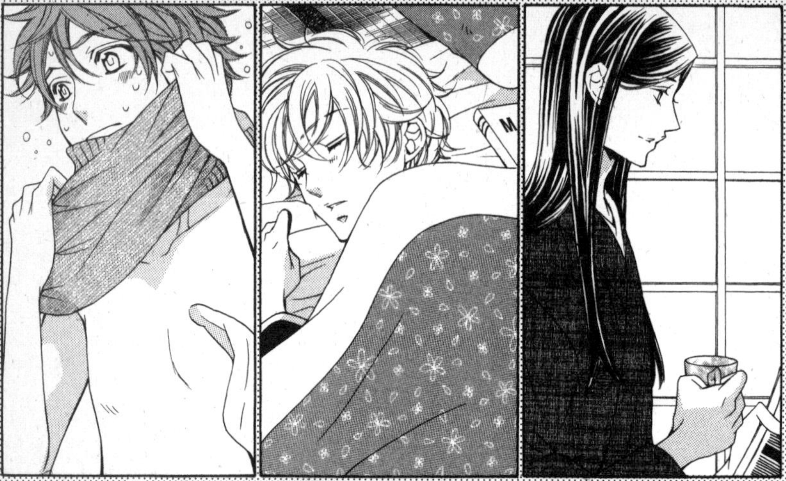

La Corda d'Oro

MEASURE 60

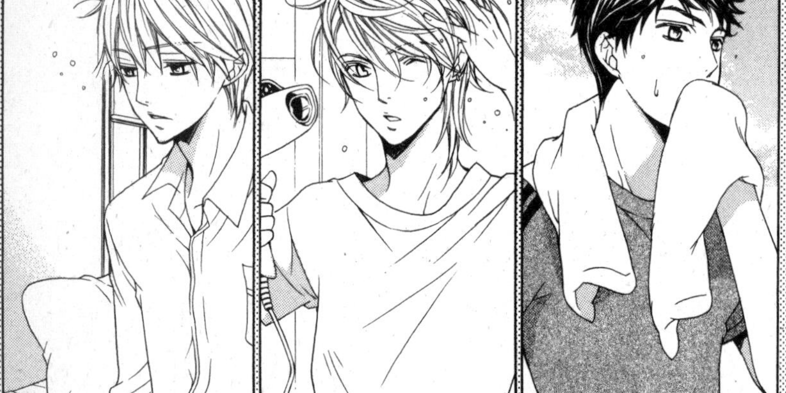

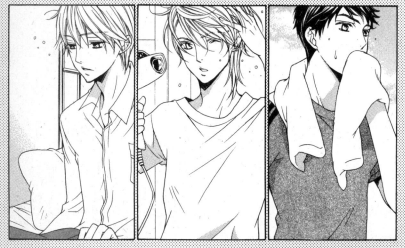

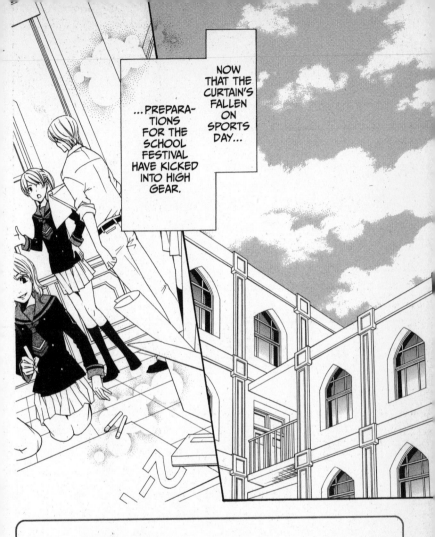

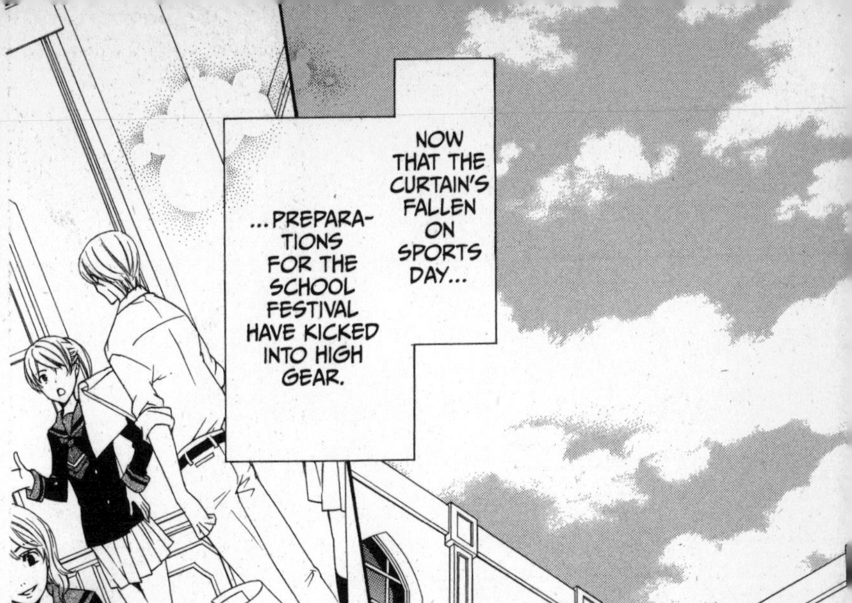
NOW THAT THE CURTAIN'S FALLEN ON SPORTS DAY...
...PREPARATIONS FOR THE SCHOOL FESTIVAL HAVE KICKED INTO HIGH GEAR.

Daily Happenings 47

Swag...

When I open my cupboard, I realize that over half of my mugs are La Corda mugs. I always get two or three as samples. I really use them!

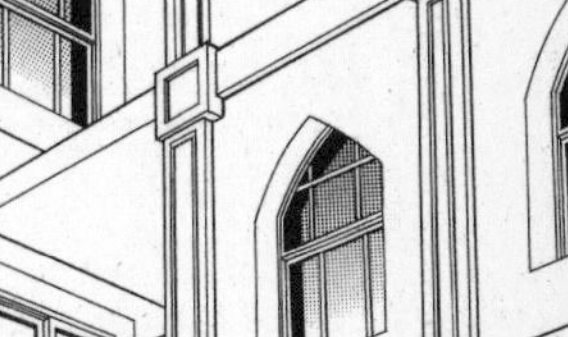

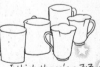

I think there's a 7:3 ratio of La Corda swag and everything else.

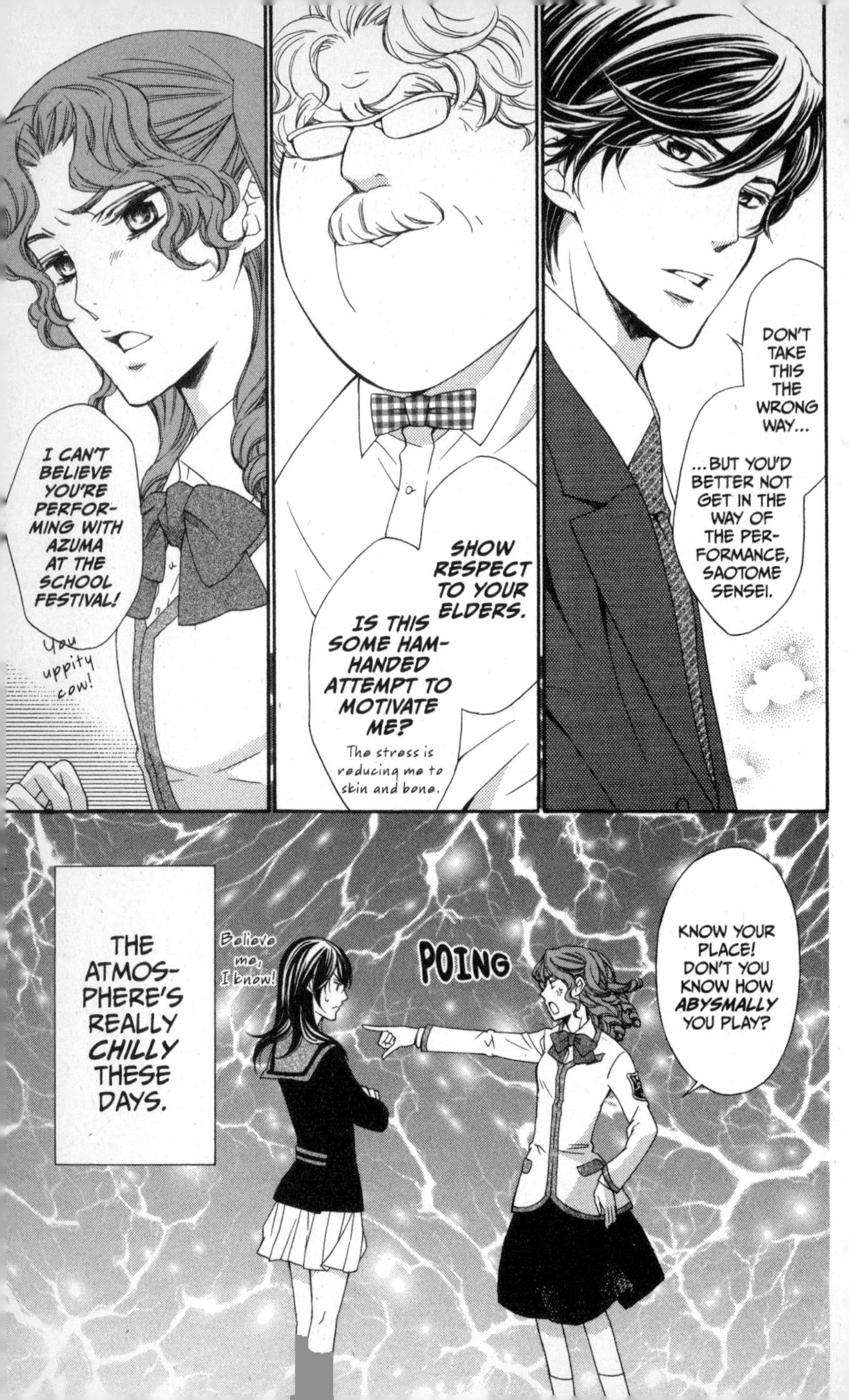
DON'T TAKE THIS THE WRONG WAY...
...BUT YOU'D BETTER NOT GET IN THE WAY OF THE PER-FORMANCE, SAOTOME SENSEI.
SHOW RESPECT TO YOUR ELDERS.
IS THIS SOME HAM-HANDED ATTEMPT TO MOTIVATE ME?
The stress is reducing me to skin and bone.
I CAN'T BELIEVE YOU'RE PERFOR-MING WITH AZUMA AT THE SCHOOL FESTIVAL!
You uppity cow!
KNOW YOUR PLACE! DON'T YOU KNOW HOW ABYSMALLY YOU PLAY?
POING
Believe me, I know!
THE ATMOS-PHERE'S REALLY CHILLY THESE DAYS.

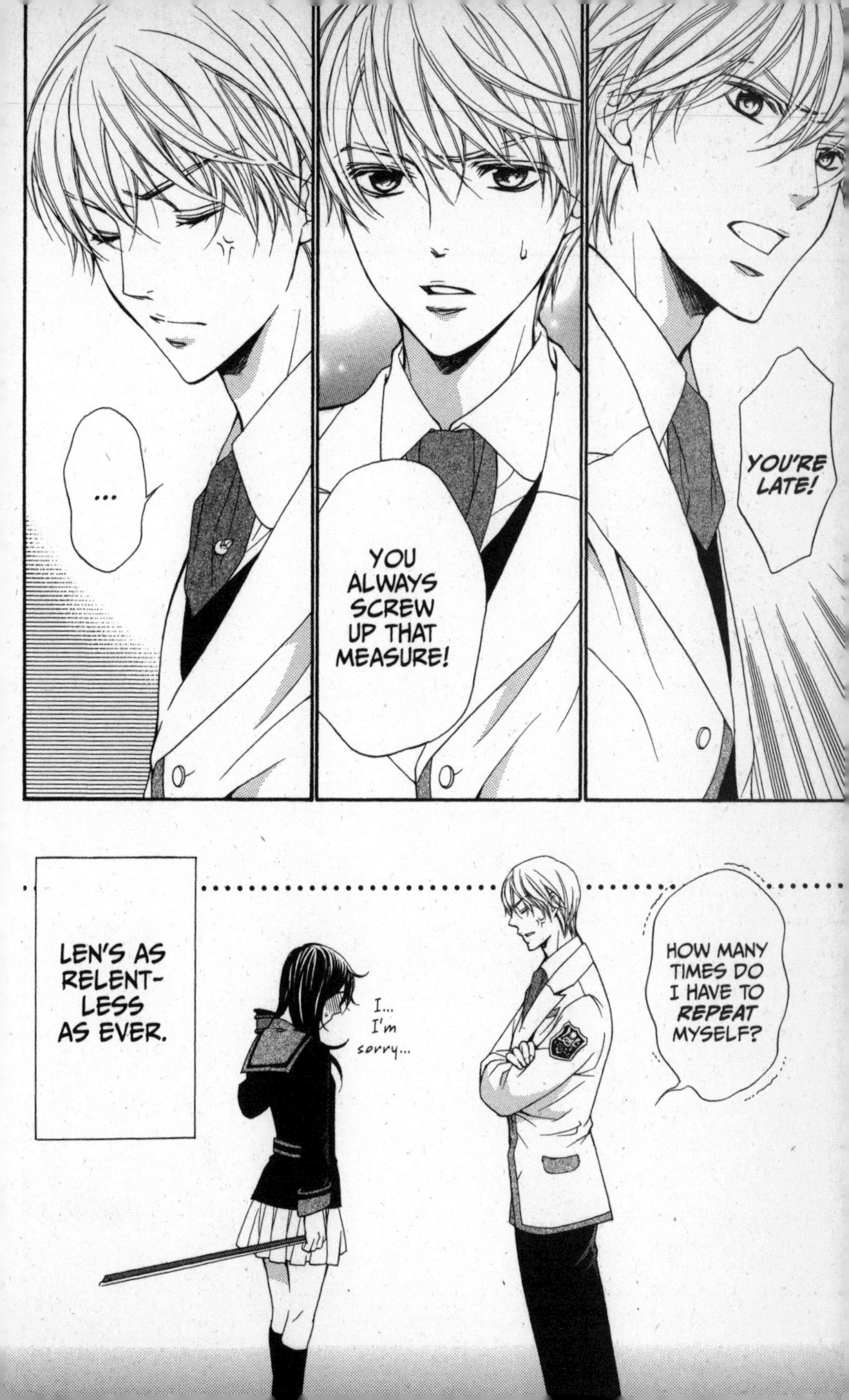
YOU'RE LATE!
YOU ALWAYS SCREW UP THAT MEASURE!
...
HOW MANY TIMES DO I HAVE TO *REPEAT* MYSELF?
I... I'm sorry...
LEN'S AS RELENT-LESS AS EVER.

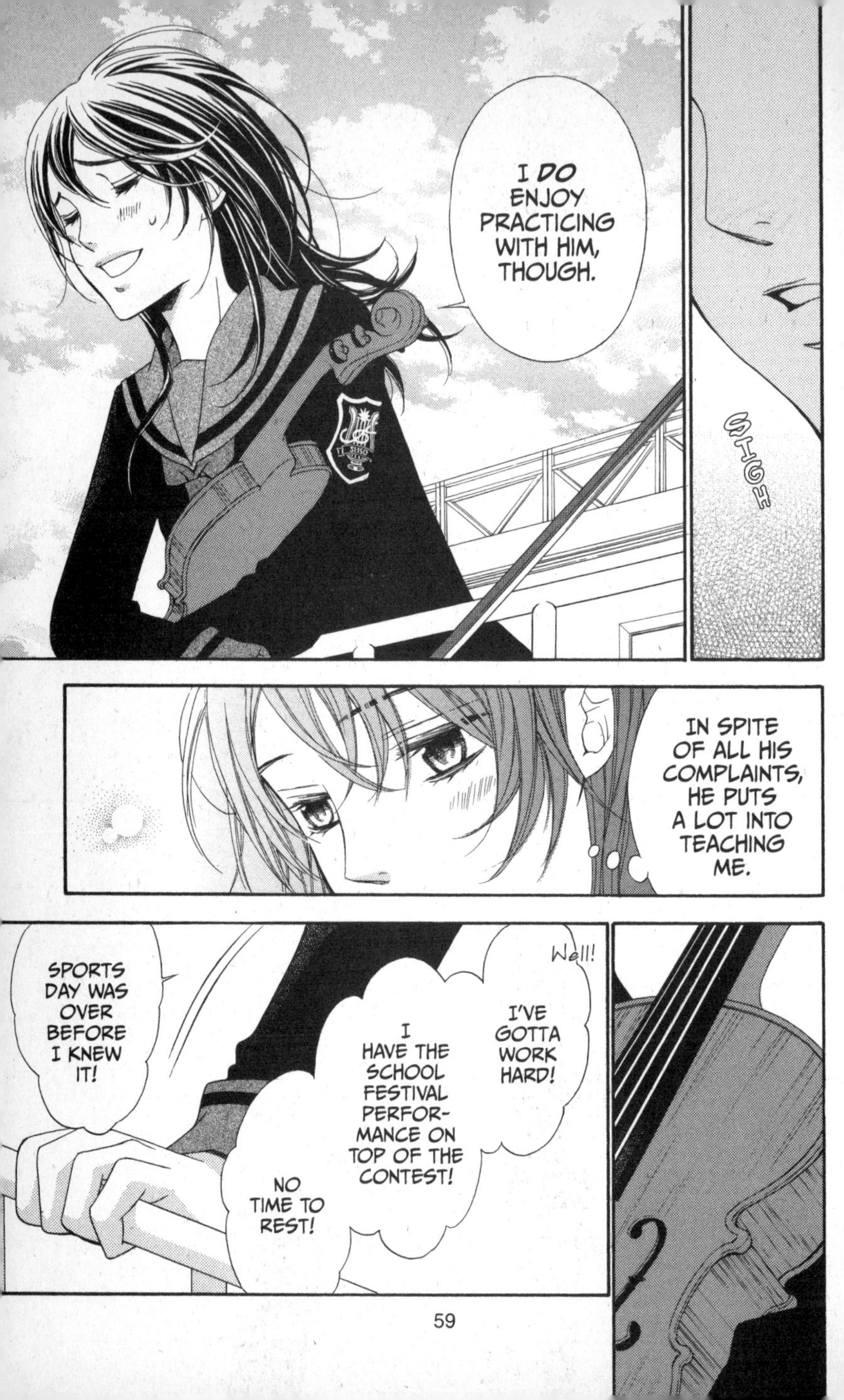
SIGH
I DO ENJOY PRACTICING WITH HIM, THOUGH.
IN SPITE OF ALL HIS COMPLAINTS, HE PUTS A LOT INTO TEACHING ME.
Well!
I'VE GOTTA WORK HARD!
SPORTS DAY WAS OVER BEFORE I KNEW IT!
I HAVE THE SCHOOL FESTIVAL PERFORMANCE ON TOP OF THE CONTEST!
NO TIME TO REST!

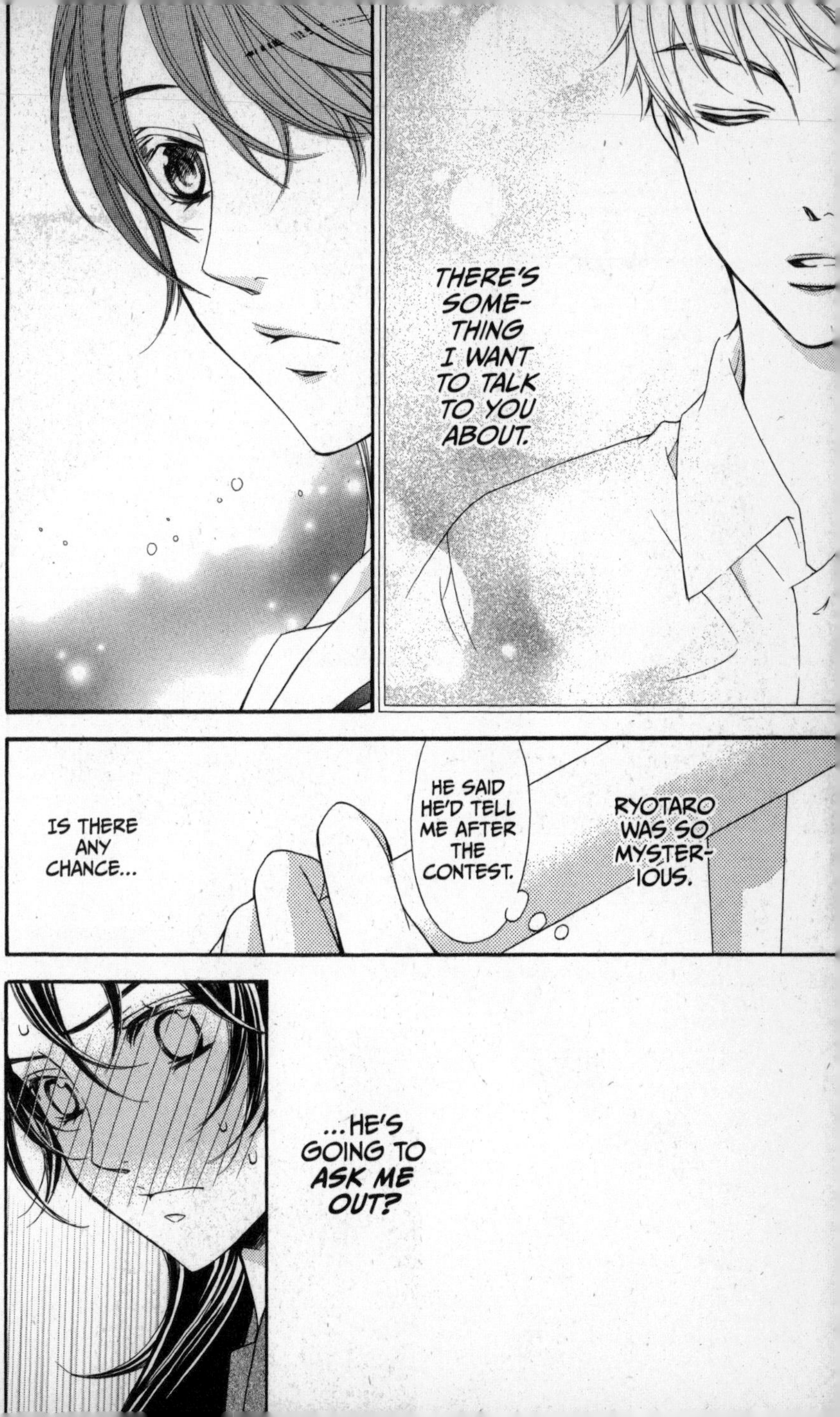
THERE'S SOMETHING I WANT TO TALK TO YOU ABOUT.
RYOTARO WAS SO MYSTERIOUS.
HE SAID HE'D TELL ME AFTER THE CONTEST.
IS THERE ANY CHANCE...
...HE'S GOING TO ASK ME OUT?

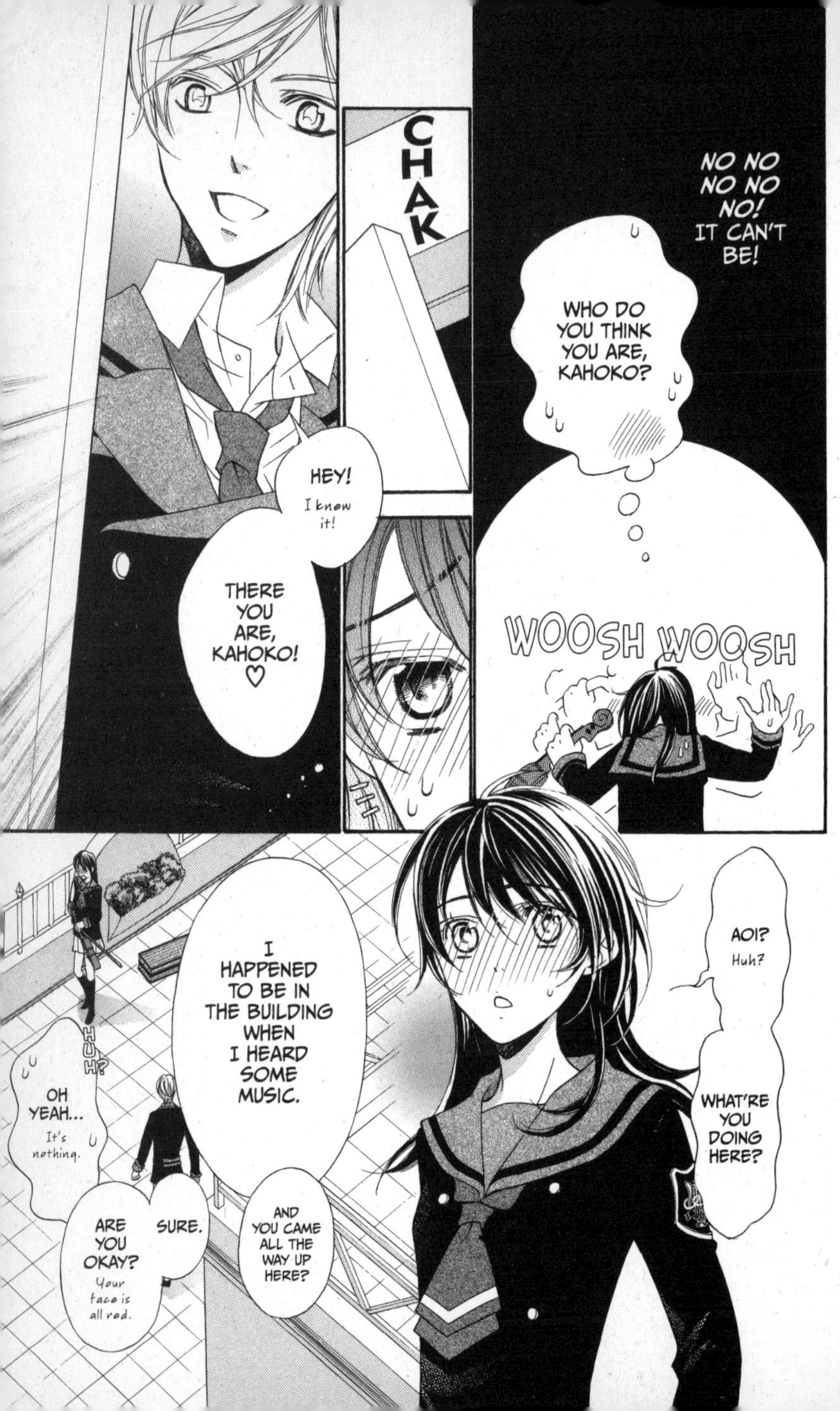
NO NO NO NO NO! IT CAN'T BE!
WHO DO YOU THINK YOU ARE, KAHOKO?
WOOSH WOOSH
CHAK
HEY! I knew it!
THERE YOU ARE, KAHOKO! ♡
AOI? Huh?
WHAT'RE YOU DOING HERE?
I HAPPENED TO BE IN THE BUILDING WHEN I HEARD SOME MUSIC.
AND YOU CAME ALL THE WAY UP HERE?
SURE.
ARE YOU OKAY? Your face is all red.
HUH?
OH YEAH... It's nothing.

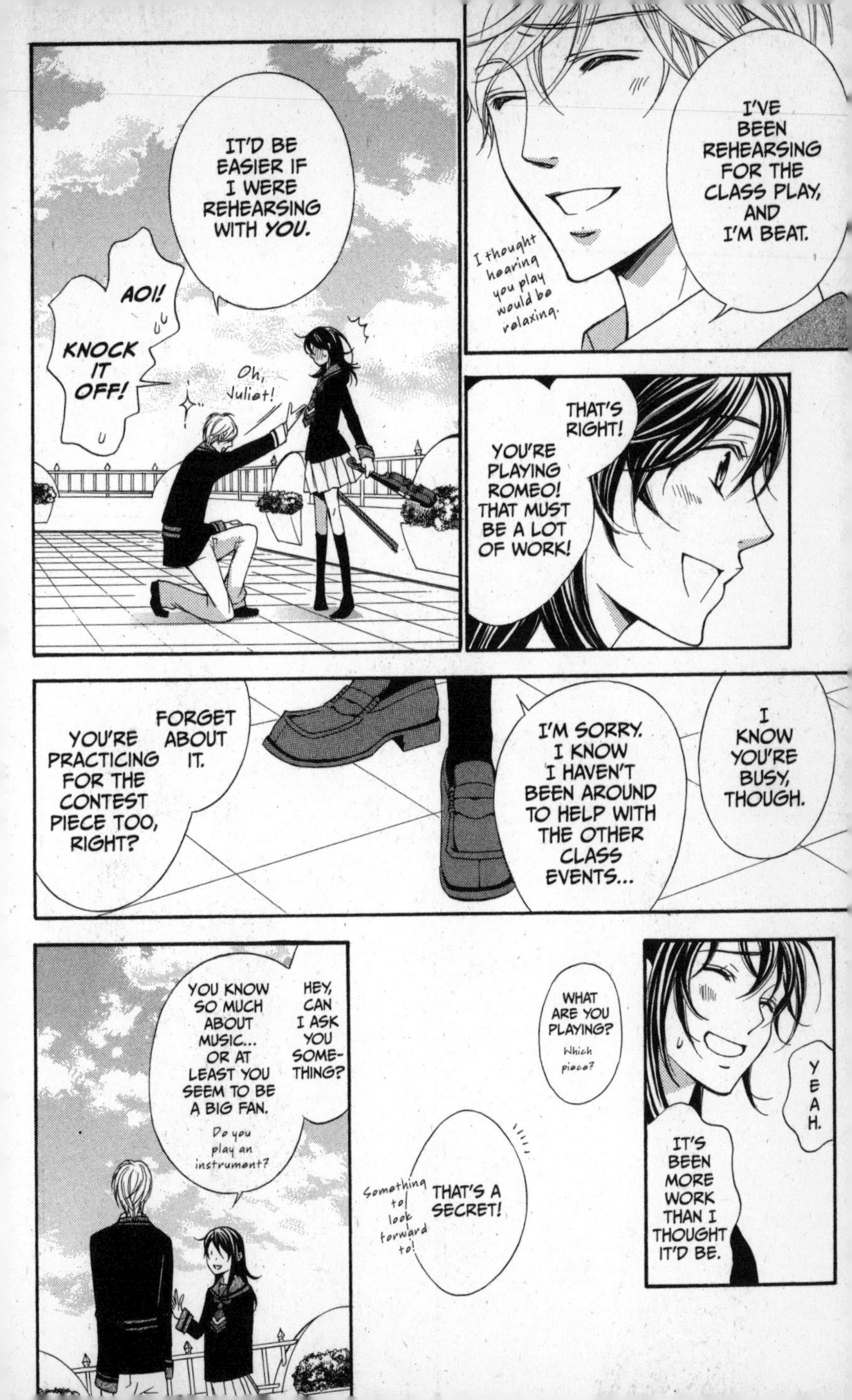
I'VE BEEN REHEARSING FOR THE CLASS PLAY, AND I'M BEAT.
I thought hearing you play would be relaxing.
THAT'S RIGHT! YOU'RE PLAYING ROMEO! THAT MUST BE A LOT OF WORK!
IT'D BE EASIER IF I WERE REHEARSING WITH *YOU.*
AOI! KNOCK IT OFF!
Oh, Juliet!
I KNOW YOU'RE BUSY, THOUGH.
I'M SORRY. I KNOW I HAVEN'T BEEN AROUND TO HELP WITH THE OTHER CLASS EVENTS...
FORGET ABOUT IT.
YOU'RE PRACTICING FOR THE CONTEST PIECE TOO, RIGHT?
YEAH.
IT'S BEEN MORE WORK THAN I THOUGHT IT'D BE.
WHAT ARE YOU PLAYING?
Which piece?
THAT'S A SECRET!
Something to look forward to!
HEY, CAN I ASK YOU SOMETHING?
YOU KNOW SO MUCH ABOUT MUSIC... OR AT LEAST YOU SEEM TO BE A BIG FAN.
Do you play an instrument?

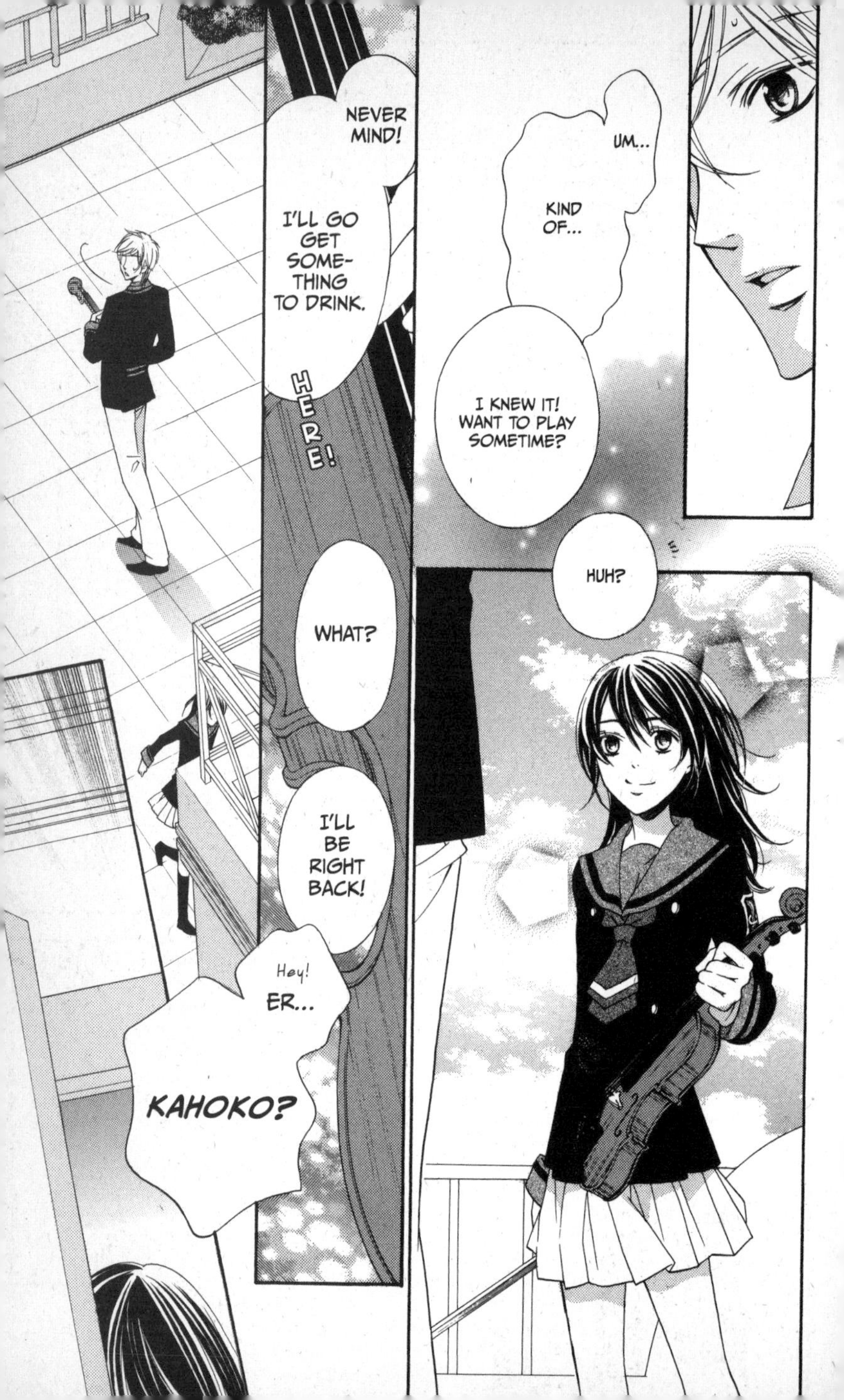
UM...
KIND OF...
I KNEW IT! WANT TO PLAY SOMETIME?
HUH?
NEVER MIND!
I'LL GO GET SOME-THING TO DRINK.
HERE!
WHAT?
I'LL BE RIGHT BACK!
Hey!
ER...
KAHOKO?

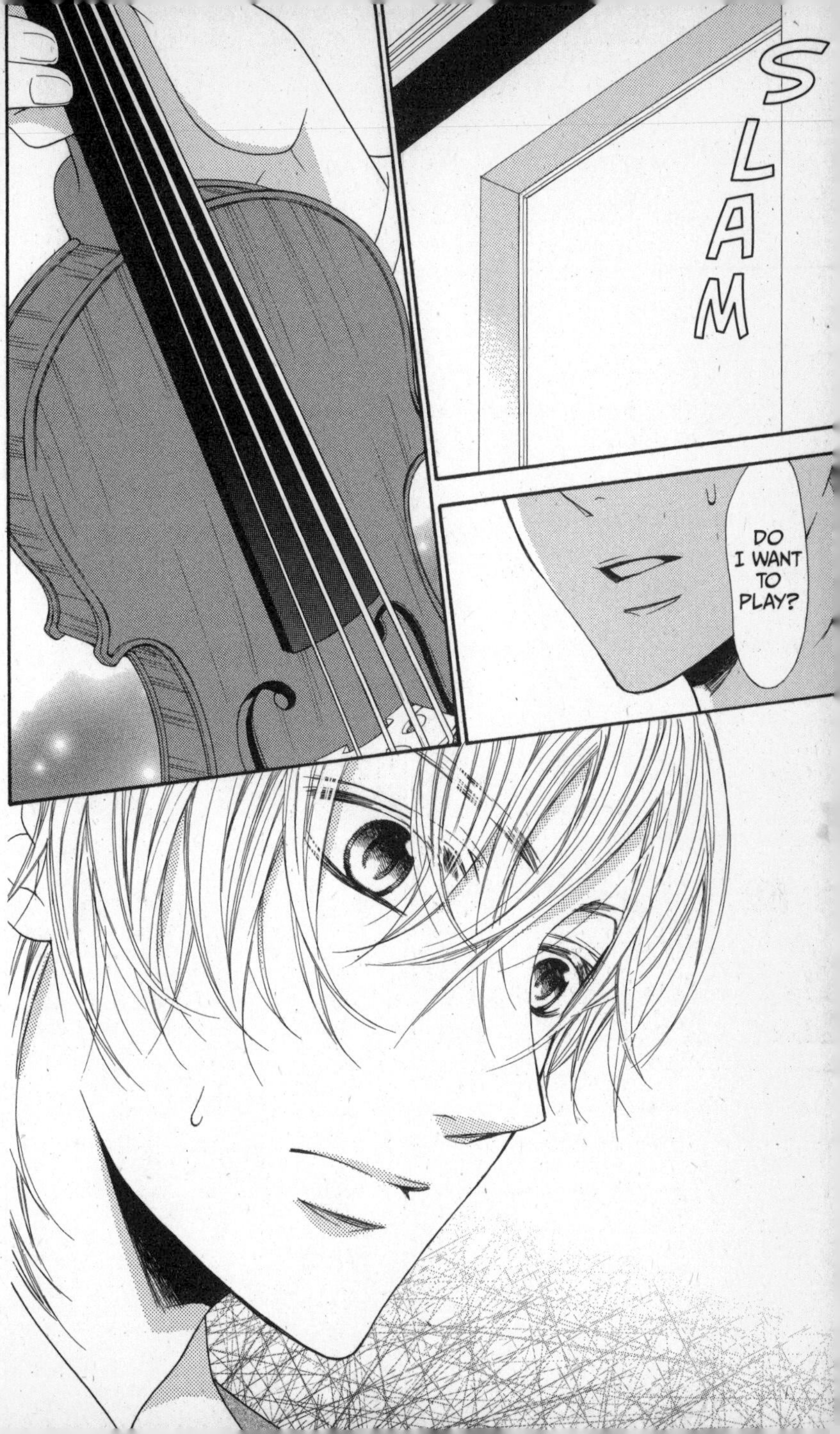
SLAM
DO I WANT TO PLAY?

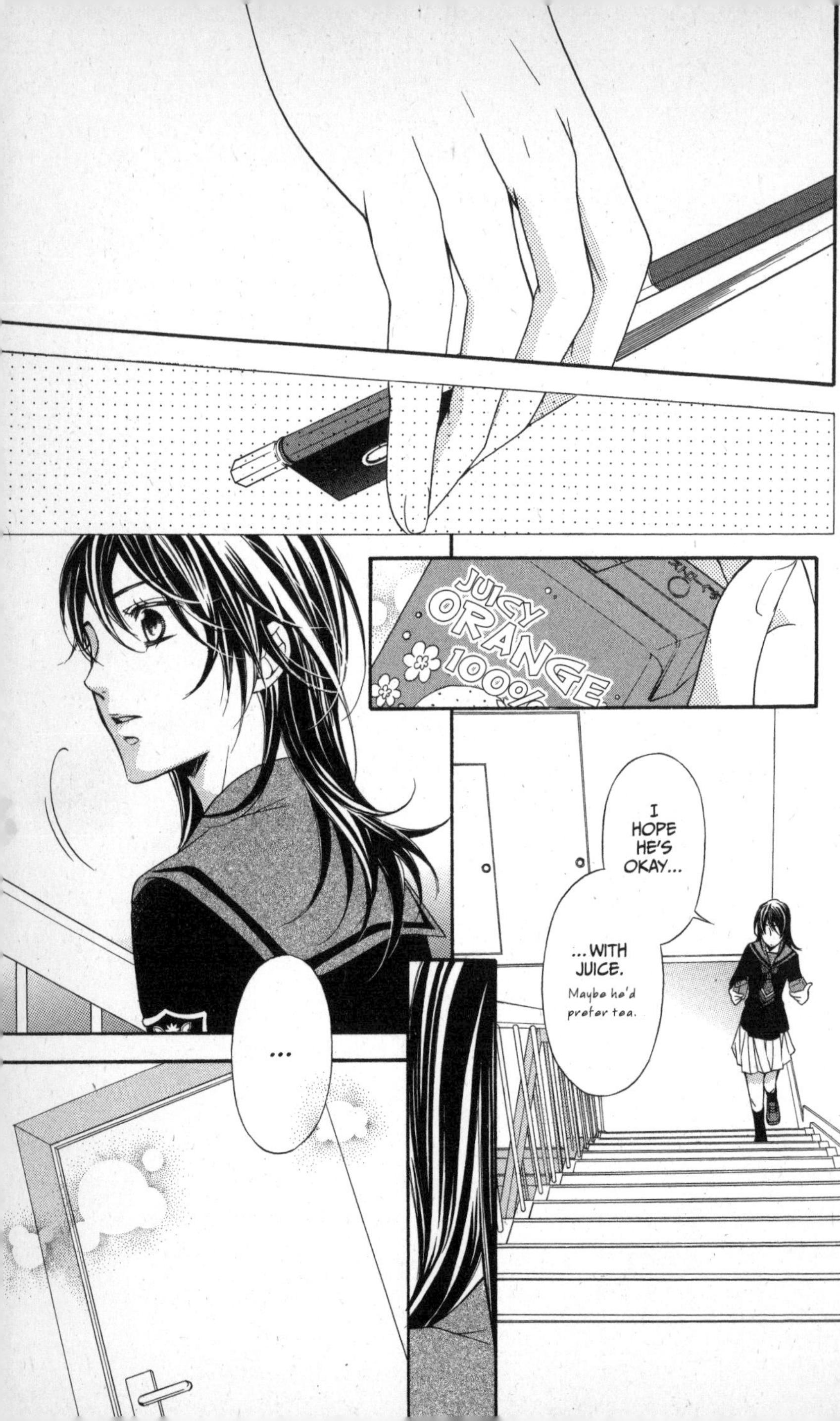
JUICY ORANGE 100%
I HOPE HE'S OKAY...
...WITH JUICE. Maybe he'd prefer tea.
...

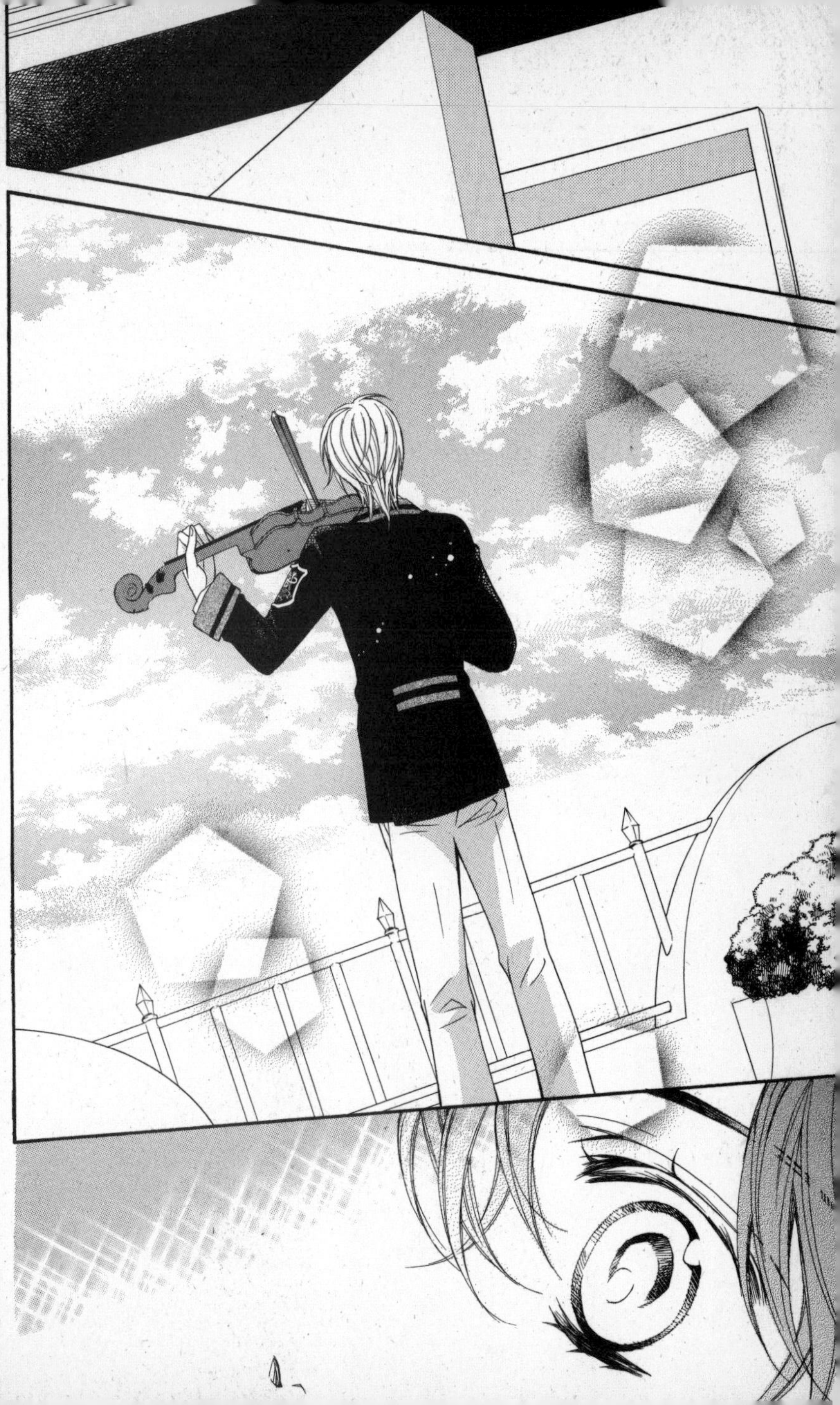

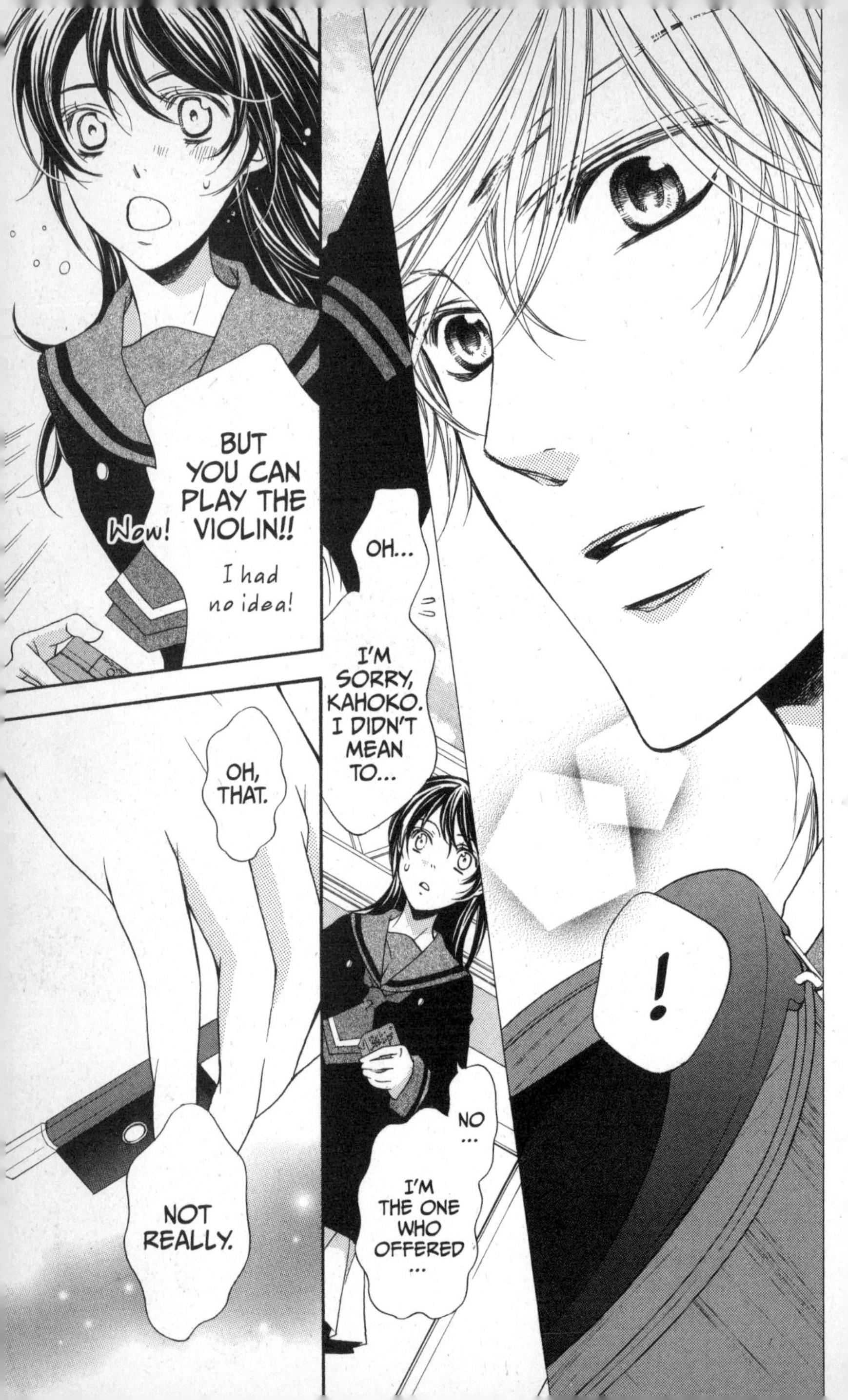
!
OH...
I'M SORRY, KAHOKO. I DIDN'T MEAN TO...
NO ...
I'M THE ONE WHO OFFERED ...
Wow!
BUT YOU CAN PLAY THE VIOLIN!!
I had no idea!
OH, THAT.
NOT REALLY.

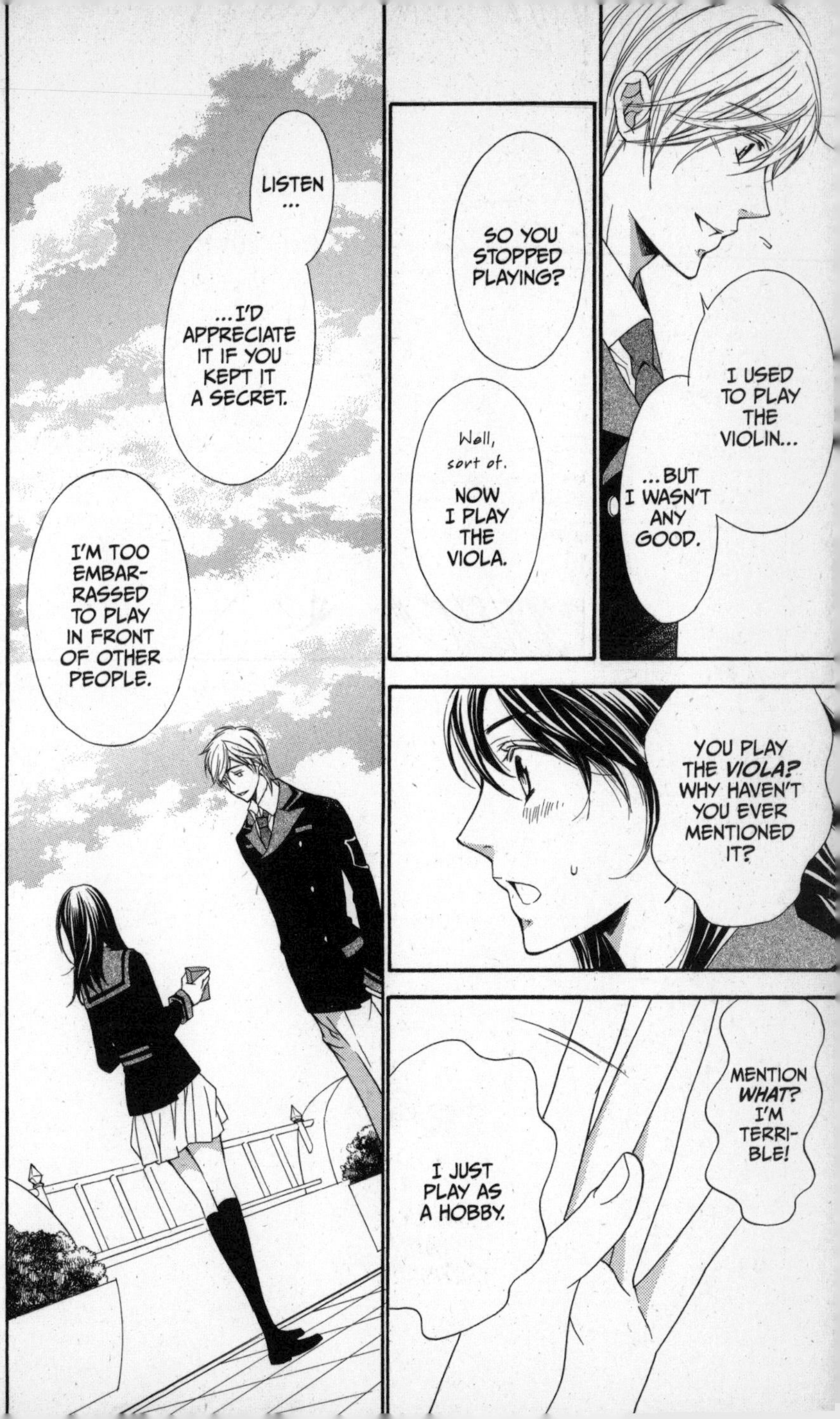

I USED TO PLAY THE VIOLIN...
...BUT I WASN'T ANY GOOD.
SO YOU STOPPED PLAYING?
Well, sort of.
NOW I PLAY THE VIOLA.
YOU PLAY THE *VIOLA?* WHY HAVEN'T YOU EVER MENTIONED IT?
MENTION *WHAT?* I'M TERRI-BLE!
I JUST PLAY AS A HOBBY.
LISTEN...
...I'D APPRECIATE IT IF YOU KEPT IT A SECRET.
I'M TOO EMBAR-RASSED TO PLAY IN FRONT OF OTHER PEOPLE.

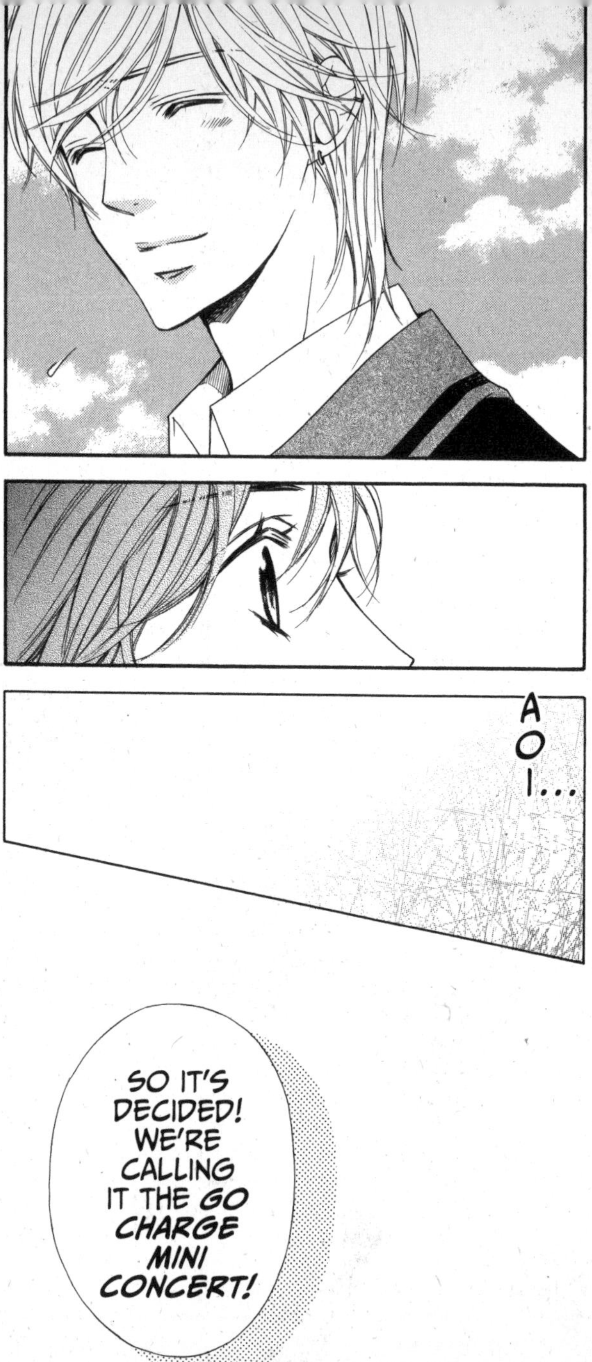
AOI...
SO IT'S DECIDED! WE'RE CALLING IT THE *GO CHARGE MINI CONCERT!*

Author's note:
The title page for Measure 60 shows everyone in the morning light. Azuma, Ryotaro and Aoi seem like guys who wouldn't have a problem getting up in the morning, but I feel like Keiichi is a different breed.

By the way, I've used this space to continue the kiddie sketch series I started in volume 13. Here's Nami. ↓

Young Nami

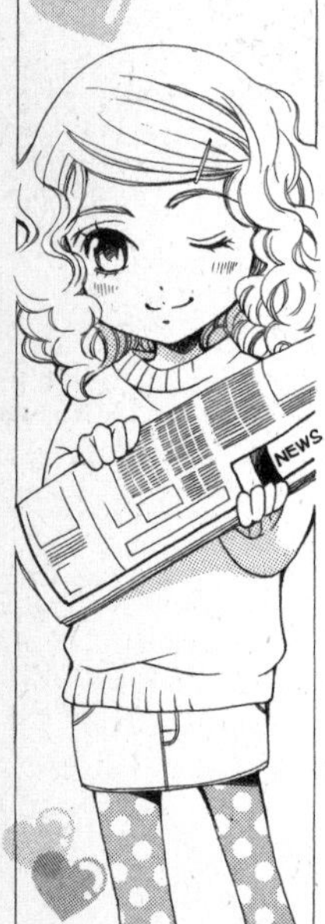
NEWS

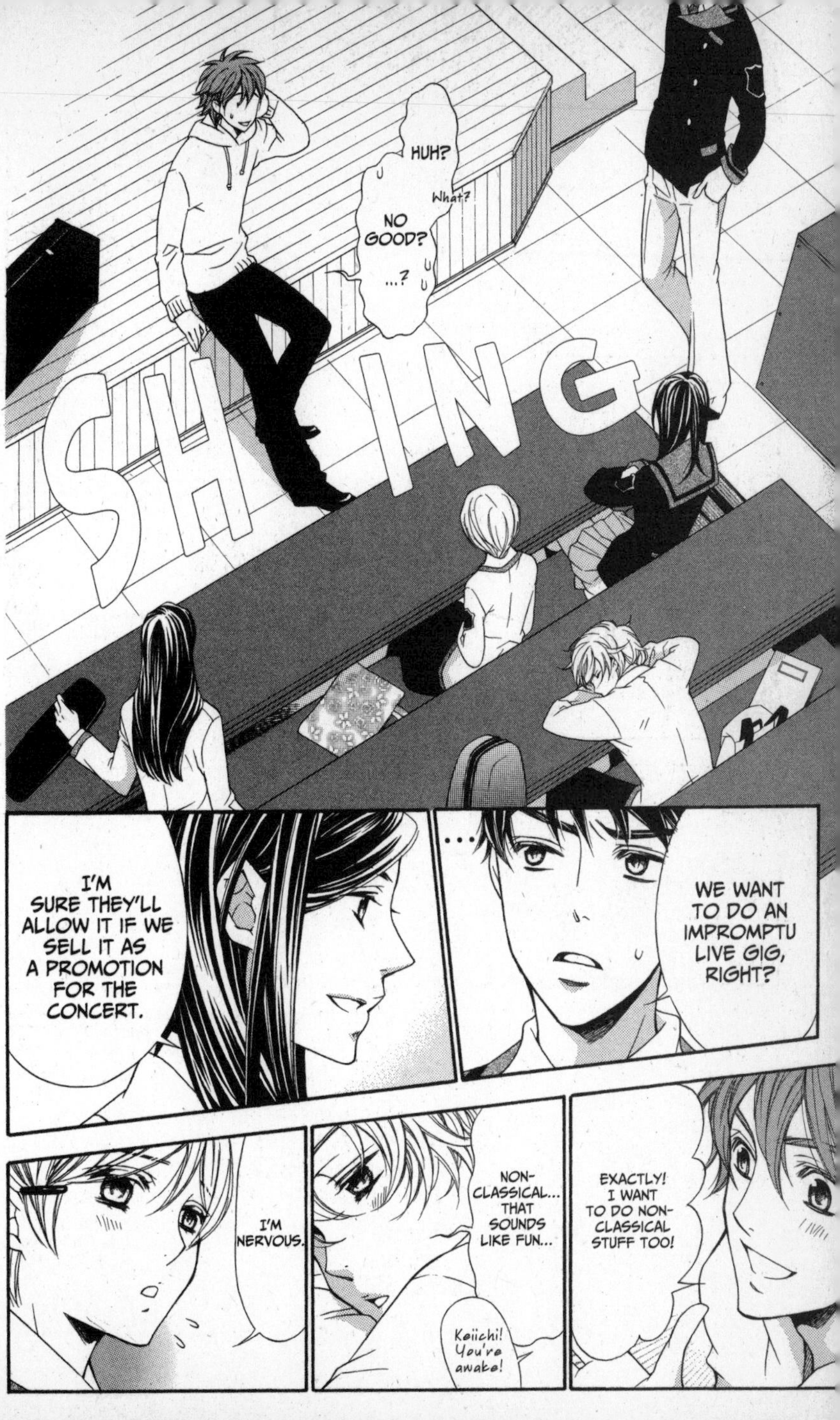
HUH?
What?
NO GOOD?
...?
SHING
WE WANT TO DO AN IMPROMPTU LIVE GIG, RIGHT?
...
I'M SURE THEY'LL ALLOW IT IF WE SELL IT AS A PROMOTION FOR THE CONCERT.
EXACTLY! I WANT TO DO NON-CLASSICAL STUFF TOO!
NON-CLASSICAL... THAT SOUNDS LIKE FUN...
Keiichi! You're awake!
I'M NERVOUS.

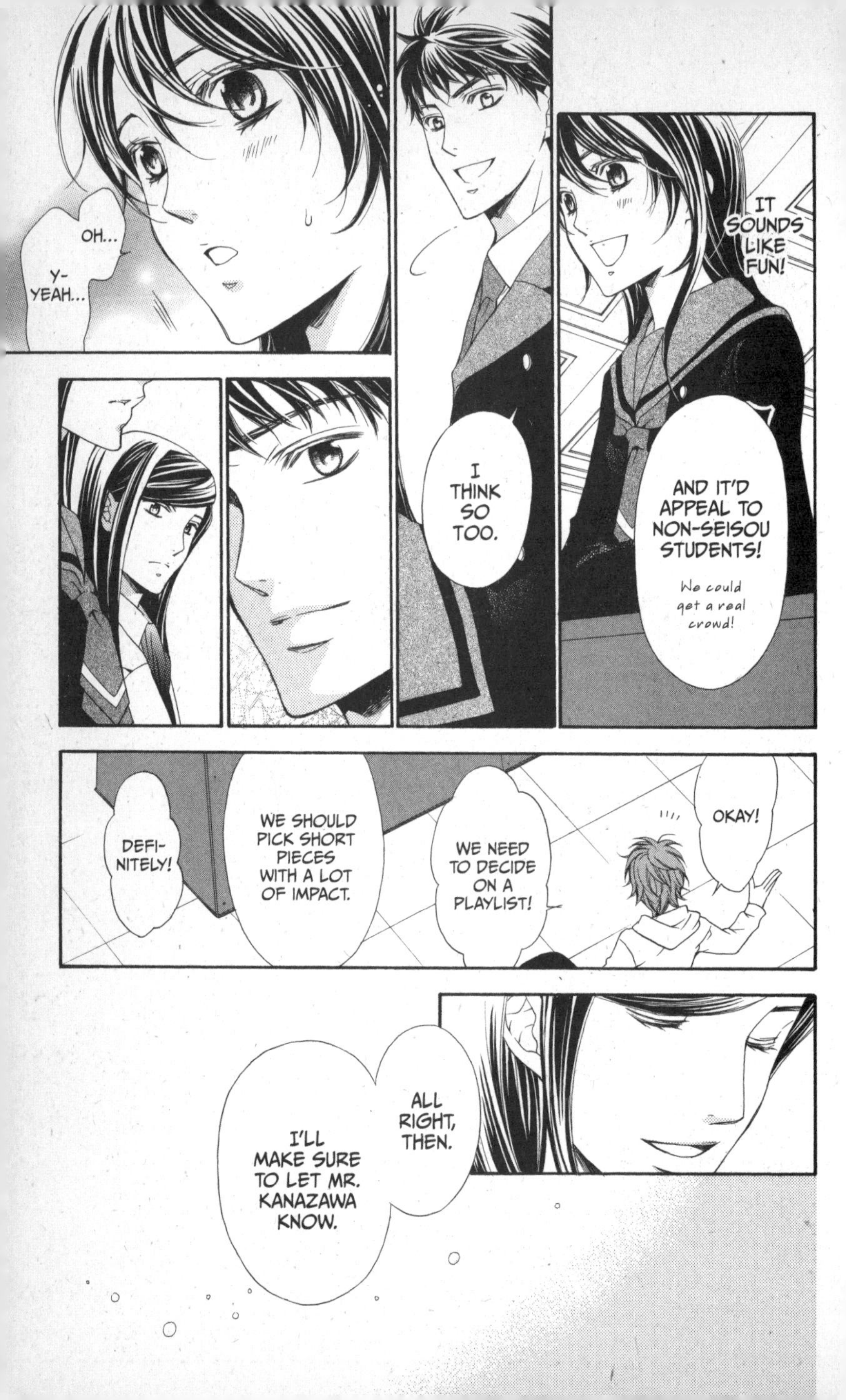
IT SOUNDS LIKE FUN!
AND IT'D APPEAL TO NON-SEISOU STUDENTS!
We could get a real crowd!
I THINK SO TOO.
OH...
Y-YEAH...
OKAY!
WE NEED TO DECIDE ON A PLAYLIST!
WE SHOULD PICK SHORT PIECES WITH A LOT OF IMPACT.
DEFI-NITELY!
ALL RIGHT, THEN.
I'LL MAKE SURE TO LET MR. KANAZAWA KNOW.

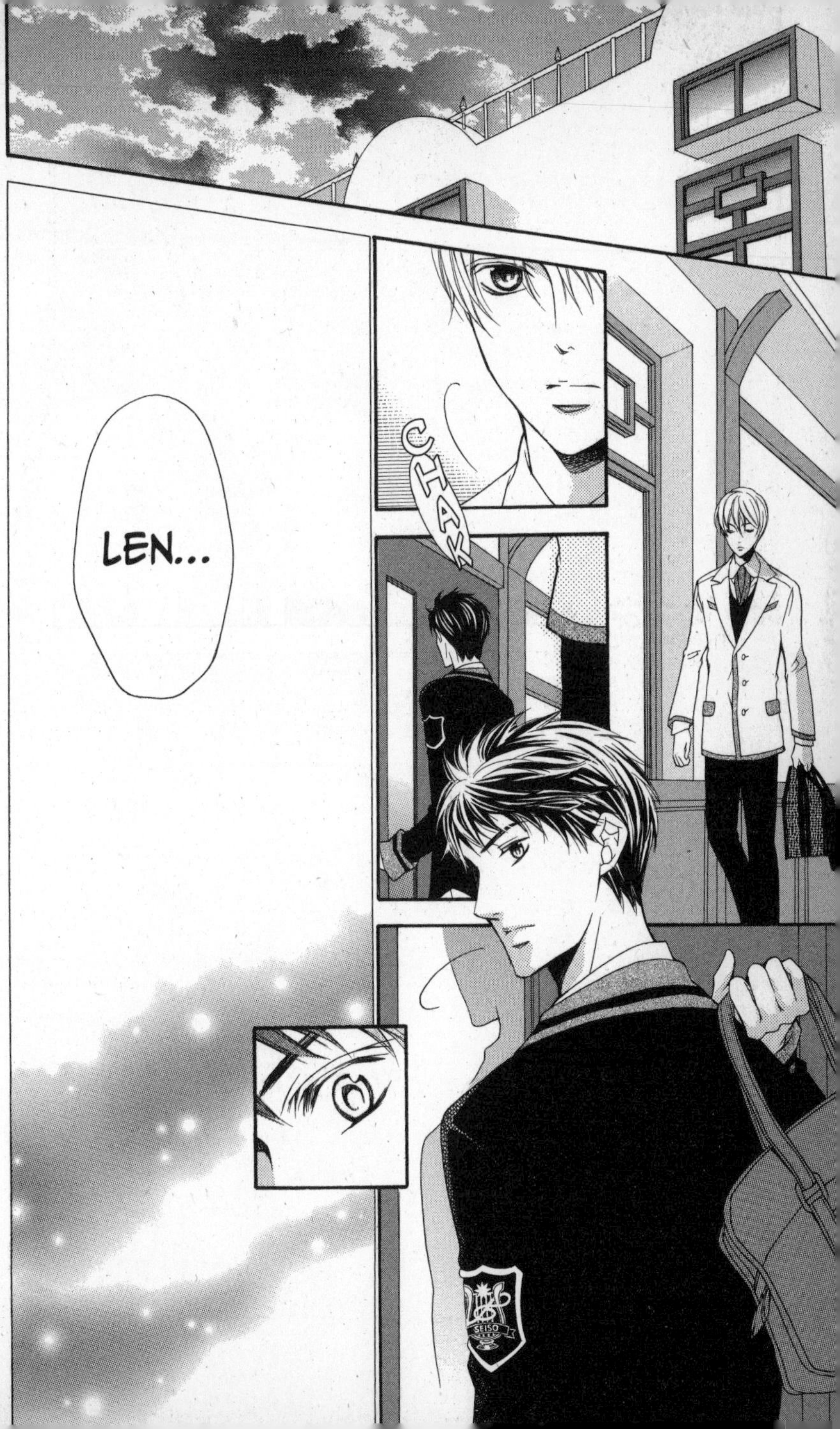
CHAK
LEN...

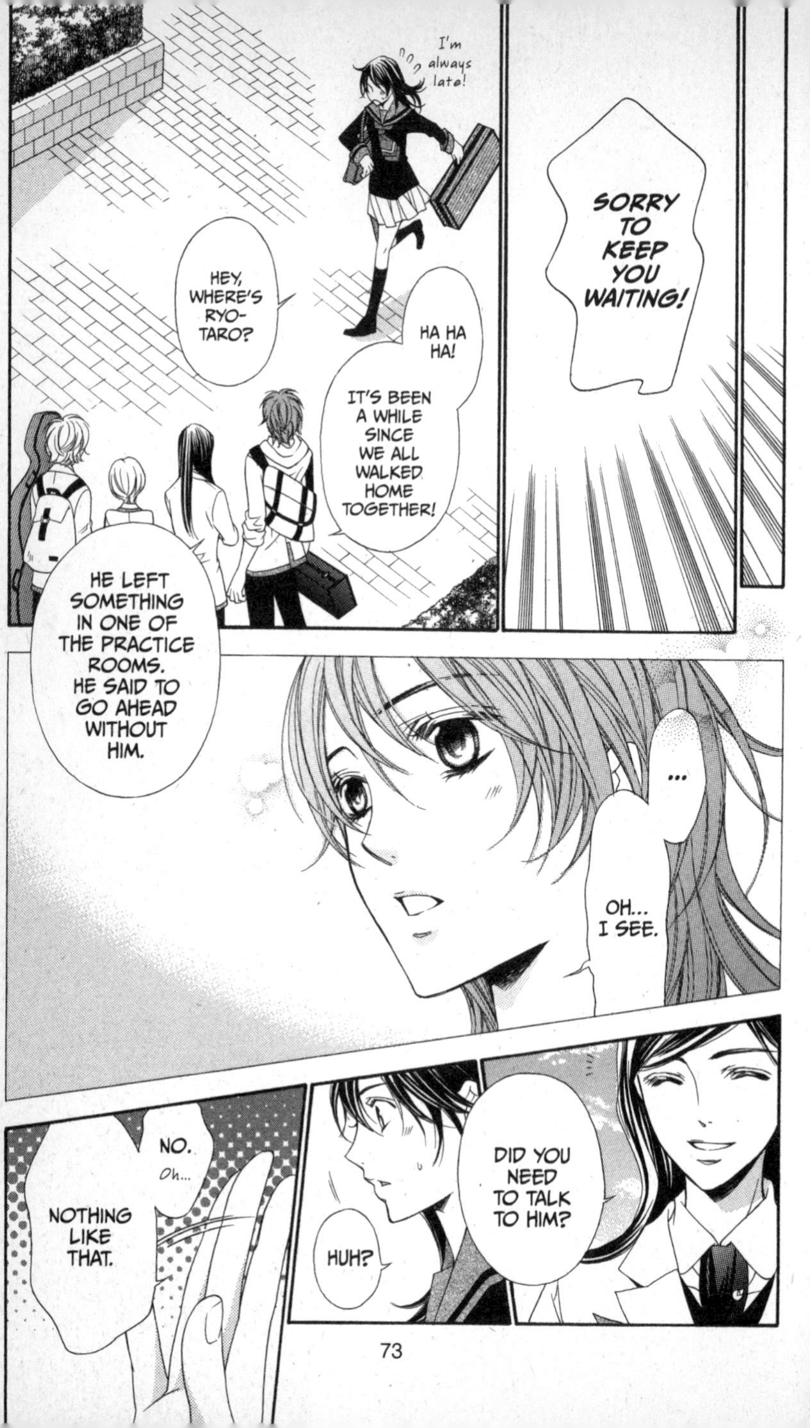
SORRY TO KEEP YOU WAITING!
I'm always late!
HA HA HA!
IT'S BEEN A WHILE SINCE WE ALL WALKED HOME TOGETHER!
HEY, WHERE'S RYO-TARO?
HE LEFT SOMETHING IN ONE OF THE PRACTICE ROOMS. HE SAID TO GO AHEAD WITHOUT HIM.
...
OH... I SEE.
DID YOU NEED TO TALK TO HIM?
HUH?
NO.
Oh...
NOTHING LIKE THAT.

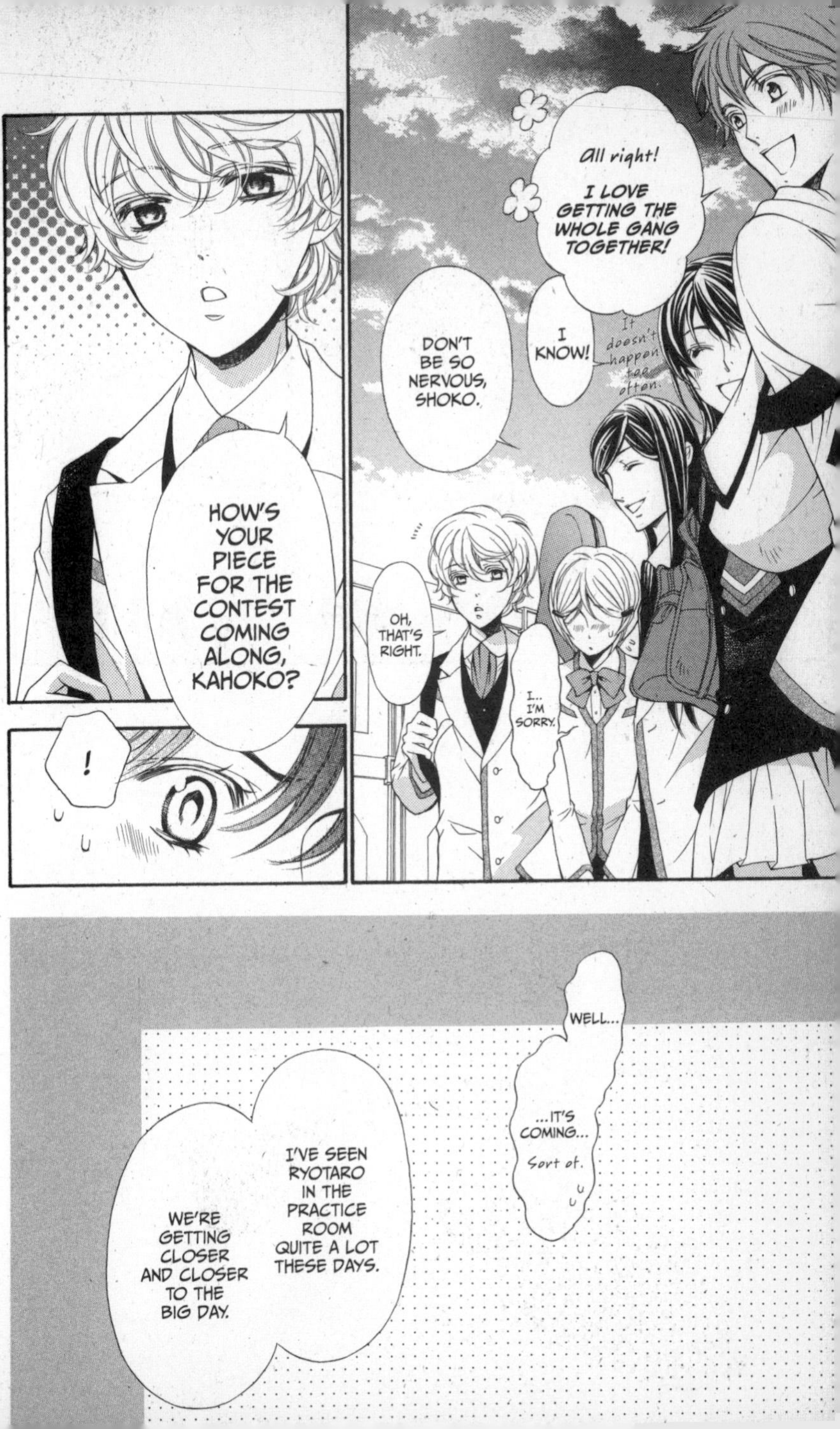
All right!
I LOVE GETTING THE WHOLE GANG TOGETHER!
I KNOW!
It doesn't happen too often.
DON'T BE SO NERVOUS, SHOKO.
I... I'M SORRY.
OH, THAT'S RIGHT.
HOW'S YOUR PIECE FOR THE CONTEST COMING ALONG, KAHOKO?
!
WELL...
...IT'S COMING...
Sort of.
I'VE SEEN RYOTARO IN THE PRACTICE ROOM QUITE A LOT THESE DAYS.
WE'RE GETTING CLOSER AND CLOSER TO THE BIG DAY.

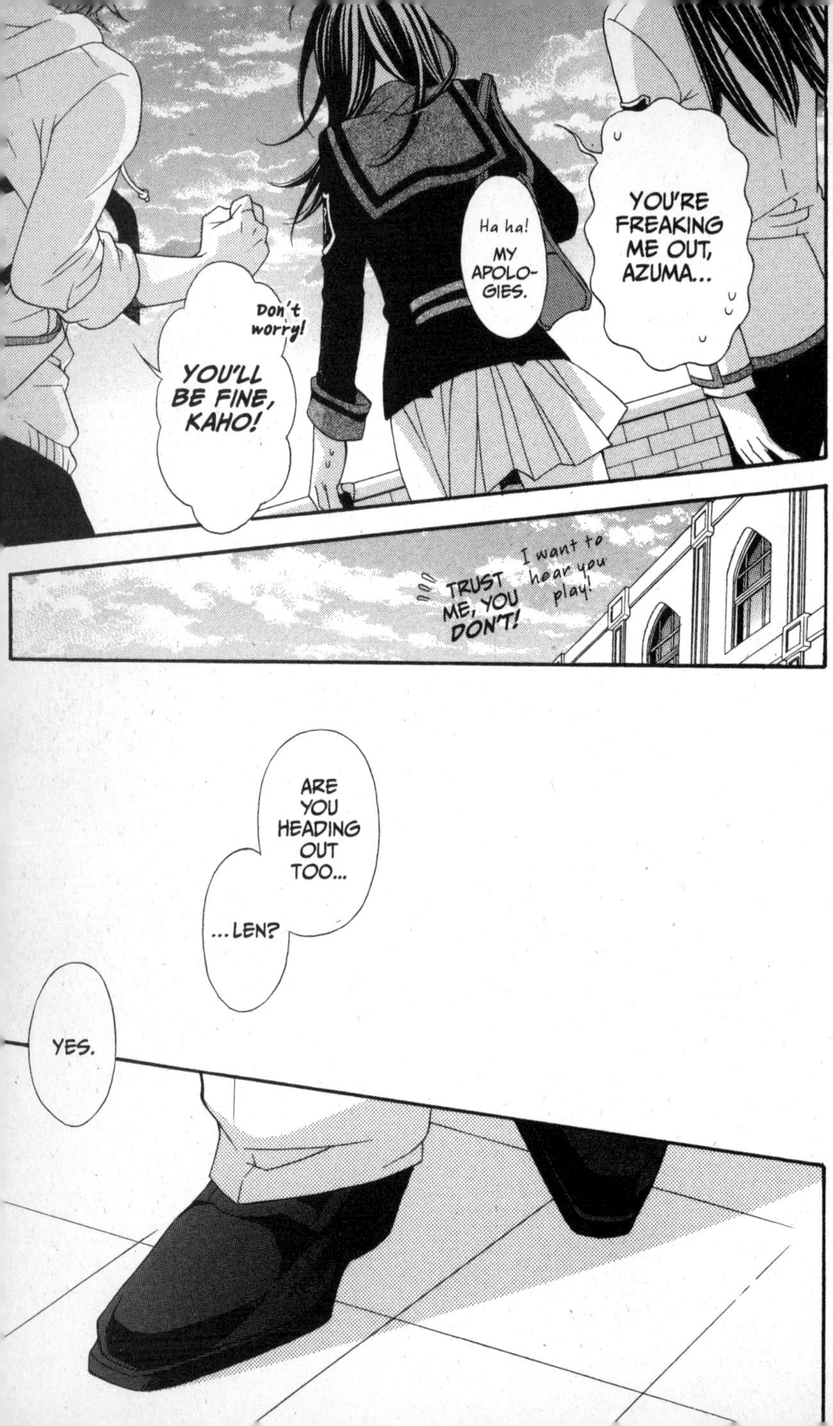
YOU'RE FREAKING ME OUT, AZUMA...
Ha ha! MY APOLOGIES.
Don't worry! YOU'LL BE FINE, KAHO!
I want to hear you play!
TRUST ME, YOU DON'T!
ARE YOU HEADING OUT TOO...
...LEN?
YES.

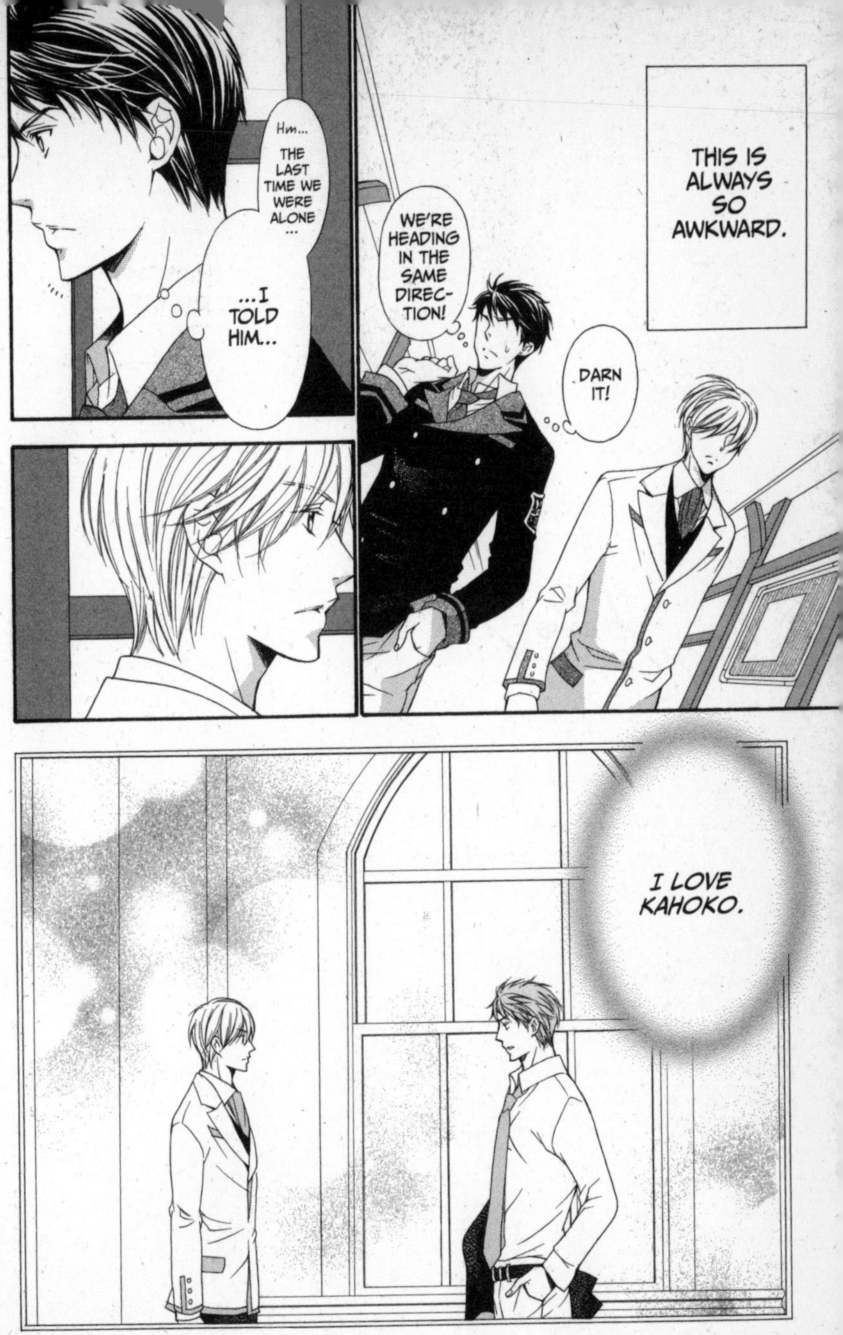
THIS IS ALWAYS SO AWKWARD.
WE'RE HEADING IN THE SAME DIRECTION!
DARN IT!
Hm... THE LAST TIME WE WERE ALONE...
...I TOLD HIM...
I LOVE KAHOKO.

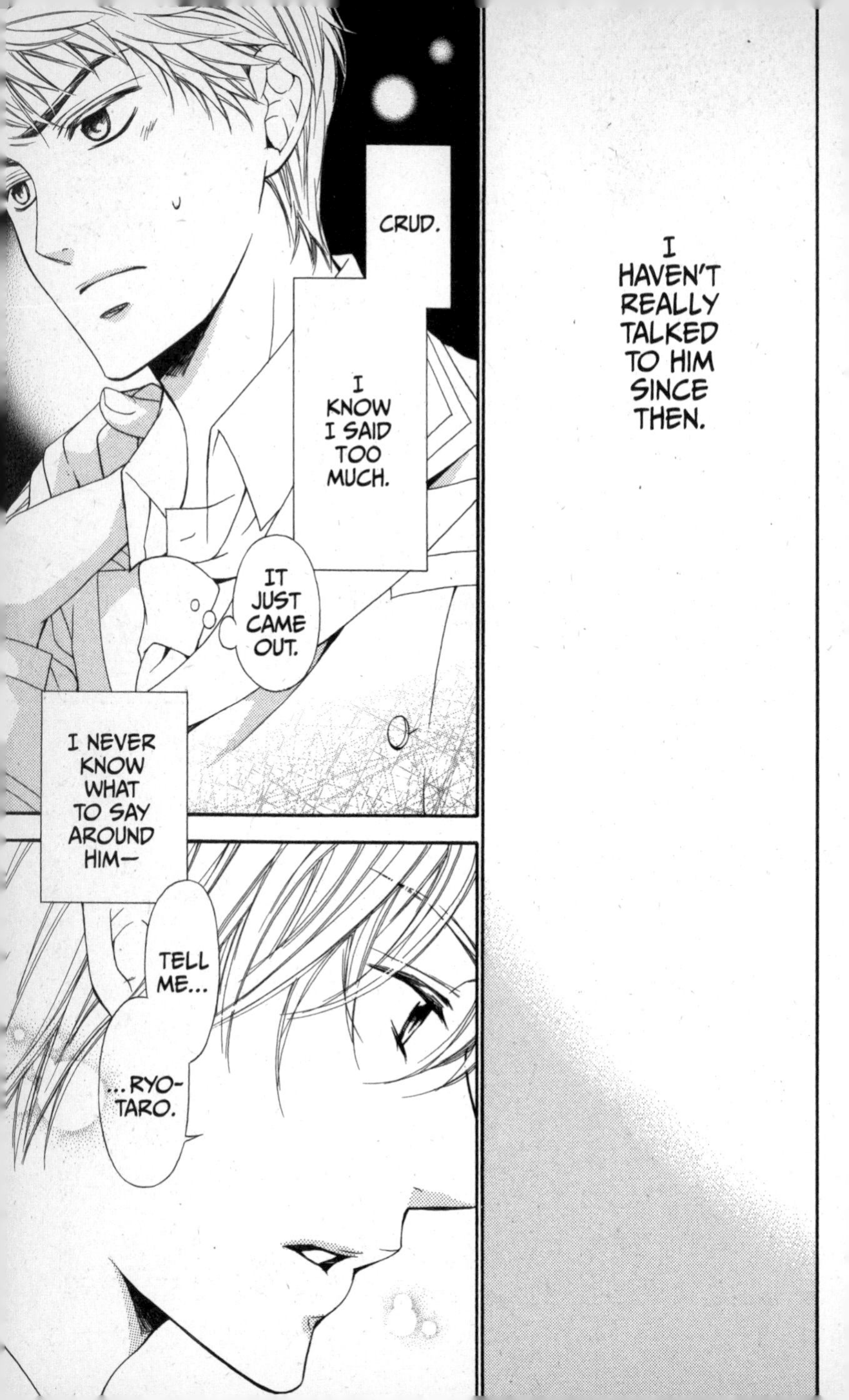
I HAVEN'T REALLY TALKED TO HIM SINCE THEN.
CRUD.
I KNOW I SAID TOO MUCH.
IT JUST CAME OUT.
I NEVER KNOW WHAT TO SAY AROUND HIM—
TELL ME...
...RYO-TARO.

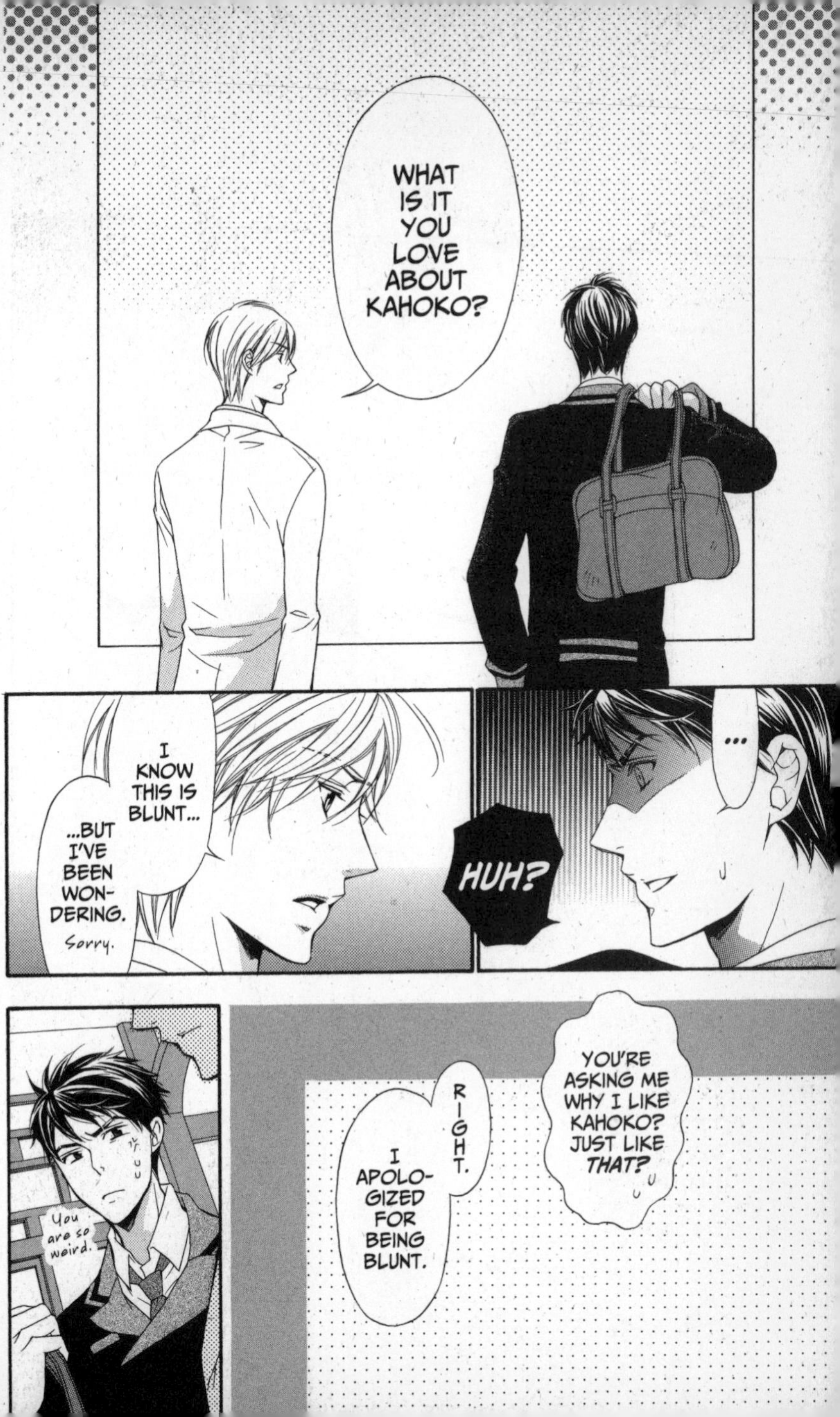
WHAT IS IT YOU LOVE ABOUT KAHOKO?
...
HUH?
I KNOW THIS IS BLUNT...
...BUT I'VE BEEN WON-DERING.
Sorry.
YOU'RE ASKING ME WHY I LIKE KAHOKO? JUST LIKE *THAT?*
RIGHT.
I APOLOGIZED FOR BEING BLUNT.
You are so weird.

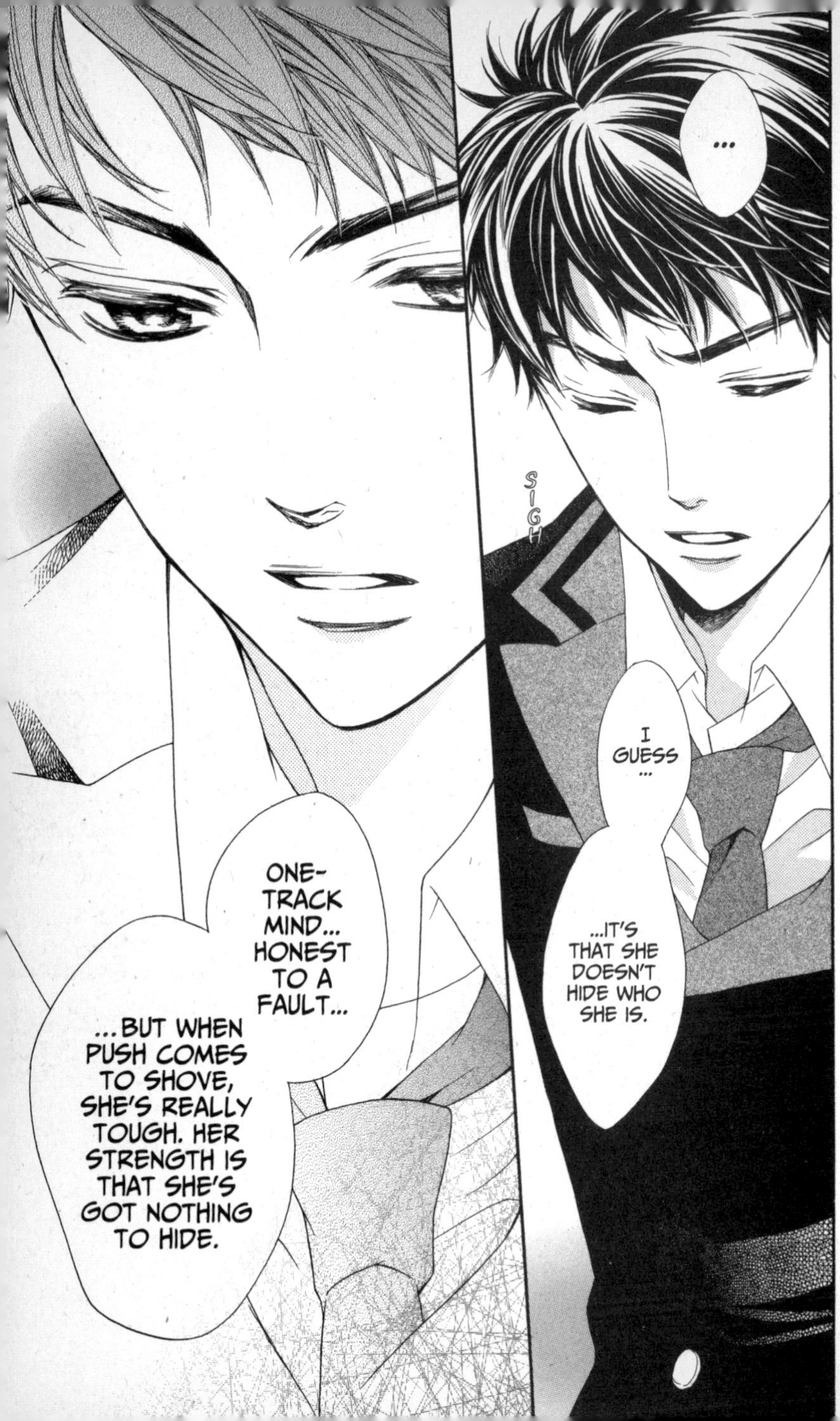
...
SIGH
I GUESS...
...IT'S THAT SHE DOESN'T HIDE WHO SHE IS.
ONE-TRACK MIND... HONEST TO A FAULT...
...BUT WHEN PUSH COMES TO SHOVE, SHE'S REALLY TOUGH. HER STRENGTH IS THAT SHE'S GOT NOTHING TO HIDE.

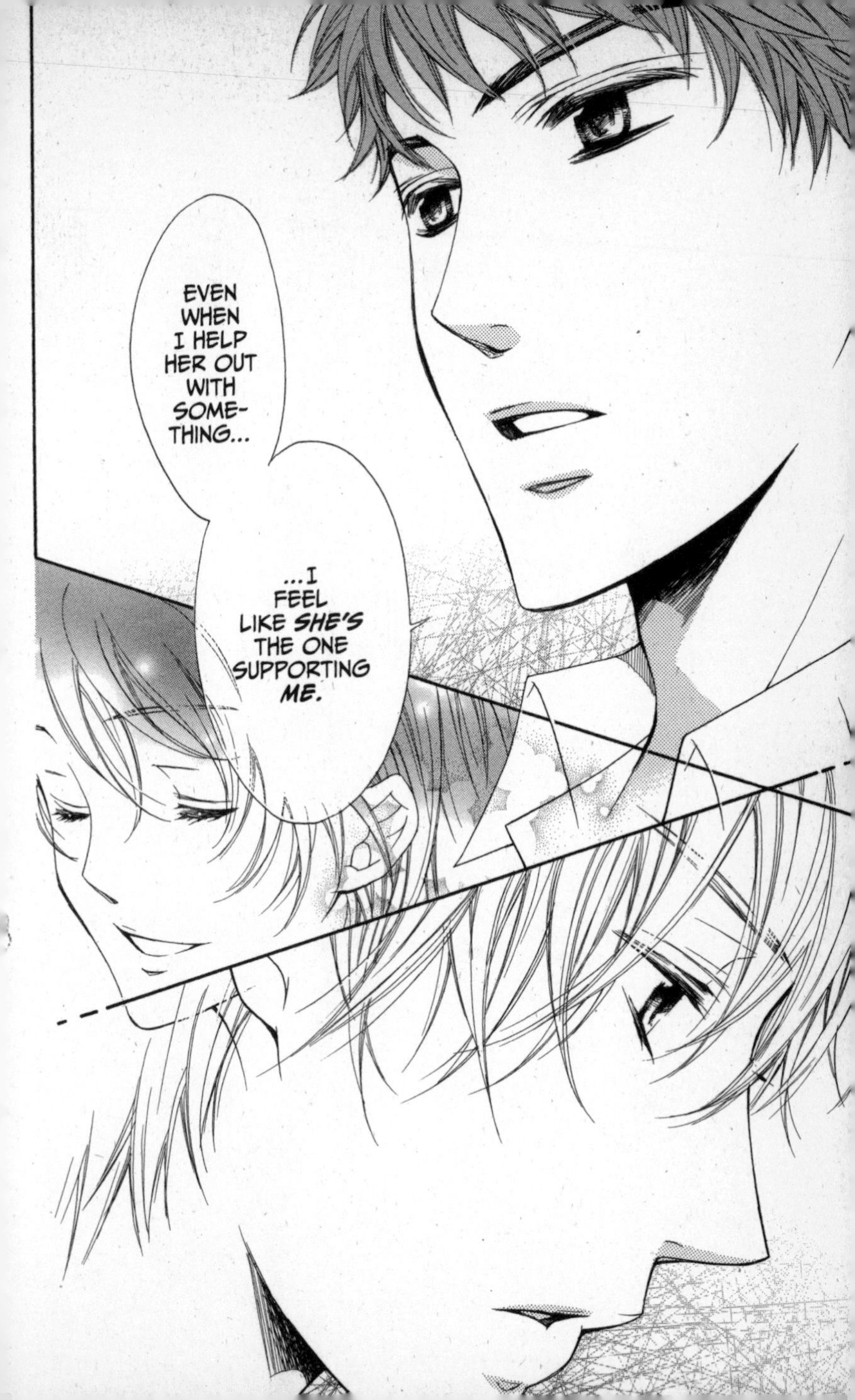
EVEN WHEN I HELP HER OUT WITH SOME-THING...
...I FEEL LIKE *SHE'S* THE ONE SUPPORTING *ME.*

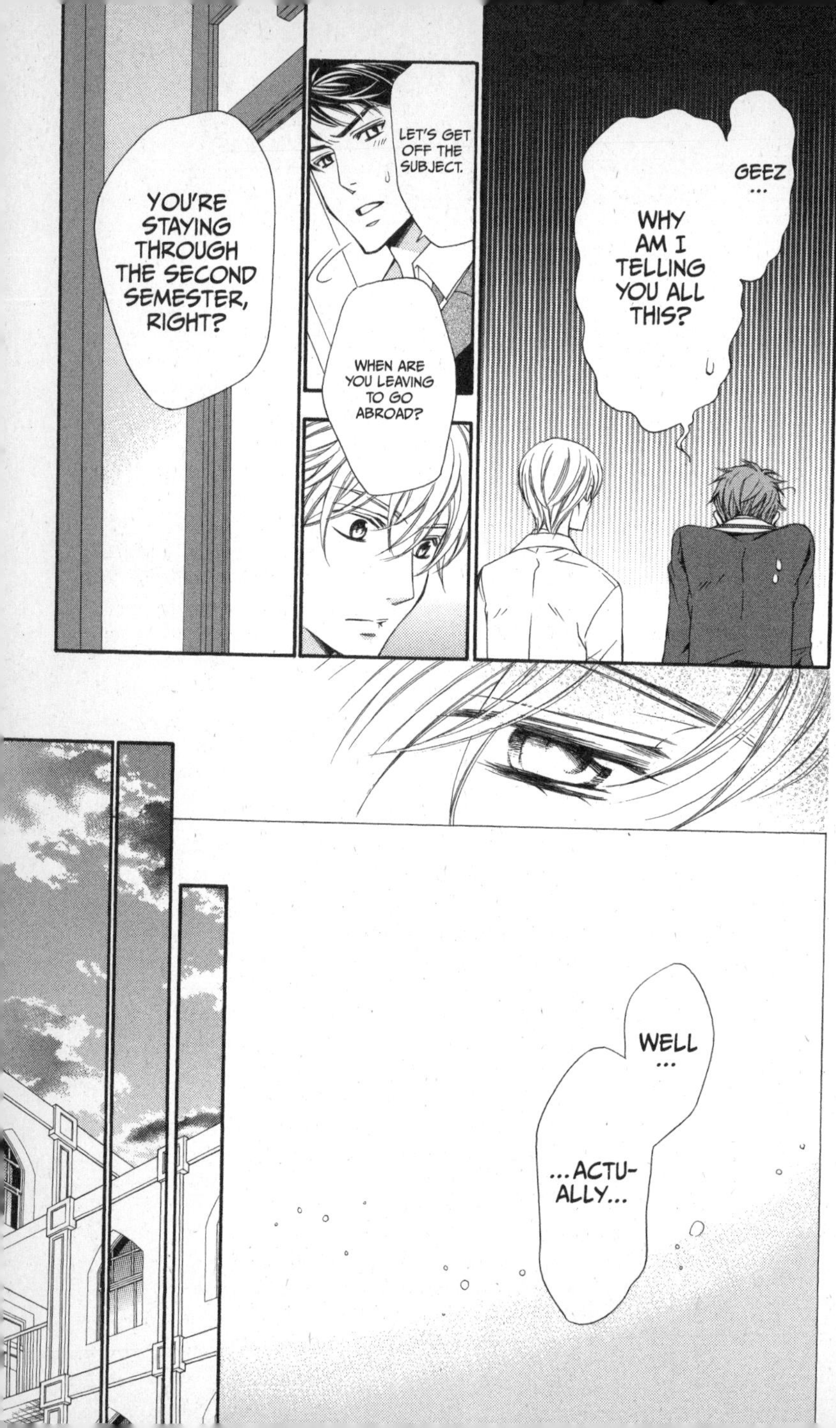
GEEZ...
WHY AM I TELLING YOU ALL THIS?
LET'S GET OFF THE SUBJECT.
WHEN ARE YOU LEAVING TO GO ABROAD?
YOU'RE STAYING THROUGH THE SECOND SEMESTER, RIGHT?
WELL...
...ACTU-ALLY...

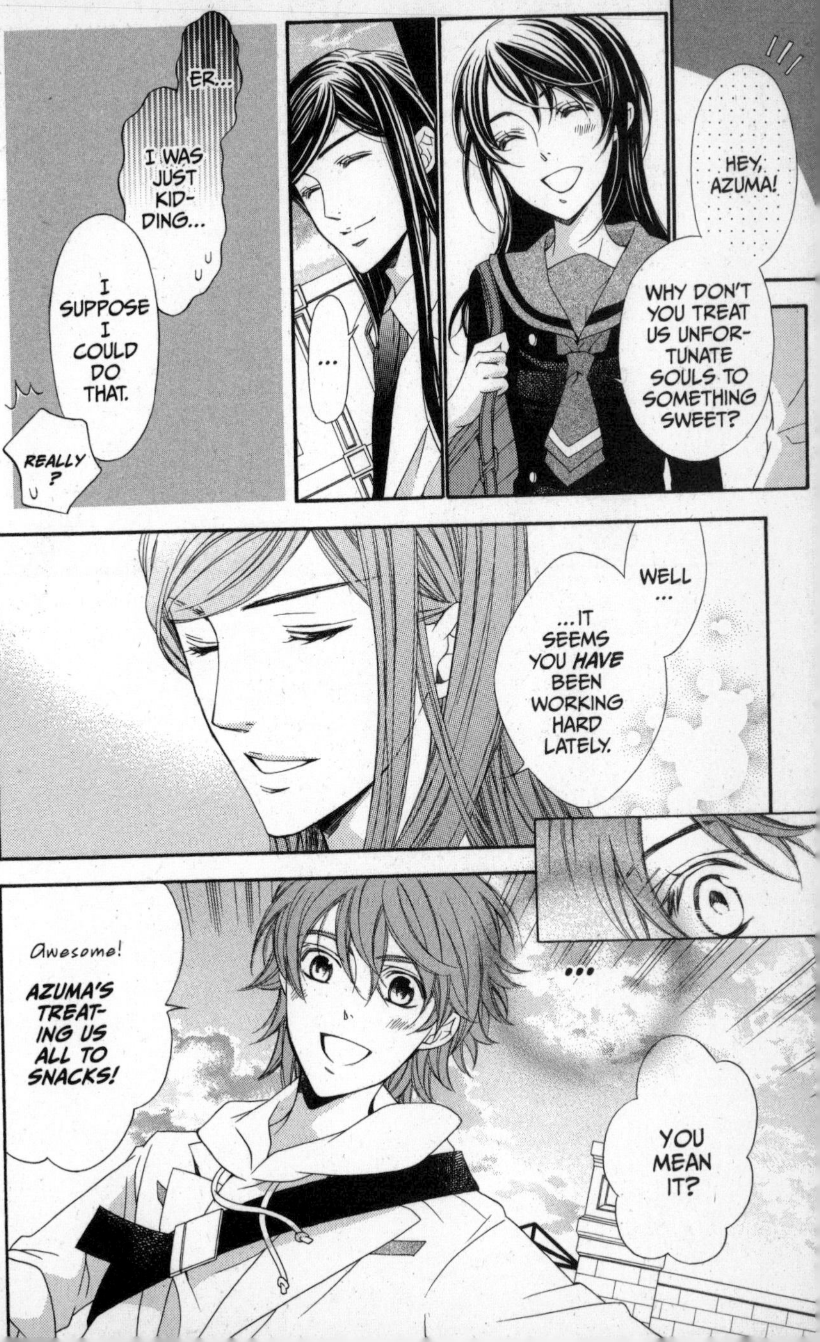
HEY, AZUMA!
WHY DON'T YOU TREAT US UNFORTUNATE SOULS TO SOMETHING SWEET?
...
ER...
I WAS JUST KIDDING...
I SUPPOSE I COULD DO THAT.
REALLY?
WELL...
...IT SEEMS YOU *HAVE* BEEN WORKING HARD LATELY.
...
YOU MEAN IT?
Awesome!
AZUMA'S TREATING US ALL TO SNACKS!

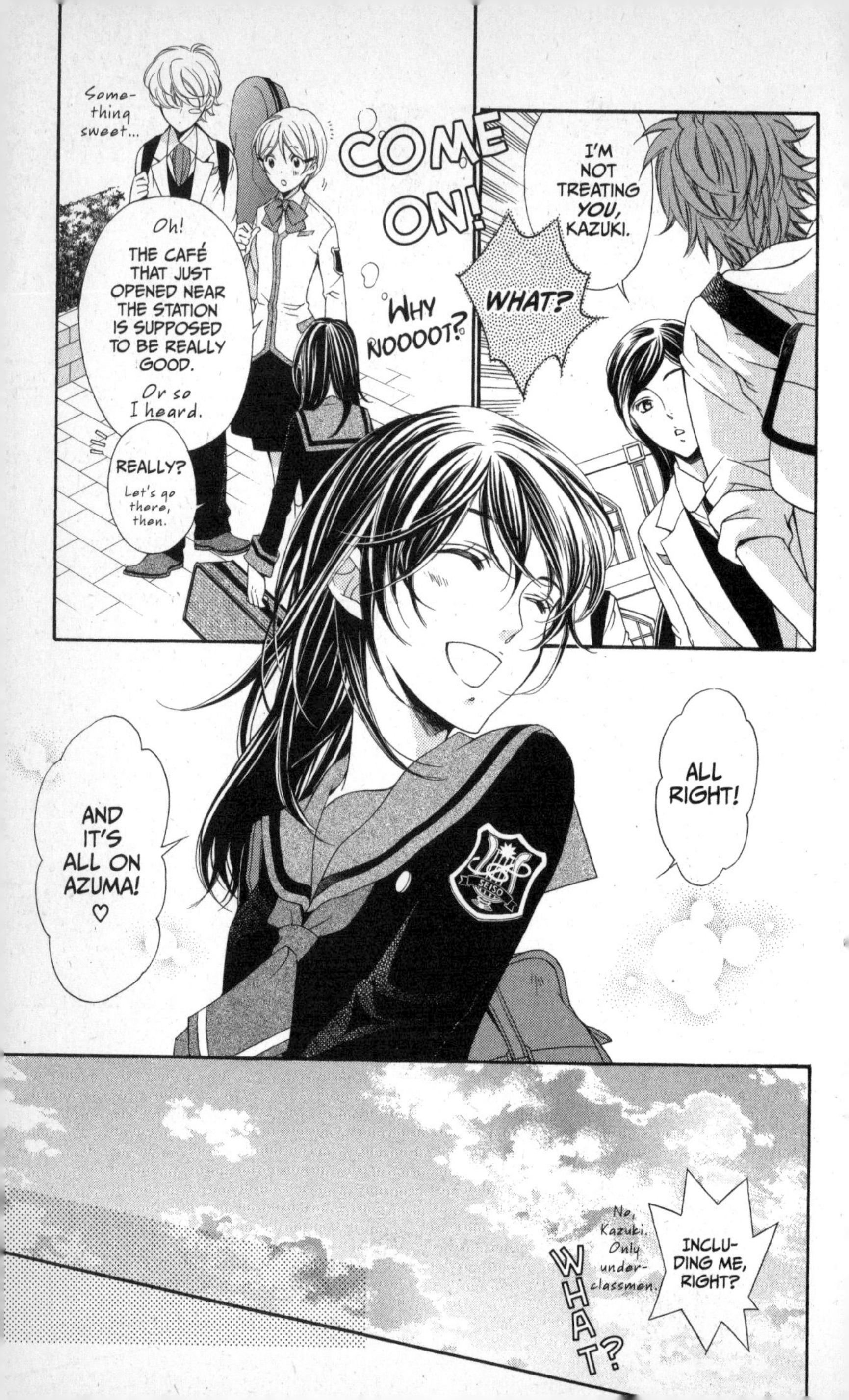

I'M NOT TREATING YOU, KAZUKI.
WHAT?
COME ON!
WHY NOOOOT?
Something sweet...
Oh! THE CAFÉ THAT JUST OPENED NEAR THE STATION IS SUPPOSED TO BE REALLY GOOD. Or so I heard.
REALLY? Let's go there, then.
ALL RIGHT!
AND IT'S ALL ON AZUMA! ♡
INCLUDING ME, RIGHT?
No, Kazuki. Only underclassmen.
WHAT?

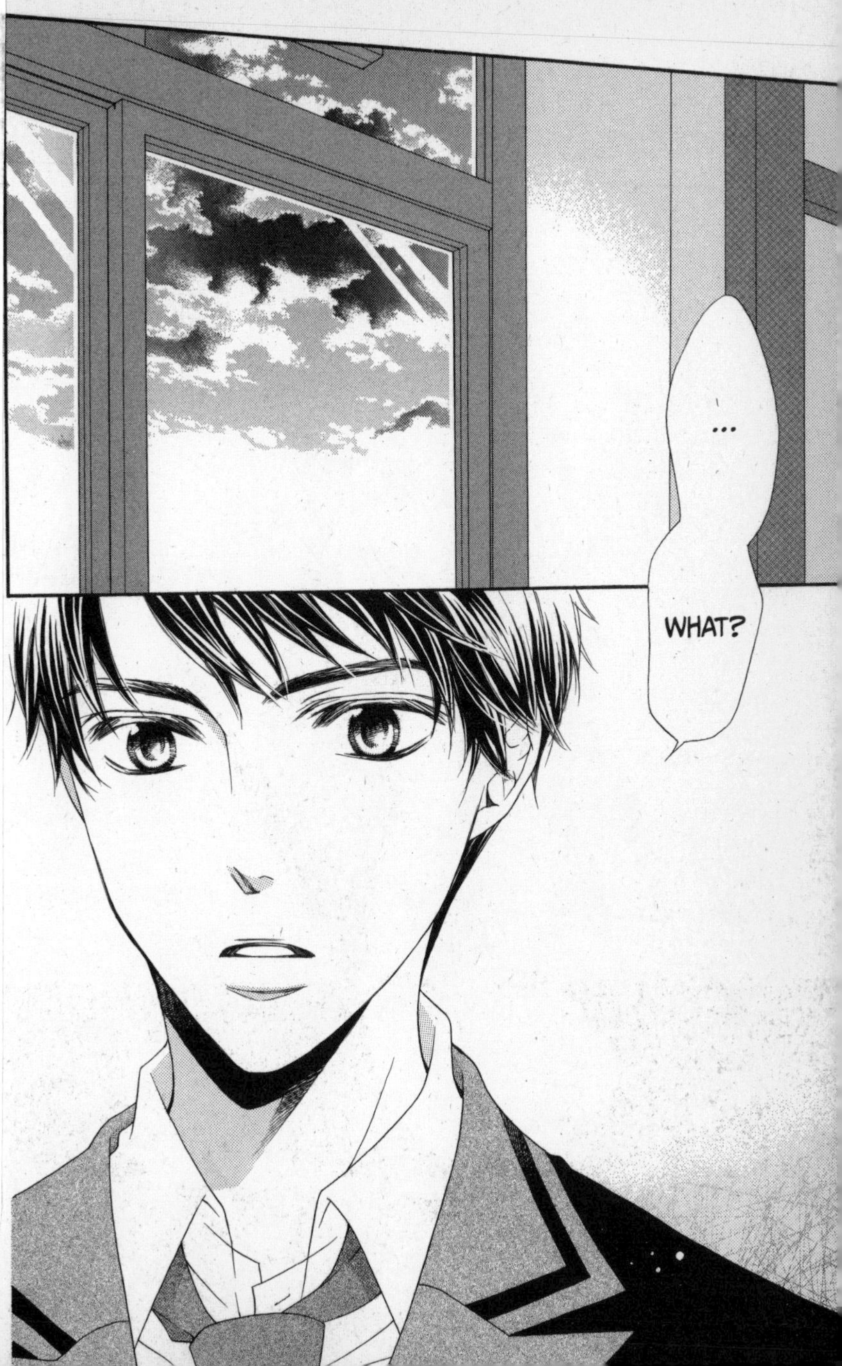
...
WHAT?

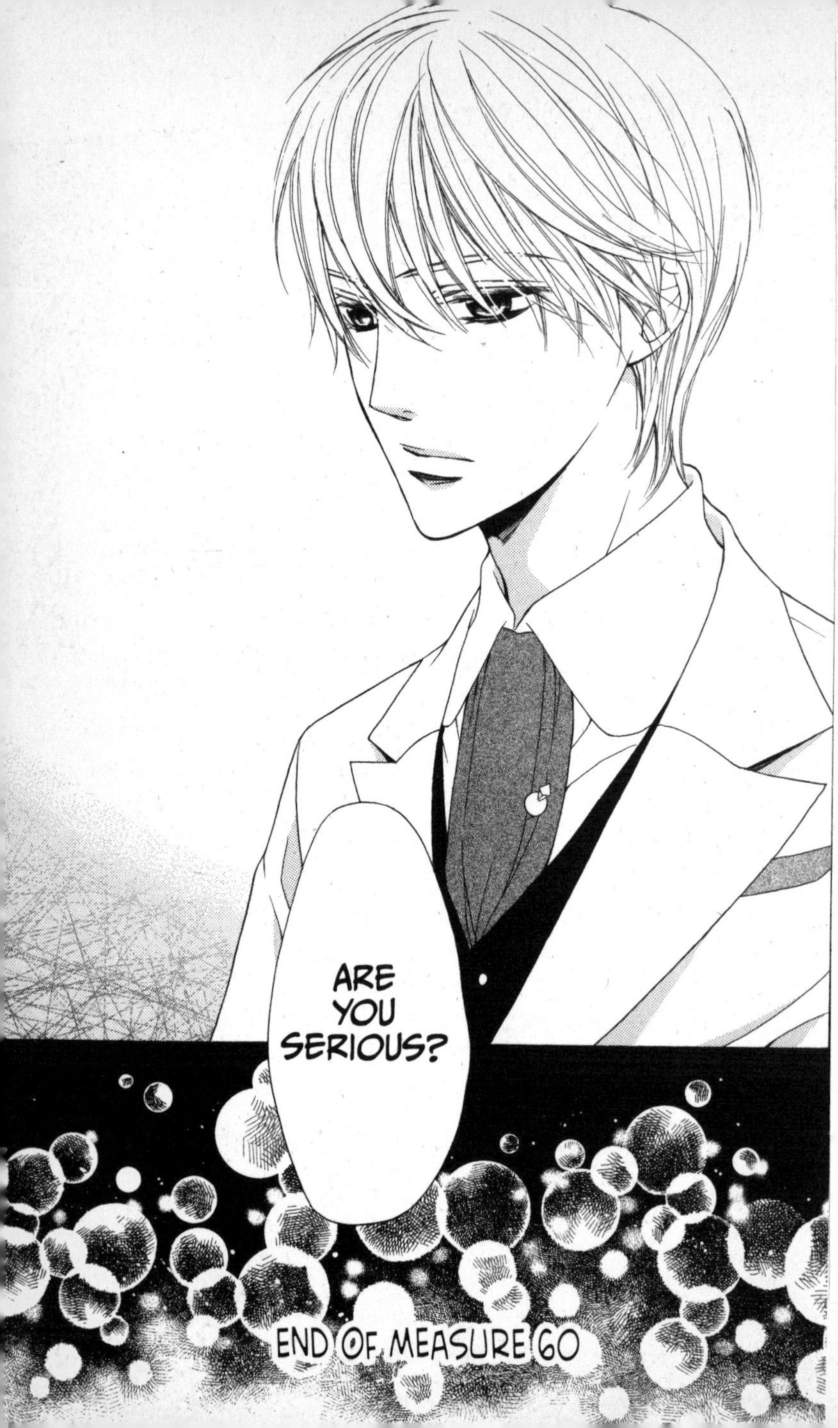
ARE YOU SERIOUS?
END OF MEASURE 60

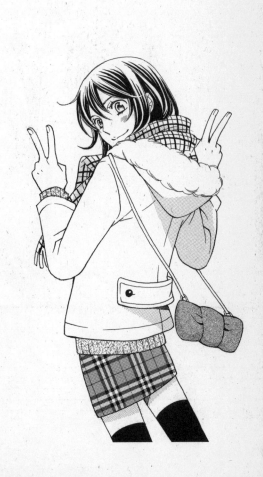

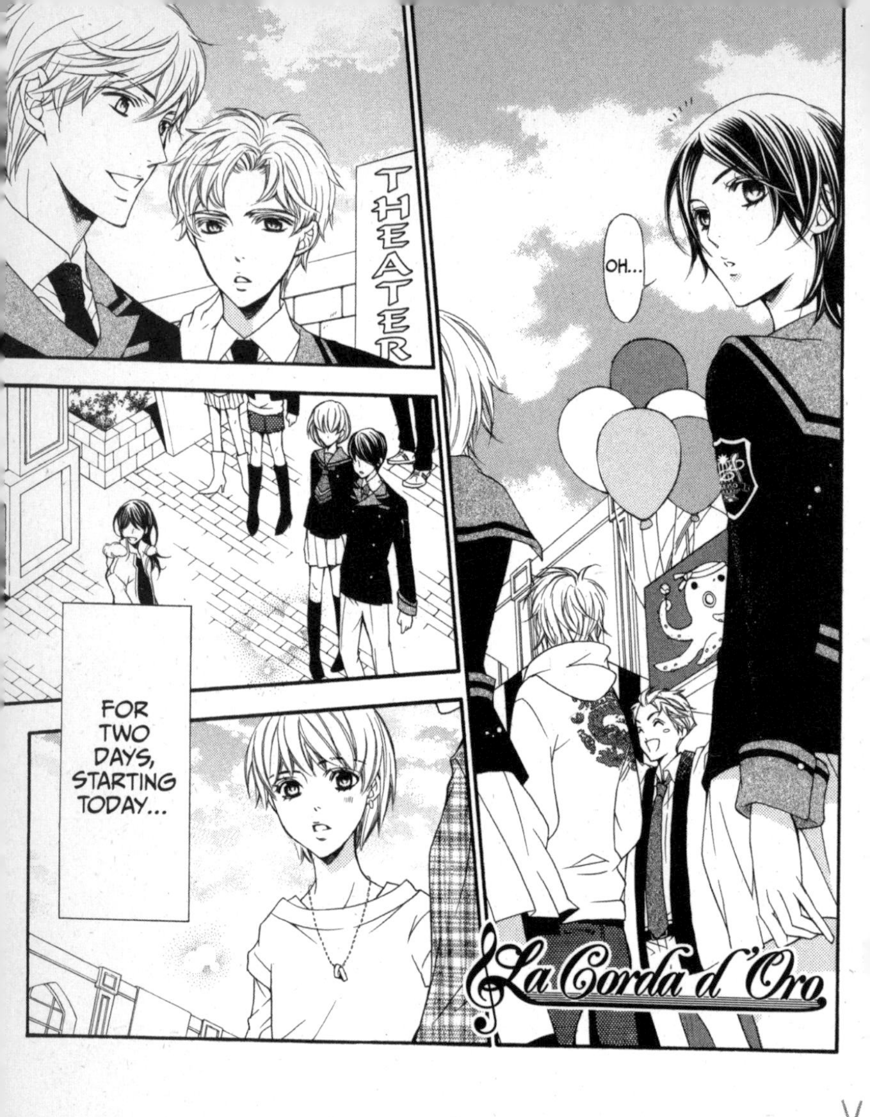
OH...
La Corda d'Oro
THEATER
FOR TWO DAYS, STARTING TODAY...

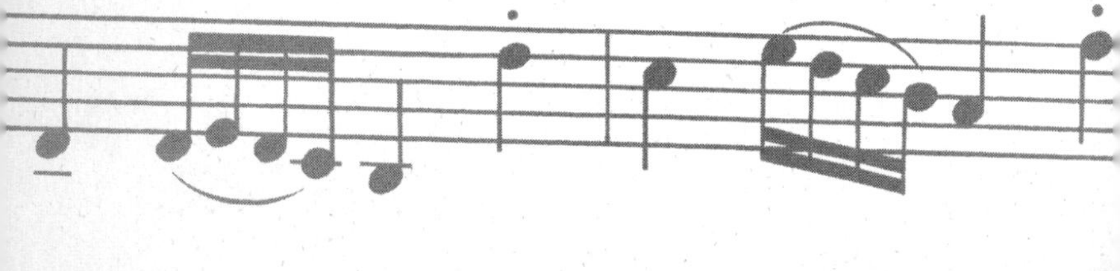

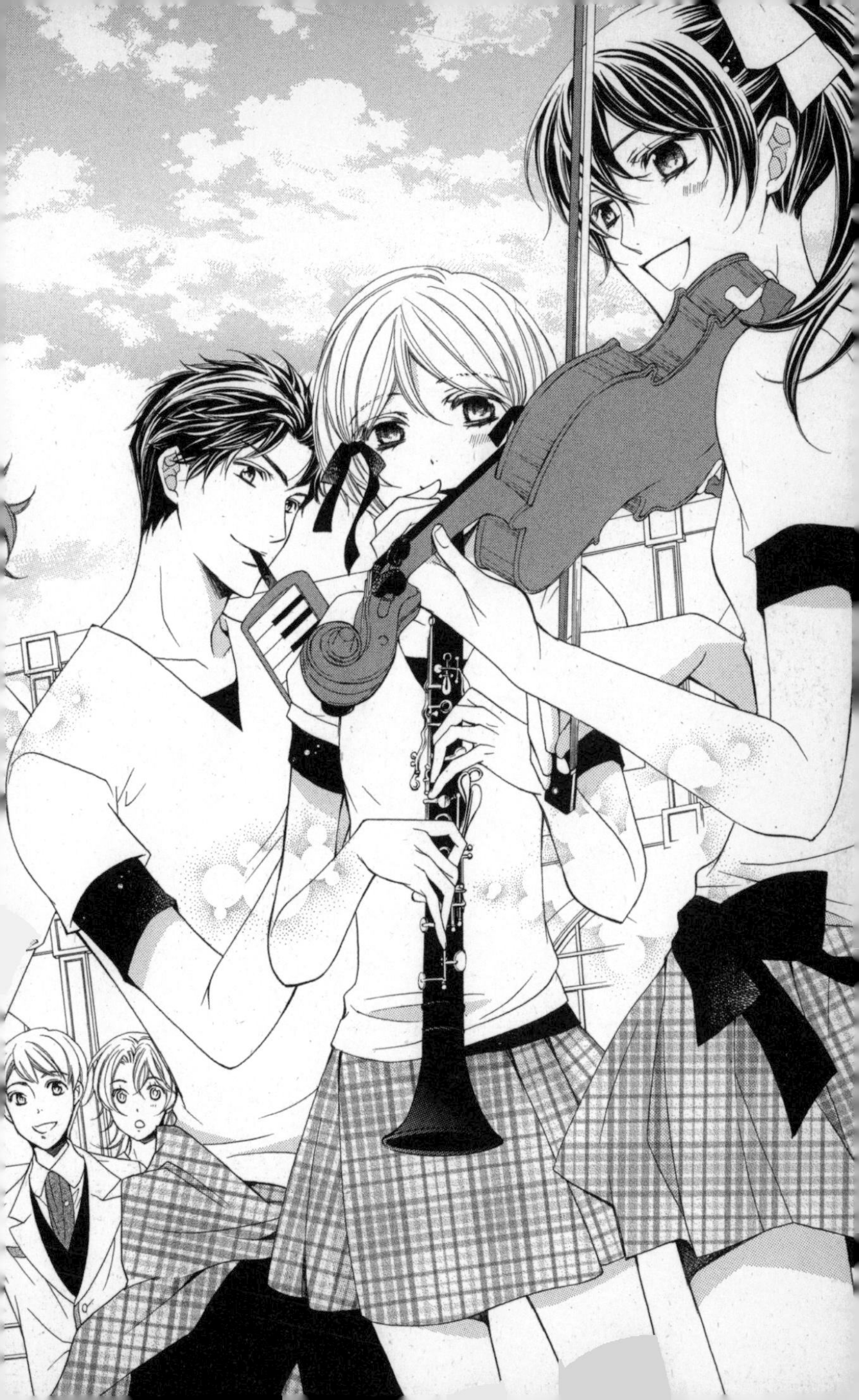

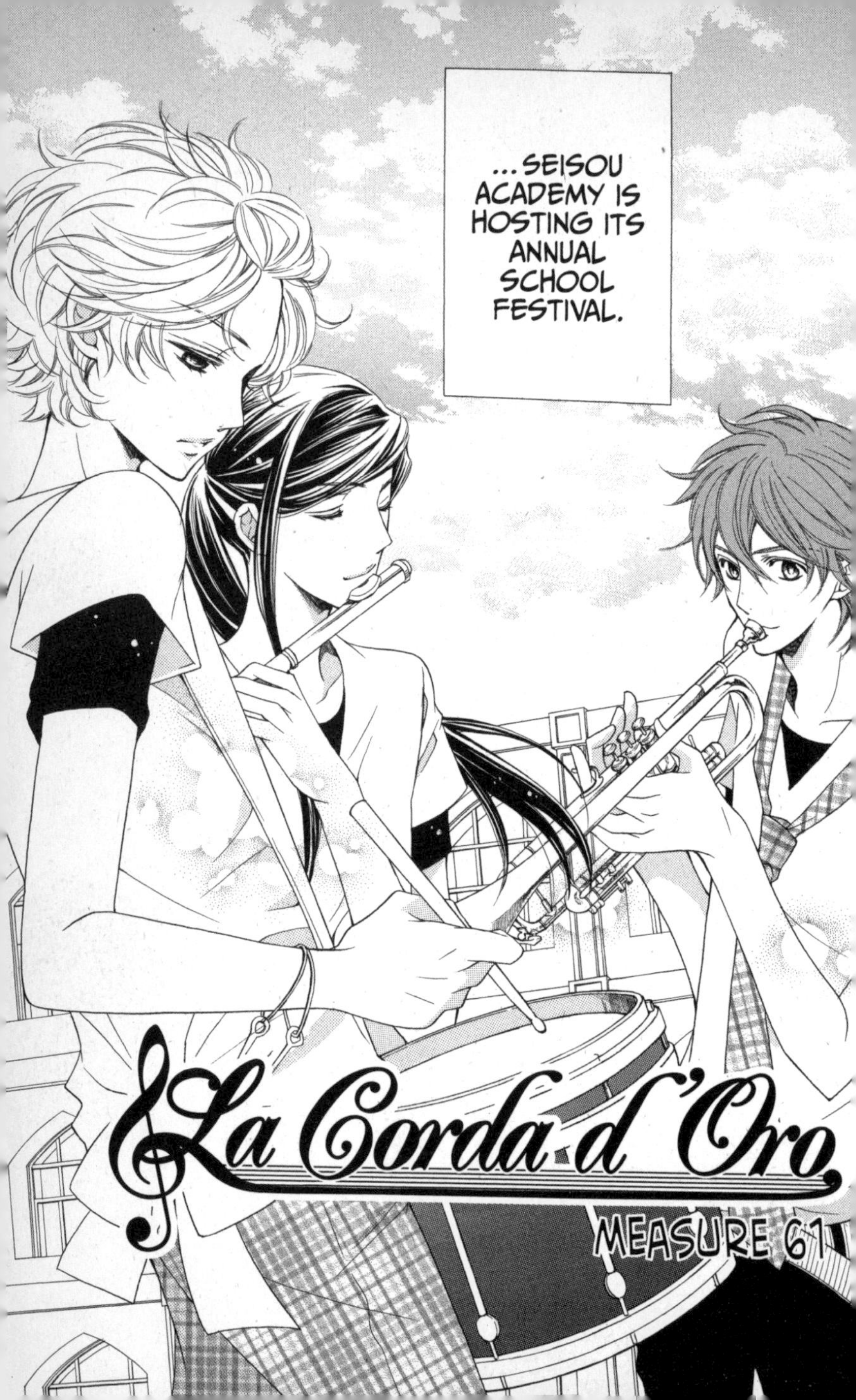
...SEISOU ACADEMY IS HOSTING ITS ANNUAL SCHOOL FESTIVAL.
La Corda d'Oro
MEASURE 61

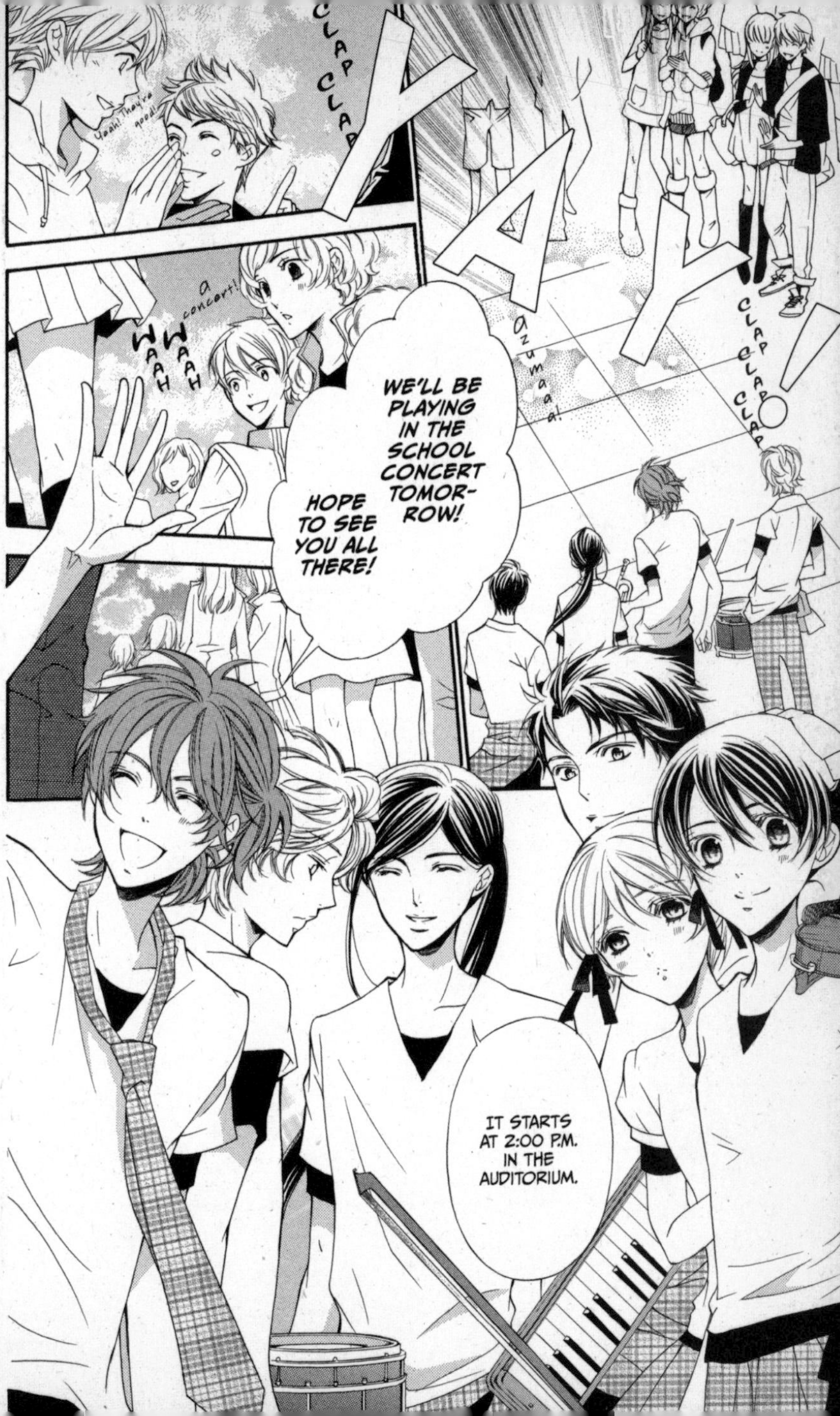
YAY!
CLAP CLAP
CLAP CLAP CLAP
Azumaaaa!
WE'LL BE PLAYING IN THE SCHOOL CONCERT TOMORROW!
HOPE TO SEE YOU ALL THERE!
Yeah! They're good!
a concert!
WAAH WAAH
IT STARTS AT 2:00 P.M. IN THE AUDITORIUM.

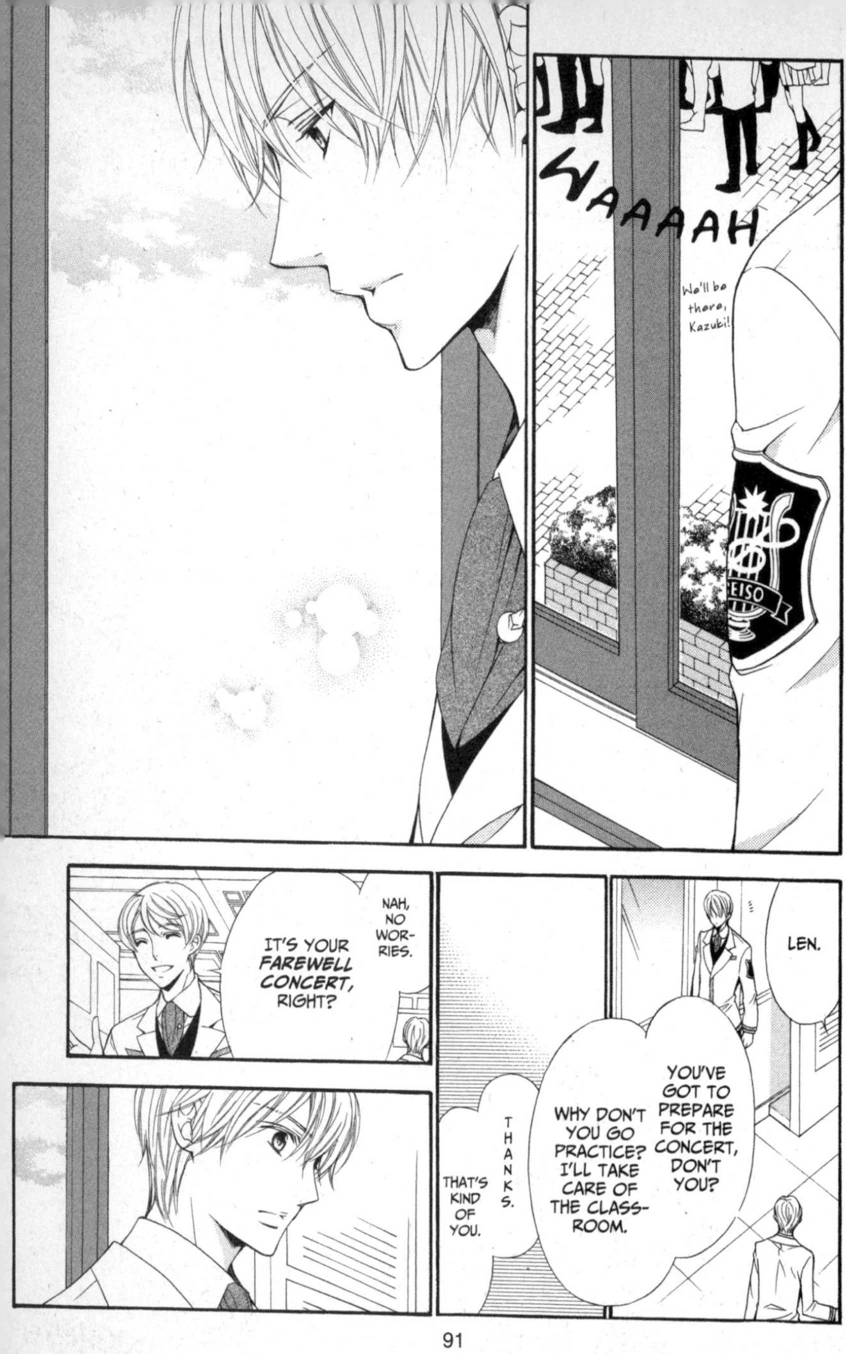
WAAAAH
We'll be there, Kazuki!
LEN.
YOU'VE GOT TO PREPARE FOR THE CONCERT, DON'T YOU?
WHY DON'T YOU GO PRACTICE? I'LL TAKE CARE OF THE CLASSROOM.
THANKS.
THAT'S KIND OF YOU.
NAH, NO WORRIES.
IT'S YOUR *FAREWELL CONCERT*, RIGHT?

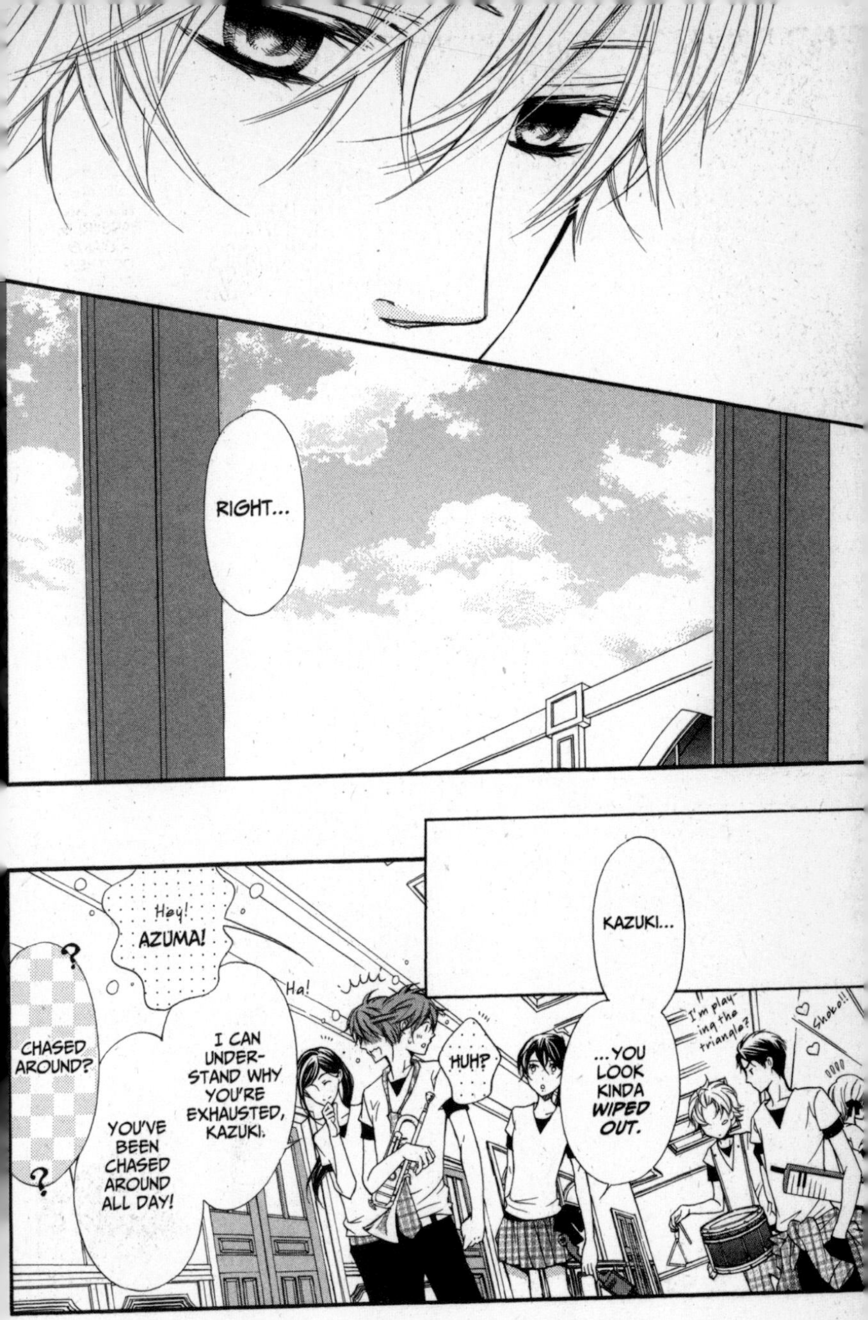
RIGHT...
KAZUKI...
Shoko!!
I'm play-ing the triangle?
...YOU LOOK KINDA WIPED OUT.
HUH?
Hey! AZUMA!
Ha!
I CAN UNDER-STAND WHY YOU'RE EXHAUSTED, KAZUKI.
YOU'VE BEEN CHASED AROUND ALL DAY!
CHASED AROUND?

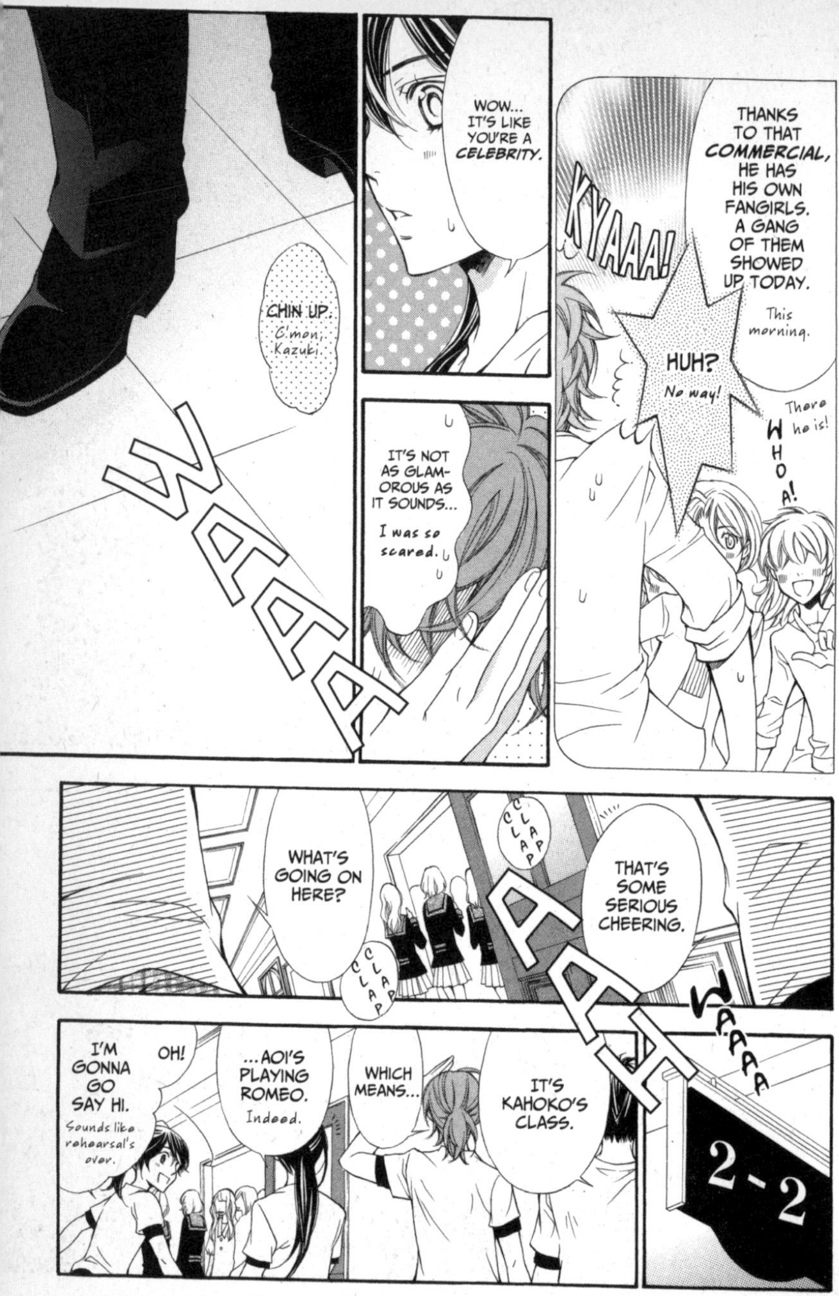
THANKS TO THAT COMMERCIAL, HE HAS HIS OWN FANGIRLS. A GANG OF THEM SHOWED UP TODAY.
This morning.
KYAAA!
HUH?
No way!
There he is!
WHOA!
WOW... IT'S LIKE YOU'RE A CELEBRITY.
IT'S NOT AS GLAMOROUS AS IT SOUNDS...
I was so scared.
CHIN UP.
C'mon, Kazuki.
WAAA
THAT'S SOME SERIOUS CHEERING.
CLAP CLAP
AAAH
WHAT'S GOING ON HERE?
CLAP CLAP
WAAAA
2-2
IT'S KAHOKO'S CLASS.
WHICH MEANS...
...AOI'S PLAYING ROMEO.
Indeed.
OH!
I'M GONNA GO SAY HI.
Sounds like rehearsal's over.

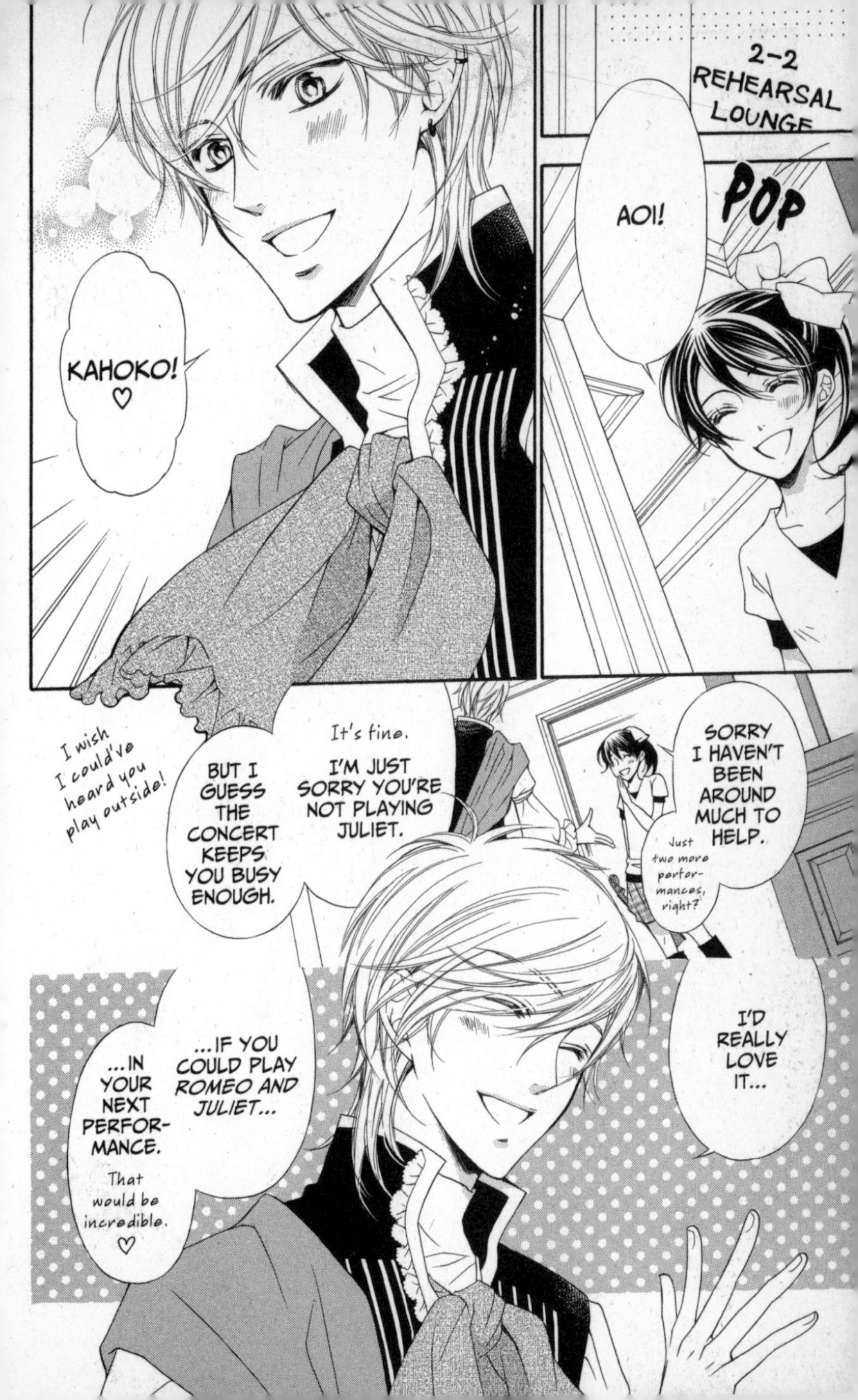
2-2 REHEARSAL LOUNGE
POP
AOI!
KAHOKO! ♡
SORRY I HAVEN'T BEEN AROUND MUCH TO HELP.
Just two more performances, right?
It's fine.
I'M JUST SORRY YOU'RE NOT PLAYING JULIET.
BUT I GUESS THE CONCERT KEEPS YOU BUSY ENOUGH.
I wish I could've heard you play outside!
I'D REALLY LOVE IT...
...IF YOU COULD PLAY ROMEO AND JULIET...
...IN YOUR NEXT PERFORMANCE.
That would be incredible. ♡

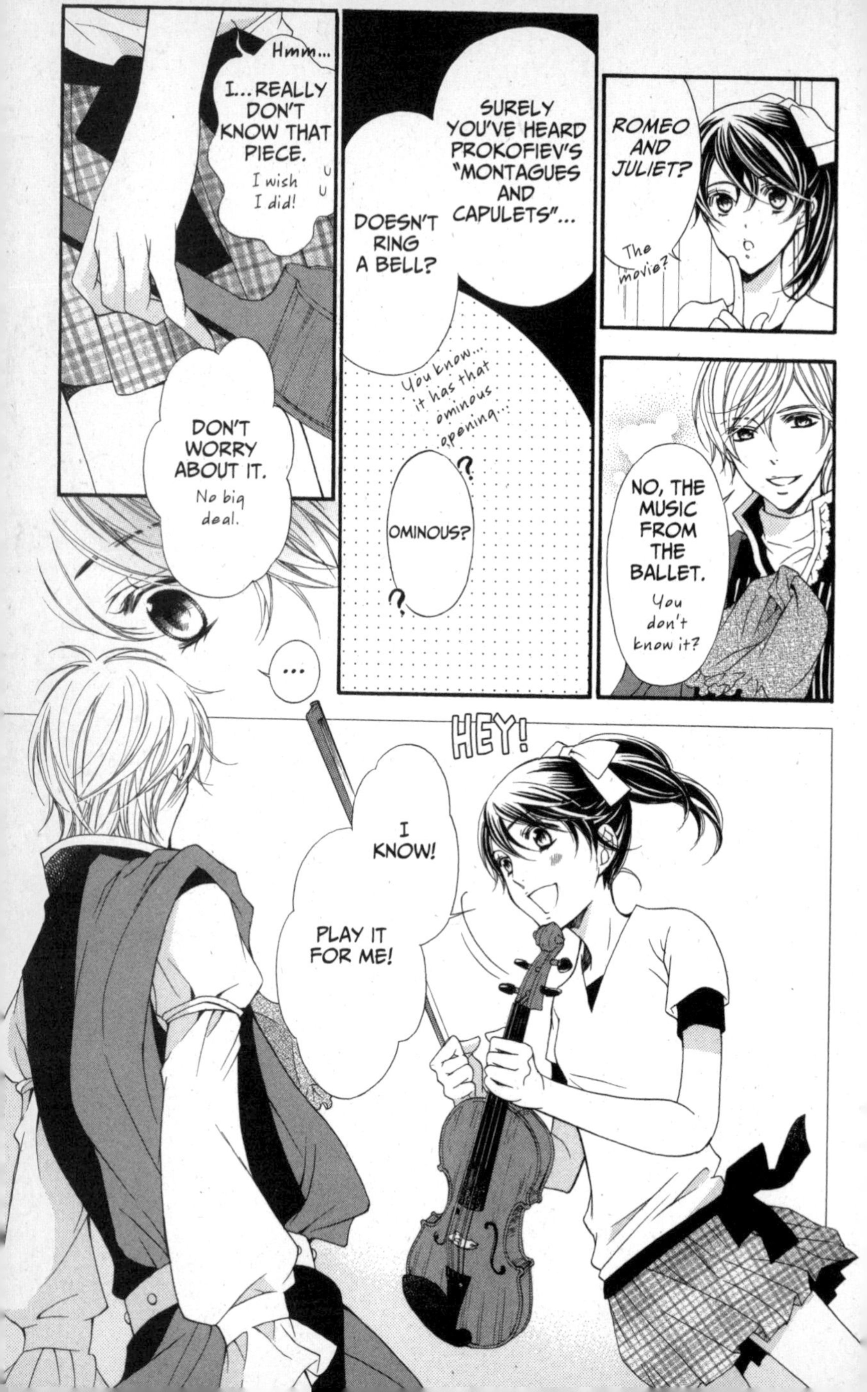
ROMEO AND JULIET?
The movie?
NO, THE MUSIC FROM THE BALLET.
You don't know it?
SURELY YOU'VE HEARD PROKOFIEV'S "MONTAGUES AND CAPULETS"...
DOESN'T RING A BELL?
You know... it has that ominous opening...
OMINOUS?
Hmm...
I...REALLY DON'T KNOW THAT PIECE.
I wish I did!
DON'T WORRY ABOUT IT.
No big deal.
...
HEY!
I KNOW!
PLAY IT FOR ME!

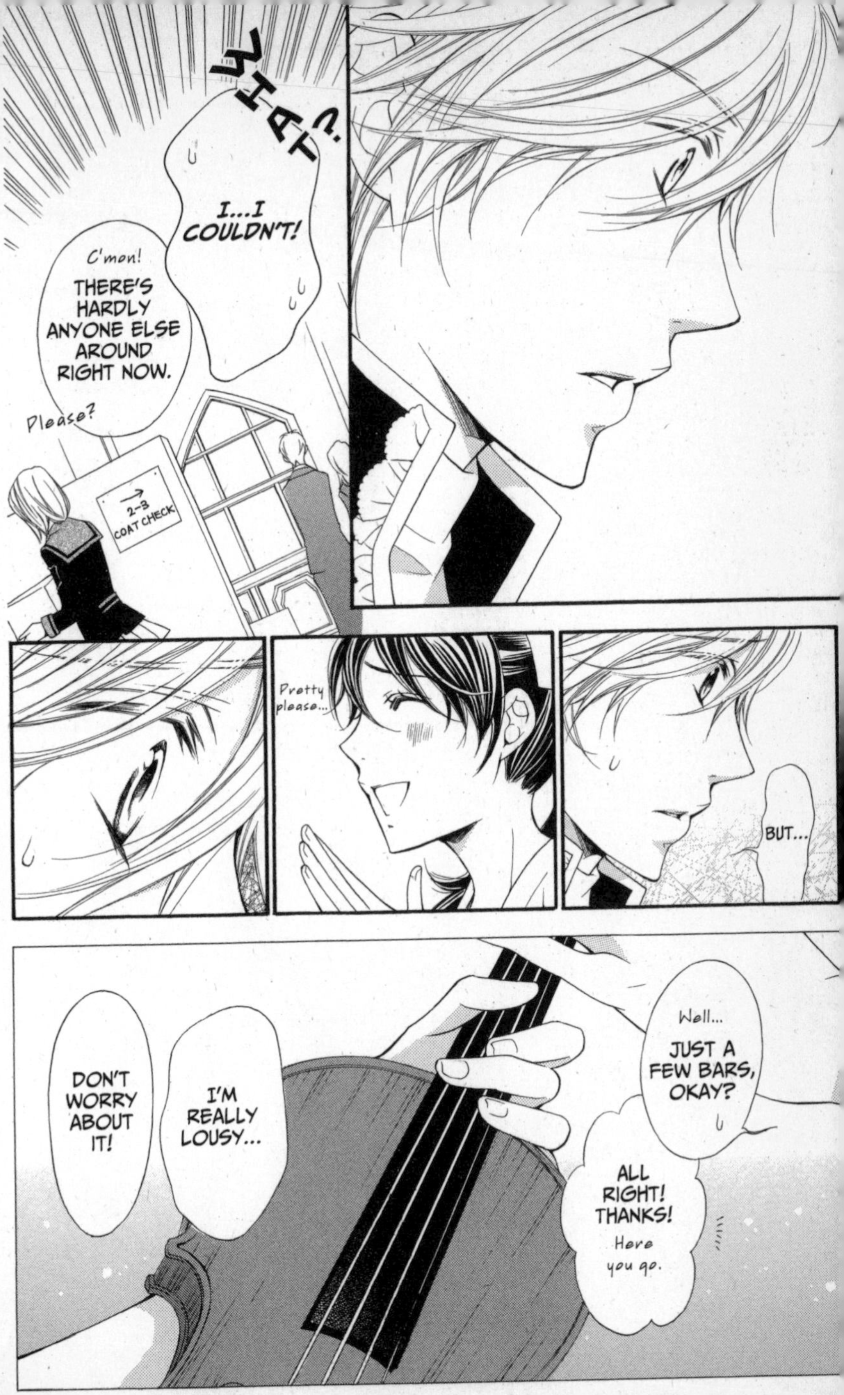
WHAT?
I...I COULDN'T!
C'mon!
THERE'S HARDLY ANYONE ELSE AROUND RIGHT NOW.
Please?
2-3 COAT CHECK
BUT...
Pretty please...
Well...
JUST A FEW BARS, OKAY?
ALL RIGHT! THANKS!
Here you go.
I'M REALLY LOUSY...
DON'T WORRY ABOUT IT!

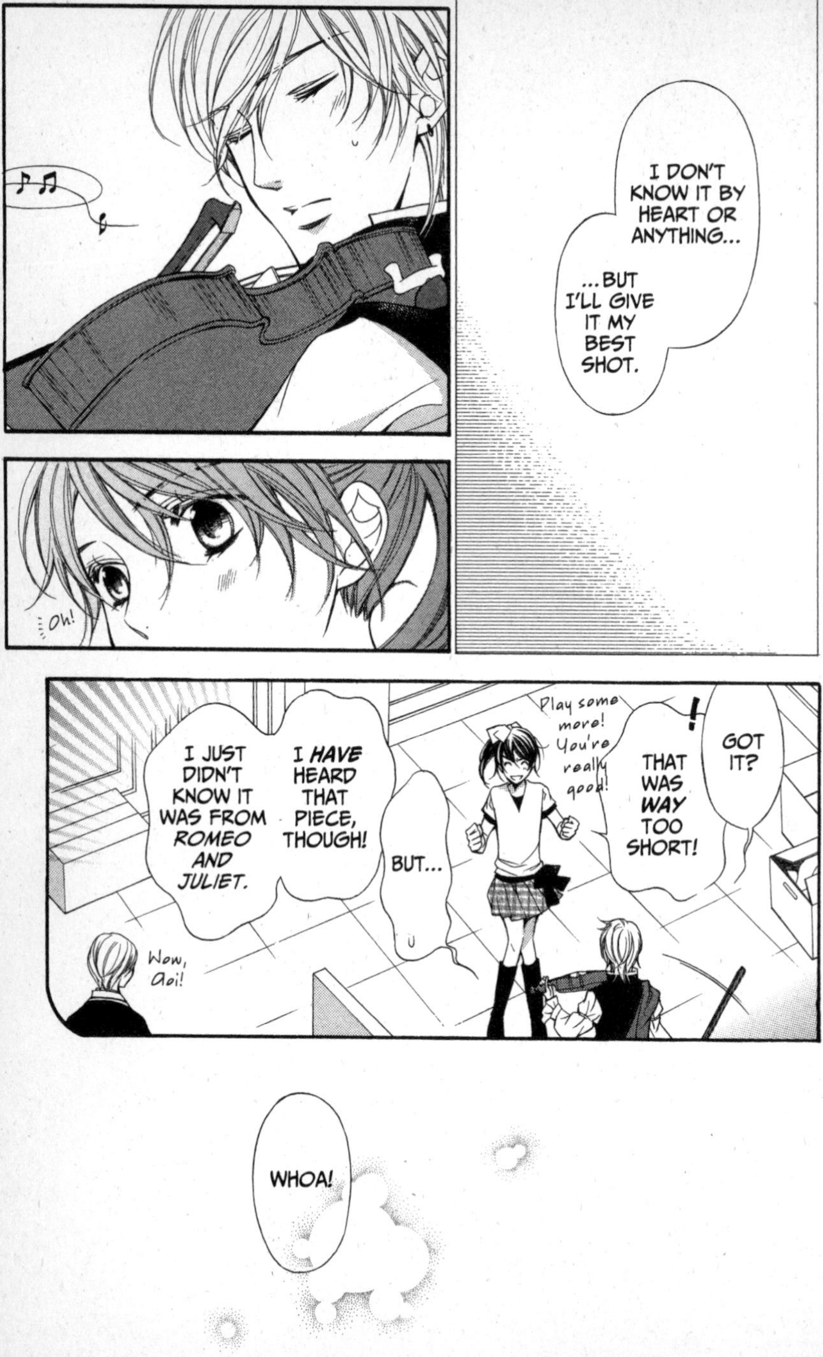
I DON'T KNOW IT BY HEART OR ANYTHING...
...BUT I'LL GIVE IT MY BEST SHOT.
Oh!
GOT IT?
!
THAT WAS *WAY* TOO SHORT!
Play some more! You're really good!
BUT...
I *HAVE* HEARD THAT PIECE, THOUGH!
I JUST DIDN'T KNOW IT WAS FROM *ROMEO AND JULIET.*
Wow, Aoi!
WHOA!

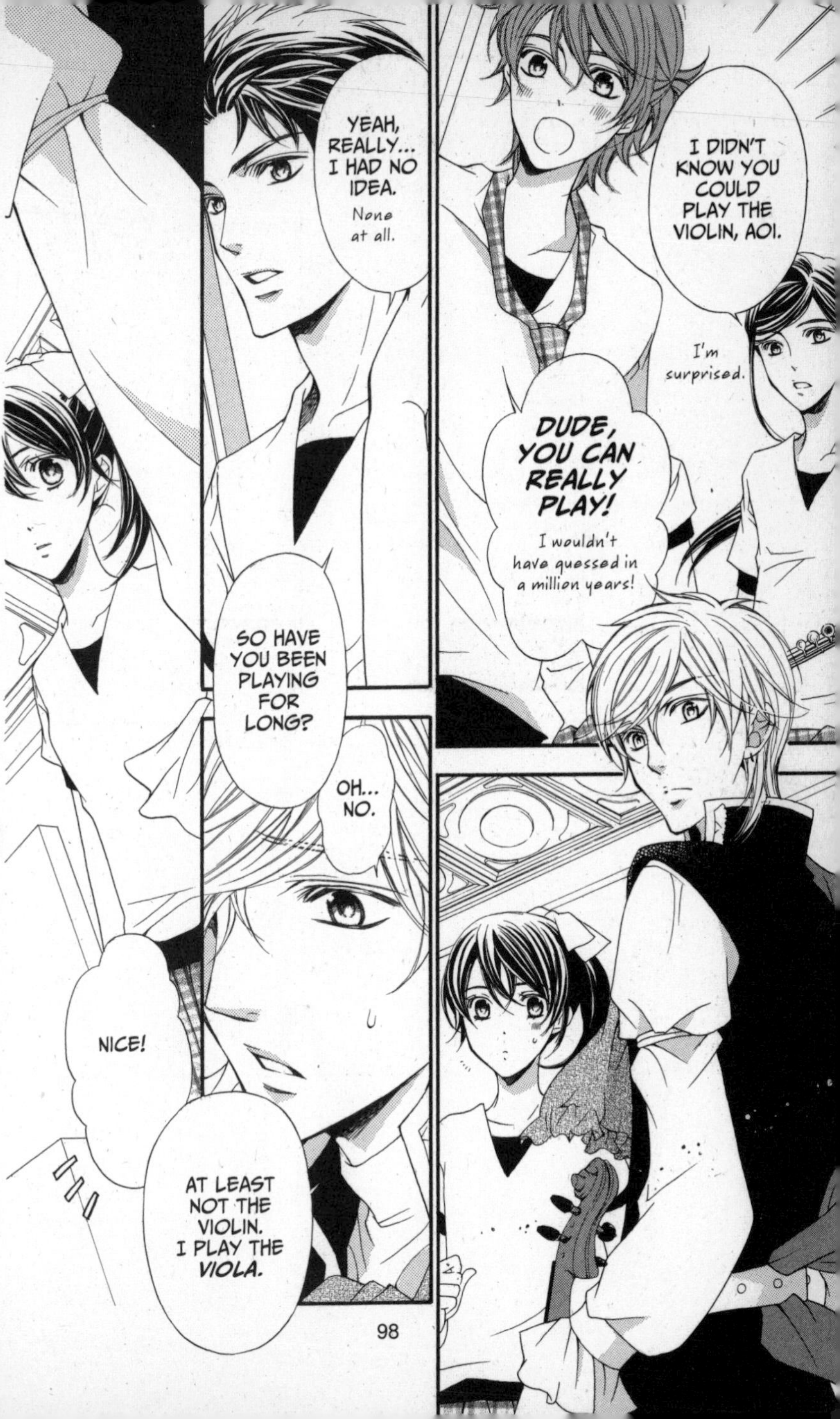

I DIDN'T KNOW YOU COULD PLAY THE VIOLIN, AOI.
I'm surprised.
DUDE, YOU CAN REALLY PLAY!
I wouldn't have guessed in a million years!
YEAH, REALLY... I HAD NO IDEA.
None at all.
SO HAVE YOU BEEN PLAYING FOR LONG?
OH... NO.
AT LEAST NOT THE VIOLIN. I PLAY THE *VIOLA*.
NICE!

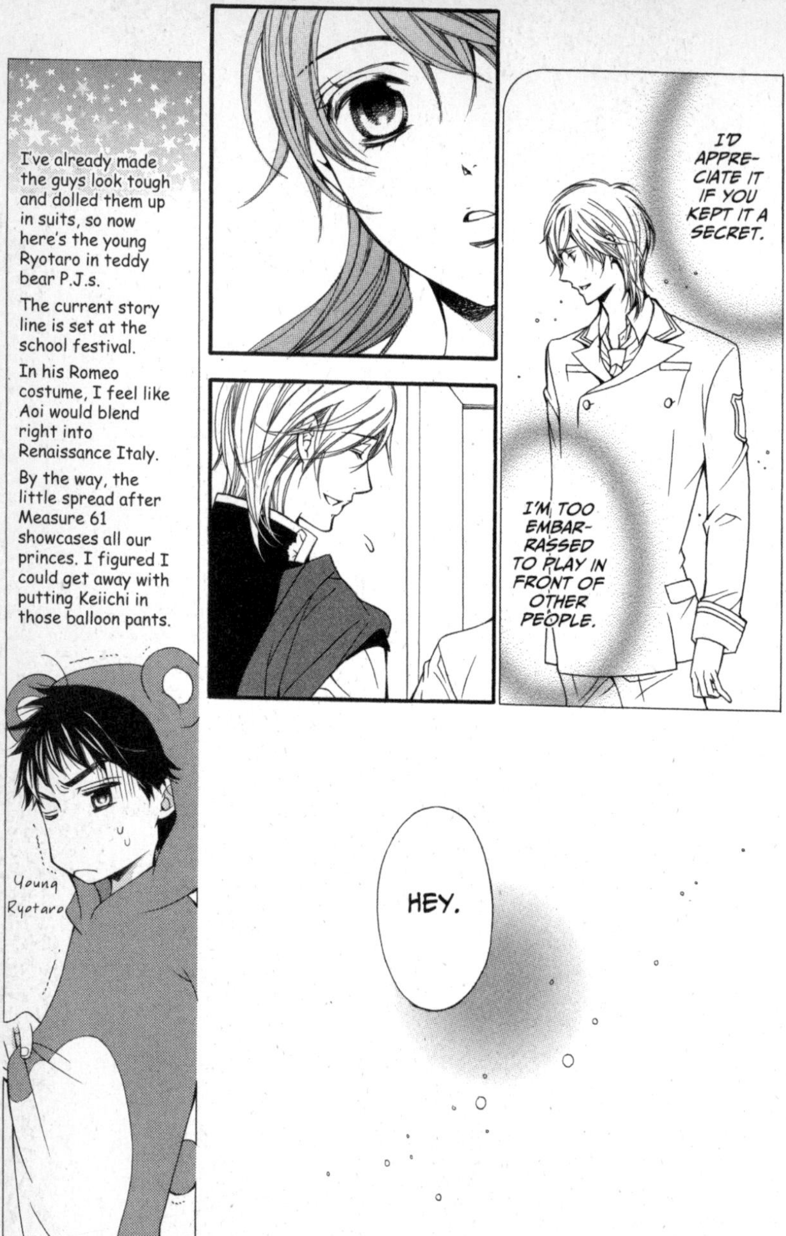
I'D APPRECIATE IT IF YOU KEPT IT A SECRET.
I'M TOO EMBARRASSED TO PLAY IN FRONT OF OTHER PEOPLE.
HEY.
I've already made the guys look tough and dolled them up in suits, so now here's the young Ryotaro in teddy bear P.J.s.
The current story line is set at the school festival.
In his Romeo costume, I feel like Aoi would blend right into Renaissance Italy.
By the way, the little spread after Measure 61 showcases all our princes. I figured I could get away with putting Keiichi in those balloon pants.
Young Ryotaro

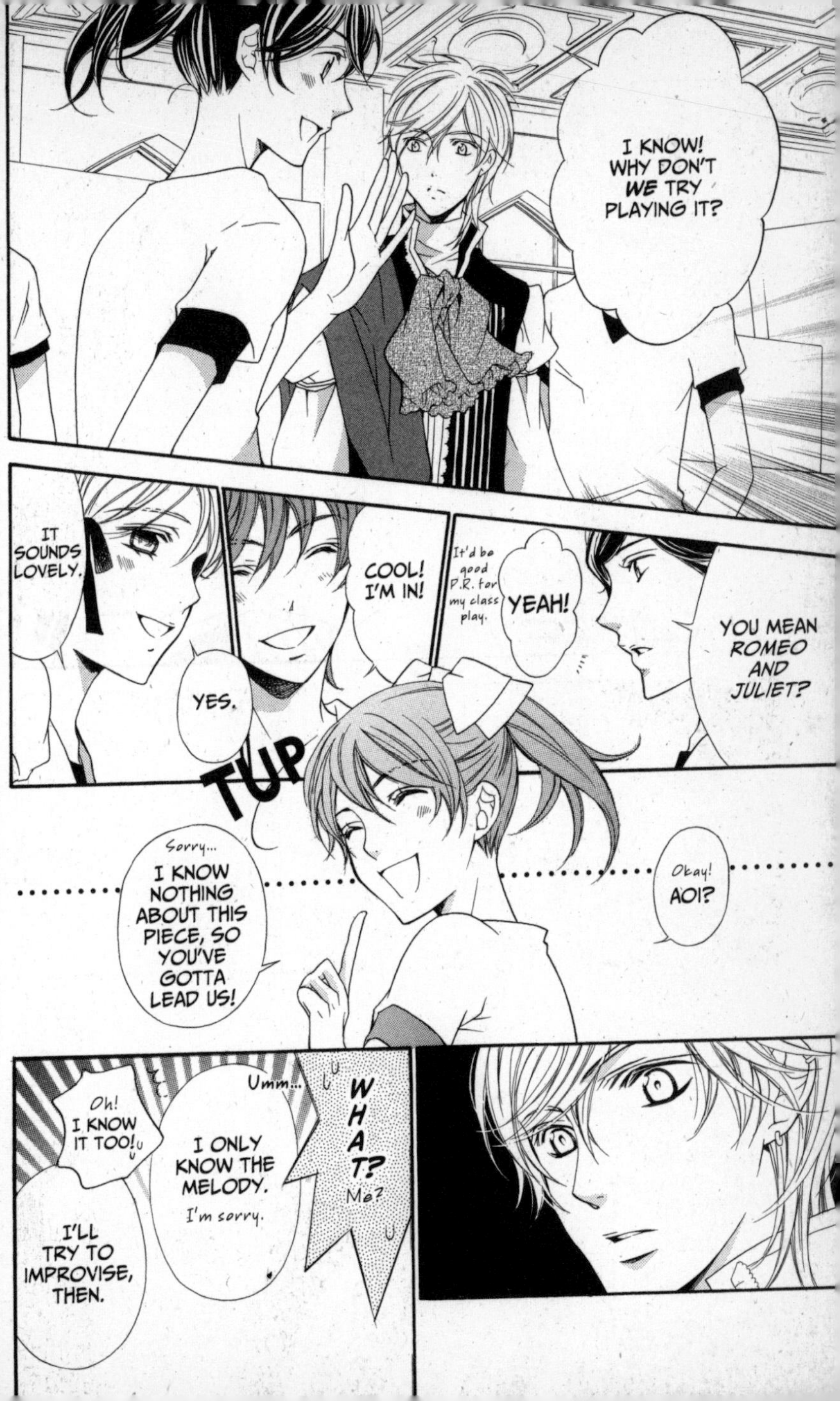
I KNOW! WHY DON'T WE TRY PLAYING IT?
YOU MEAN ROMEO AND JULIET?
YEAH!
It'd be good P.R. for my class play.
COOL! I'M IN!
IT SOUNDS LOVELY.
YES.
TUP
Okay! AOI?
Sorry...
I KNOW NOTHING ABOUT THIS PIECE, SO YOU'VE GOTTA LEAD US!
WHAT? Me?
Umm...
I ONLY KNOW THE MELODY.
I'm sorry.
Oh! I KNOW IT TOO!
I'LL TRY TO IMPROVISE, THEN.

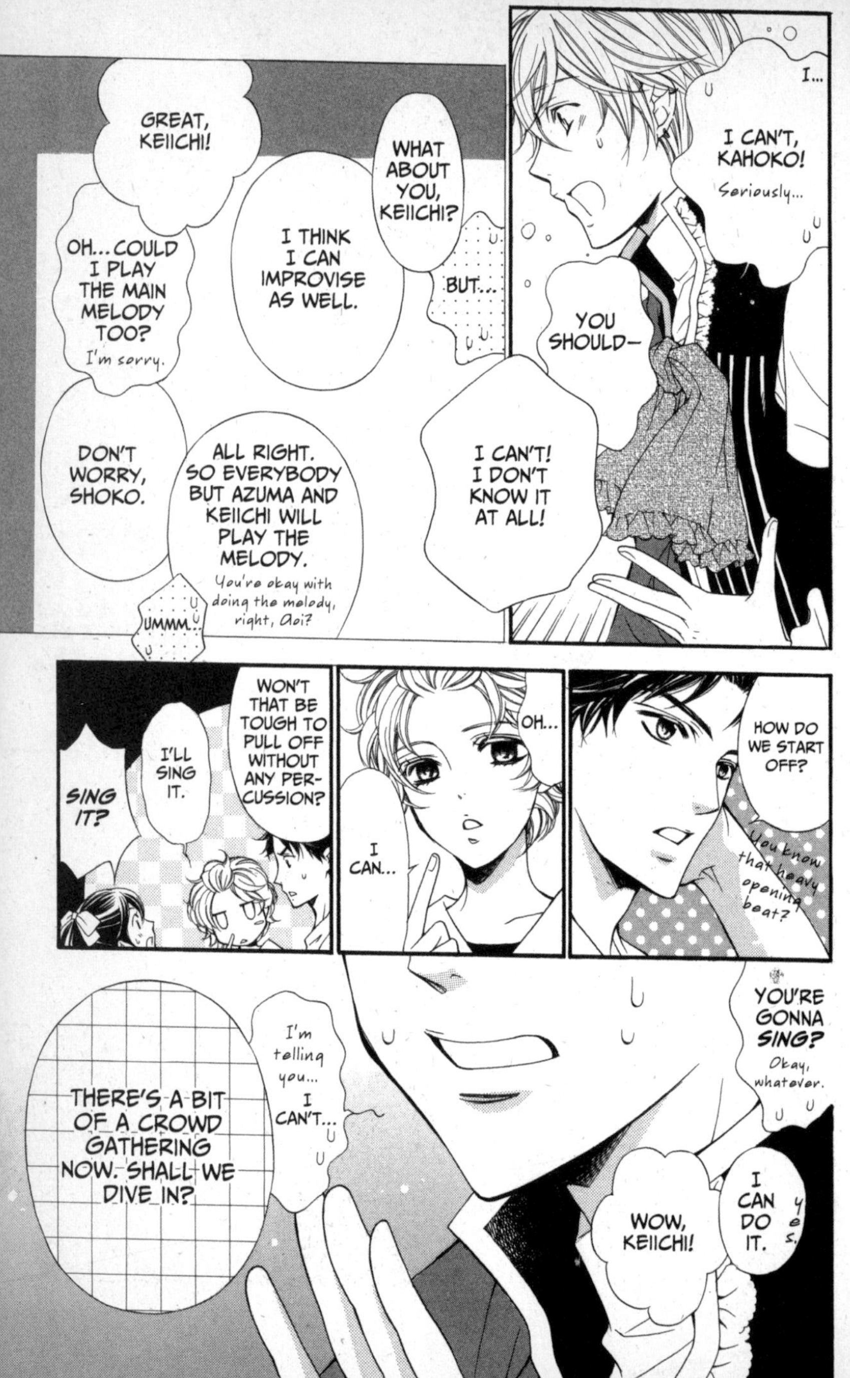
I...
I CAN'T, KAHOKO!
Seriously...
YOU SHOULD—
I CAN'T! I DON'T KNOW IT AT ALL!
WHAT ABOUT YOU, KEIICHI?
BUT...
GREAT, KEIICHI!
I THINK I CAN IMPROVISE AS WELL.
OH...COULD I PLAY THE MAIN MELODY TOO?
I'm sorry.
DON'T WORRY, SHOKO.
ALL RIGHT. SO EVERYBODY BUT AZUMA AND KEIICHI WILL PLAY THE MELODY.
You're okay with doing the melody, right, Aoi?
UMMM...
HOW DO WE START OFF?
You know that heavy opening beat?
OH...
I CAN...
WON'T THAT BE TOUGH TO PULL OFF WITHOUT ANY PER-CUSSION?
I'LL SING IT.
SING IT?
YOU'RE GONNA SING?
Okay, whatever.
I CAN DO IT.
yes.
WOW, KEIICHI!
I'm telling you... I CAN'T...
THERE'S A BIT OF A CROWD GATHERING NOW. SHALL WE DIVE IN?

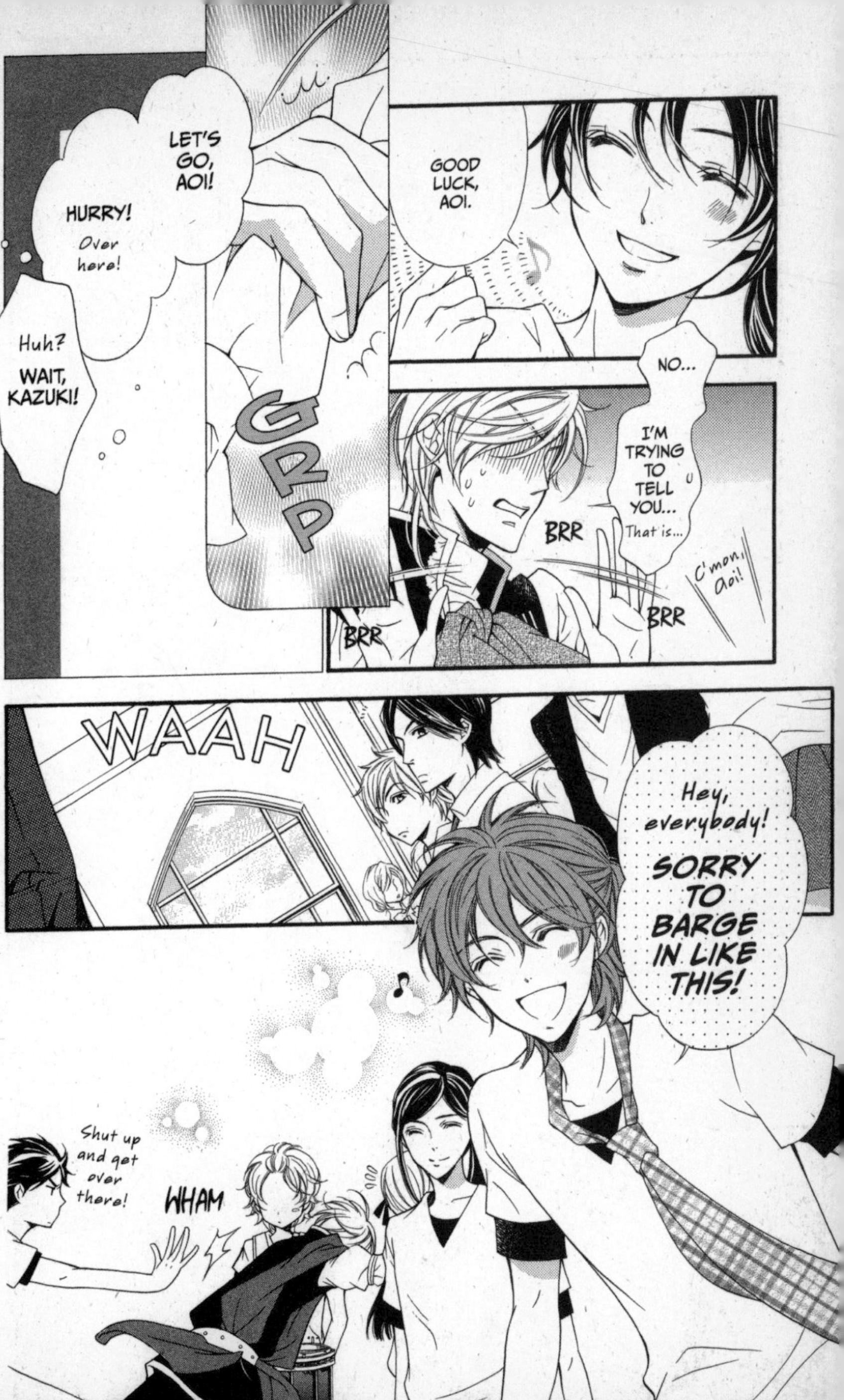
GOOD LUCK, AOI.
NO...
I'M TRYING TO TELL YOU...
That is...
C'mon, Aoi!
BRR
BRR
BRR
LET'S GO, AOI!
HURRY!
Over here!
GRP
Huh?
WAIT, KAZUKI!
WAAH
Hey, everybody!
SORRY TO BARGE IN LIKE THIS!
WHAM
Shut up and get over there!

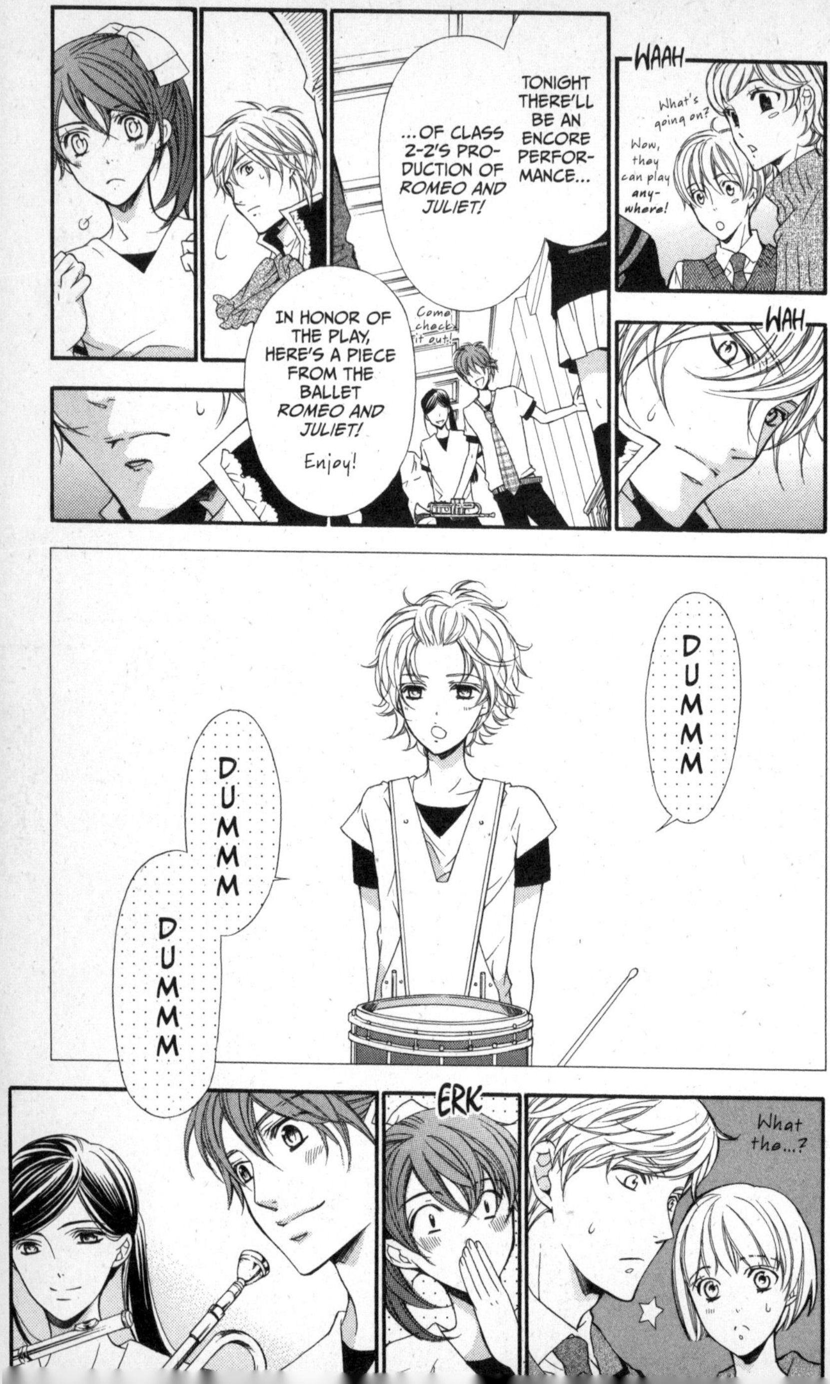
WAAH
What's going on?
Wow, they can play anywhere!
TONIGHT THERE'LL BE AN ENCORE PERFORMANCE...
...OF CLASS 2-2'S PRODUCTION OF ROMEO AND JULIET!
WAH
Come check it out!
IN HONOR OF THE PLAY, HERE'S A PIECE FROM THE BALLET ROMEO AND JULIET!
Enjoy!
DUMMM
DUMMM
DUMMM
What the...?
ERK

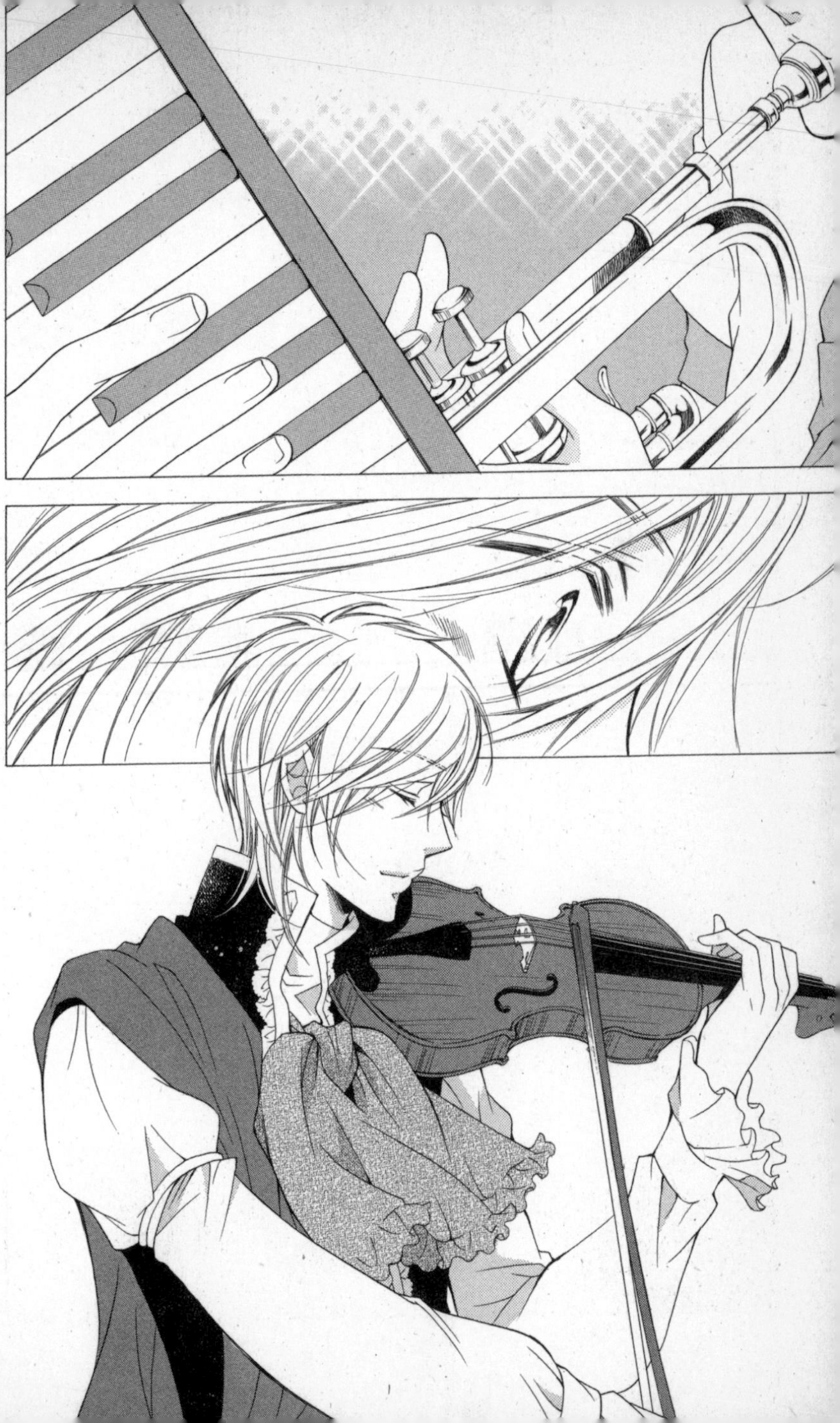

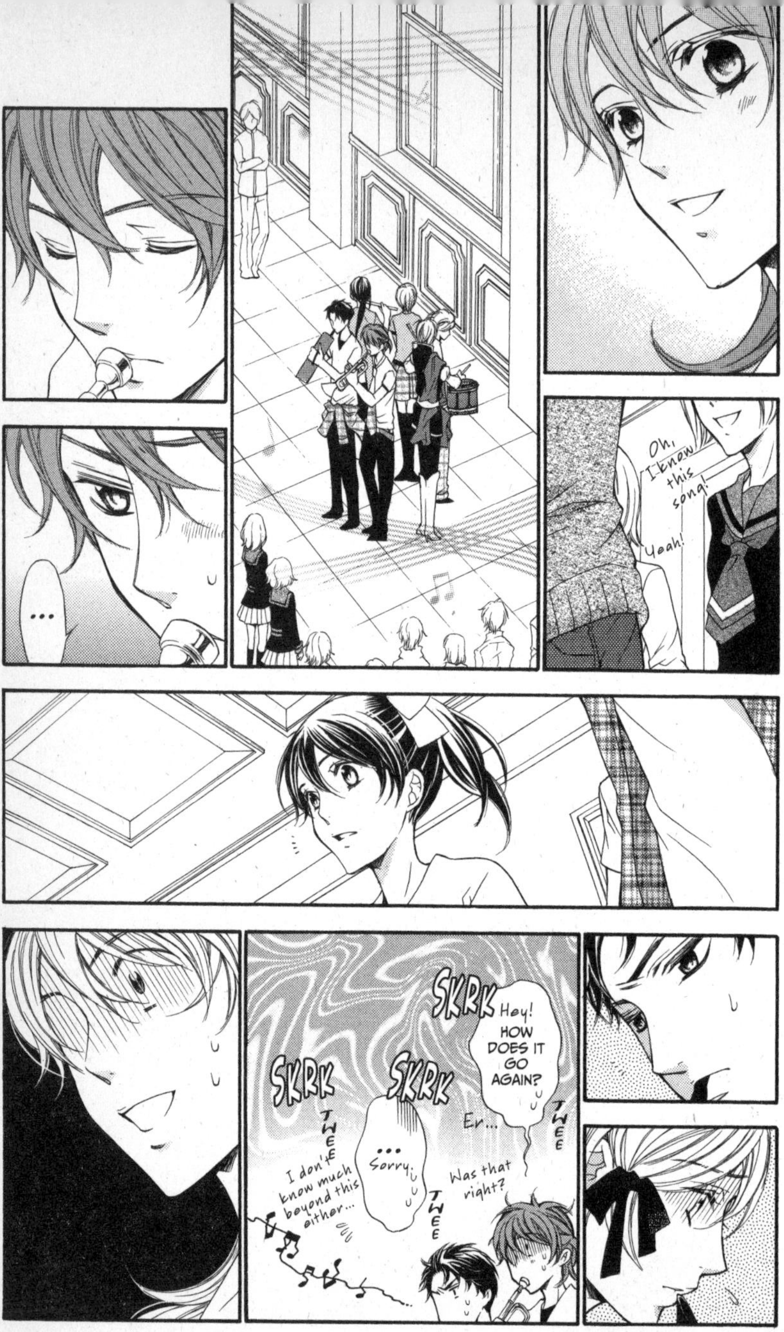
Oh, I know this song!
Yeah!
...
SKRK
Hey! HOW DOES IT GO AGAIN?
SKRK
SKRK
TWEE
Er...
Was that right?
TWEE
... Sorry.
TWEE
I don't know much beyond this either...

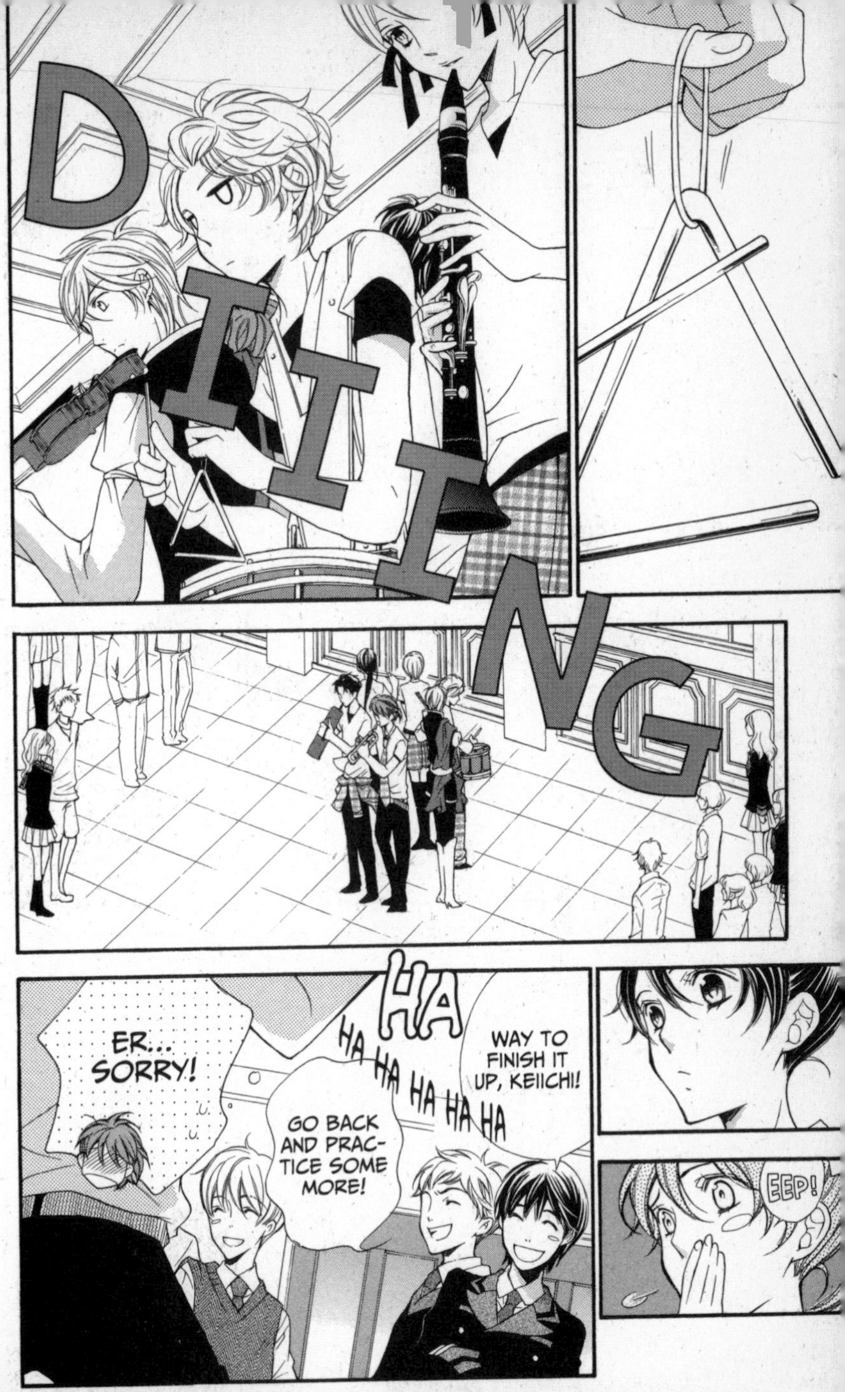
DIIING
EEP!
WAY TO FINISH IT UP, KEIICHI!
HA HA HA HA HA HA
GO BACK AND PRAC-TICE SOME MORE!
ER... SORRY!

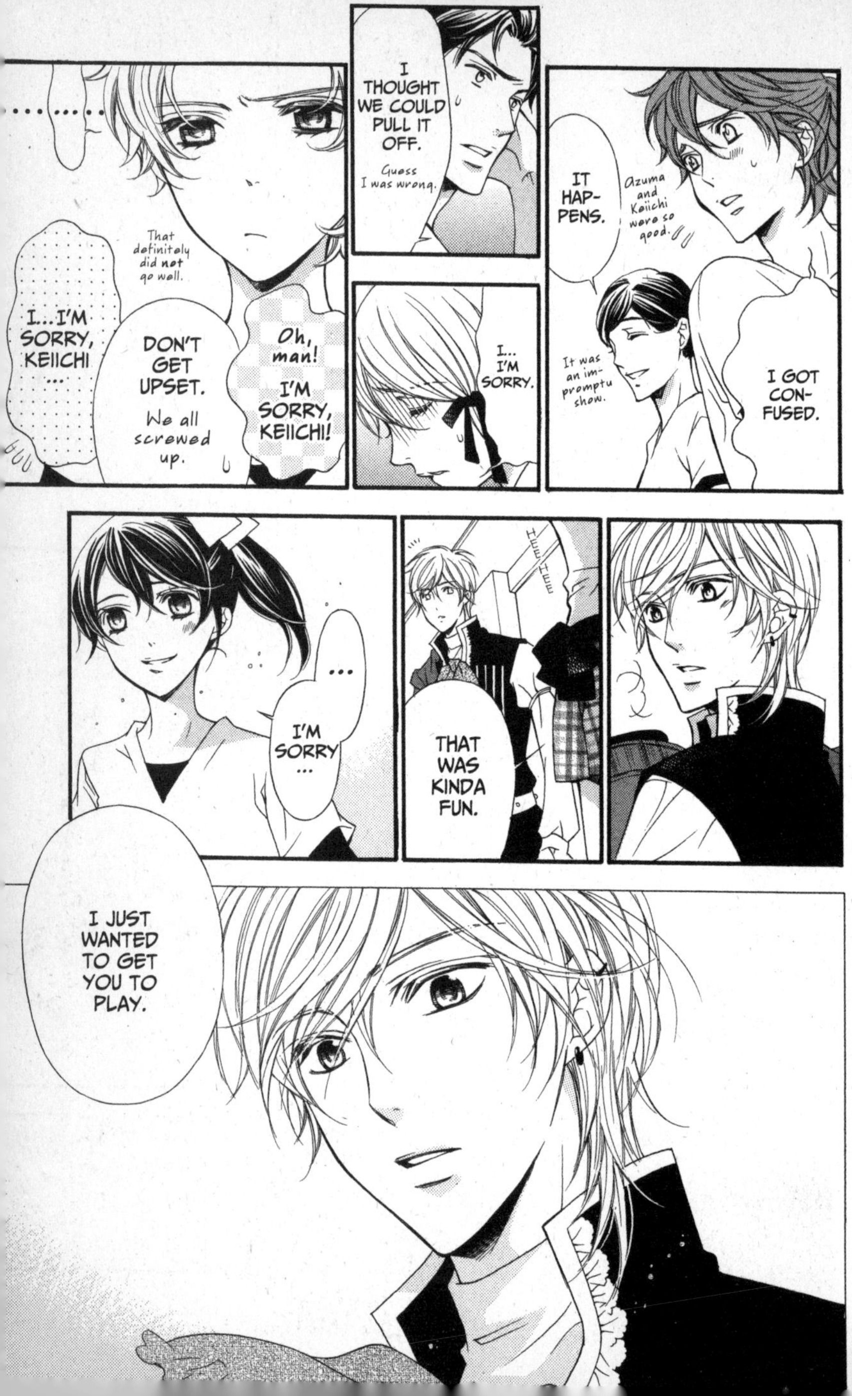
Azuma and Keiichi were so good.
IT HAP-PENS.
I GOT CON-FUSED.
It was an im-promptu show.
I THOUGHT WE COULD PULL IT OFF.
Guess I was wrong.
I... I'M SORRY.
......
That definitely did not go well.
Oh, man! I'M SORRY, KEIICHI!
DON'T GET UPSET. We all screwed up.
I...I'M SORRY, KEIICHI...
HEE HEE
THAT WAS KINDA FUN.
...
I'M SORRY...
I JUST WANTED TO GET YOU TO PLAY.

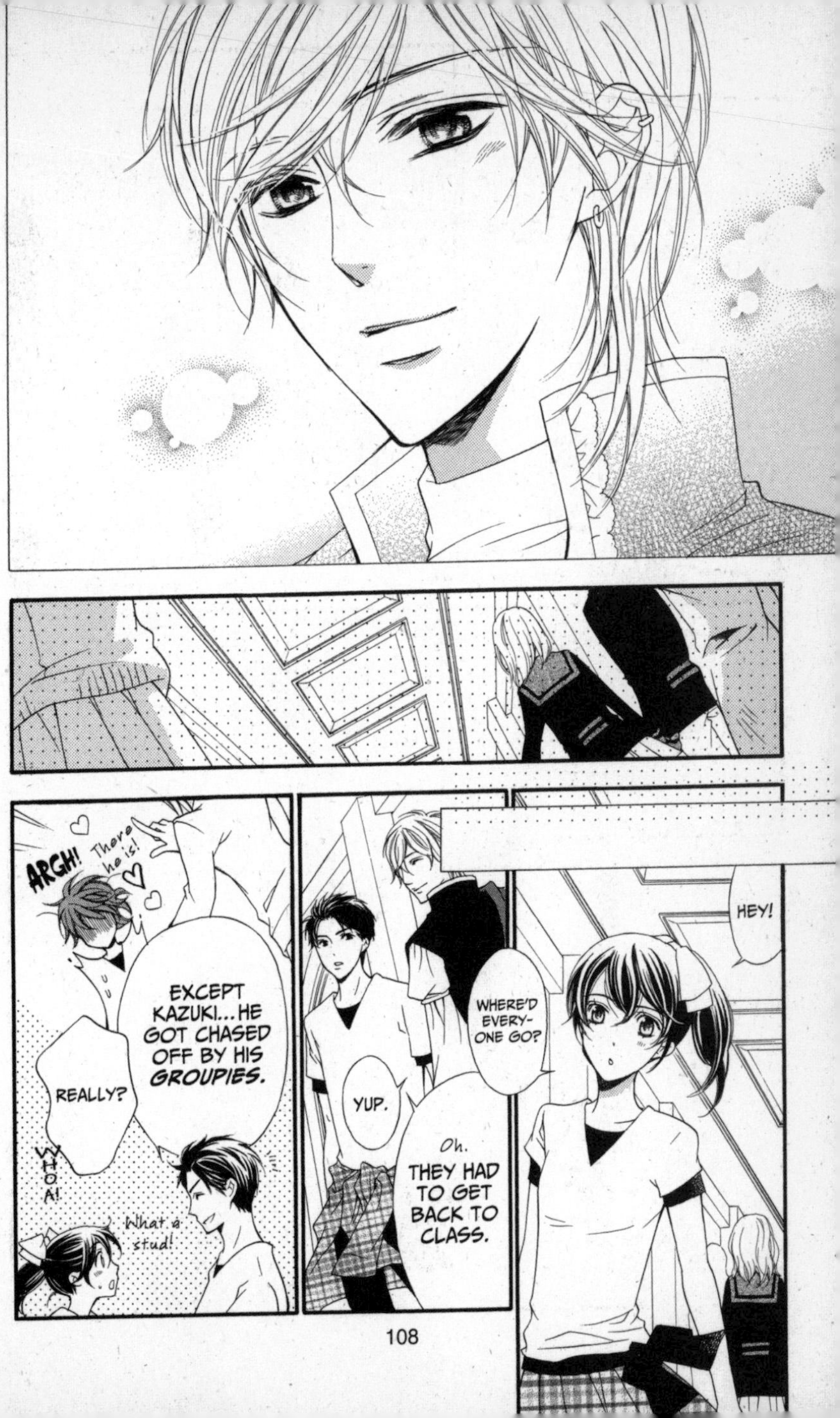
HEY!
WHERE'D EVERY-ONE GO?
Oh.
THEY HAD TO GET BACK TO CLASS.
YUP.
EXCEPT KAZUKI...HE GOT CHASED OFF BY HIS *GROUPIES.*
REALLY?
There he is!
ARGH!
WHOA!
What a stud!

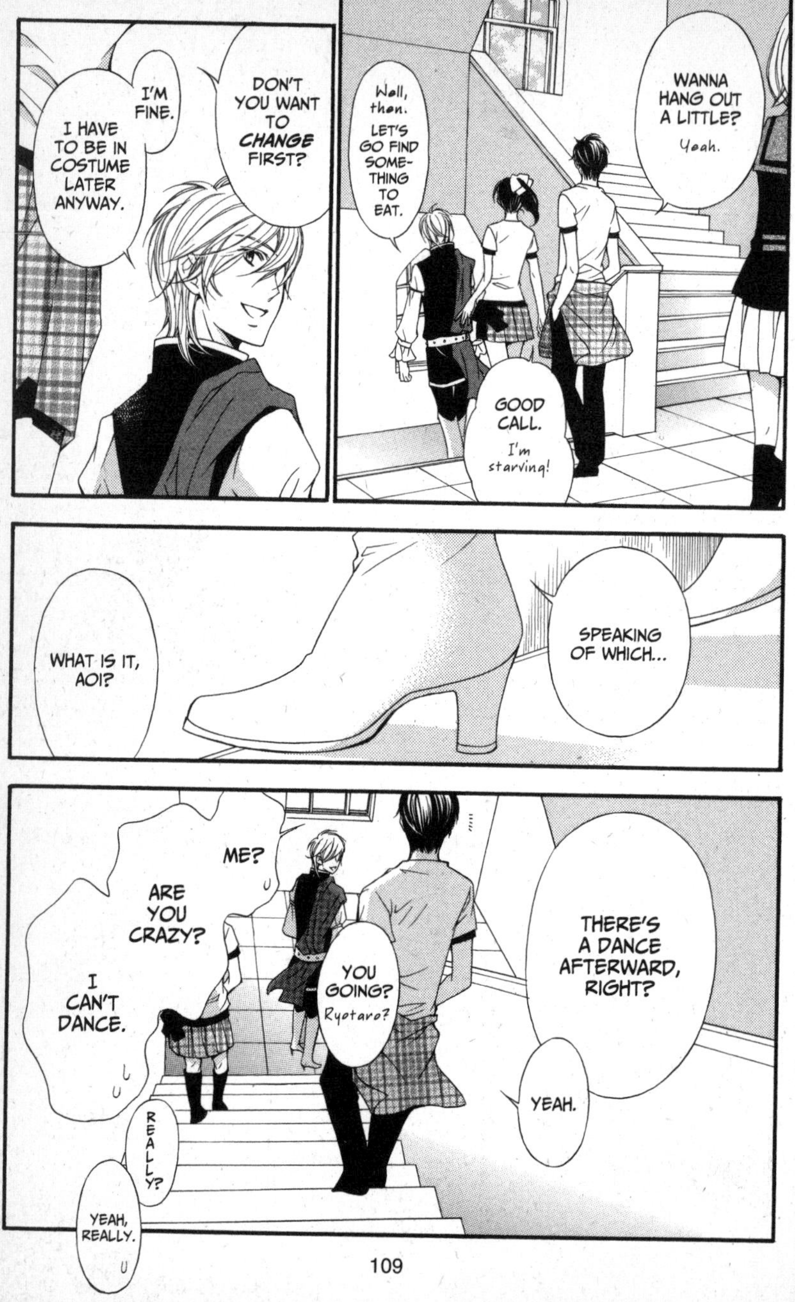
WANNA HANG OUT A LITTLE?
Yeah.
Well, then. LET'S GO FIND SOME-THING TO EAT.
GOOD CALL.
I'm starving!
DON'T YOU WANT TO *CHANGE* FIRST?
I'M FINE.
I HAVE TO BE IN COSTUME LATER ANYWAY.
SPEAKING OF WHICH...
WHAT IS IT, AOI?
THERE'S A DANCE AFTERWARD, RIGHT?
YEAH.
YOU GOING?
Ryotaro?
ME?
ARE YOU CRAZY?
I CAN'T DANCE.
REALLY?
YEAH, REALLY.

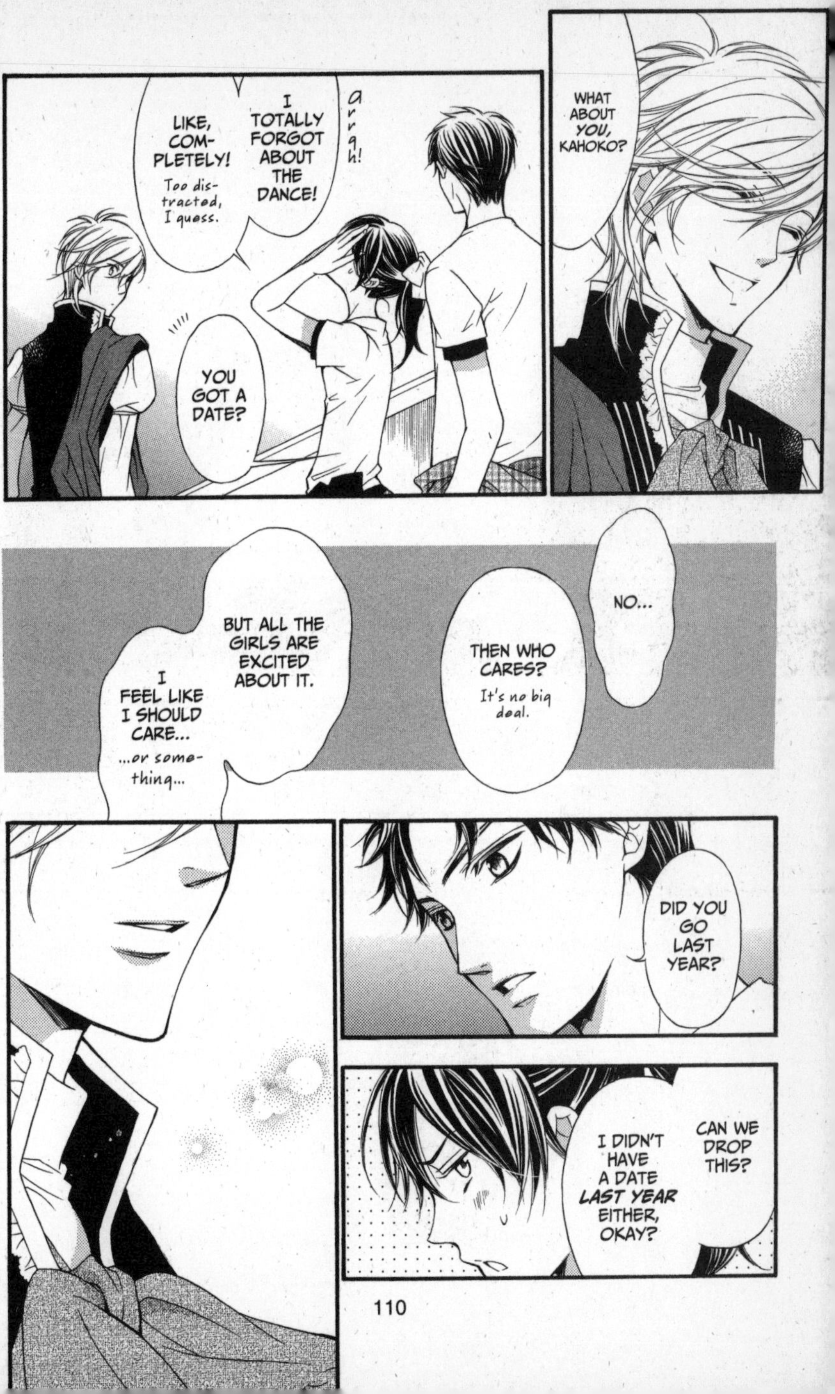

WHAT ABOUT *YOU*, KAHOKO?
Arrgh!
I TOTALLY FORGOT ABOUT THE DANCE!
LIKE, COMPLETELY! Too distracted, I guess.
YOU GOT A DATE?
NO...
THEN WHO CARES? It's no big deal.
BUT ALL THE GIRLS ARE EXCITED ABOUT IT.
I FEEL LIKE I SHOULD CARE... ...or something...
DID YOU GO LAST YEAR?
CAN WE DROP THIS?
I DIDN'T HAVE A DATE *LAST YEAR* EITHER, OKAY?

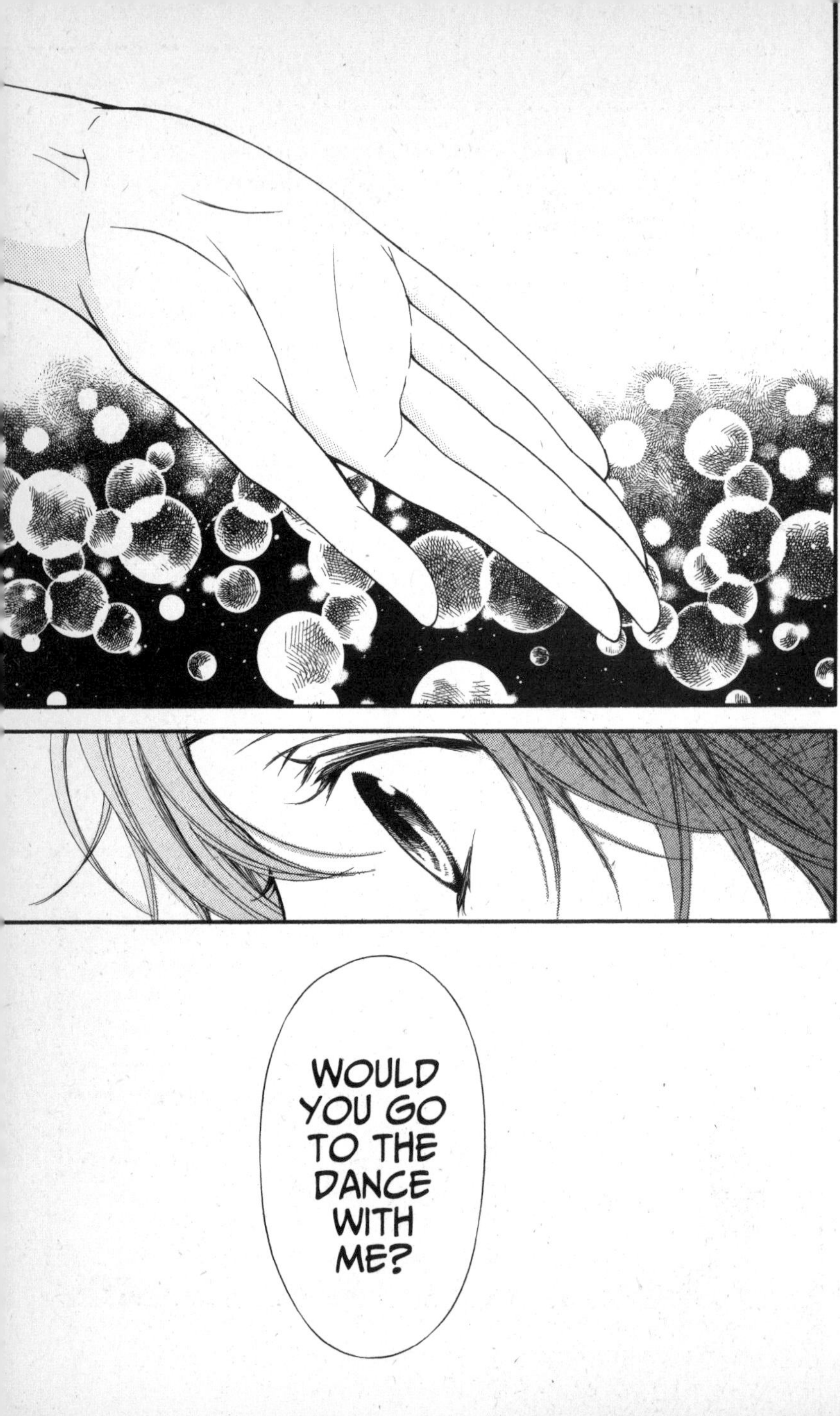
WOULD YOU GO TO THE DANCE WITH ME?

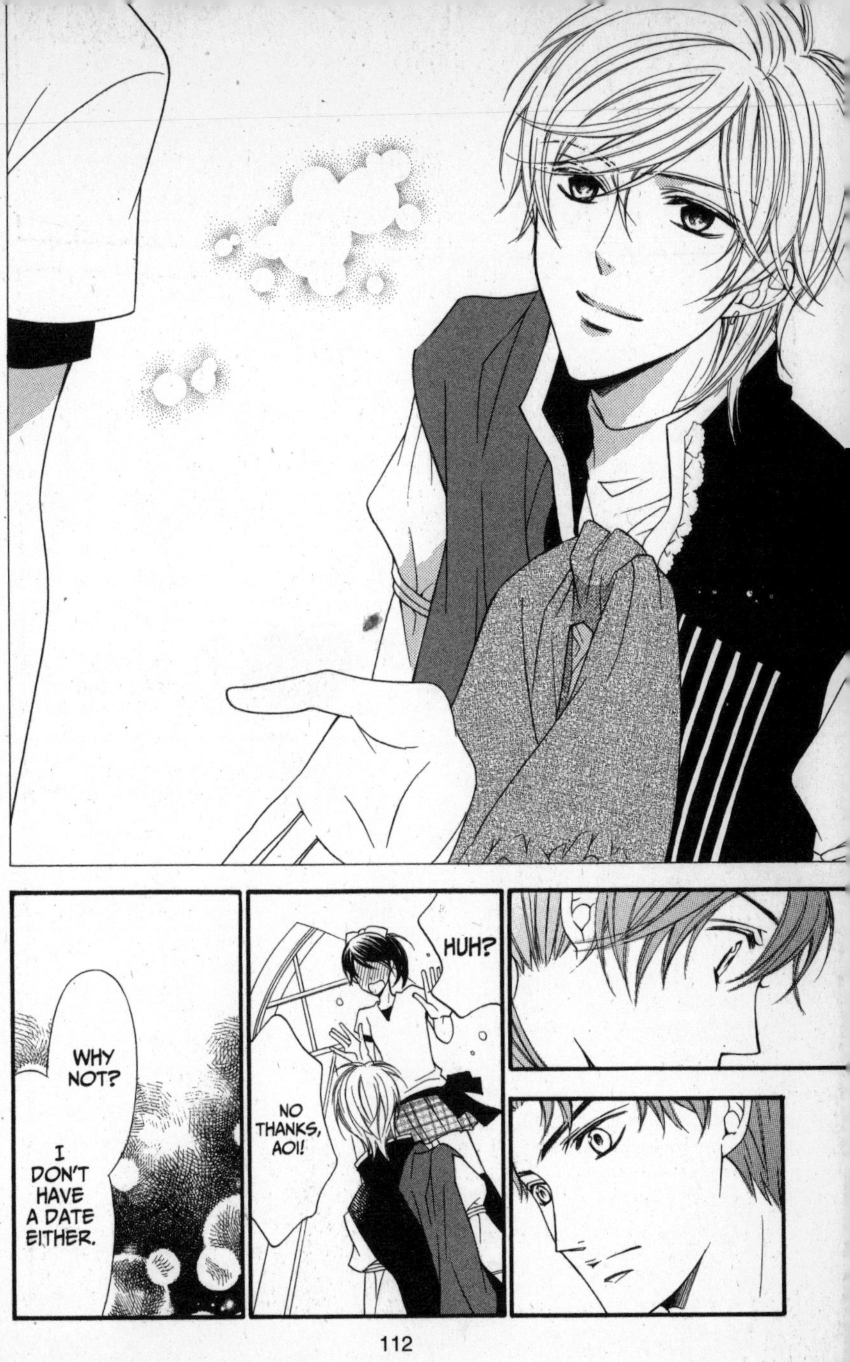
HUH?
NO THANKS, AOI!
WHY NOT?
I DON'T HAVE A DATE EITHER.

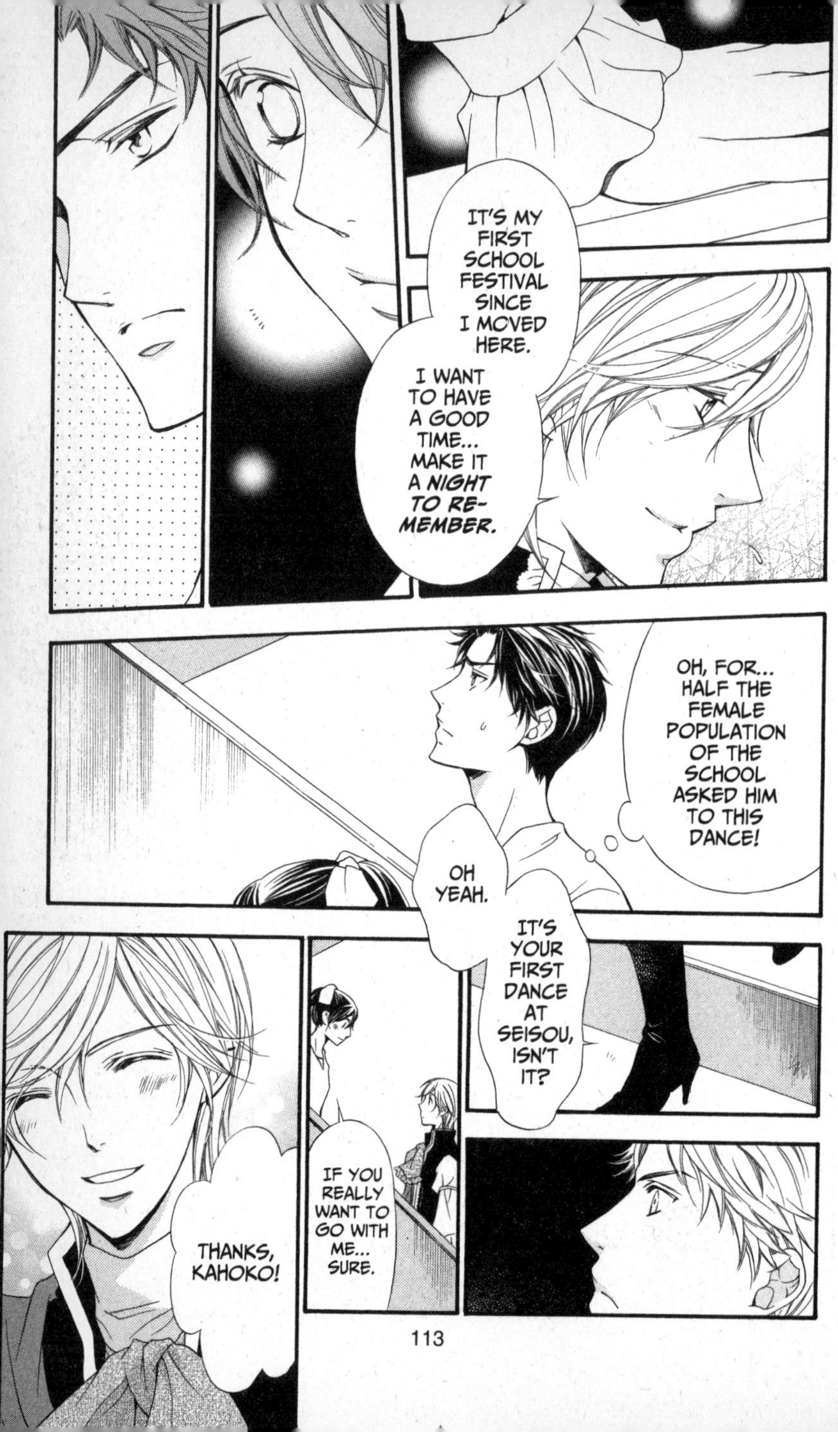
IT'S MY FIRST SCHOOL FESTIVAL SINCE I MOVED HERE.
I WANT TO HAVE A GOOD TIME... MAKE IT A *NIGHT TO RE-MEMBER.*
OH, FOR... HALF THE FEMALE POPULATION OF THE SCHOOL ASKED HIM TO THIS DANCE!
OH YEAH.
IT'S YOUR FIRST DANCE AT SEISOU, ISN'T IT?
IF YOU REALLY WANT TO GO WITH ME... SURE.
THANKS, KAHOKO!

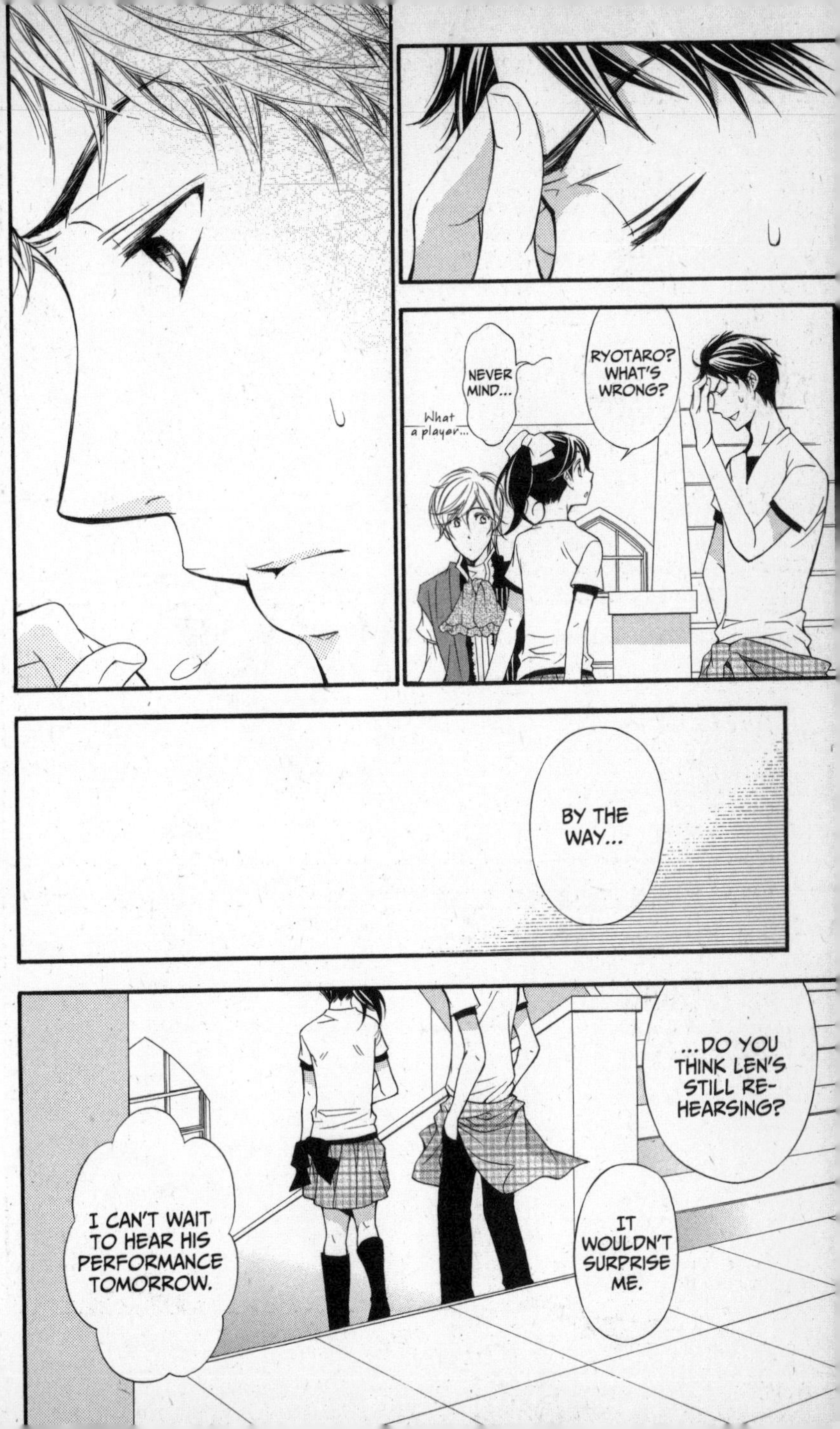
RYOTARO? WHAT'S WRONG?
NEVER MIND...
What a player...
BY THE WAY...
...DO YOU THINK LEN'S STILL RE-HEARSING?
IT WOULDN'T SURPRISE ME.
I CAN'T WAIT TO HEAR HIS PERFORMANCE TOMORROW.

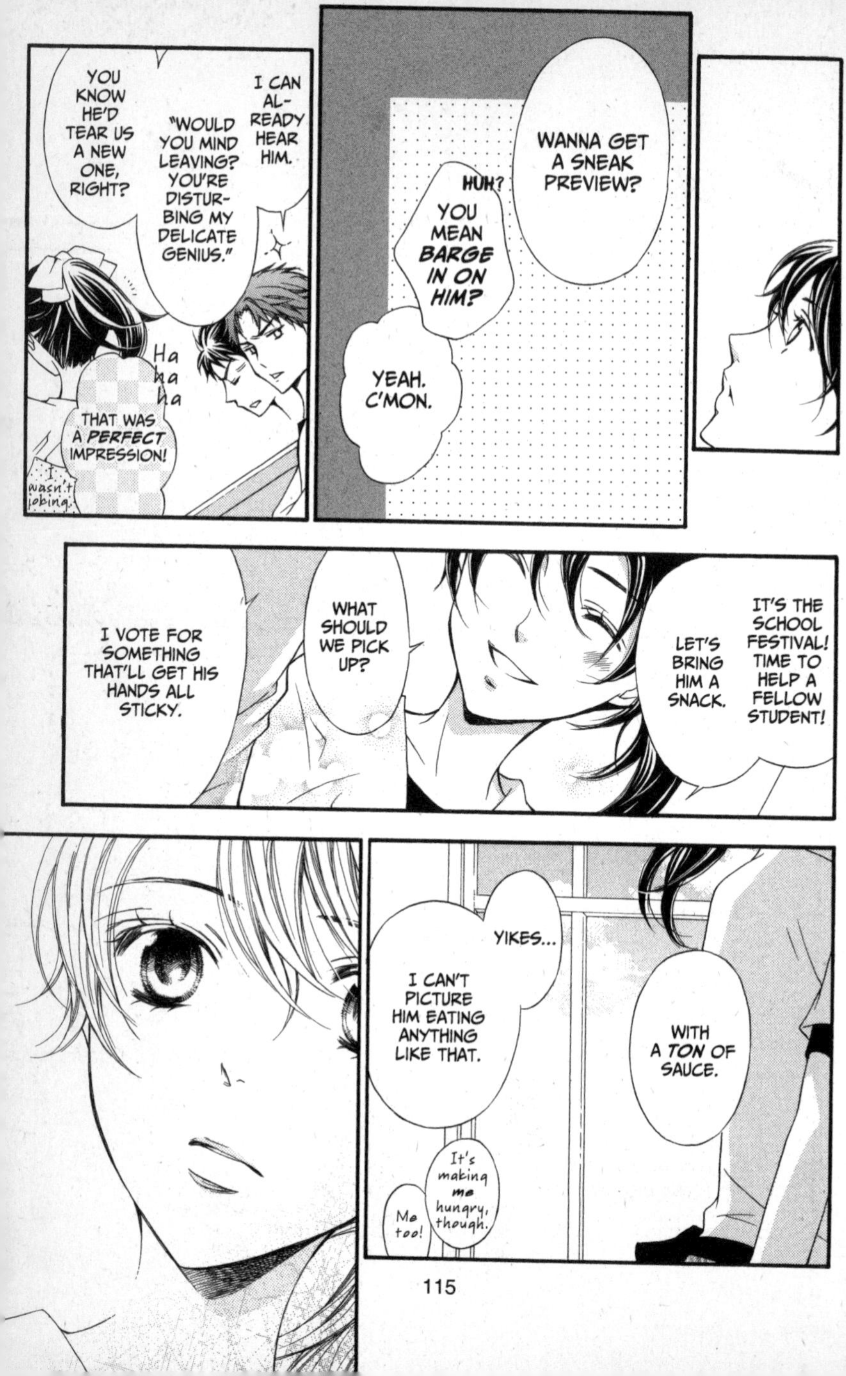
WANNA GET A SNEAK PREVIEW?
HUH? YOU MEAN *BARGE IN ON HIM?*
YEAH. C'MON.
I CAN AL-READY HEAR HIM.
"WOULD YOU MIND LEAVING? YOU'RE DISTUR-BING MY DELICATE GENIUS."
YOU KNOW HE'D TEAR US A NEW ONE, RIGHT?
Ha ha ha
THAT WAS A *PERFECT* IMPRESSION!
I wasn't joking.
IT'S THE SCHOOL FESTIVAL! TIME TO HELP A FELLOW STUDENT!
LET'S BRING HIM A SNACK.
WHAT SHOULD WE PICK UP?
I VOTE FOR SOMETHING THAT'LL GET HIS HANDS ALL STICKY.
WITH A *TON* OF SAUCE.
YIKES...
I CAN'T PICTURE HIM EATING ANYTHING LIKE THAT.
It's making *me* hungry, though.
Me too!

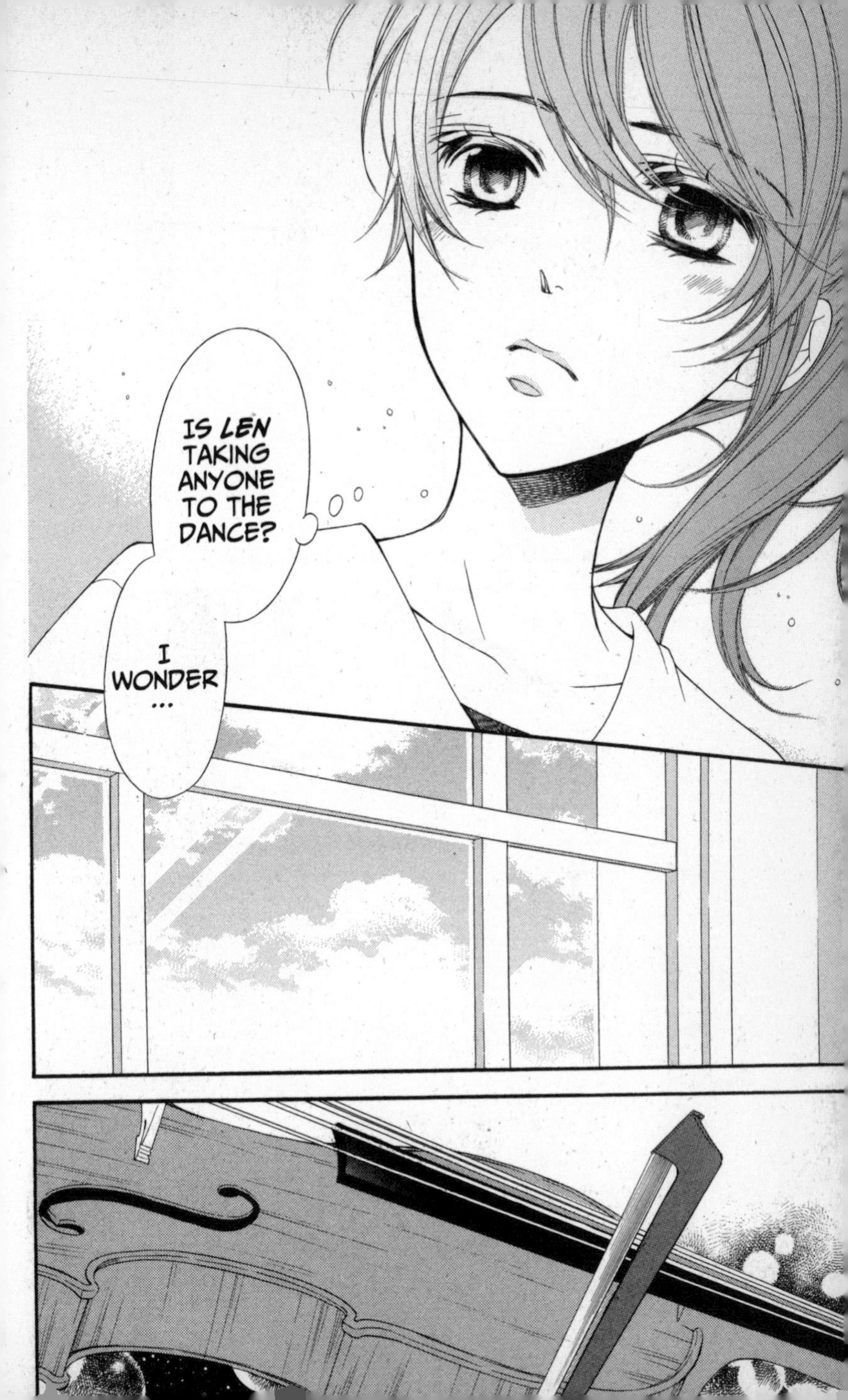
IS LEN TAKING ANYONE TO THE DANCE?
I WONDER...

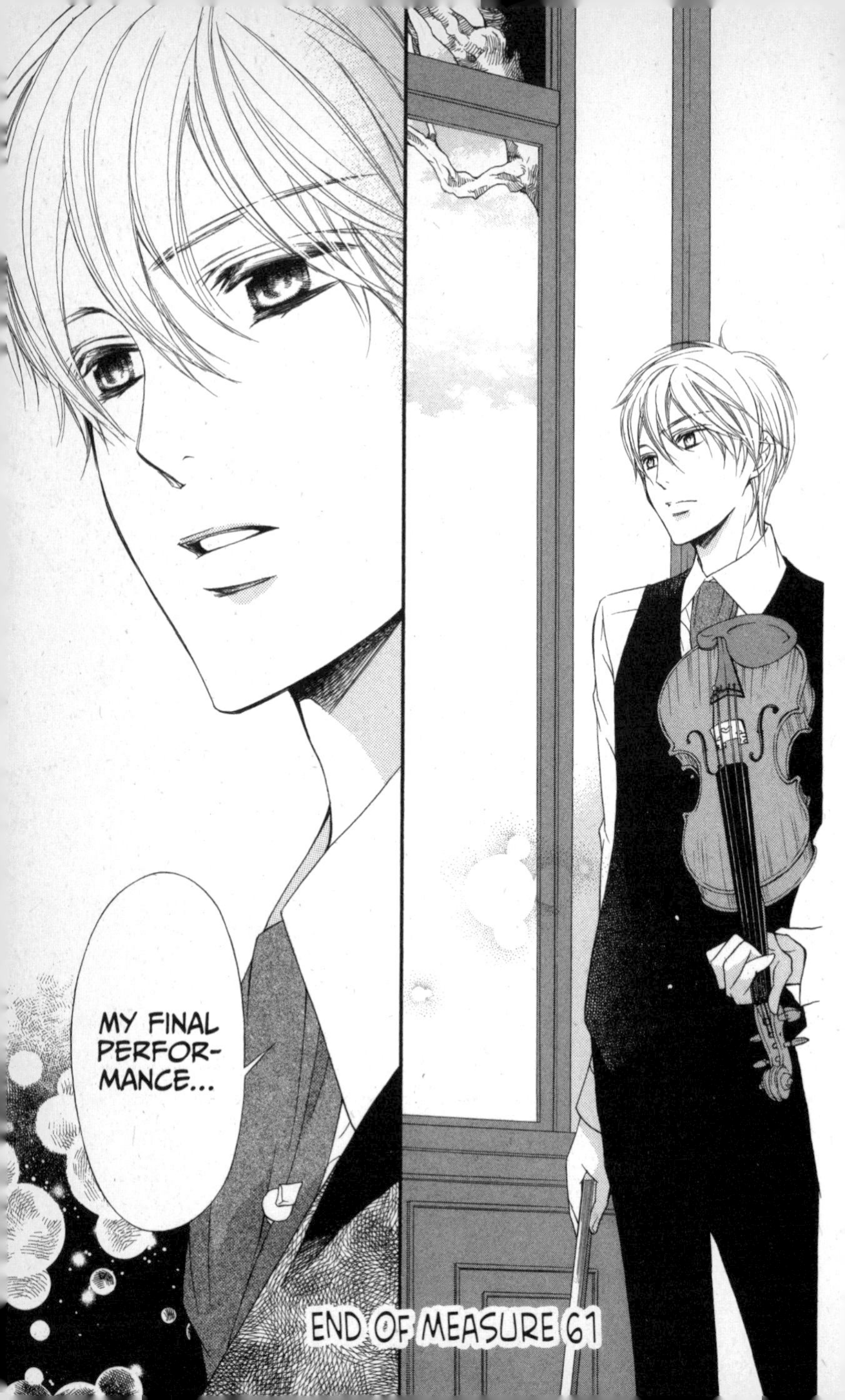
MY FINAL PERFOR-MANCE...
END OF MEASURE 61

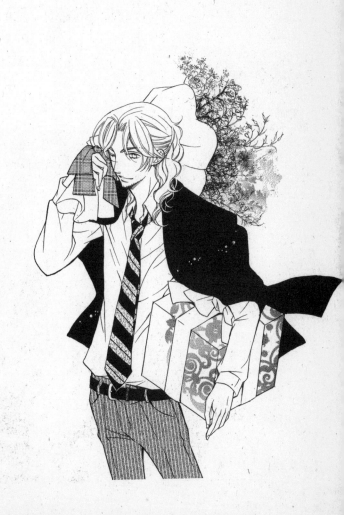

La Corda d'Oro

SCHOOL FESTIVAL SPECIAL EDITION

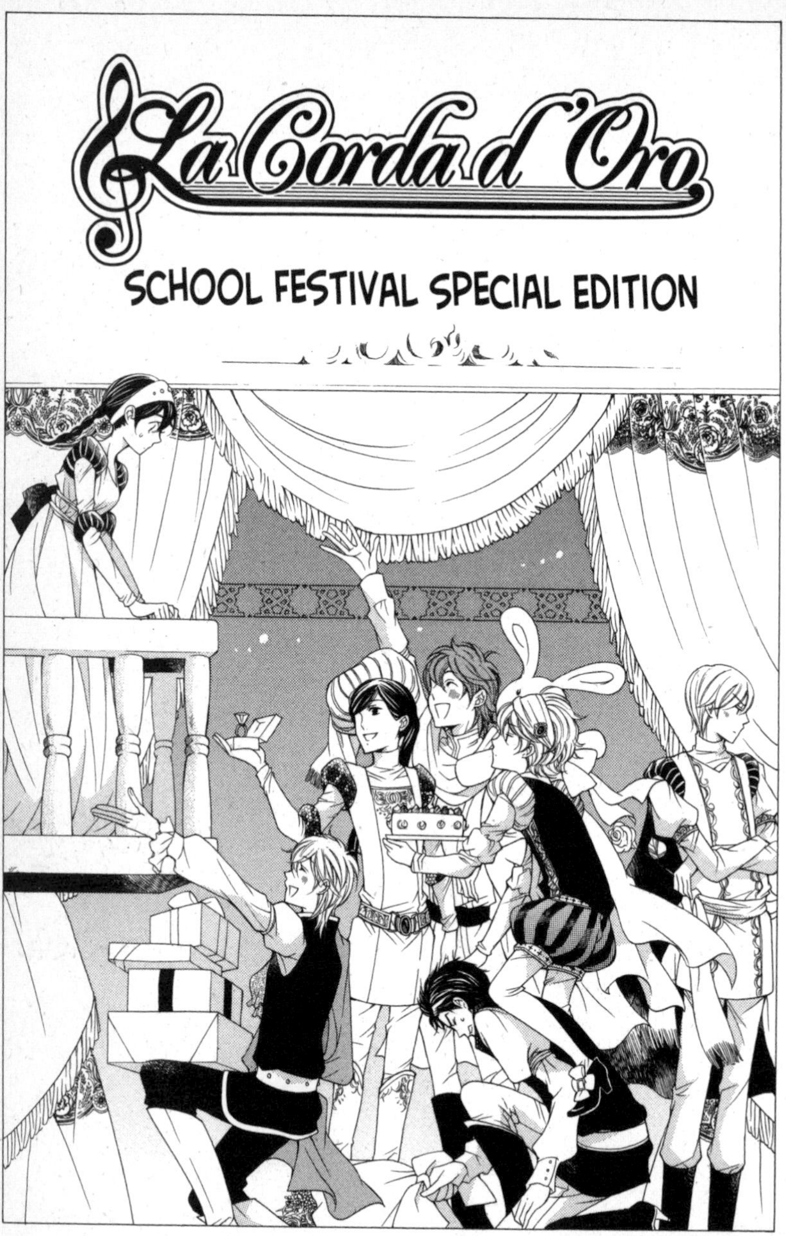

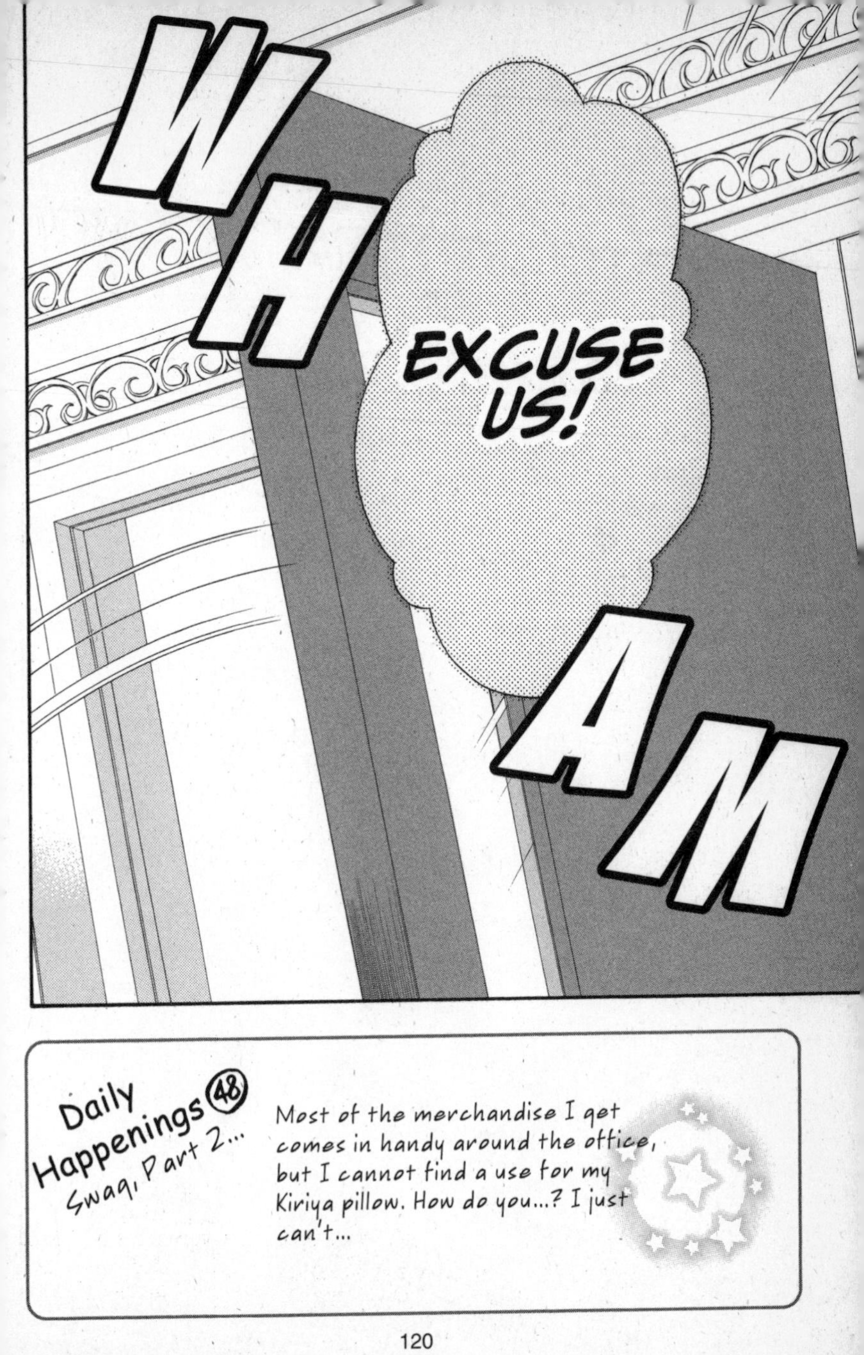
EXCUSE US!
WHAM

Daily Happenings 48
Swag, Part 2...

Most of the merchandise I get comes in handy around the office, but I cannot find a use for my Kiriya pillow. How do you...? I just can't...

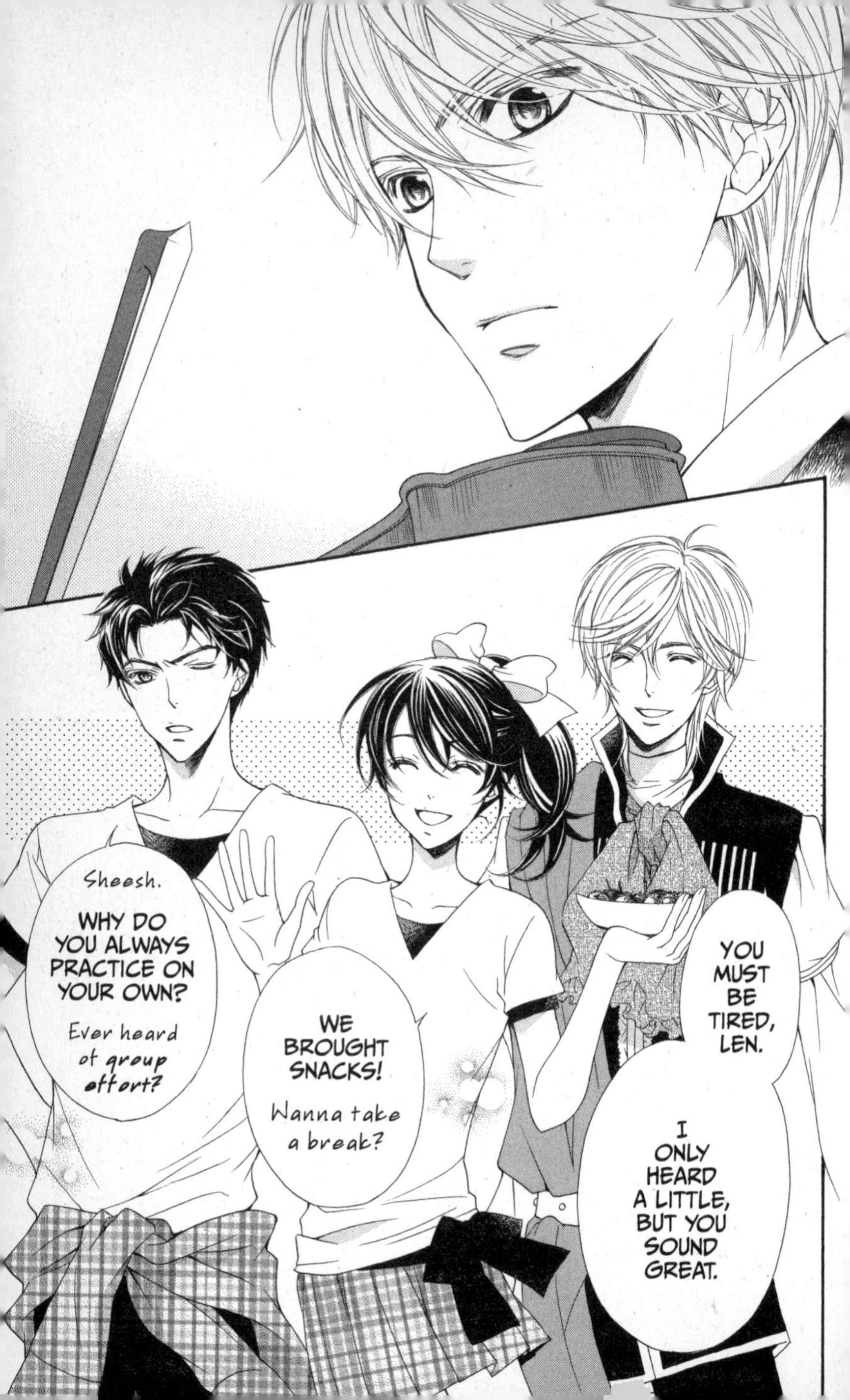
YOU MUST BE TIRED, LEN.
I ONLY HEARD A LITTLE, BUT YOU SOUND GREAT.
WE BROUGHT SNACKS!
Wanna take a break?
Sheesh.
WHY DO YOU ALWAYS PRACTICE ON YOUR OWN?
Ever heard of group effort?

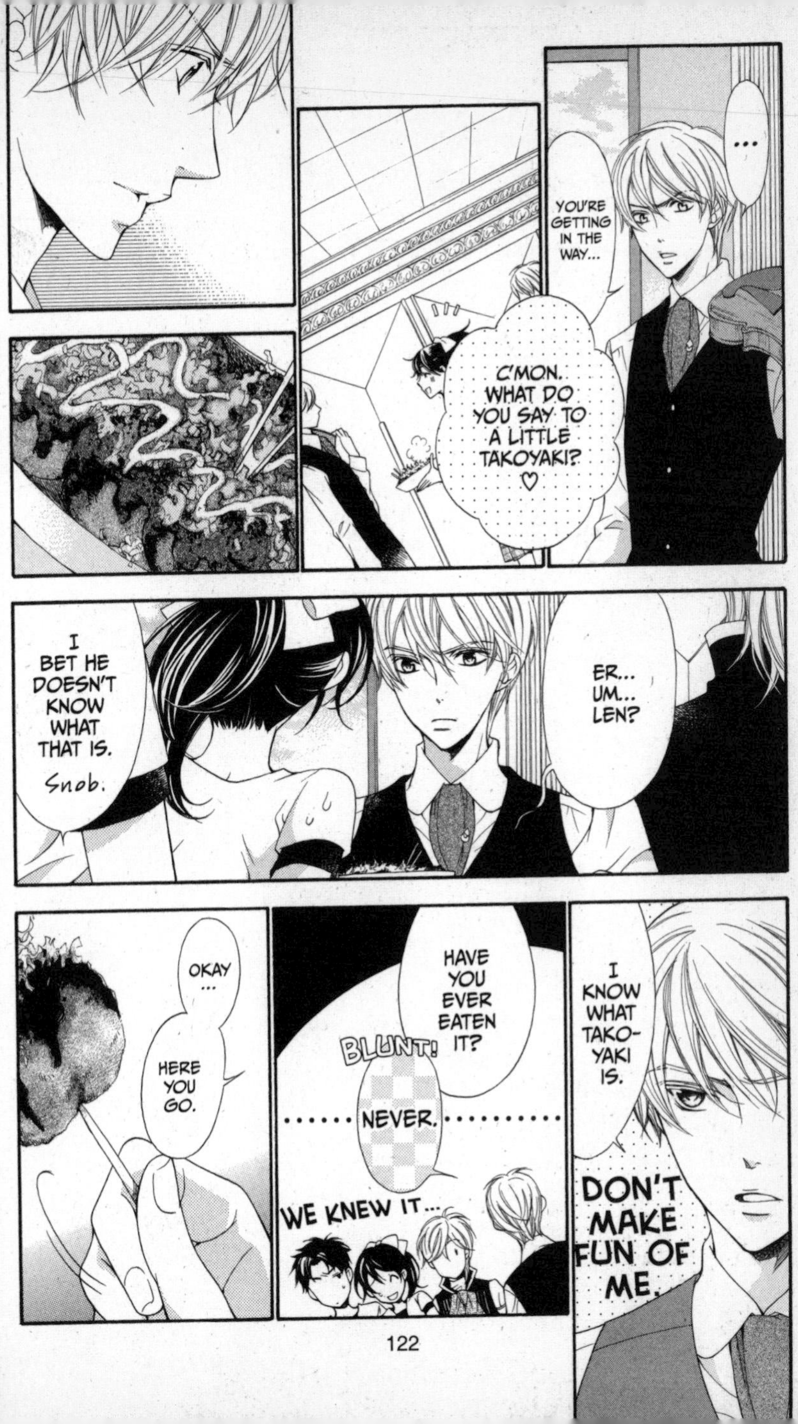
...
YOU'RE GETTING IN THE WAY...
C'MON. WHAT DO YOU SAY TO A LITTLE TAKOYAKI? ♡
ER... UM... LEN?
I BET HE DOESN'T KNOW WHAT THAT IS.
Snob.
I KNOW WHAT TAKO-YAKI IS.
DON'T MAKE FUN OF ME.
HAVE YOU EVER EATEN IT?
BLUNT!
NEVER.
WE KNEW IT...
OKAY...
HERE YOU GO.

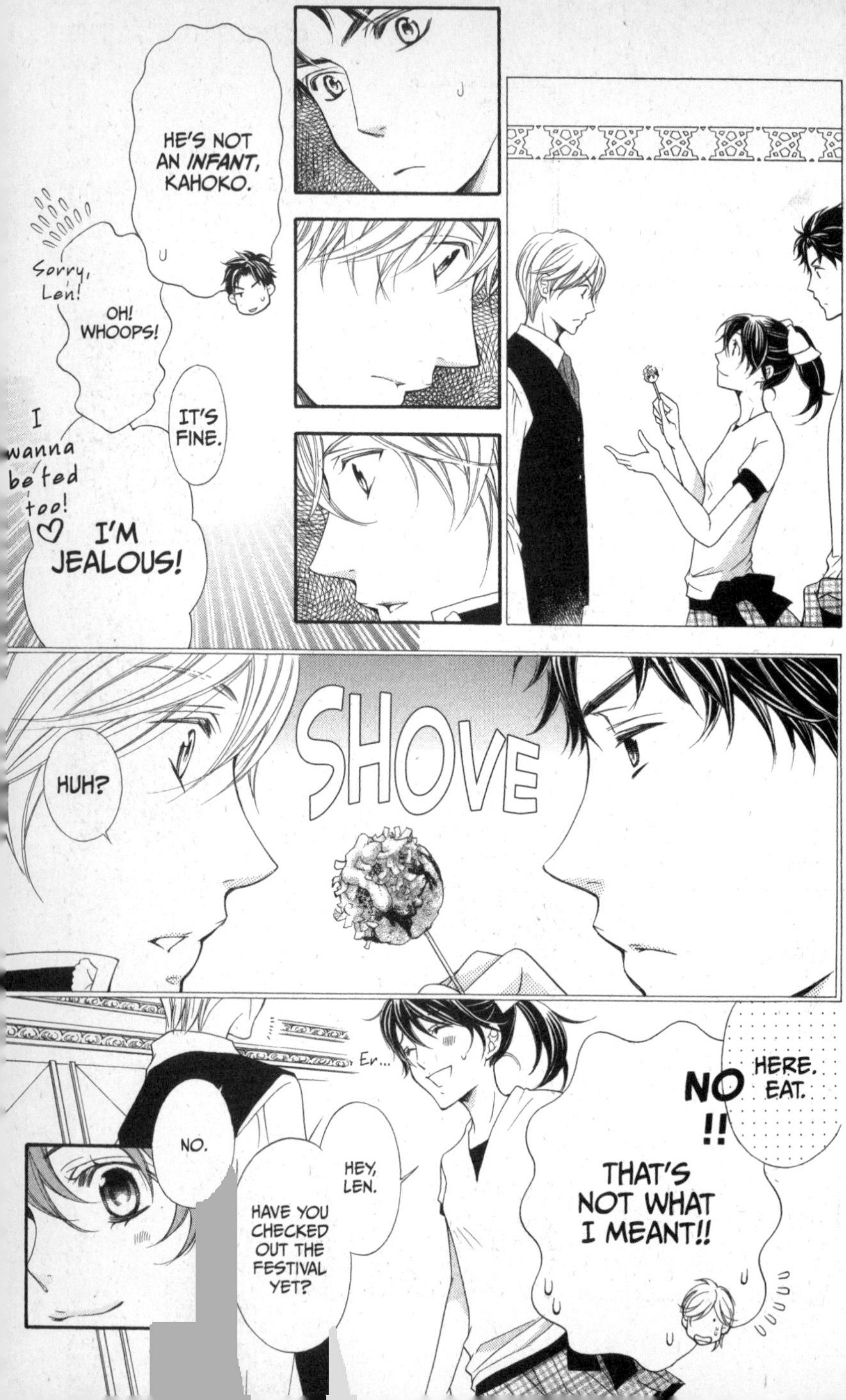
IT'S FINE.
I'M JEALOUS!
I wanna be fed too! ♡
HE'S NOT AN *INFANT*, KAHOKO.
OH! WHOOPS!
Sorry, Len!
SHOVE
HUH?
HERE. EAT.
NO!!
THAT'S NOT WHAT I MEANT!!
Er...
HEY, LEN.
HAVE YOU CHECKED OUT THE FESTIVAL YET?
NO.

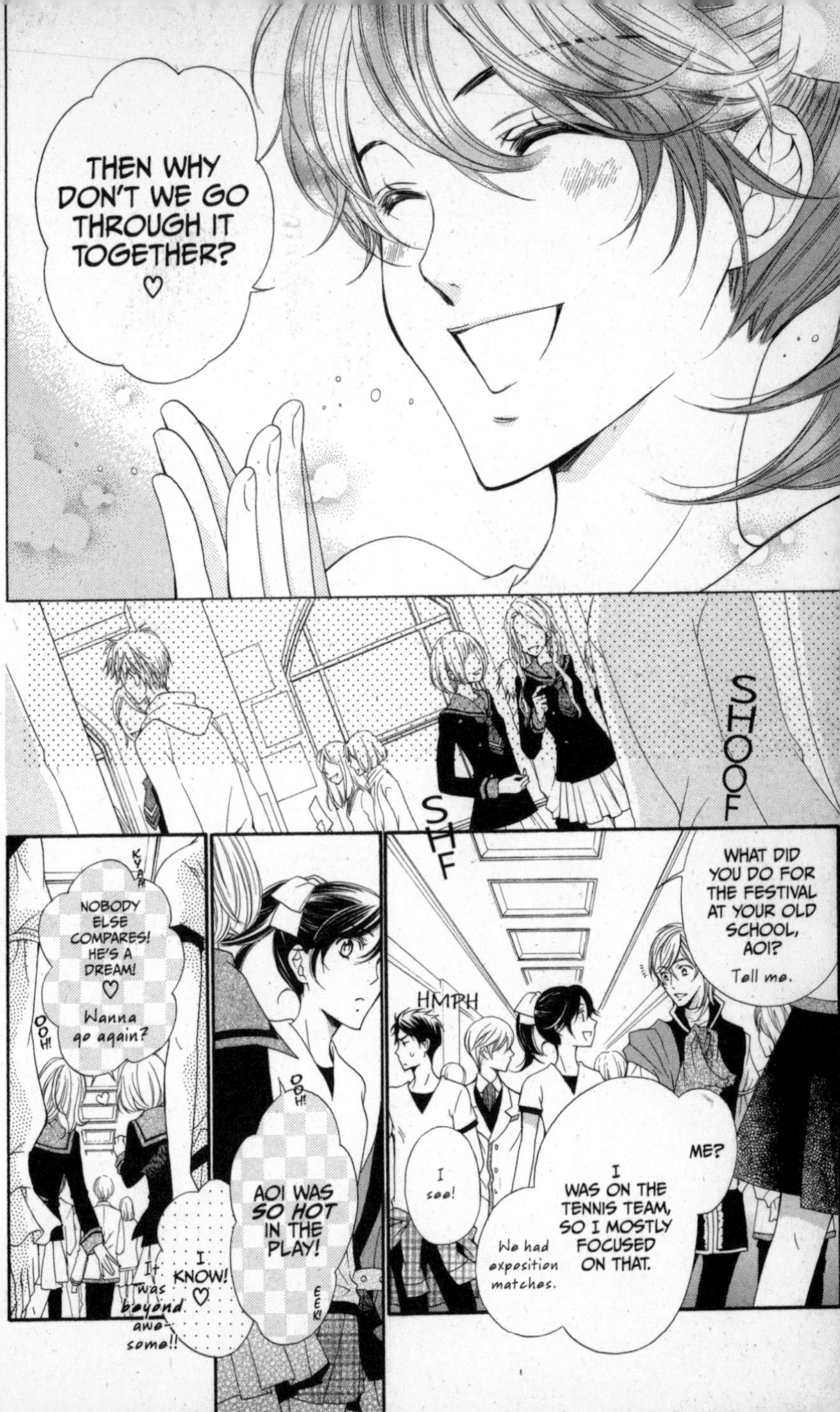
THEN WHY DON'T WE GO THROUGH IT TOGETHER? ♡
SHOOF
SHF
WHAT DID YOU DO FOR THE FESTIVAL AT YOUR OLD SCHOOL, AOI?
Tell me.
HMPH
ME?
I WAS ON THE TENNIS TEAM, SO I MOSTLY FOCUSED ON THAT.
We had exposition matches.
I see!
OOOH!
AOI WAS SO HOT IN THE PLAY!
EEK!
I KNOW! ♡
It was beyond awe-some!!
KYAA!
NOBODY ELSE COMPARES! HE'S A DREAM! ♡
Wanna go again?
OOOH!

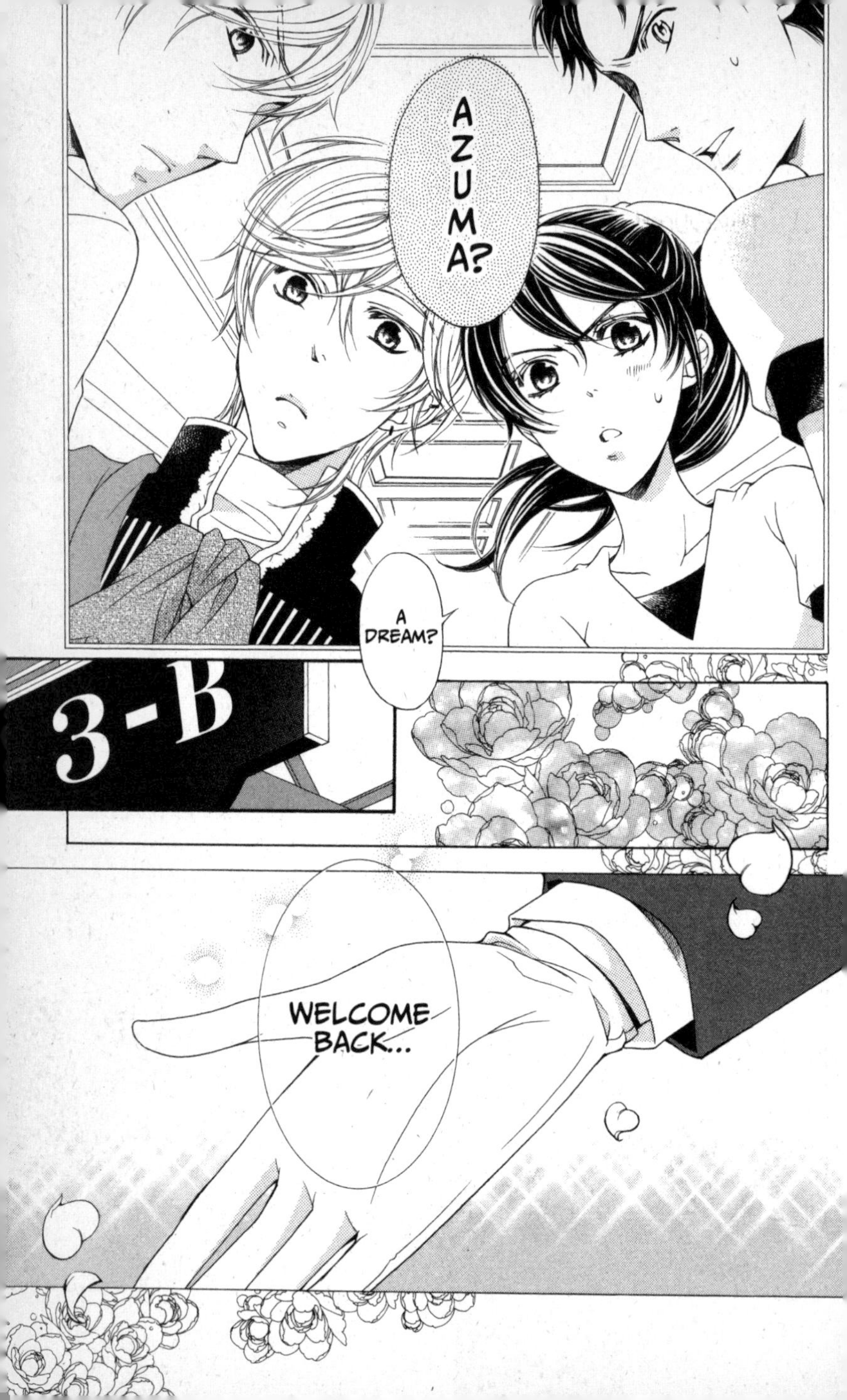
AZUMA?
A DREAM?
3-B
WELCOME BACK...

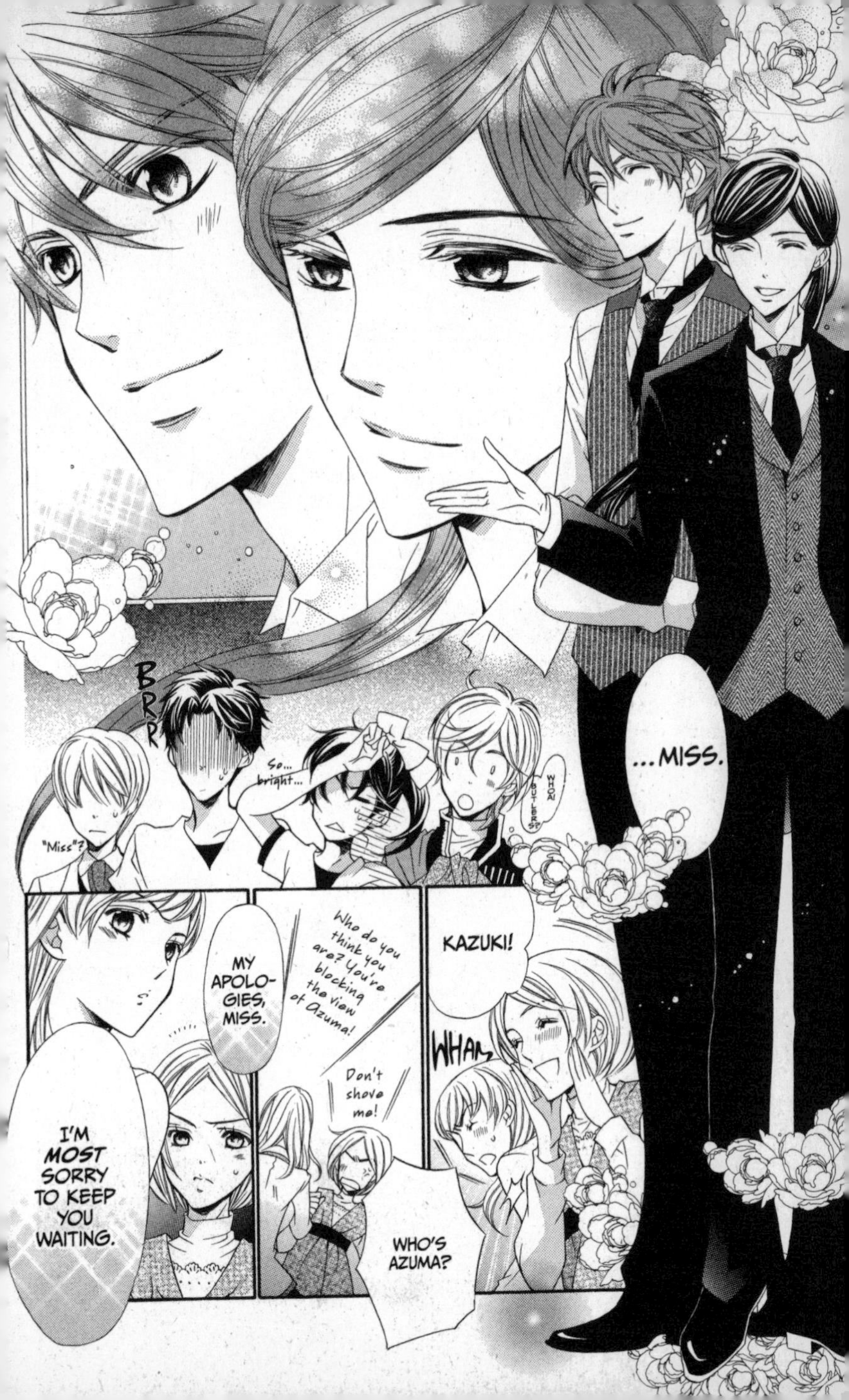
...MISS.
WHOA! BUTLERS?
So... bright...
BRR
"Miss"?
KAZUKI!
WHAM
Who do you think you are? You're blocking the view of Azuma!
Don't shove me!
WHO'S AZUMA?
MY APOLOGIES, MISS.
I'M MOST SORRY TO KEEP YOU WAITING.

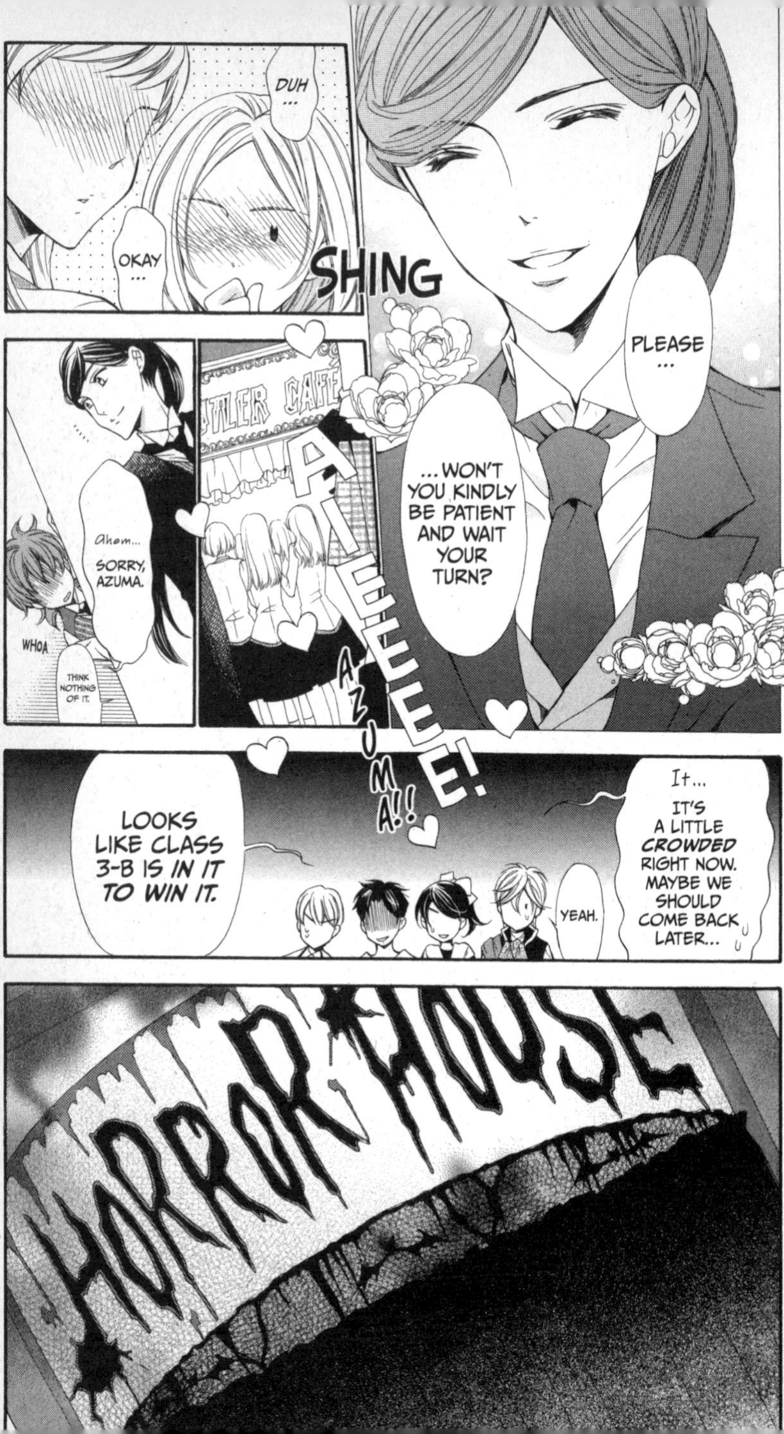
SHING
PLEASE...
...WON'T YOU KINDLY BE PATIENT AND WAIT YOUR TURN?
DUH...
OKAY...
AIEEEEEE!
AZUMA!!
BUTLER CAFE
Ahem...
SORRY, AZUMA.
WHOA
THINK NOTHING OF IT.
It... IT'S A LITTLE *CROWDED* RIGHT NOW. MAYBE WE SHOULD COME BACK LATER...
YEAH.
LOOKS LIKE CLASS 3-B IS *IN IT TO WIN IT.*
HORROR HOUSE

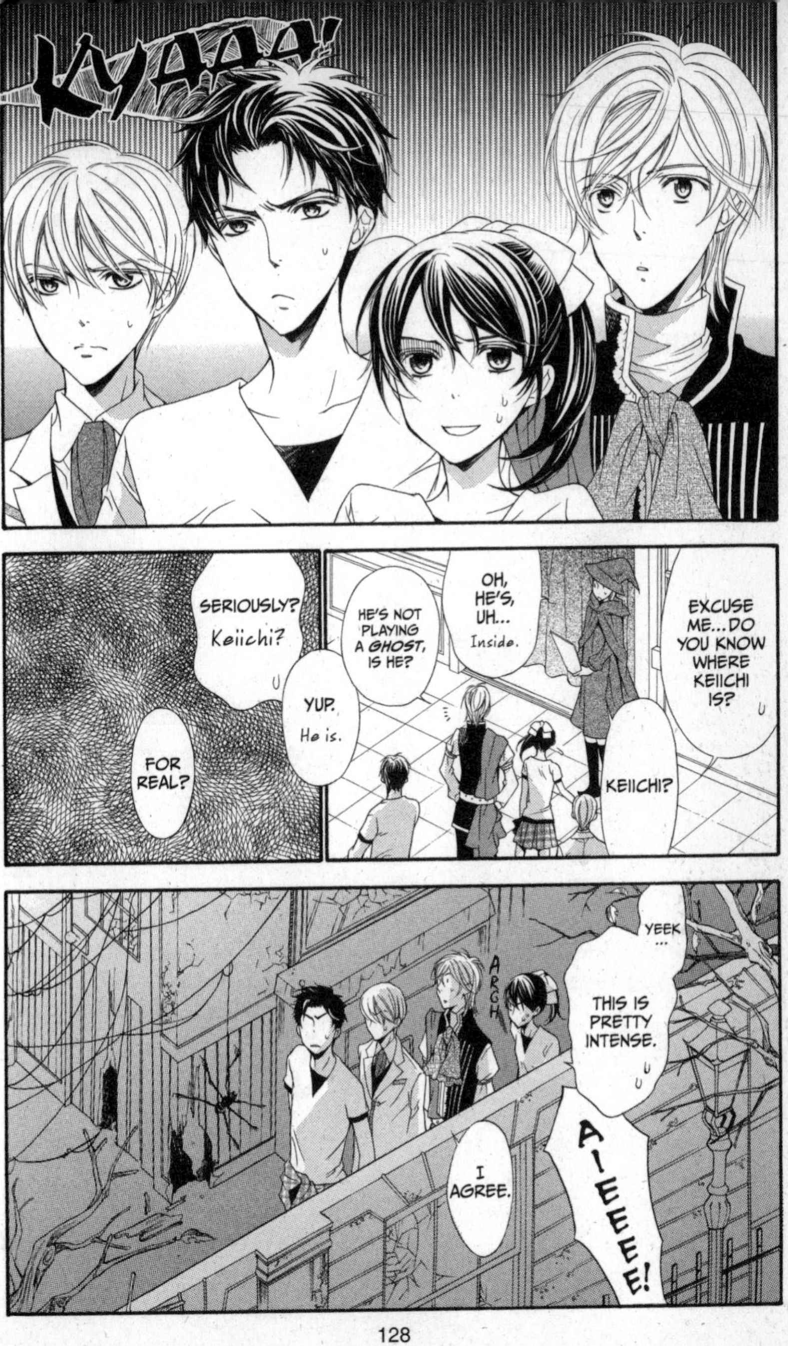
KYAAA!
EXCUSE ME...DO YOU KNOW WHERE KEIICHI IS?
KEIICHI?
OH, HE'S, UH... Inside.
HE'S NOT PLAYING A *GHOST*, IS HE?
YUP. He is.
SERIOUSLY? Keiichi?
FOR REAL?
YEEK...
ARGH
THIS IS PRETTY INTENSE.
AIEEEE!
I AGREE.

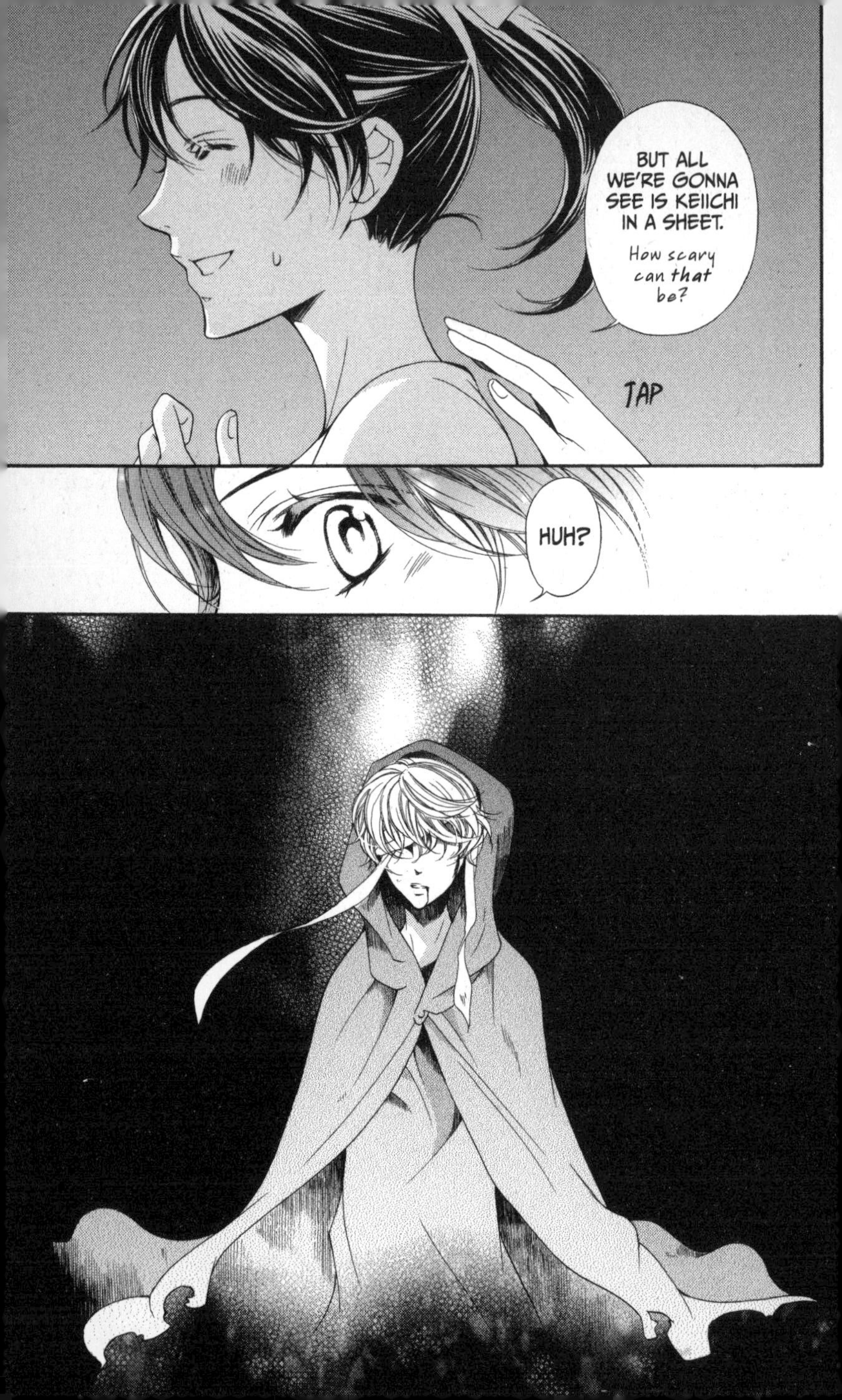
BUT ALL WE'RE GONNA SEE IS KEIICHI IN A SHEET.
How scary can *that* be?
TAP
HUH?

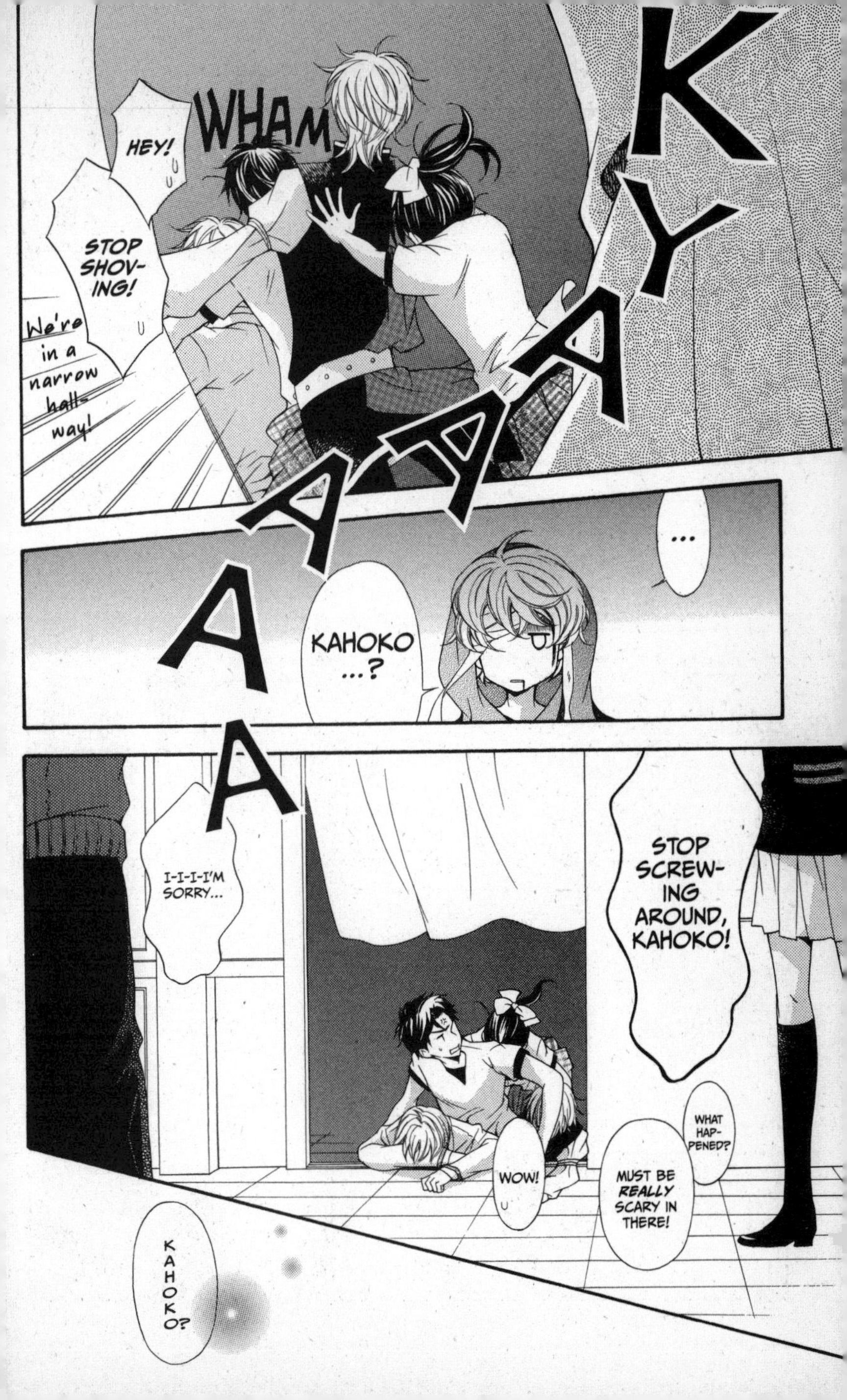
KYAAAAAAA
WHAM
HEY!
STOP SHOVING!
We're in a narrow hall-way!
...
KAHOKO ...?
STOP SCREWING AROUND, KAHOKO!
WHAT HAPPENED?
MUST BE REALLY SCARY IN THERE!
WOW!
I-I-I-I'M SORRY...
KAHOKO?

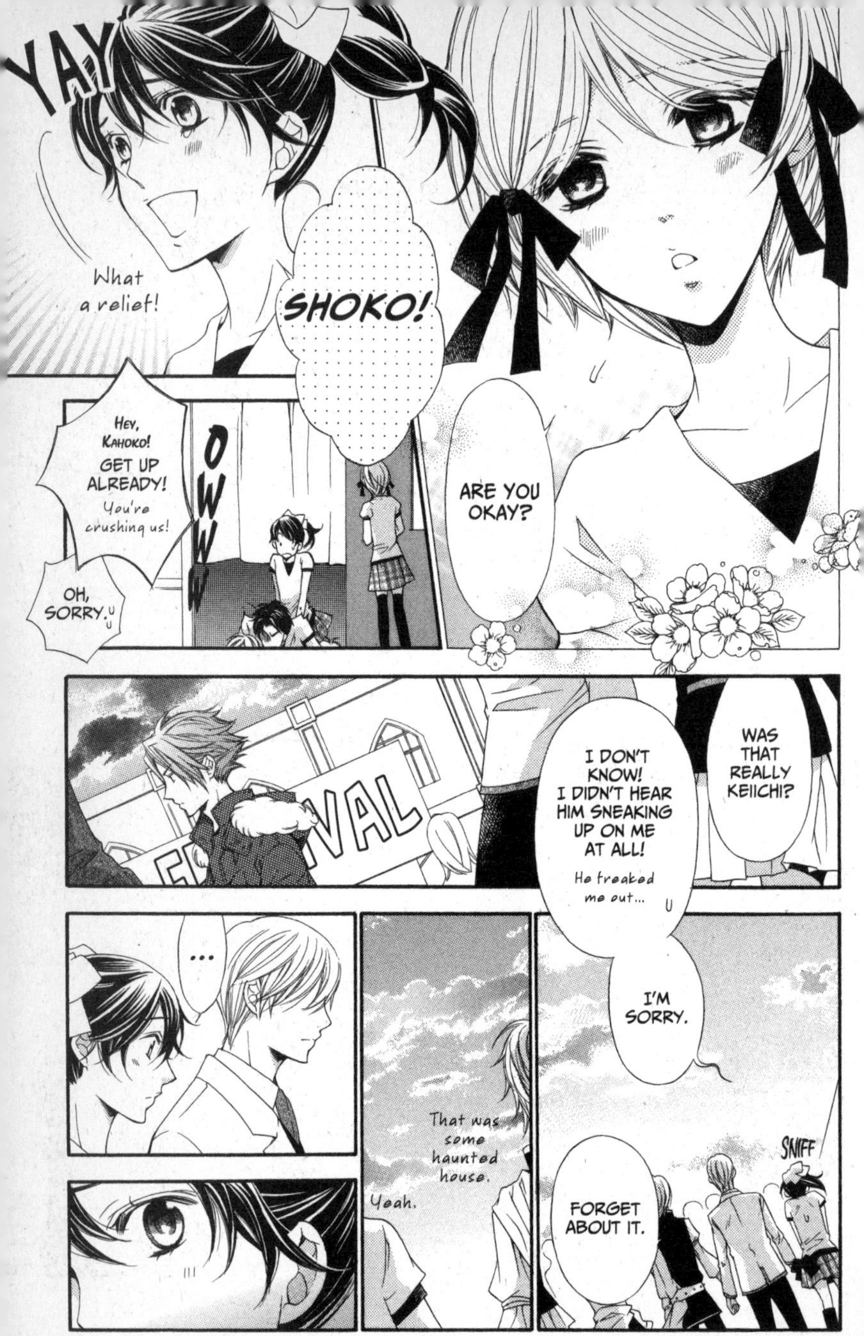
ARE YOU OKAY?
YAY
What a relief!
SHOKO!
Hey, Kahoko! GET UP ALREADY! You're crushing us!
OWWW
OH, SORRY.
WAS THAT REALLY KEIICHI?
I DON'T KNOW! I DIDN'T HEAR HIM SNEAKING UP ON ME AT ALL!
He freaked me out...
I'M SORRY.
SNIFF
FORGET ABOUT IT.
That was some haunted house.
Yeah.
...

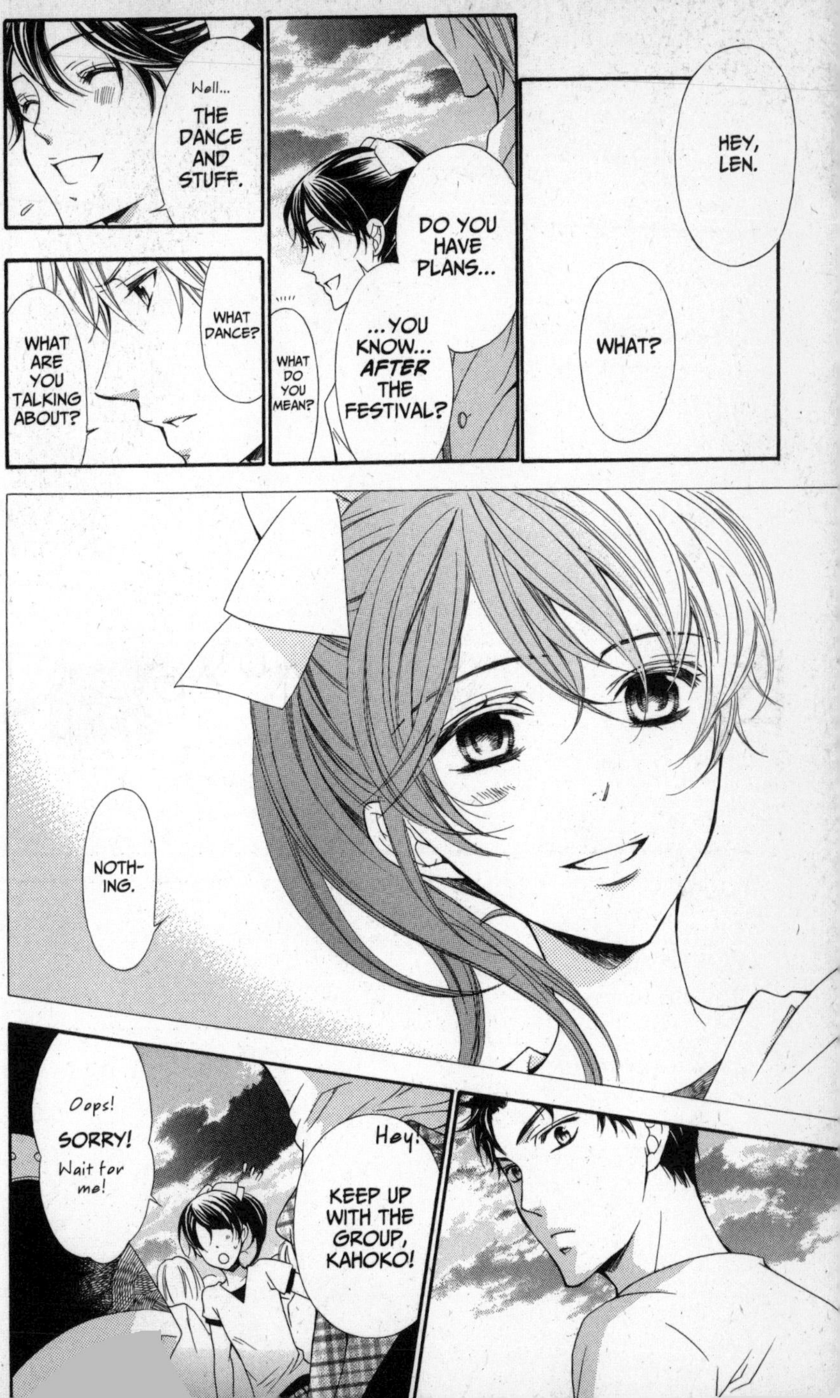
HEY, LEN.
WHAT?
DO YOU HAVE PLANS...
...YOU KNOW... AFTER THE FESTIVAL?
WHAT DO YOU MEAN?
Well... THE DANCE AND STUFF.
WHAT DANCE?
WHAT ARE YOU TALKING ABOUT?
NOTHING.
Hey! KEEP UP WITH THE GROUP, KAHOKO!
Oops! SORRY! Wait for me!

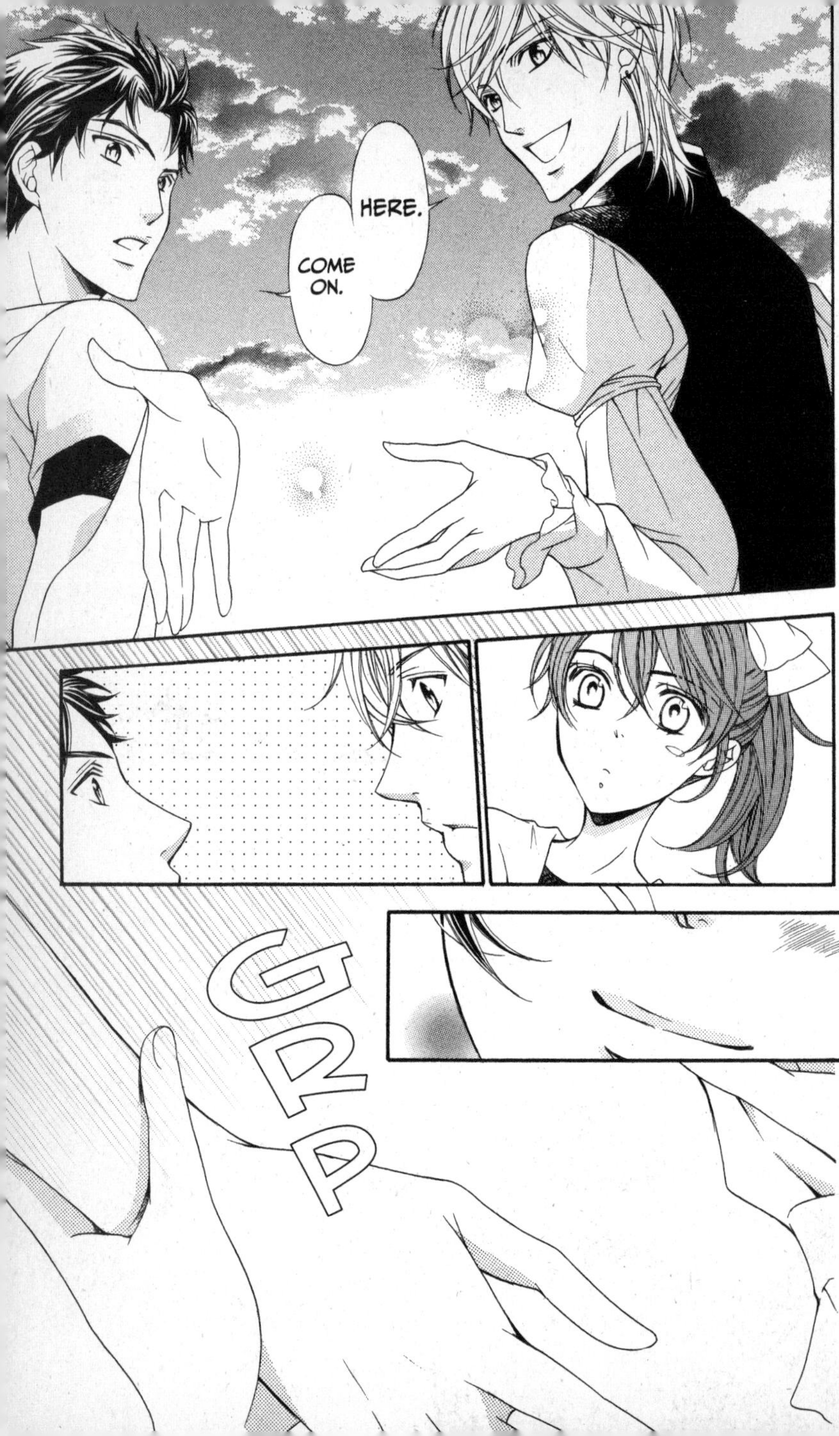
HERE.
COME ON.
GRP

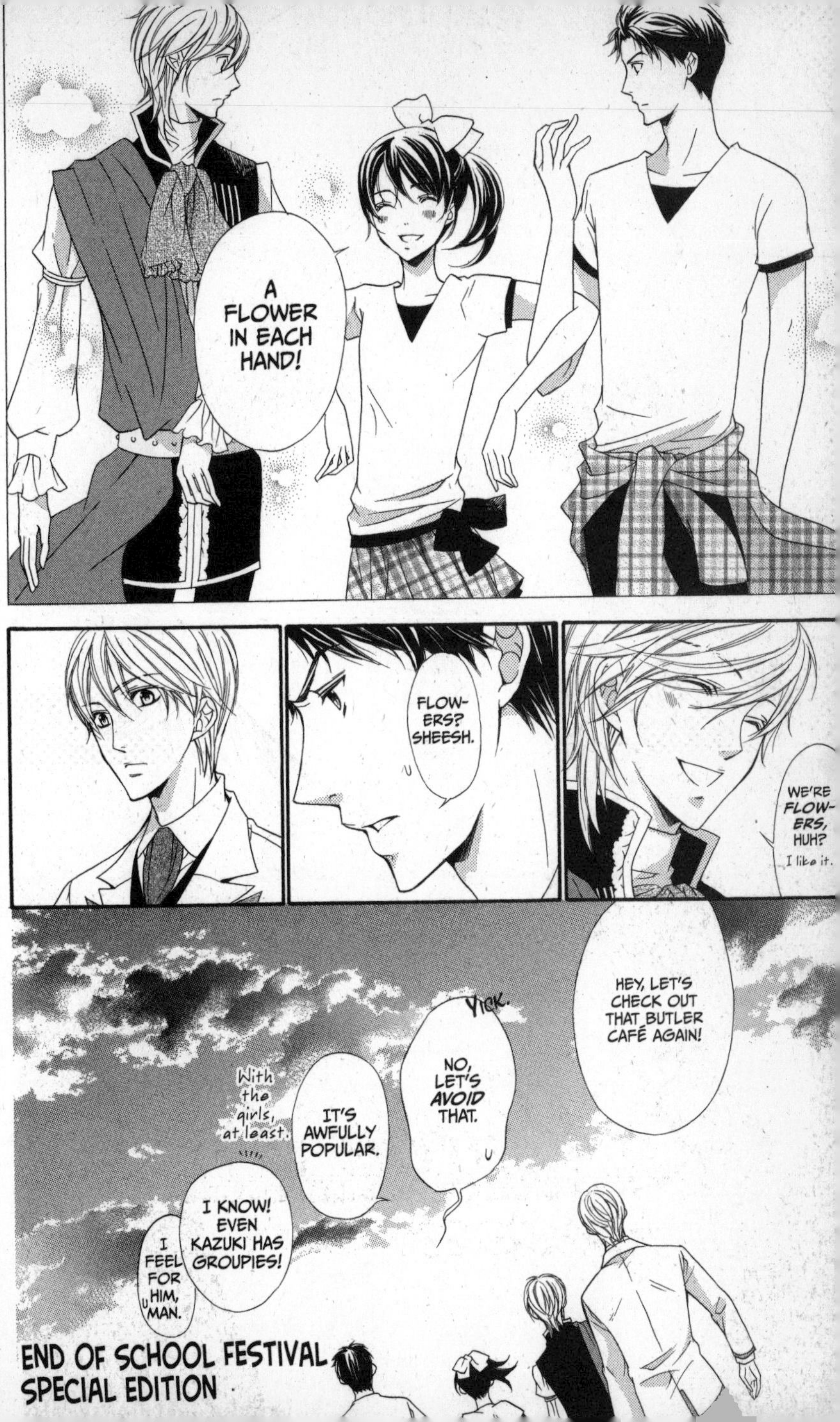
A FLOWER IN EACH HAND!
WE'RE FLOWERS, HUH?
I like it.
FLOWERS? SHEESH.
HEY, LET'S CHECK OUT THAT BUTLER CAFÉ AGAIN!
YICK.
NO, LET'S AVOID THAT.
IT'S AWFULLY POPULAR.
With the girls, at least.
I KNOW! EVEN KAZUKI HAS GROUPIES!
I FEEL FOR HIM, MAN.
END OF SCHOOL FESTIVAL SPECIAL EDITION

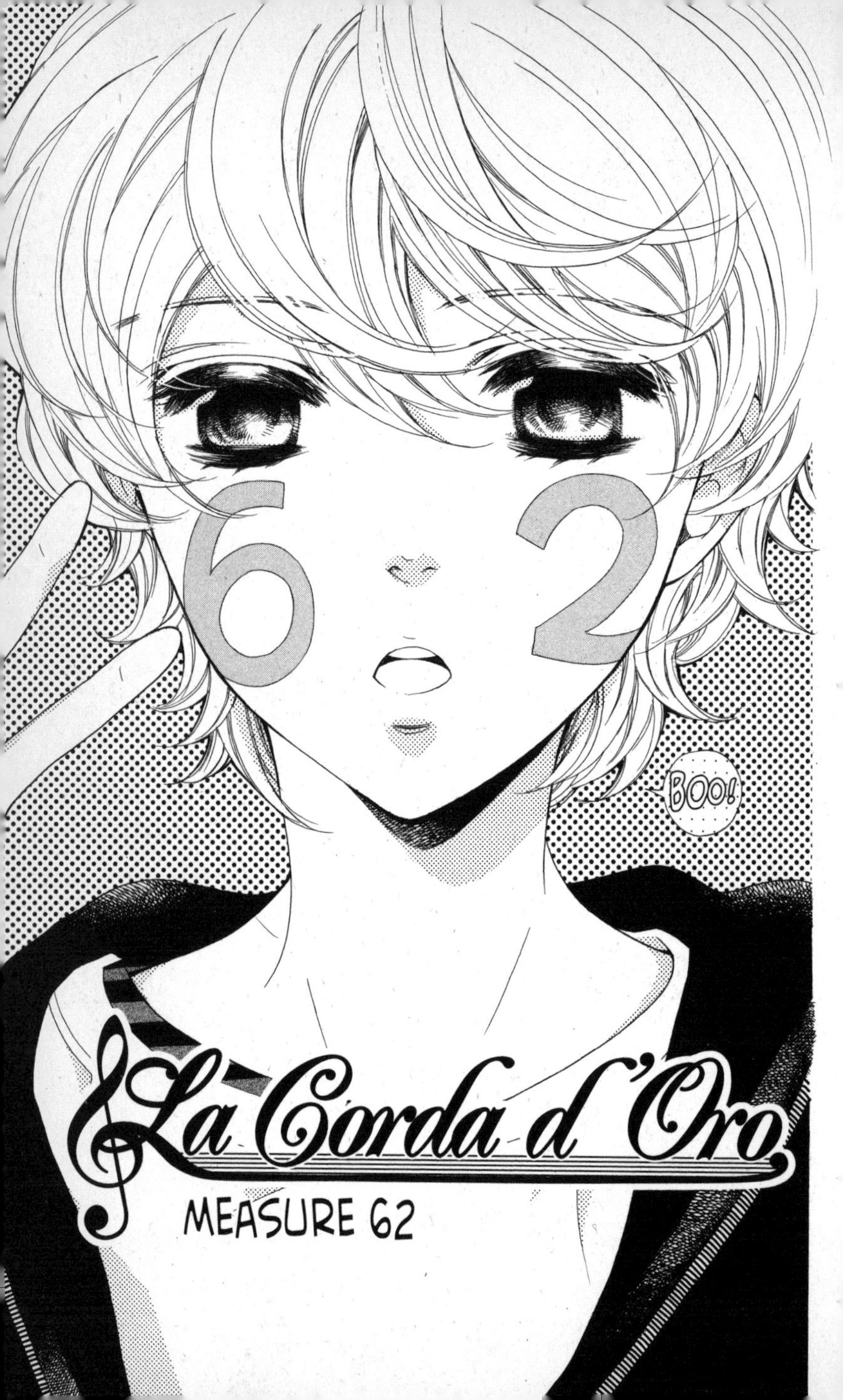
62
BOO!
La Corda d'Oro
MEASURE 62

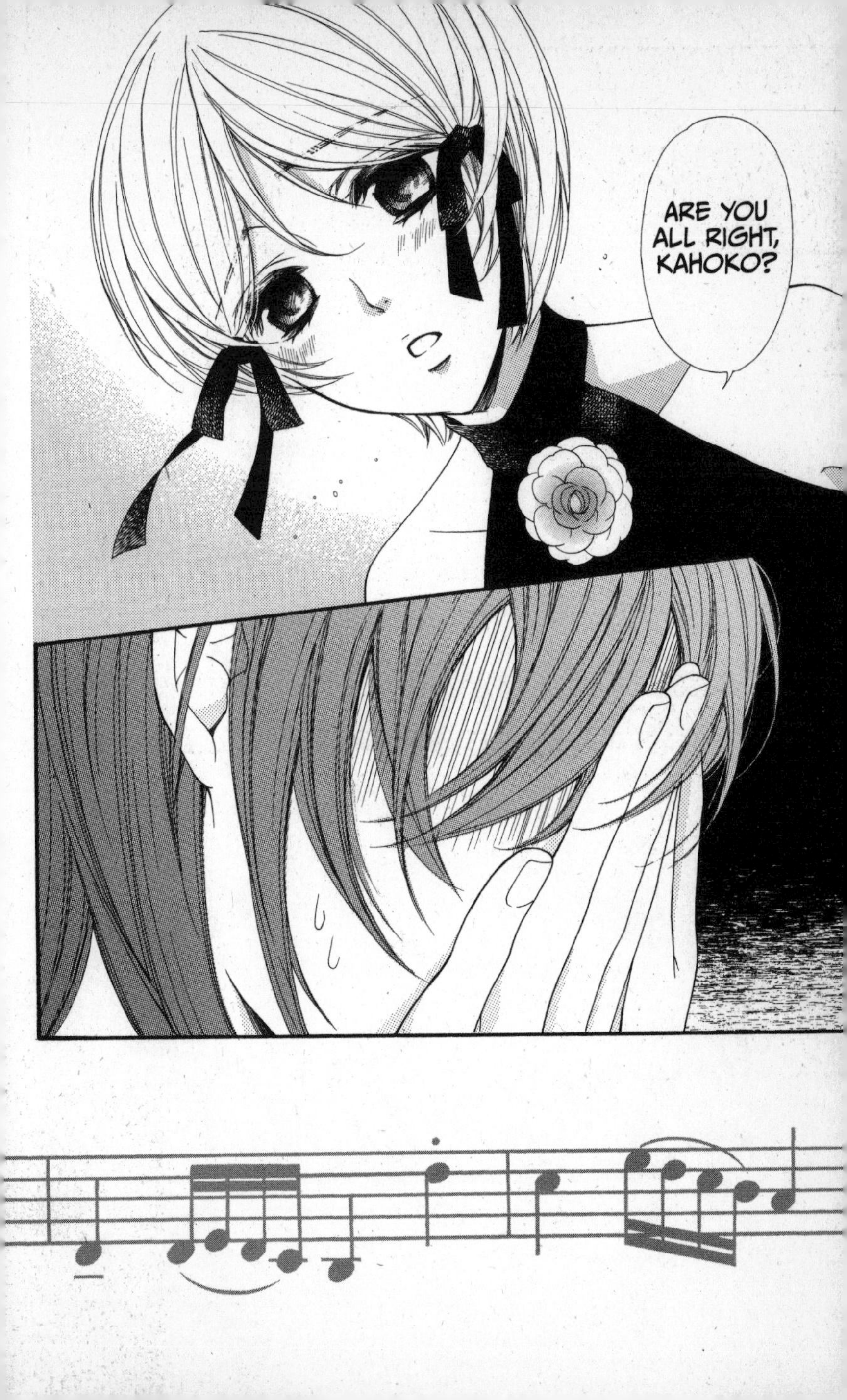
ARE YOU ALL RIGHT, KAHOKO?

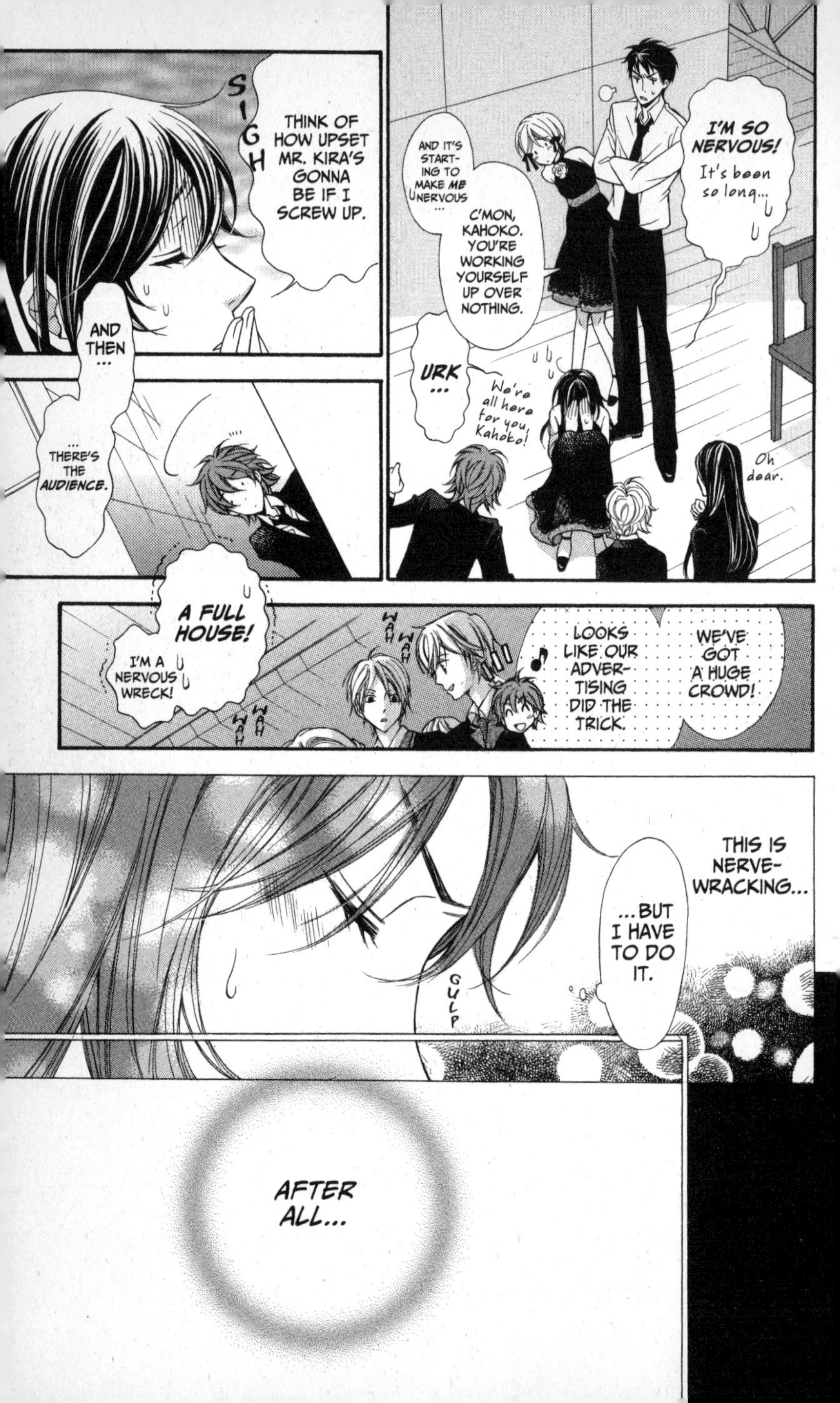
I'M SO NERVOUS! It's been so long...
C'MON, KAHOKO. YOU'RE WORKING YOURSELF UP OVER NOTHING.
AND IT'S STARTING TO MAKE ME NERVOUS...
Oh dear.
We're all here for you, Kahoko!
URK...
SIGH
THINK OF HOW UPSET MR. KIRA'S GONNA BE IF I SCREW UP.
AND THEN...
...THERE'S THE AUDIENCE.
WE'VE GOT A HUGE CROWD!
LOOKS LIKE OUR ADVERTISING DID THE TRICK.
WAH WAH
A FULL HOUSE!
I'M A NERVOUS WRECK!
WAH WAH
THIS IS NERVE-WRACKING...
...BUT I HAVE TO DO IT.
GULP
AFTER ALL...

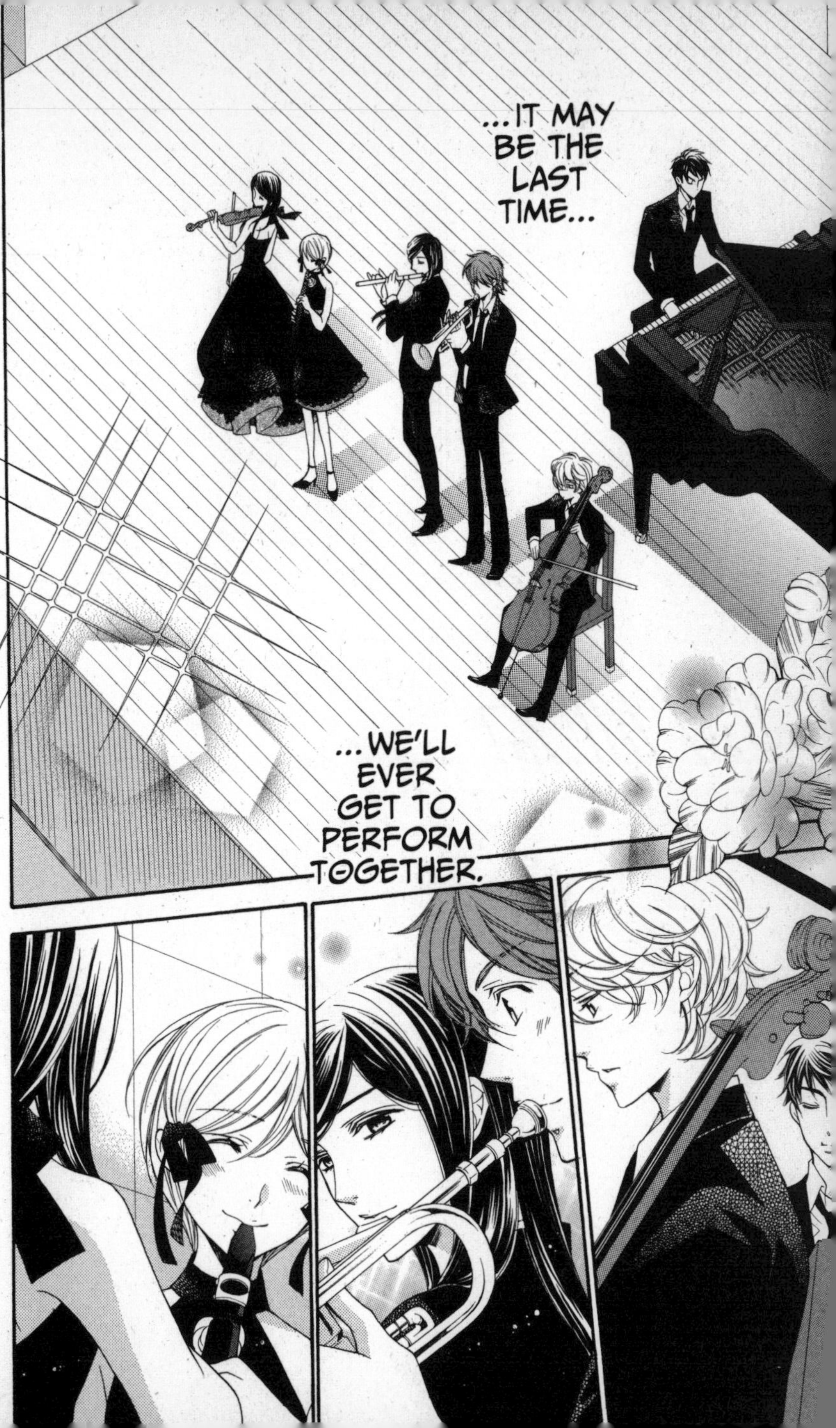
...IT MAY BE THE LAST TIME...
...WE'LL EVER GET TO PERFORM TOGETHER.

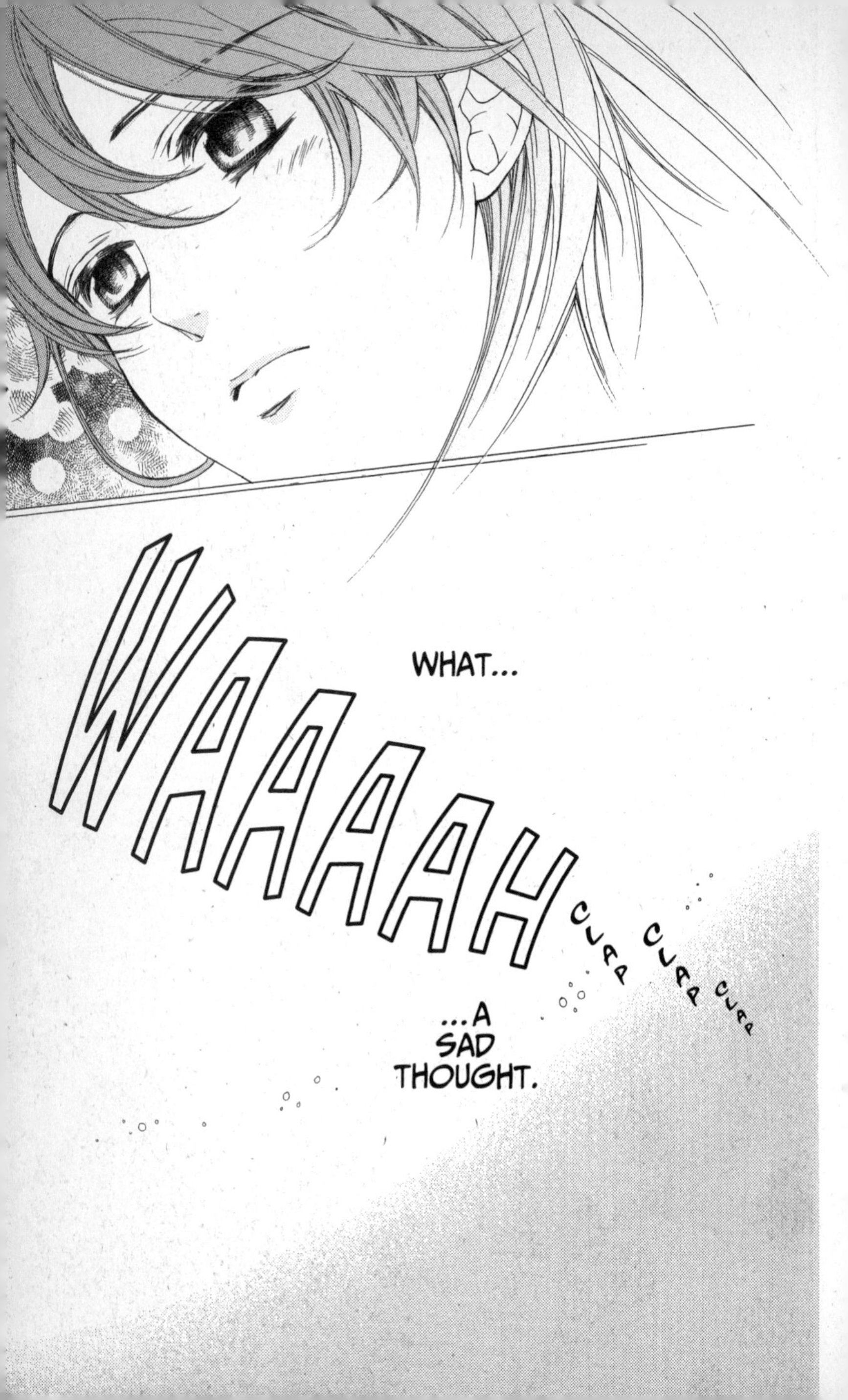
WHAT...
WAAAAAH
CLAP CLAP CLAP
...A SAD THOUGHT.

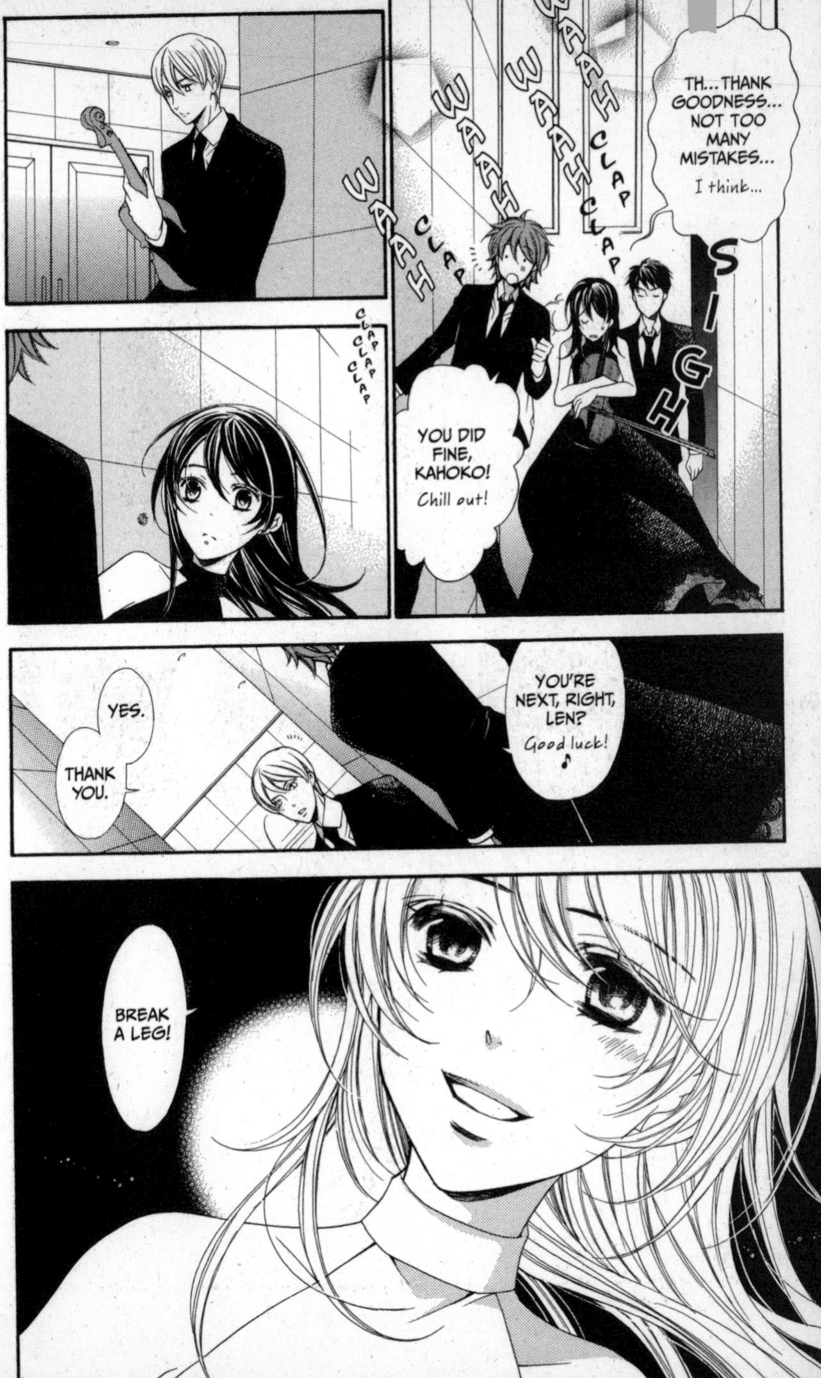
WAAH WAAH WAAH WAAH
CLAP CLAP CLAP
TH... THANK GOODNESS... NOT TOO MANY MISTAKES... I think...
SIGH
YOU DID FINE, KAHOKO! Chill out!
CLAP CLAP CLAP
YOU'RE NEXT, RIGHT, LEN? Good luck! ♪
YES.
THANK YOU.
BREAK A LEG!

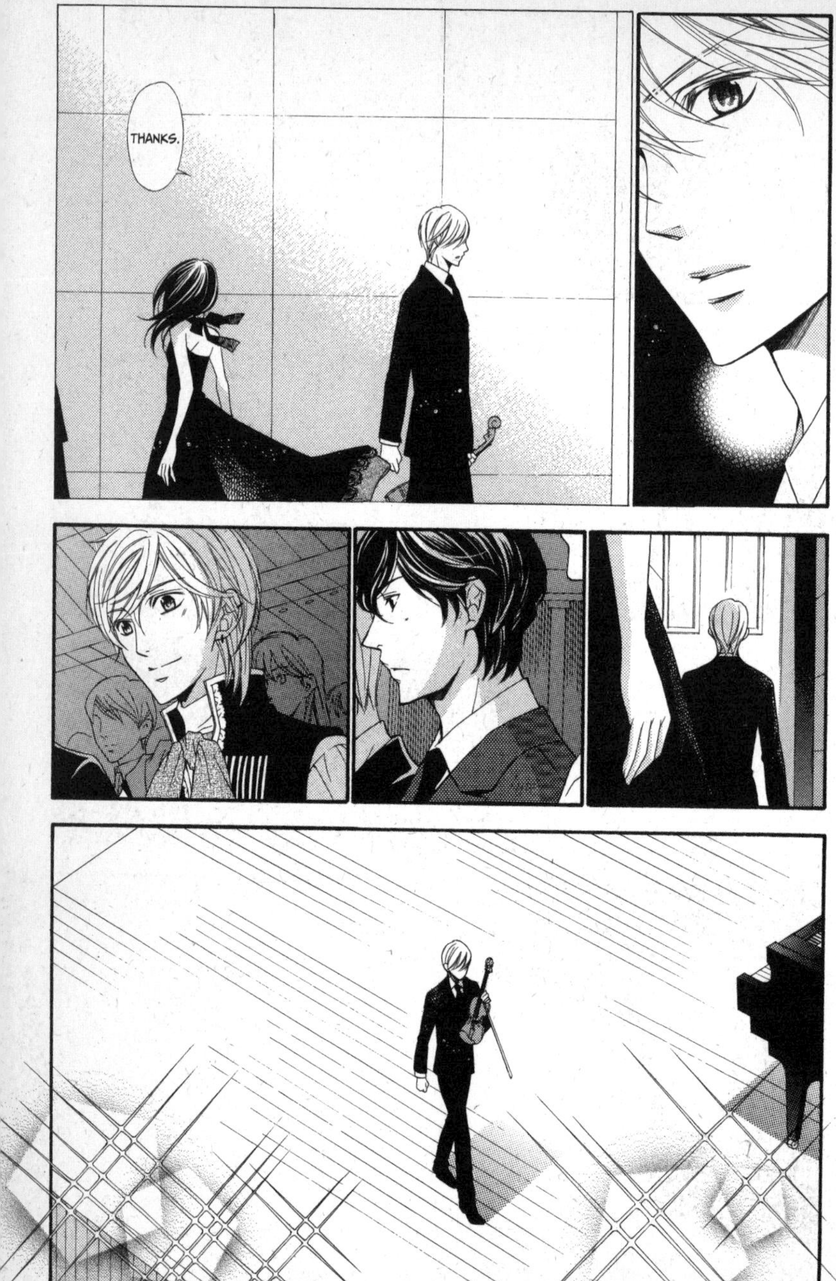
THANKS.

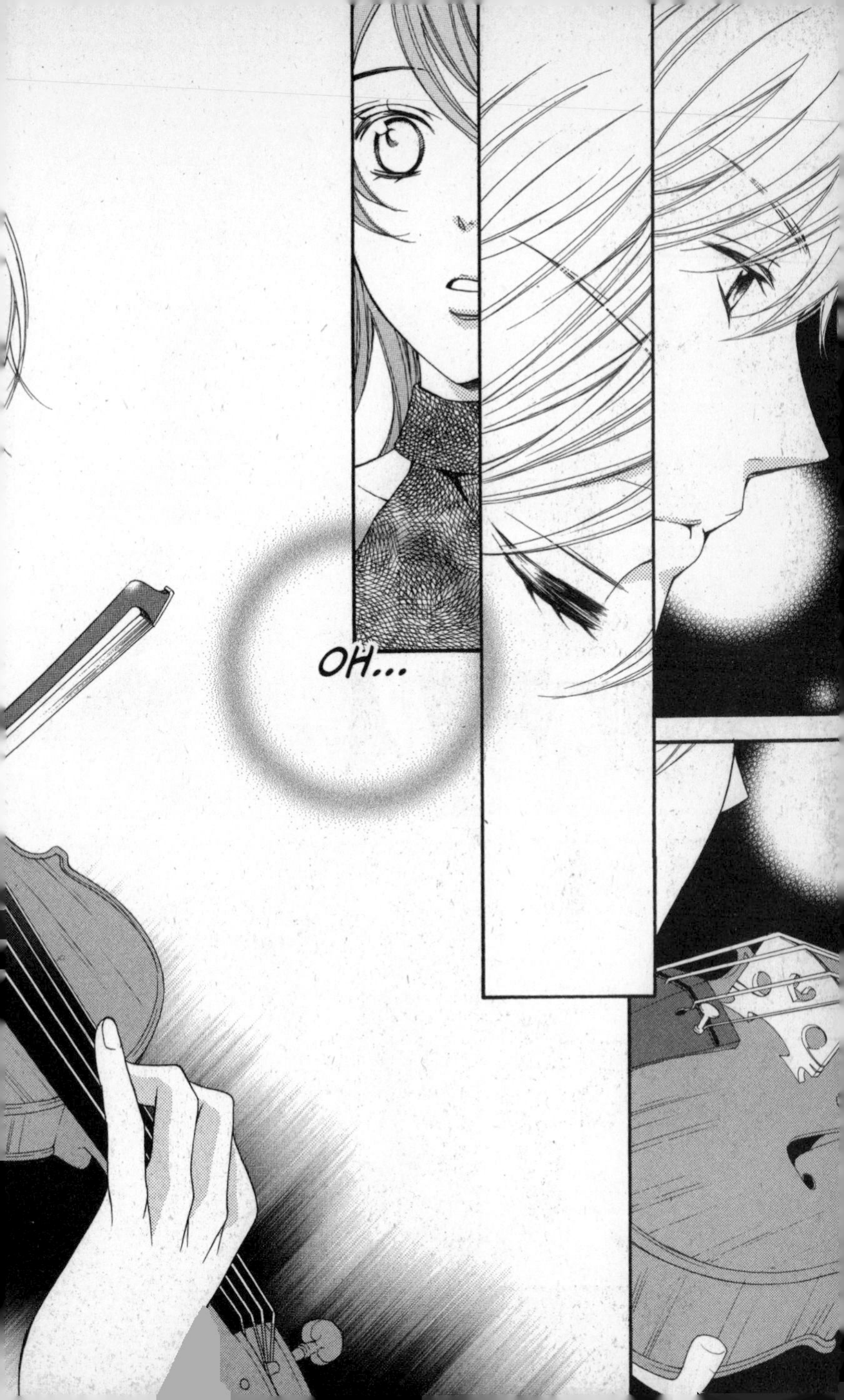
OH...

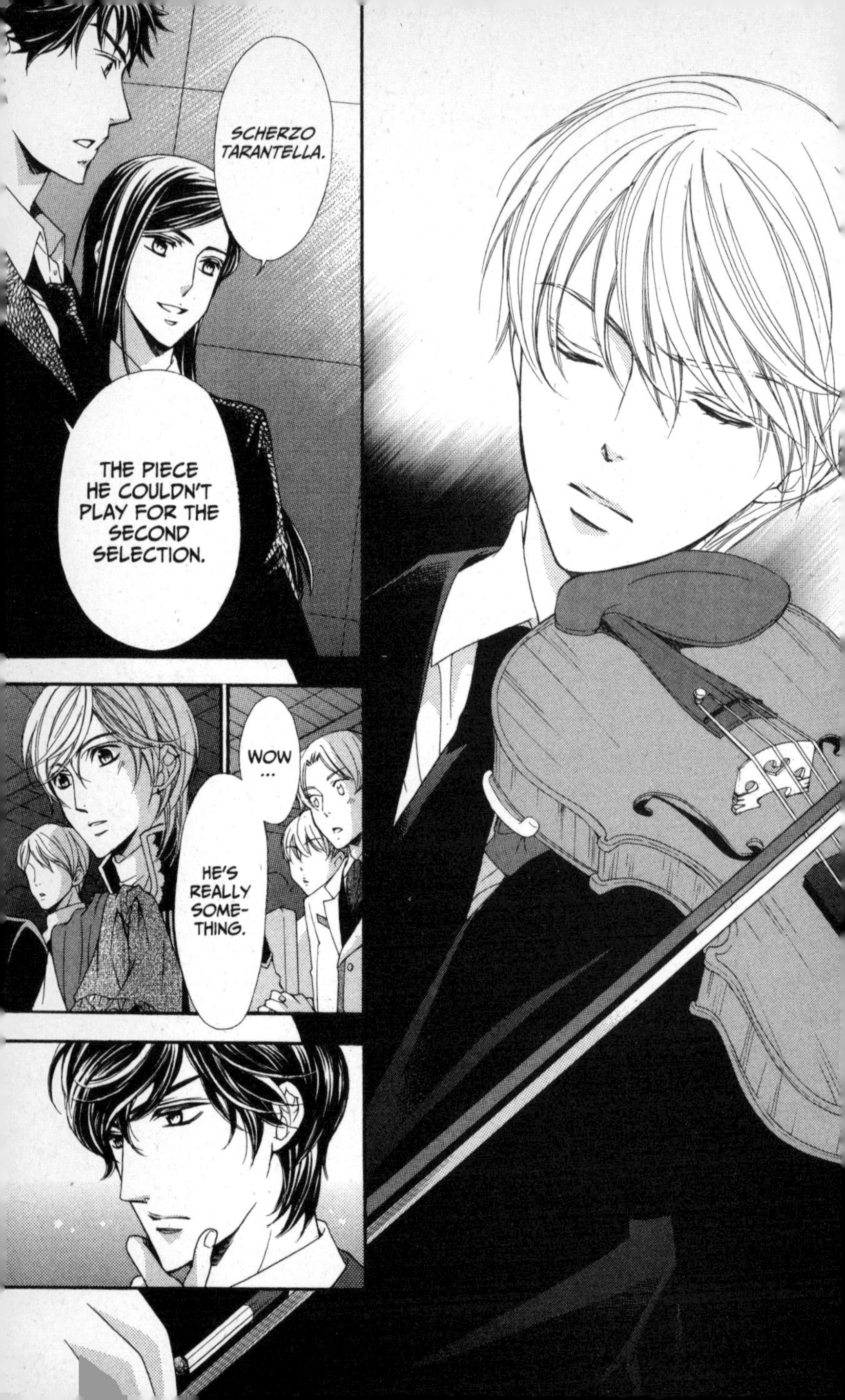
SCHERZO TARANTELLA.
THE PIECE HE COULDN'T PLAY FOR THE SECOND SELECTION.
WOW...
HE'S REALLY SOME-THING.

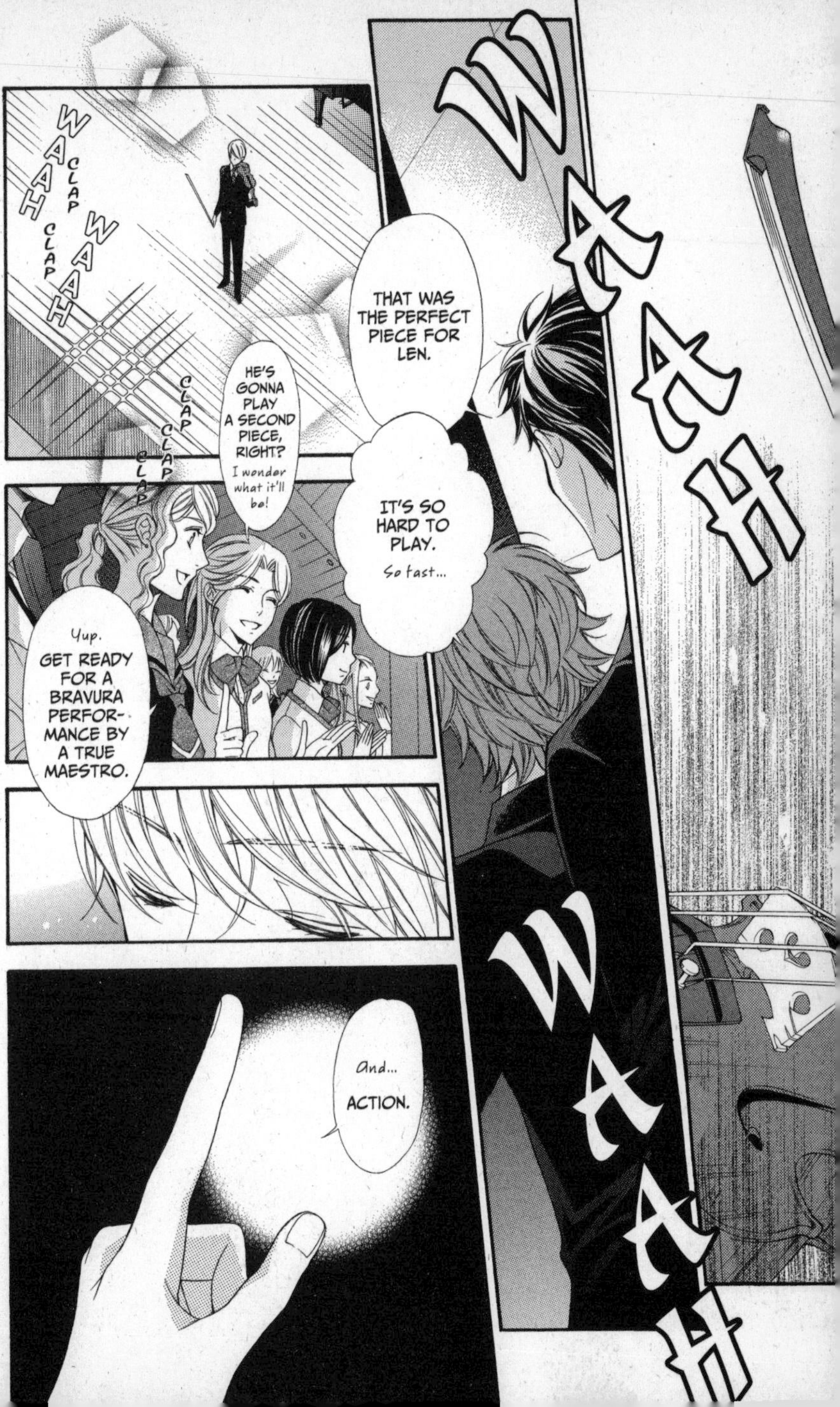
WAAH
THAT WAS THE PERFECT PIECE FOR LEN.
IT'S SO HARD TO PLAY. So fast...
WAAAH
WAAH
CLAP
CLAP
WAAH
CLAP
CLAP
CLAP
HE'S GONNA PLAY A SECOND PIECE, RIGHT? I wonder what it'll be!
Yup. GET READY FOR A BRAVURA PERFORMANCE BY A TRUE MAESTRO.
And... ACTION.

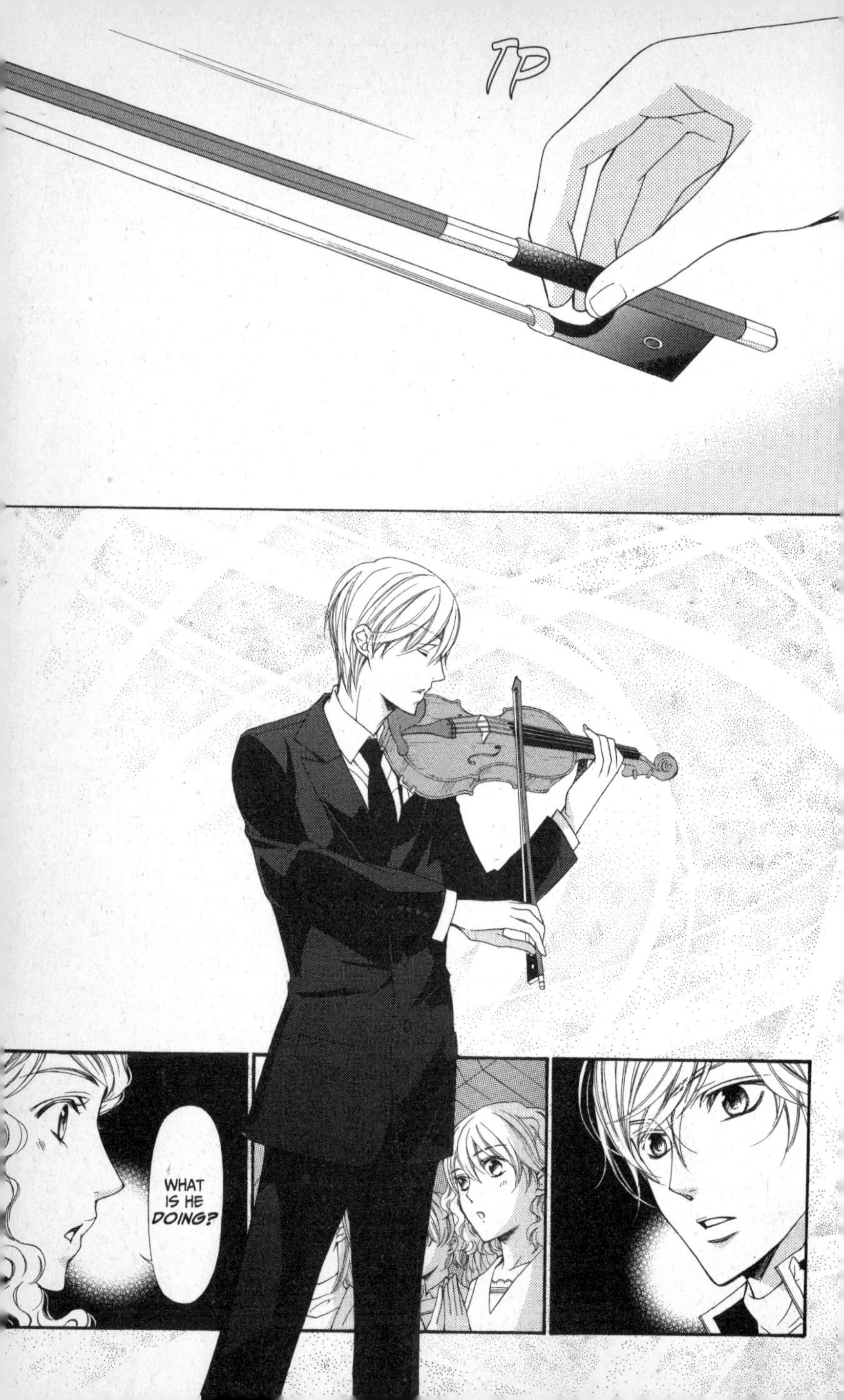
TP
WHAT IS HE DOING?

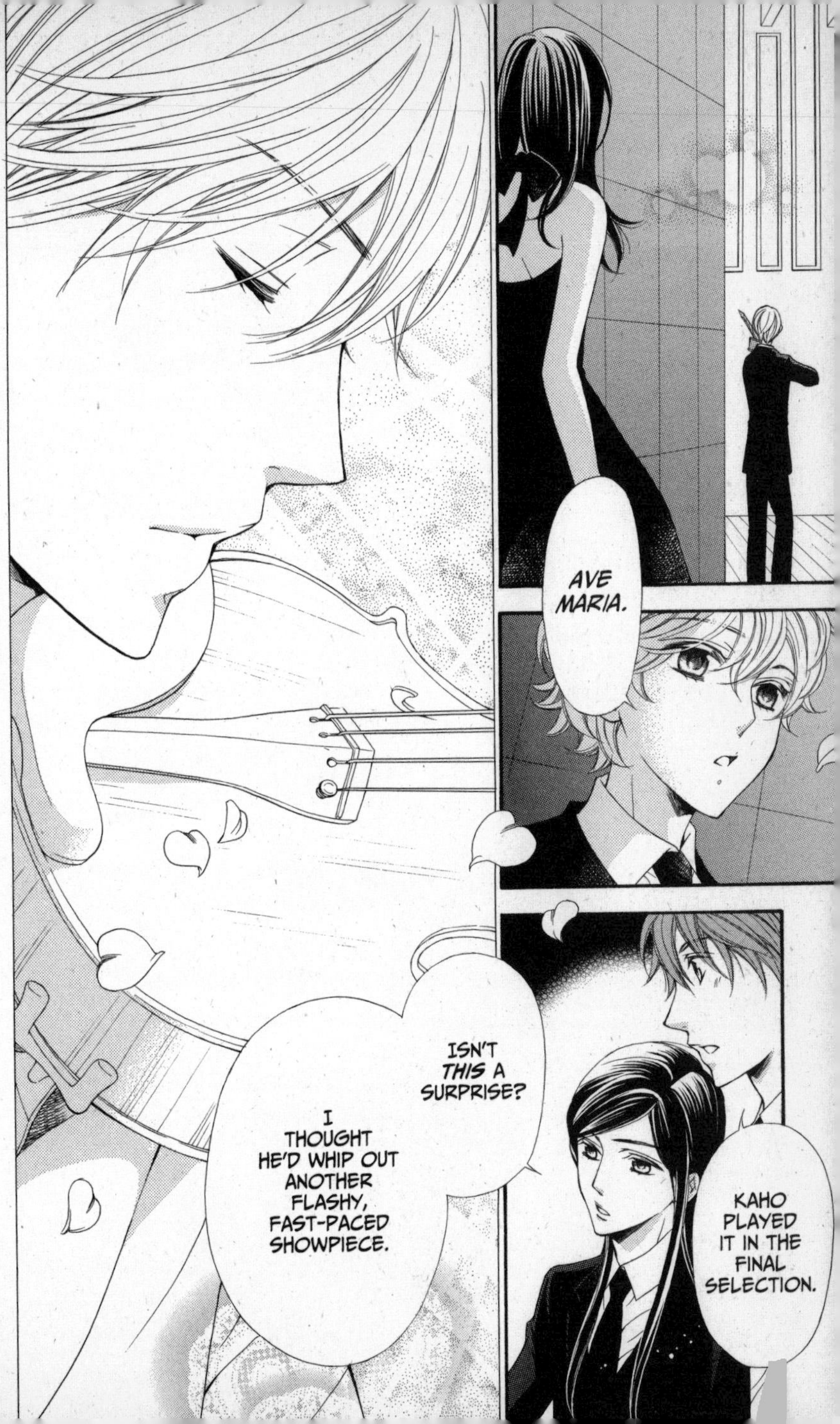
AVE MARIA.
ISN'T *THIS* A SURPRISE?
I THOUGHT HE'D WHIP OUT ANOTHER FLASHY, FAST-PACED SHOWPIECE.
KAHO PLAYED IT IN THE FINAL SELECTION.

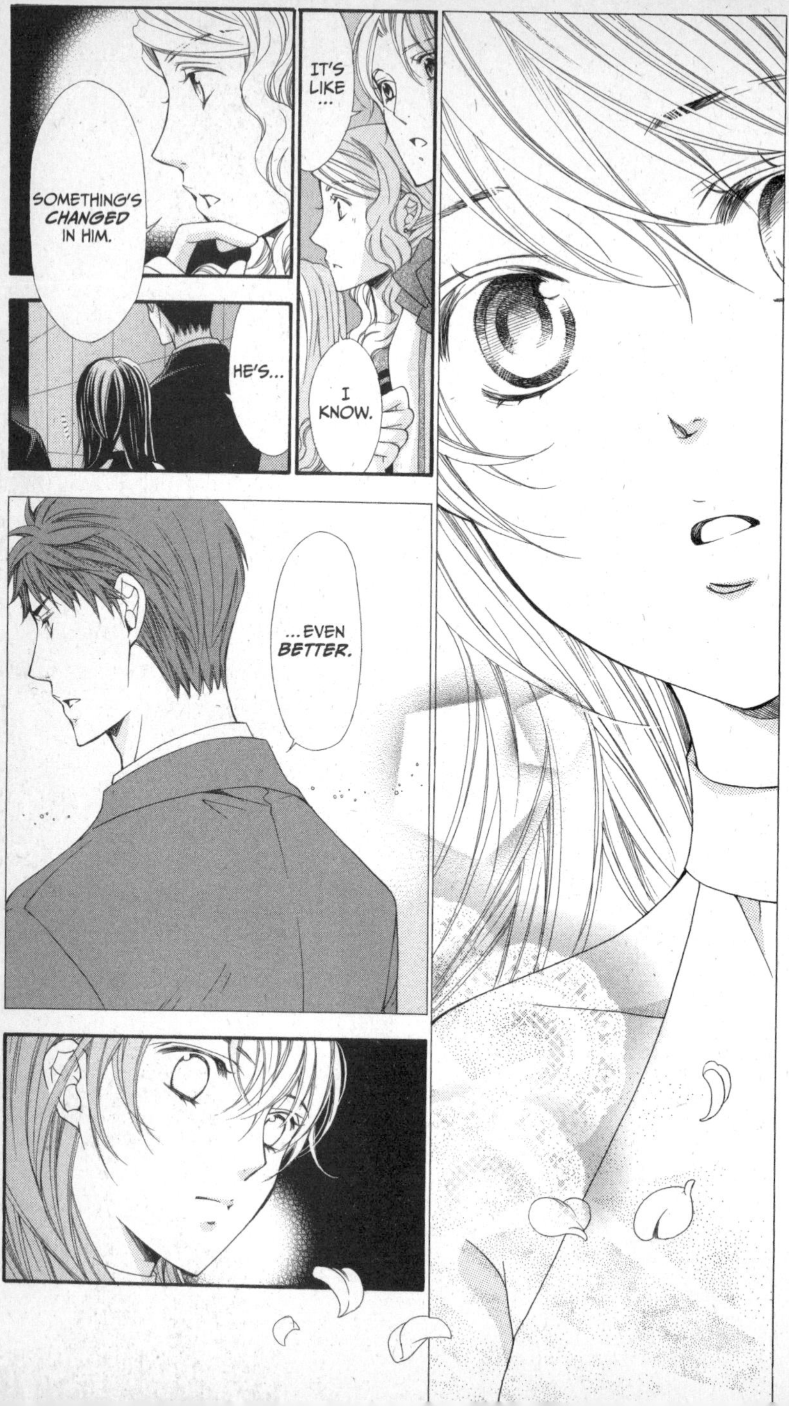
IT'S LIKE ...
I KNOW.
SOMETHING'S CHANGED IN HIM.
HE'S...
...EVEN BETTER.

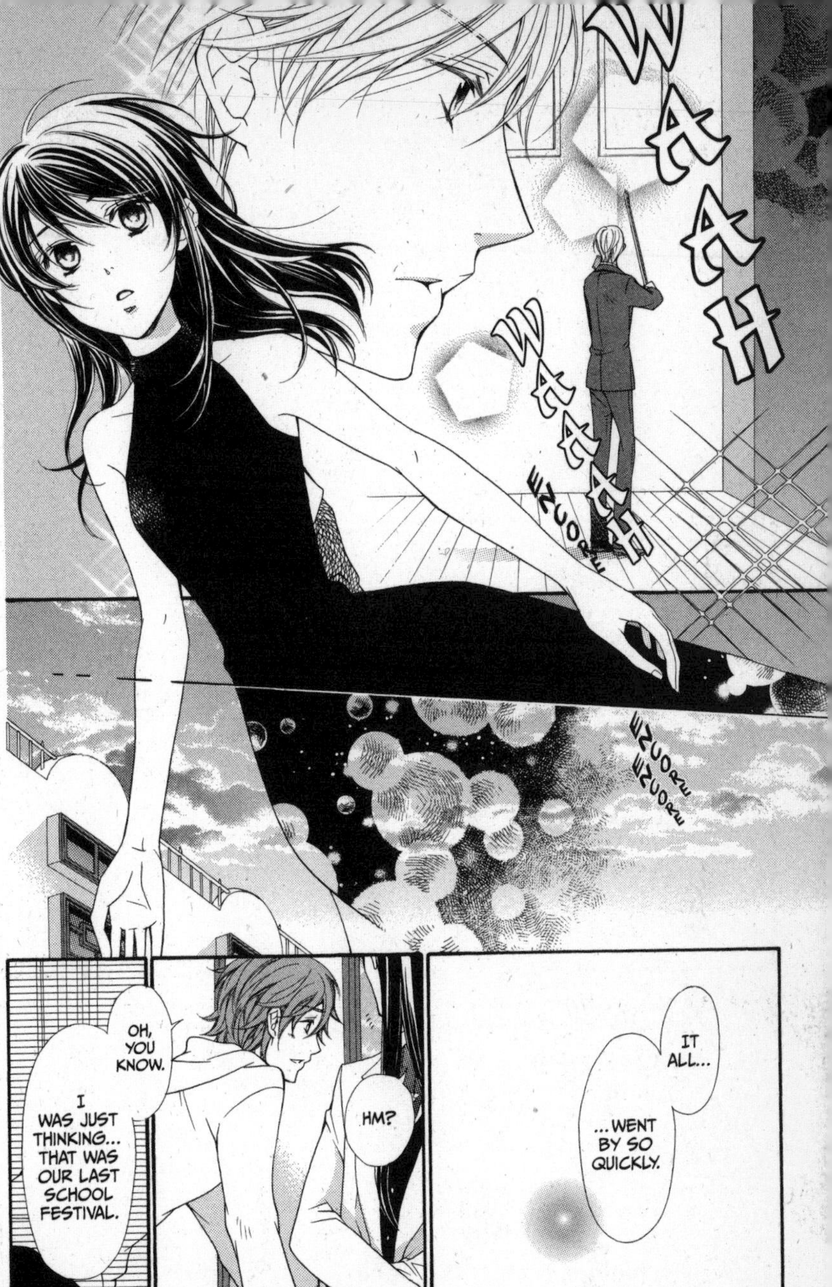
WAAH
WAAH
IT ALL...
...WENT BY SO QUICKLY.
HM?
OH, YOU KNOW.
I WAS JUST THINKING... THAT WAS OUR LAST SCHOOL FESTIVAL.

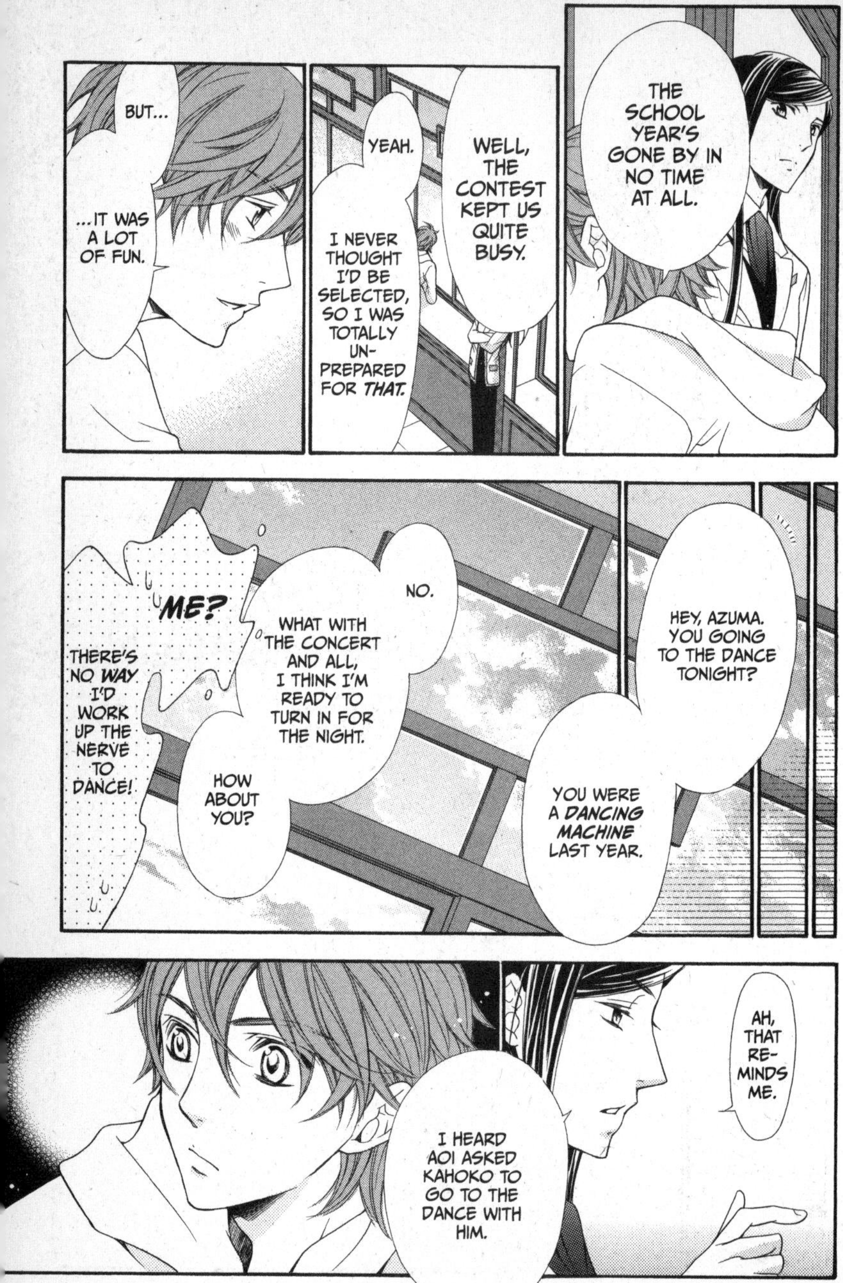
THE SCHOOL YEAR'S GONE BY IN NO TIME AT ALL.
WELL, THE CONTEST KEPT US QUITE BUSY.
YEAH.
I NEVER THOUGHT I'D BE SELECTED, SO I WAS TOTALLY UN-PREPARED FOR *THAT.*
BUT...
...IT WAS A LOT OF FUN.
HEY, AZUMA. YOU GOING TO THE DANCE TONIGHT?
YOU WERE A *DANCING MACHINE* LAST YEAR.
NO.
WHAT WITH THE CONCERT AND ALL, I THINK I'M READY TO TURN IN FOR THE NIGHT.
HOW ABOUT YOU?
ME?
THERE'S NO *WAY* I'D WORK UP THE NERVE TO DANCE!
AH, THAT RE-MINDS ME.
I HEARD AOI ASKED KAHOKO TO GO TO THE DANCE WITH HIM.

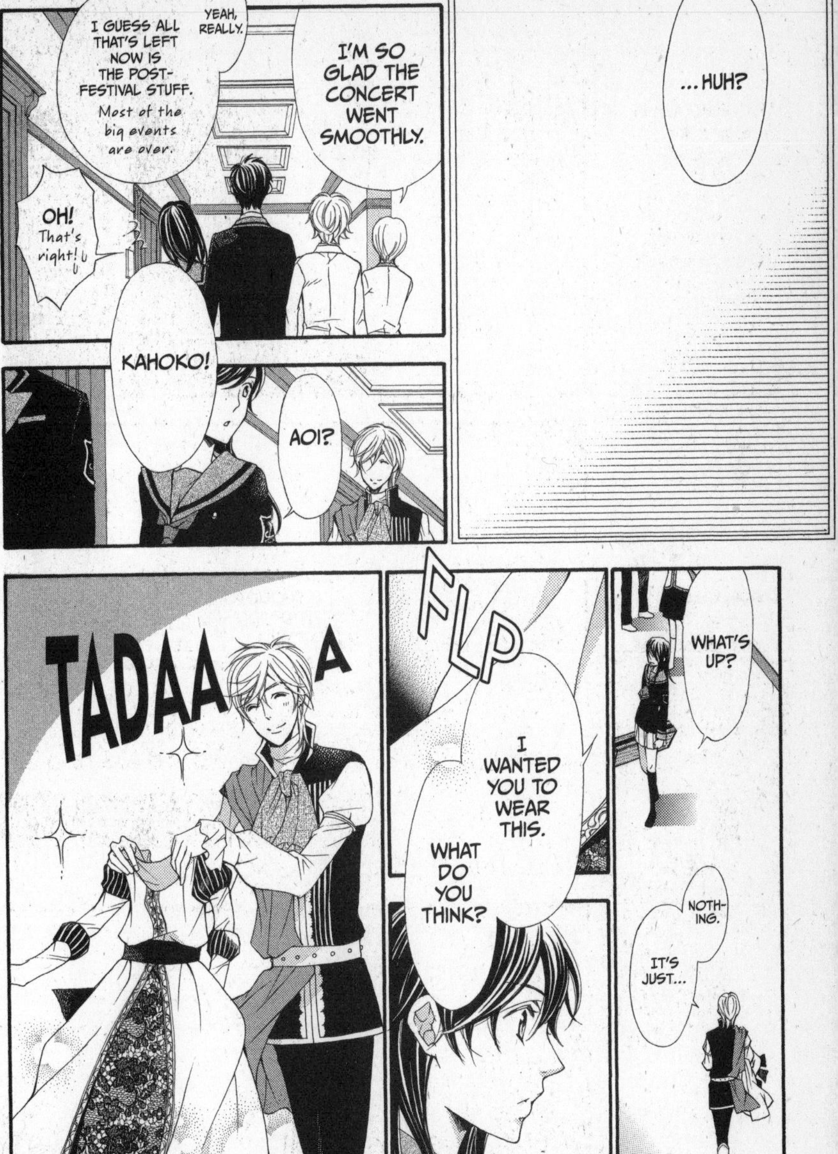
...HUH?
I'M SO GLAD THE CONCERT WENT SMOOTHLY.
YEAH, REALLY.
I GUESS ALL THAT'S LEFT NOW IS THE POST-FESTIVAL STUFF.
Most of the big events are over.
OH! That's right!
KAHOKO!
AOI?
WHAT'S UP?
NOTHING.
IT'S JUST...
FLP
I WANTED YOU TO WEAR THIS.
WHAT DO YOU THINK?
TADAAA

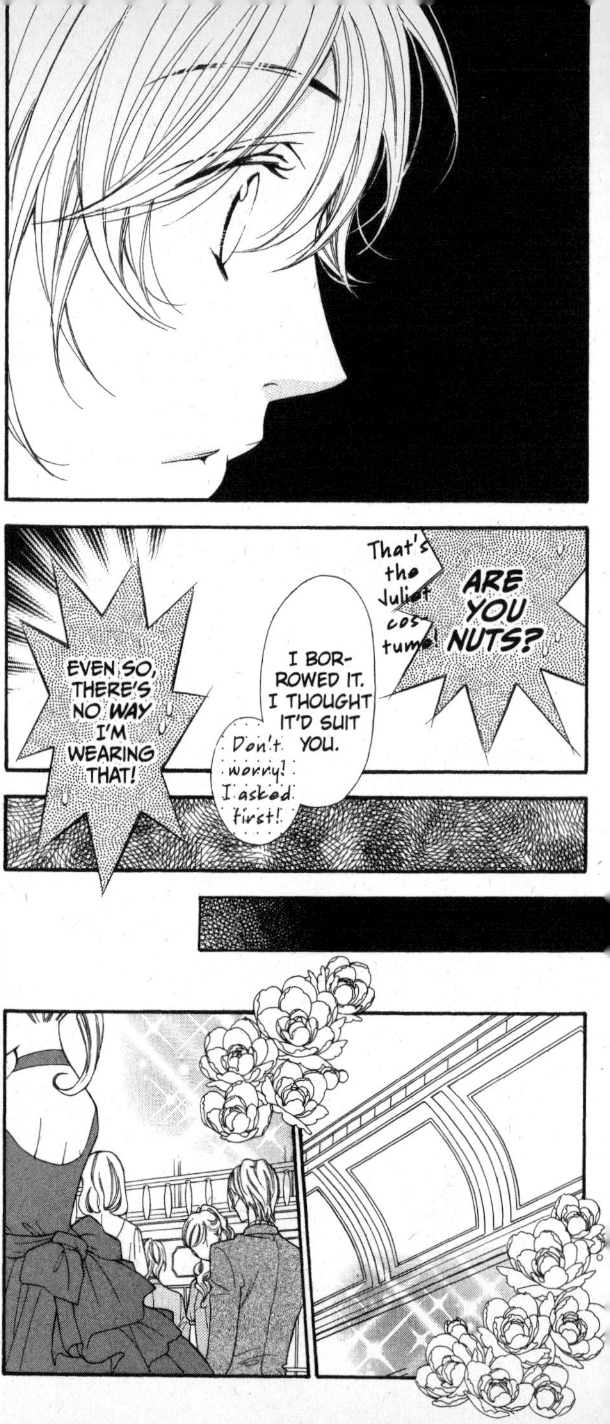

That's the Juliet costume!
ARE YOU NUTS?
I BORROWED IT. I THOUGHT IT'D SUIT YOU.
Don't worry! I asked first!
EVEN SO, THERE'S NO WAY I'M WEARING THAT!

The young Kazuki... I imagine him getting muddy every day.
Getting back to our main story, can't you imagine Keiichi being able to sneak up on people like a cat? I thought it fit his character, but what do you think?
I bet Azuma could scare the pants off people too...

Young Kazuki

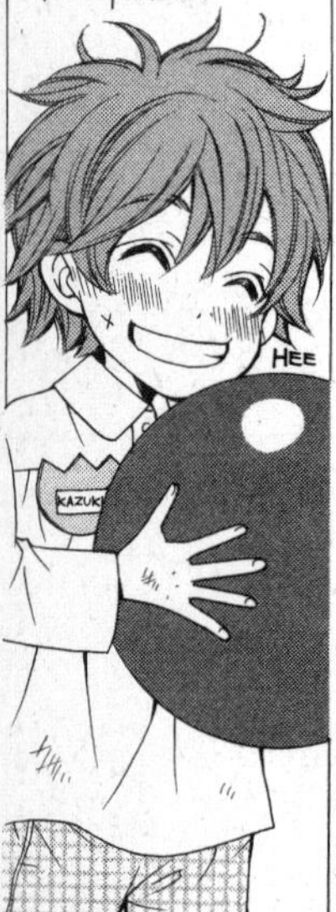

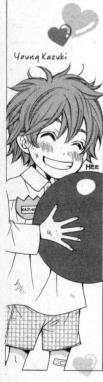

HEE
KAZUKI

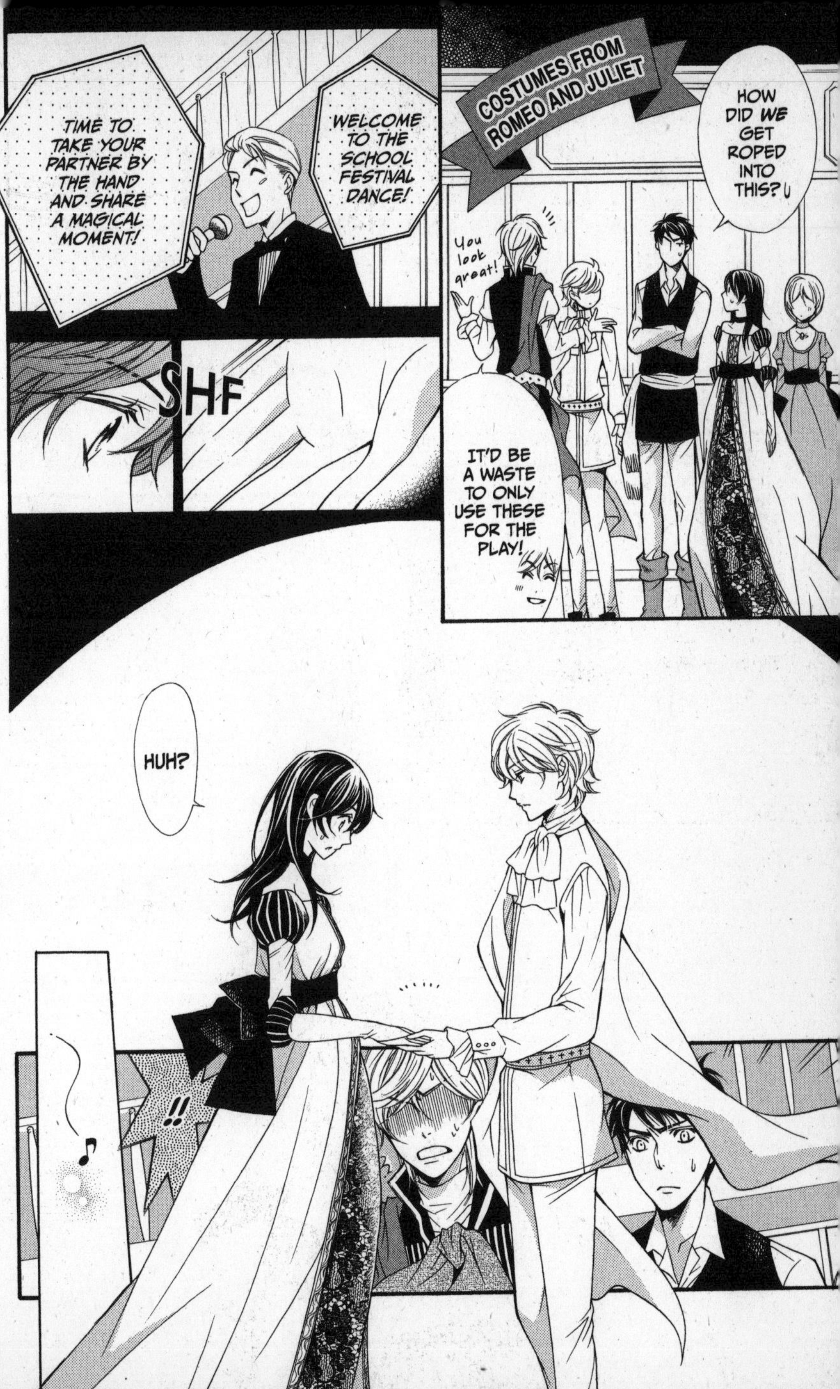
COSTUMES FROM ROMEO AND JULIET
HOW DID WE GET ROPED INTO THIS?
You look great!
IT'D BE A WASTE TO ONLY USE THESE FOR THE PLAY!
WELCOME TO THE SCHOOL FESTIVAL DANCE!
TIME TO TAKE YOUR PARTNER BY THE HAND AND SHARE A MAGICAL MOMENT!
SHF
HUH?
!!

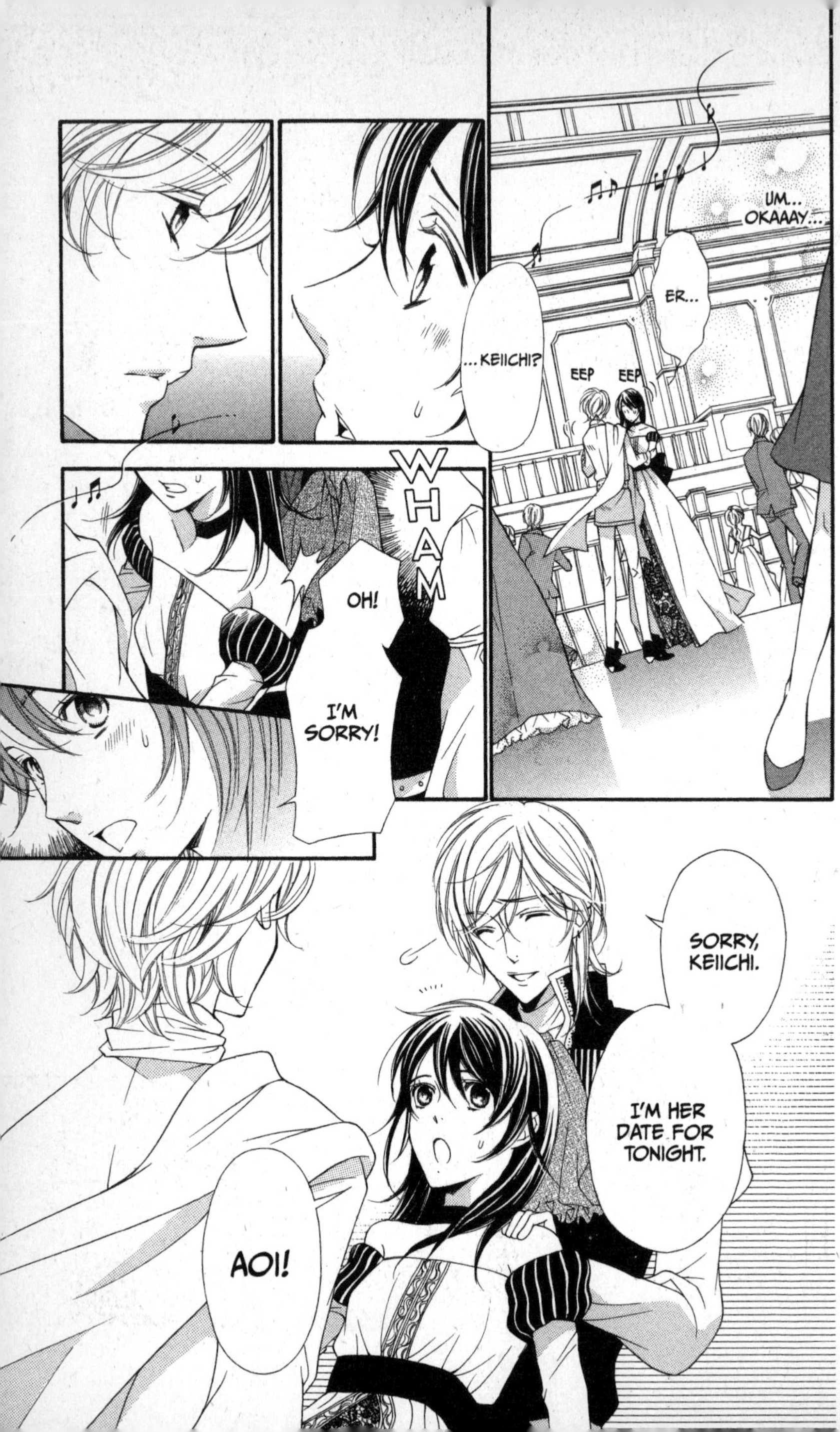
UM... OKAAAY...
ER...
...KEIICHI?
EEP
EEP
WHAM
OH!
I'M SORRY!
SORRY, KEIICHI.
I'M HER DATE FOR TONIGHT.
AOI!

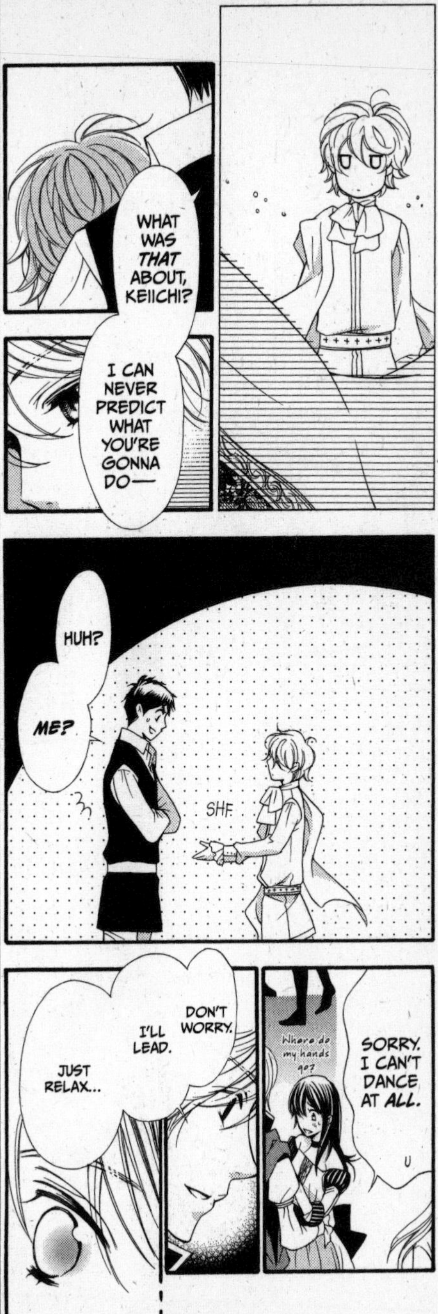
WHAT WAS THAT ABOUT, KEIICHI?
I CAN NEVER PREDICT WHAT YOU'RE GONNA DO—
HUH?
ME?
SHF.
SORRY. I CAN'T DANCE AT ALL.
Where do my hands go?
DON'T WORRY.
I'LL LEAD.
JUST RELAX...

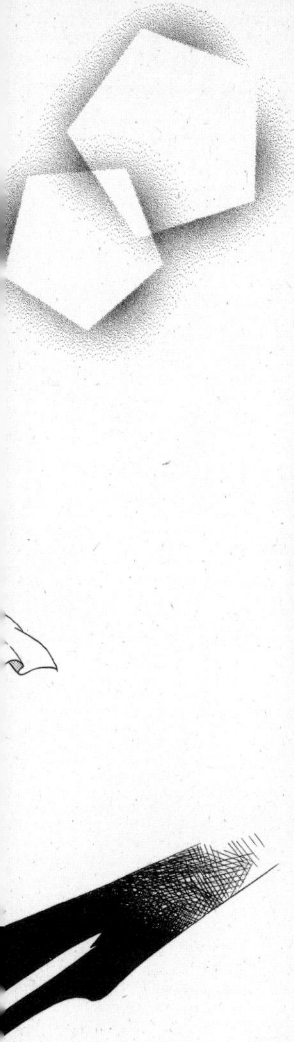

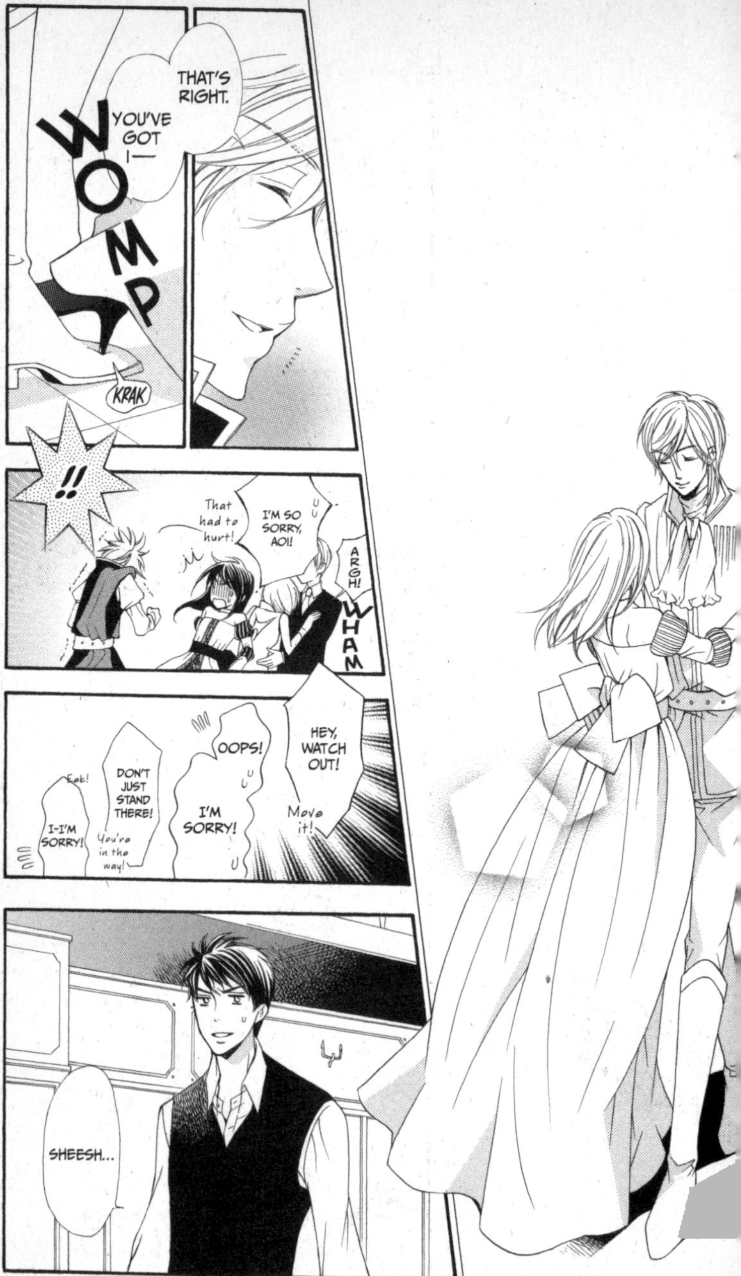
THAT'S RIGHT.
YOU'VE GOT I—
WOMP
KRAK
ARGH!
WHAM
I'M SO SORRY, AOI!
That had to hurt!
!!
HEY, WATCH OUT!
Move it!
OOPS!
I'M SORRY!
DON'T JUST STAND THERE!
You're in the way!
Eek!
I-I'M SORRY!
SHEESH...

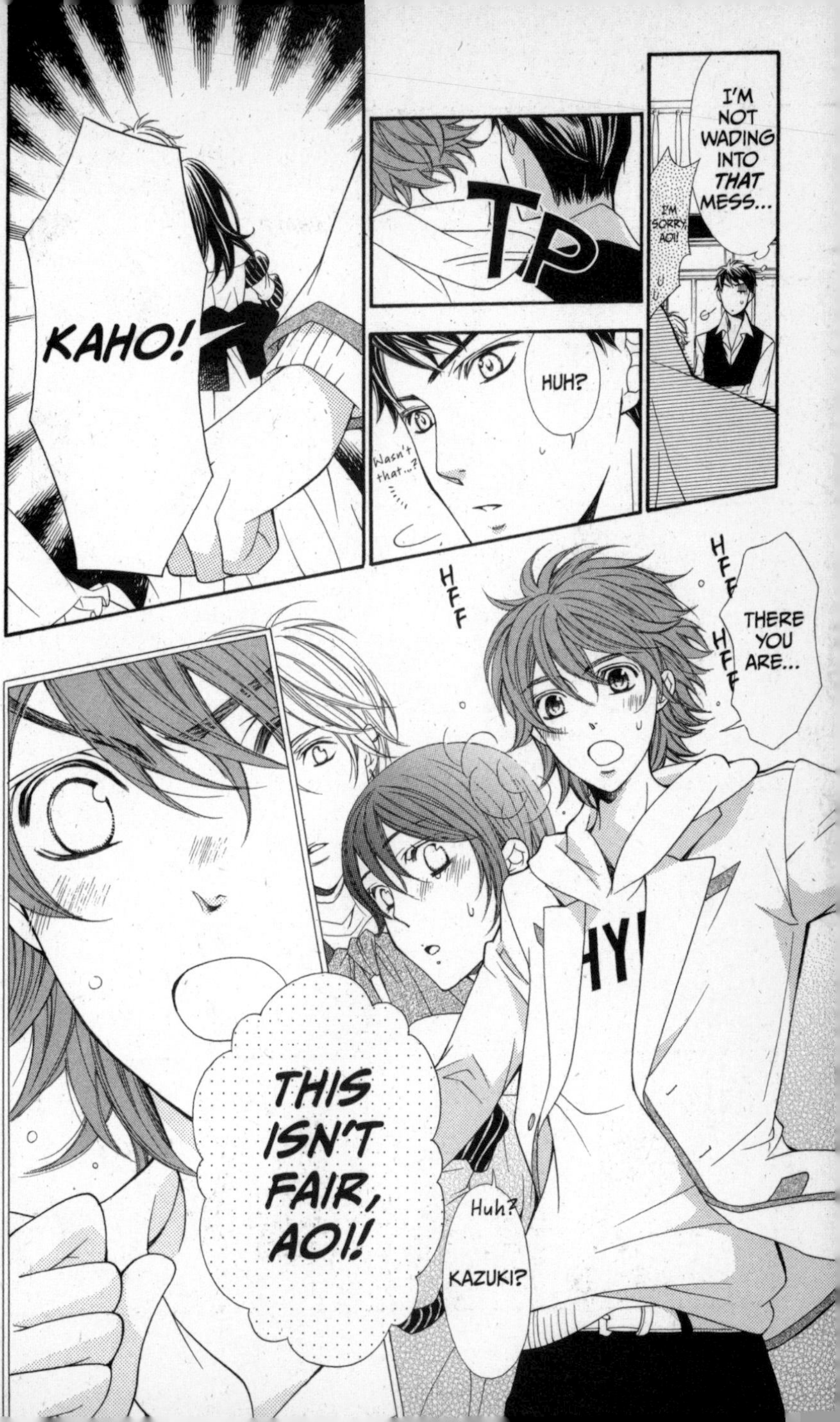
I'M NOT WADING INTO THAT MESS...
I'M SORRY, AOI!
TP
HUH?
Wasn't that...?
KAHO!
HFF HFF
THERE YOU ARE...
HFF
THIS ISN'T FAIR, AOI!
Huh?
KAZUKI?

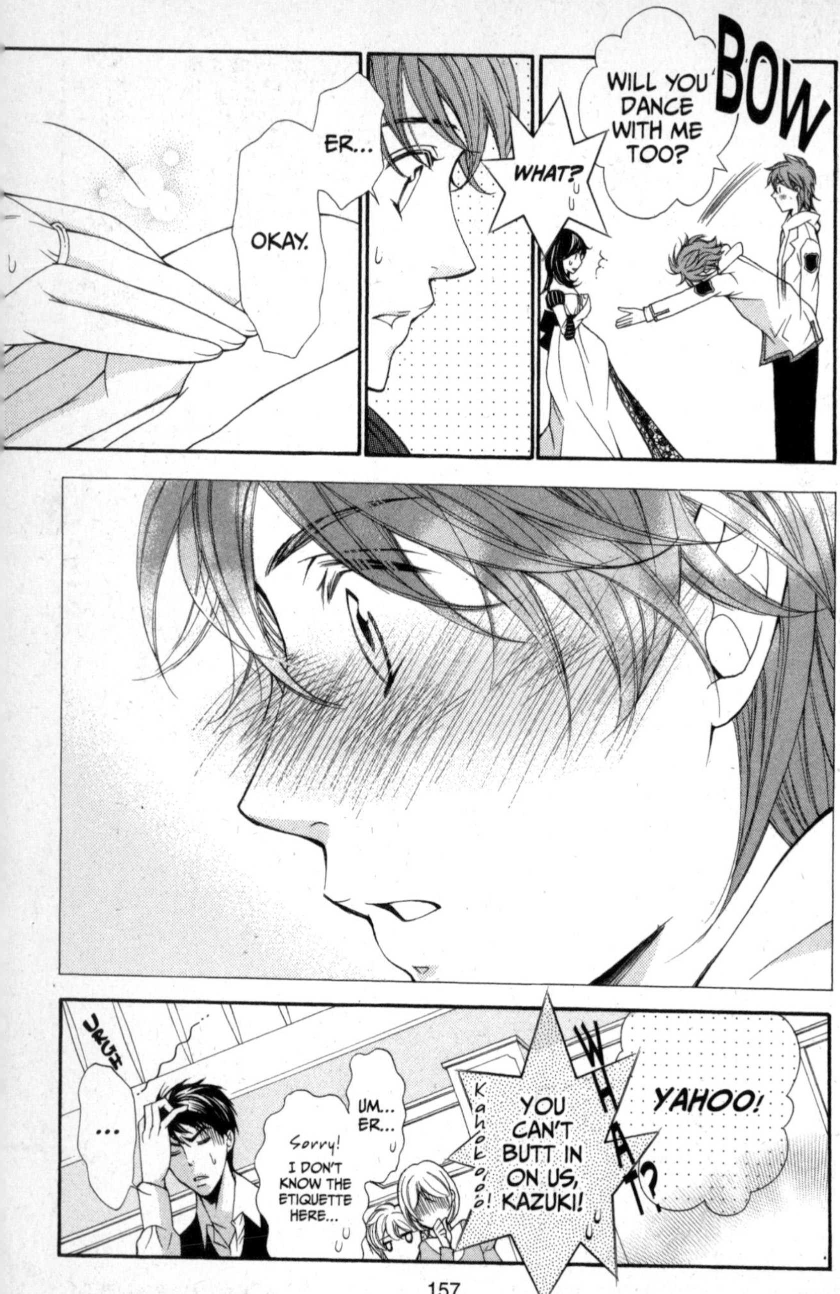
BOW
WILL YOU DANCE WITH ME TOO?
WHAT?
ER...
OKAY.
YAHOO!
WHAT?
YOU CAN'T BUTT IN ON US, KAZUKI!
Kahoooo!
UM... ER...
Sorry!
I DON'T KNOW THE ETIQUETTE HERE...
...

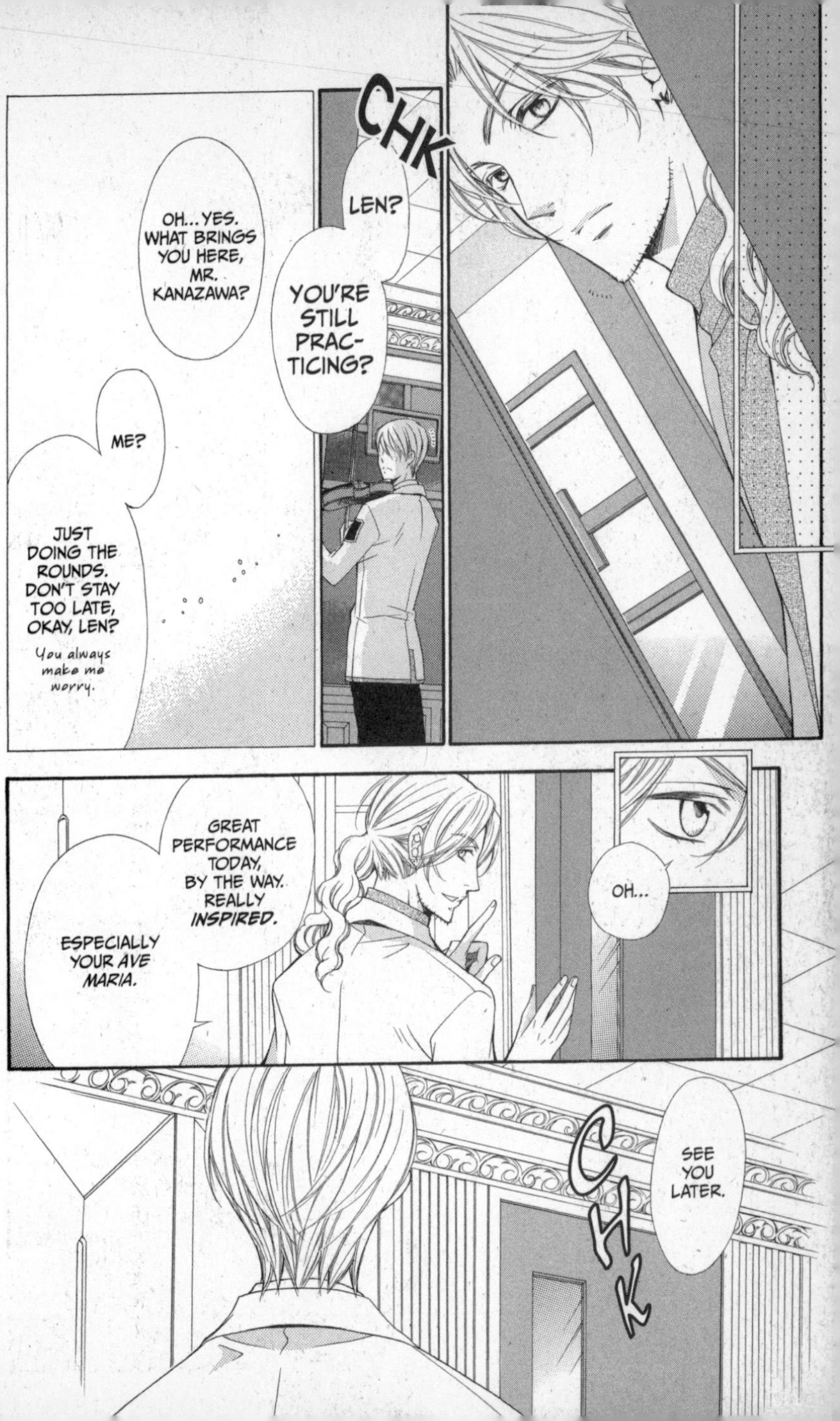
CHK
LEN?
YOU'RE STILL PRAC-TICING?
OH...YES. WHAT BRINGS YOU HERE, MR. KANAZAWA?
ME?
JUST DOING THE ROUNDS. DON'T STAY TOO LATE, OKAY, LEN?
You always make me worry.
OH...
GREAT PERFORMANCE TODAY, BY THE WAY. REALLY *INSPIRED*.
ESPECIALLY YOUR *AVE MARIA*.
SEE YOU LATER.
CHK

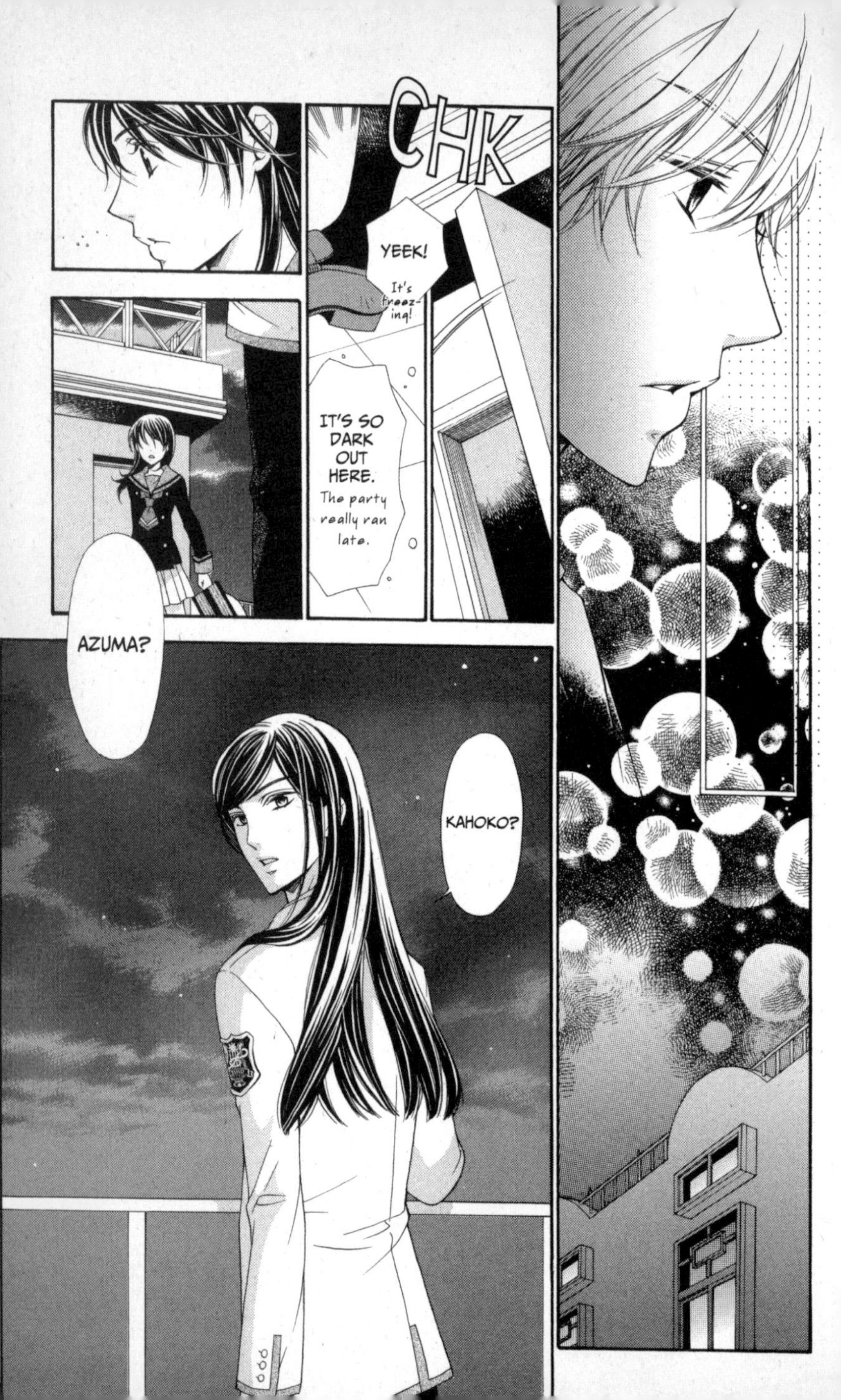
CHK
YEEK!
It's freezing!
IT'S SO DARK OUT HERE.
The party really ran late.
...
AZUMA?
KAHOKO?

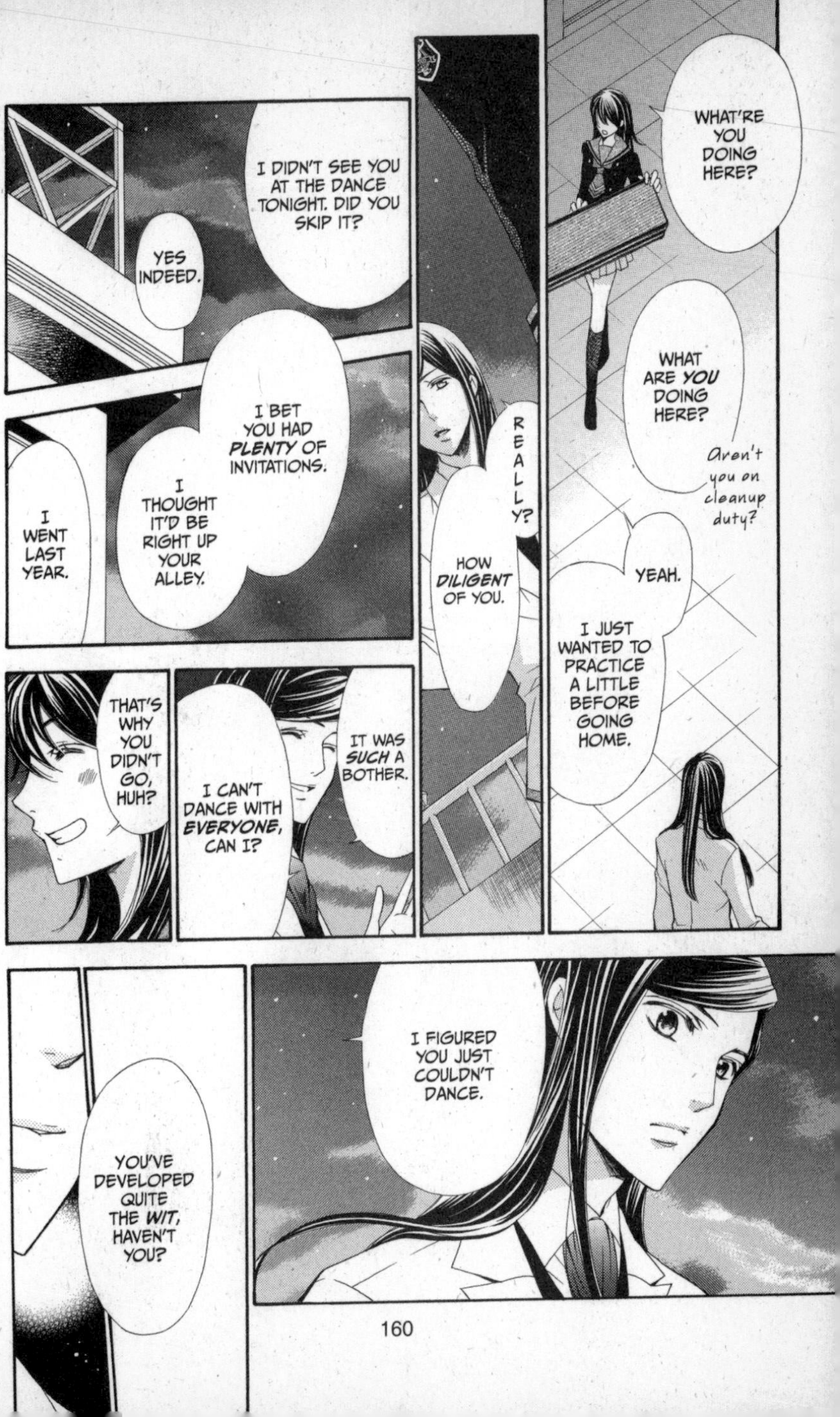
WHAT'RE YOU DOING HERE?
WHAT ARE YOU DOING HERE?
Aren't you on cleanup duty?
YEAH.
I JUST WANTED TO PRACTICE A LITTLE BEFORE GOING HOME.
REALLY?
HOW DILIGENT OF YOU.
I DIDN'T SEE YOU AT THE DANCE TONIGHT. DID YOU SKIP IT?
YES INDEED.
I BET YOU HAD PLENTY OF INVITATIONS.
I THOUGHT IT'D BE RIGHT UP YOUR ALLEY.
I WENT LAST YEAR.
IT WAS SUCH A BOTHER.
I CAN'T DANCE WITH EVERYONE, CAN I?
THAT'S WHY YOU DIDN'T GO, HUH?
I FIGURED YOU JUST COULDN'T DANCE.
YOU'VE DEVELOPED QUITE THE WIT, HAVEN'T YOU?

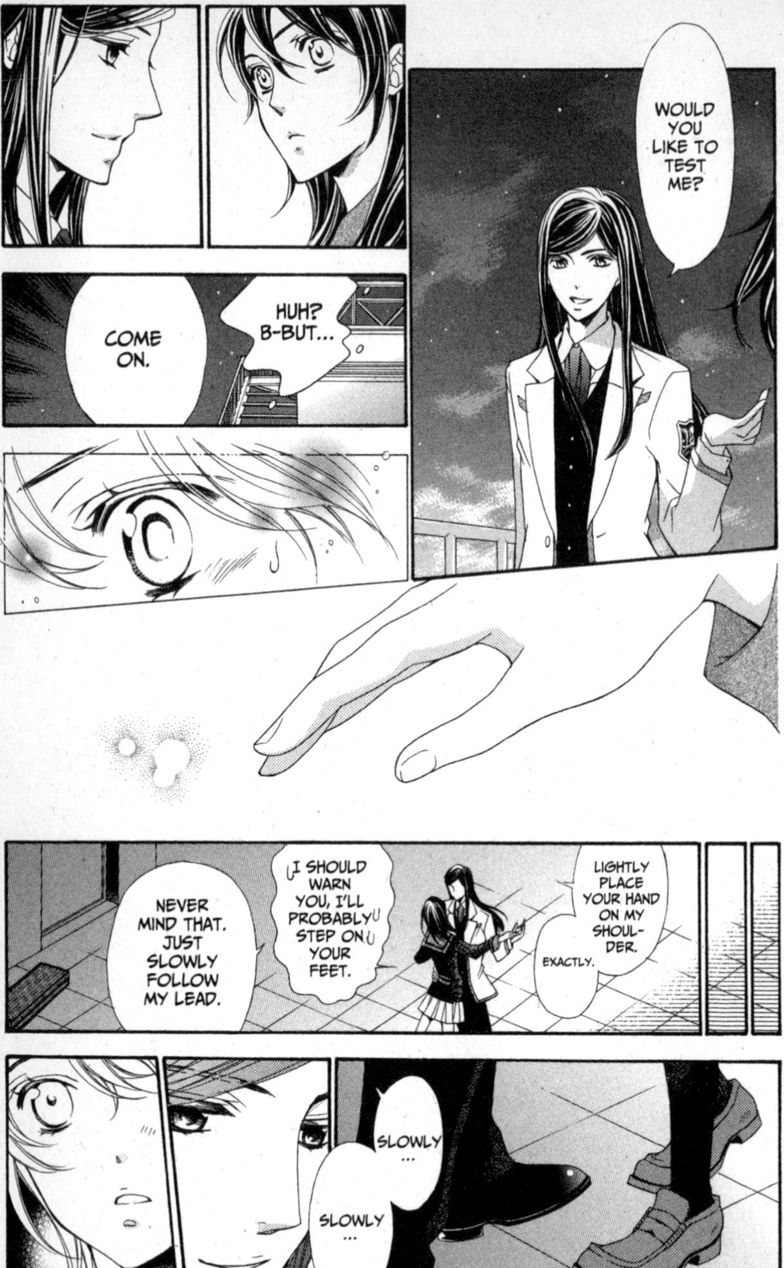
WOULD YOU LIKE TO TEST ME?
HUH? B-BUT...
COME ON.
LIGHTLY PLACE YOUR HAND ON MY SHOULDER.
EXACTLY.
I SHOULD WARN YOU, I'LL PROBABLY STEP ON YOUR FEET.
NEVER MIND THAT. JUST SLOWLY FOLLOW MY LEAD.
SLOWLY...
SLOWLY...

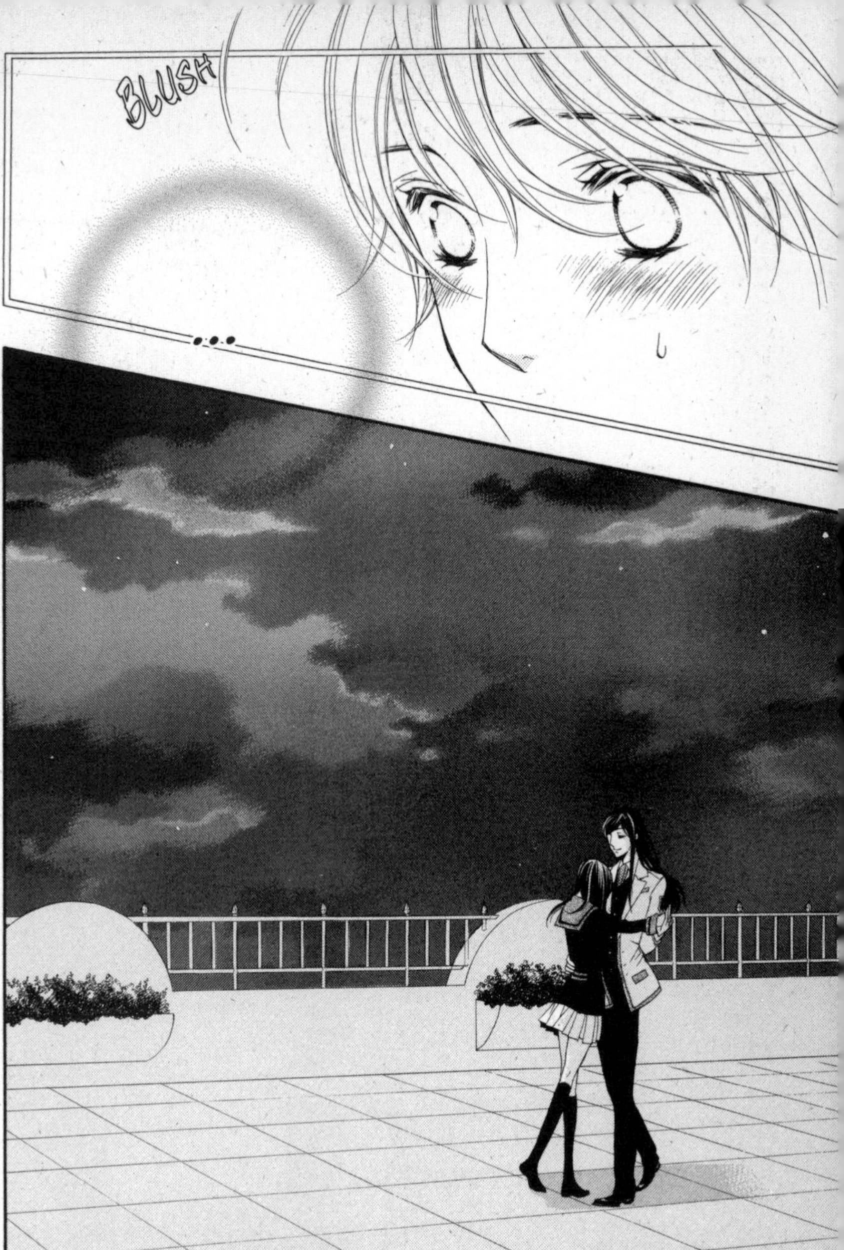
BLUSH
...

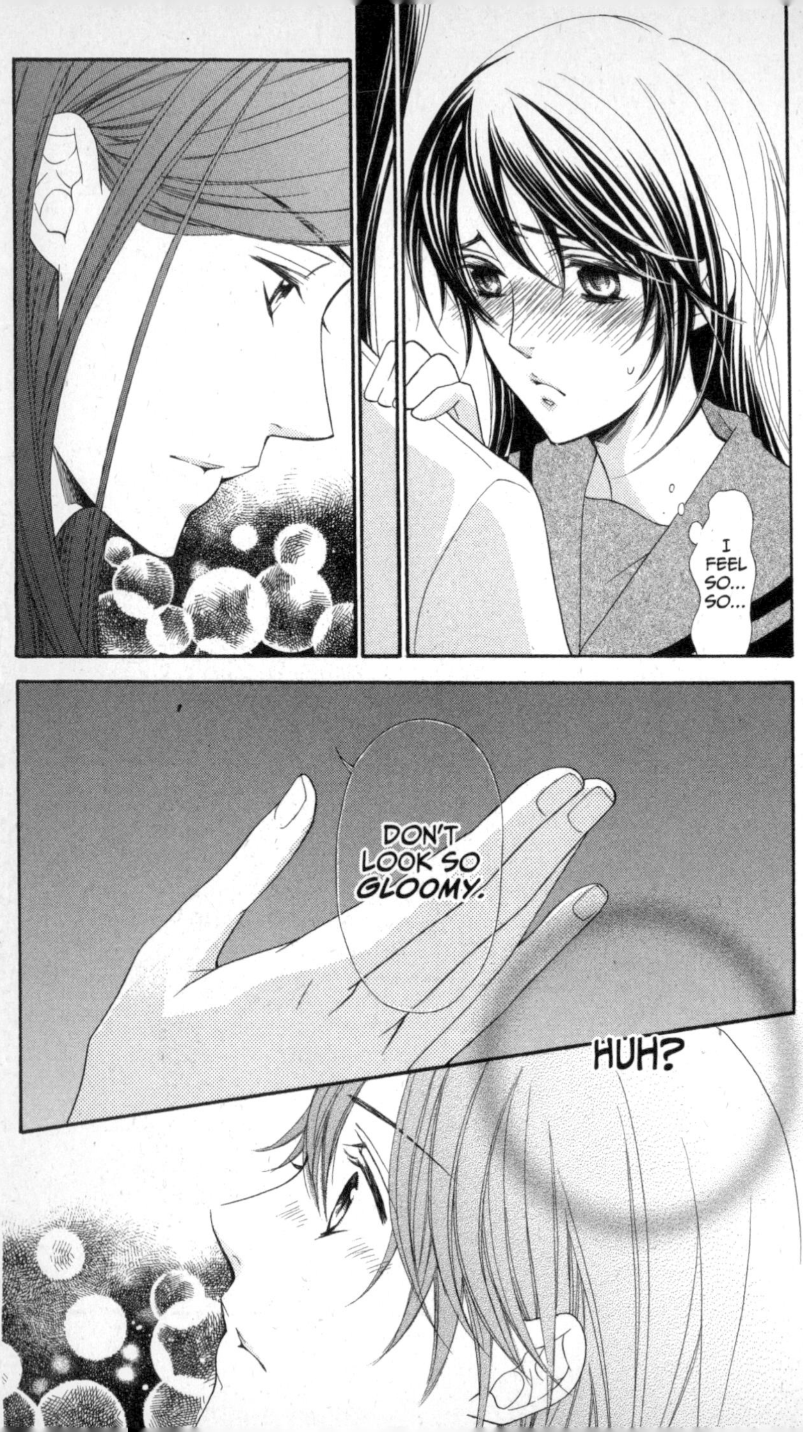
I FEEL SO... SO...
DON'T LOOK SO GLOOMY.
HUH?

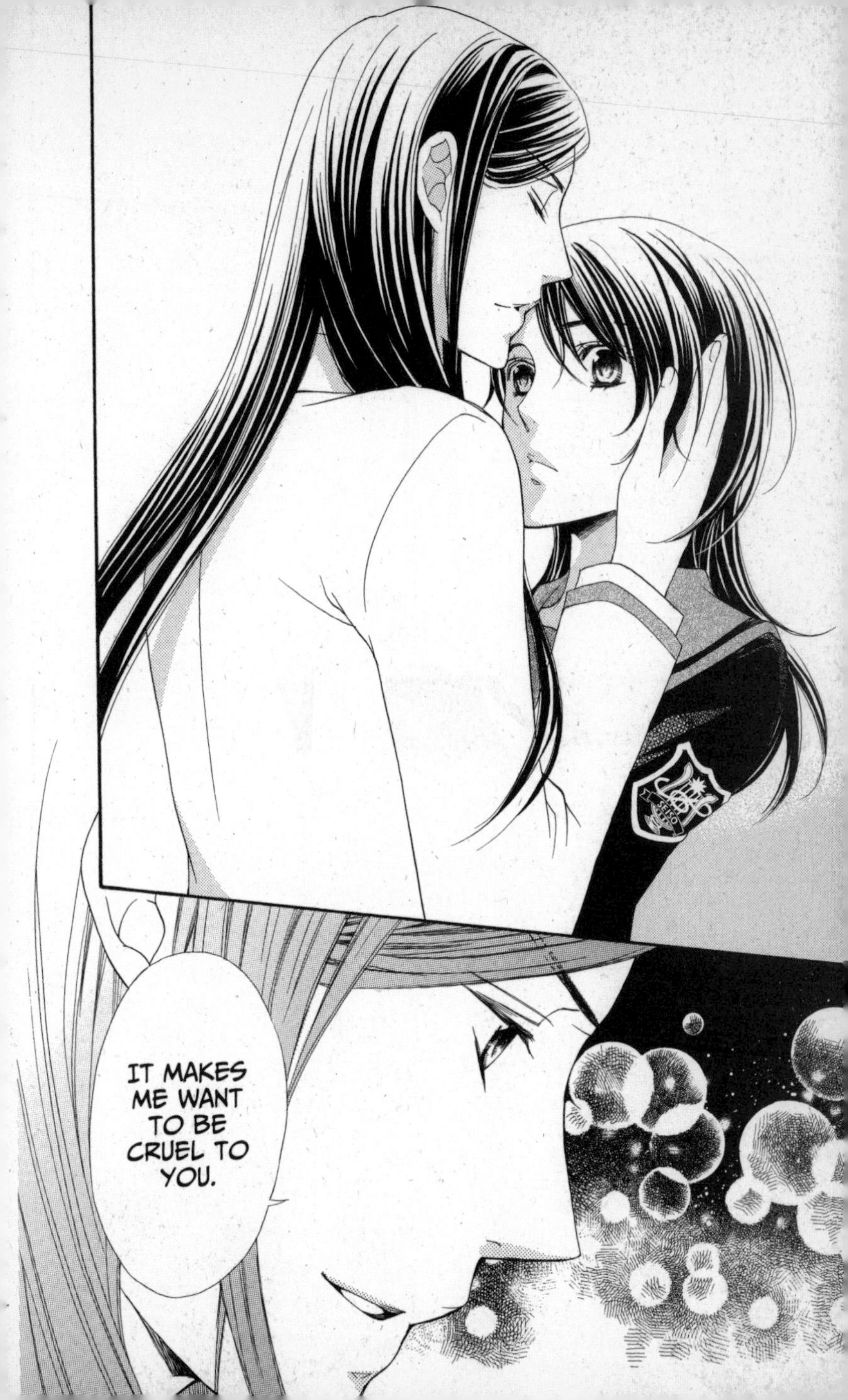
IT MAKES ME WANT TO BE CRUEL TO YOU.

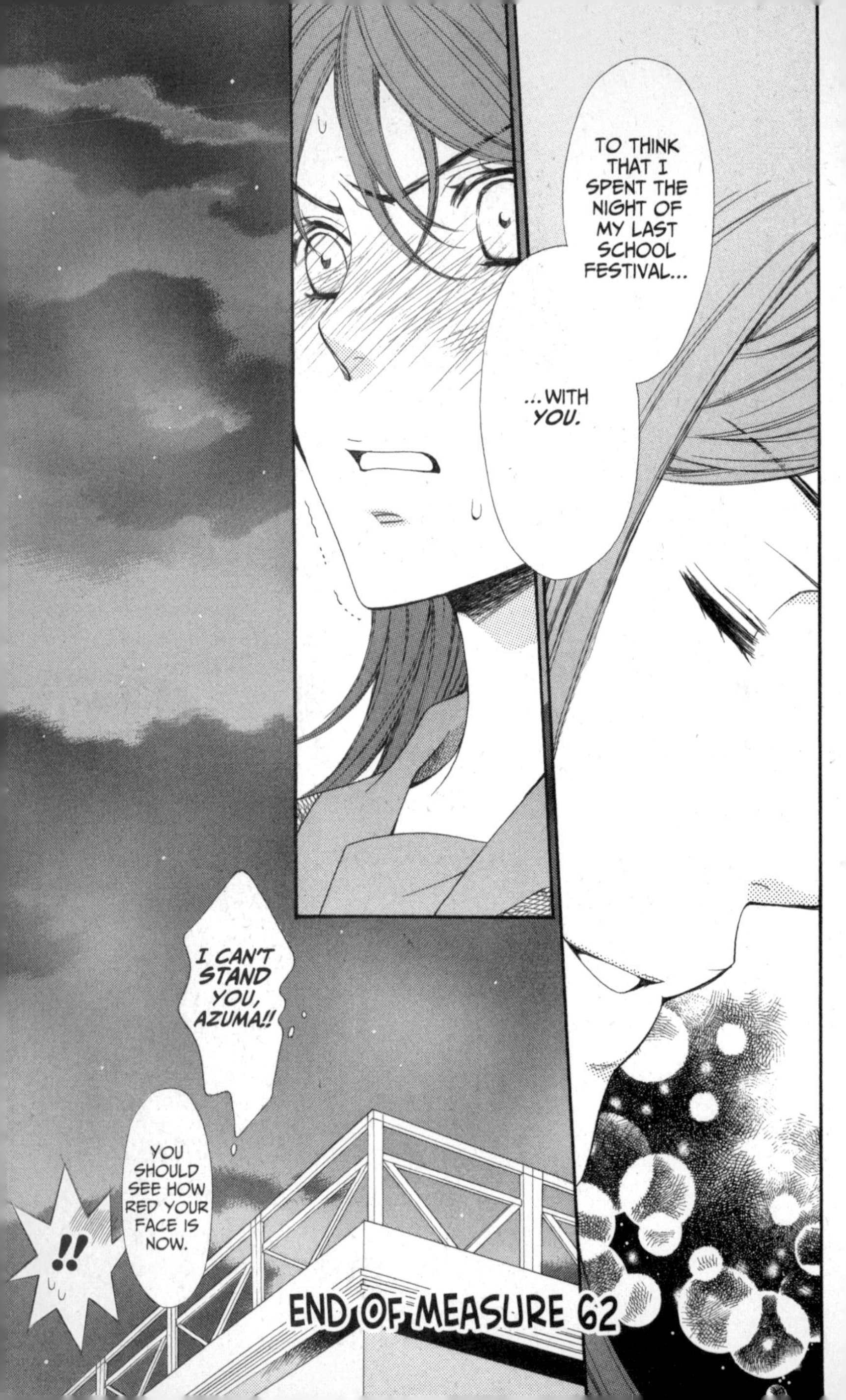
TO THINK THAT I SPENT THE NIGHT OF MY LAST SCHOOL FESTIVAL...
...WITH YOU.
I CAN'T STAND YOU, AZUMA!!
YOU SHOULD SEE HOW RED YOUR FACE IS NOW.
!!
END OF MEASURE 62

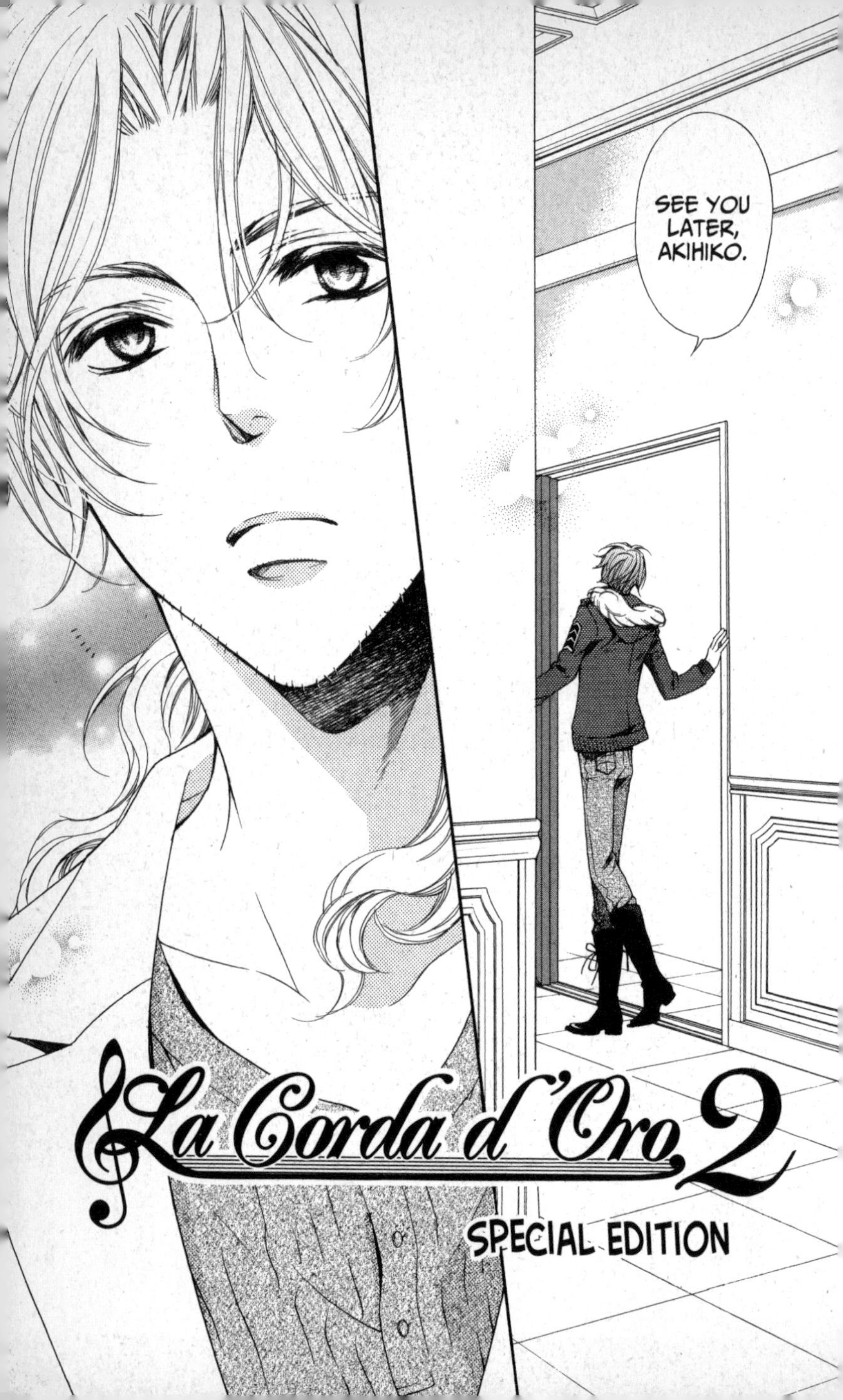
SEE YOU LATER, AKIHIKO.
La Corda d'Oro 2
SPECIAL EDITION

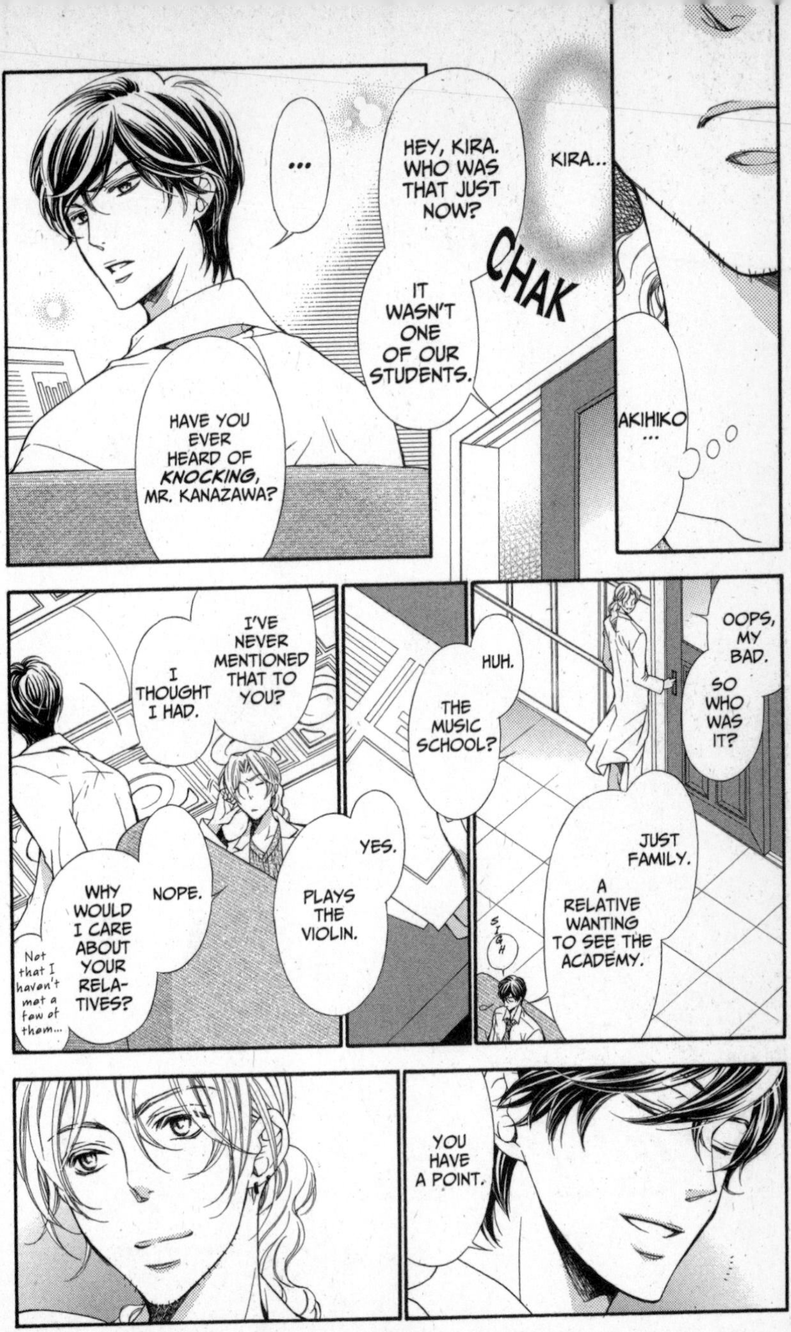
KIRA...
AKIHIKO...
HEY, KIRA. WHO WAS THAT JUST NOW?
CHAK
IT WASN'T ONE OF OUR STUDENTS.
...
HAVE YOU EVER HEARD OF *KNOCKING*, MR. KANAZAWA?
OOPS, MY BAD.
SO WHO WAS IT?
JUST FAMILY.
A RELATIVE WANTING TO SEE THE ACADEMY.
SIGH
HUH.
THE MUSIC SCHOOL?
YES.
PLAYS THE VIOLIN.
I'VE NEVER MENTIONED THAT TO YOU?
I THOUGHT I HAD.
NOPE.
WHY WOULD I CARE ABOUT YOUR RELATIVES?
Not that I haven't met a few of them...
YOU HAVE A POINT.

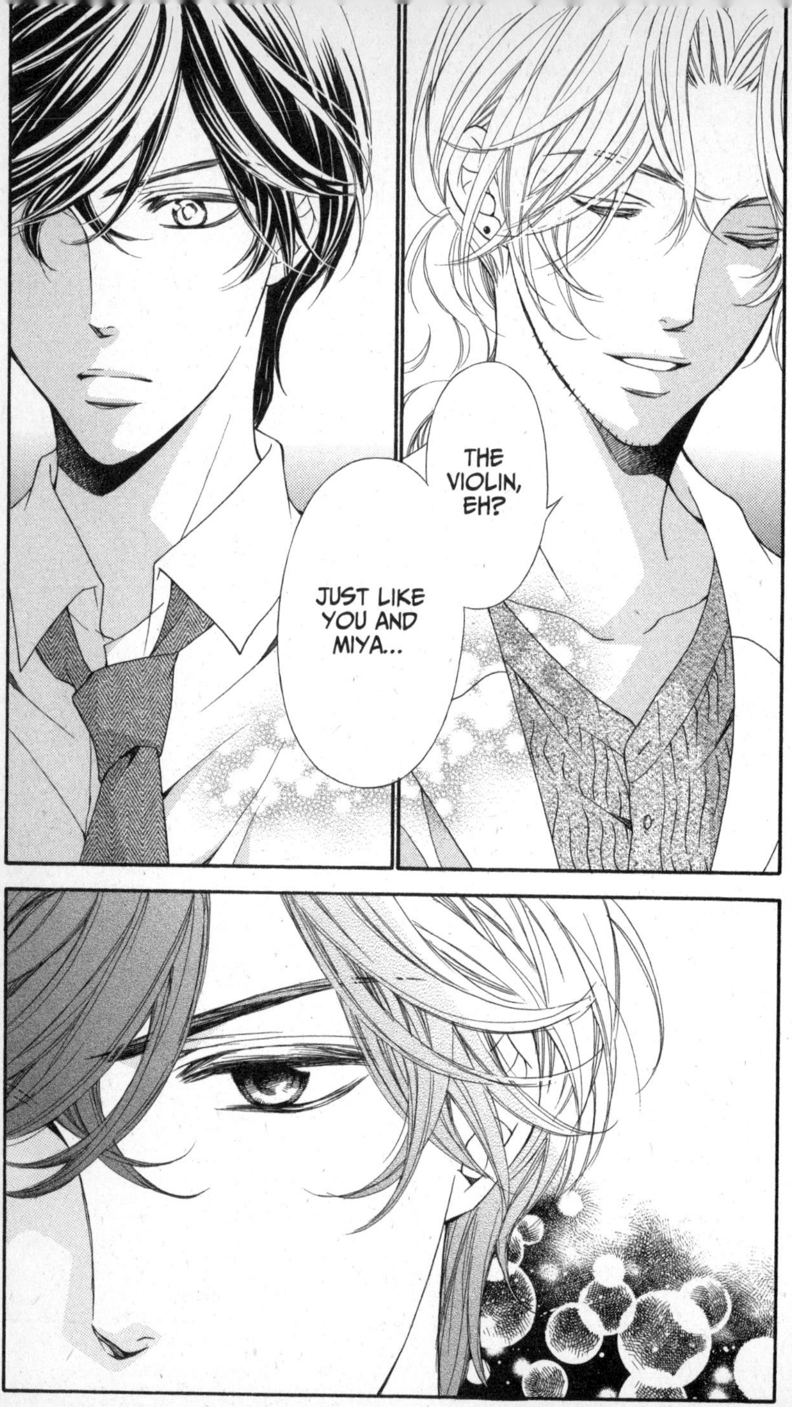
THE VIOLIN, EH?
JUST LIKE YOU AND MIYA...

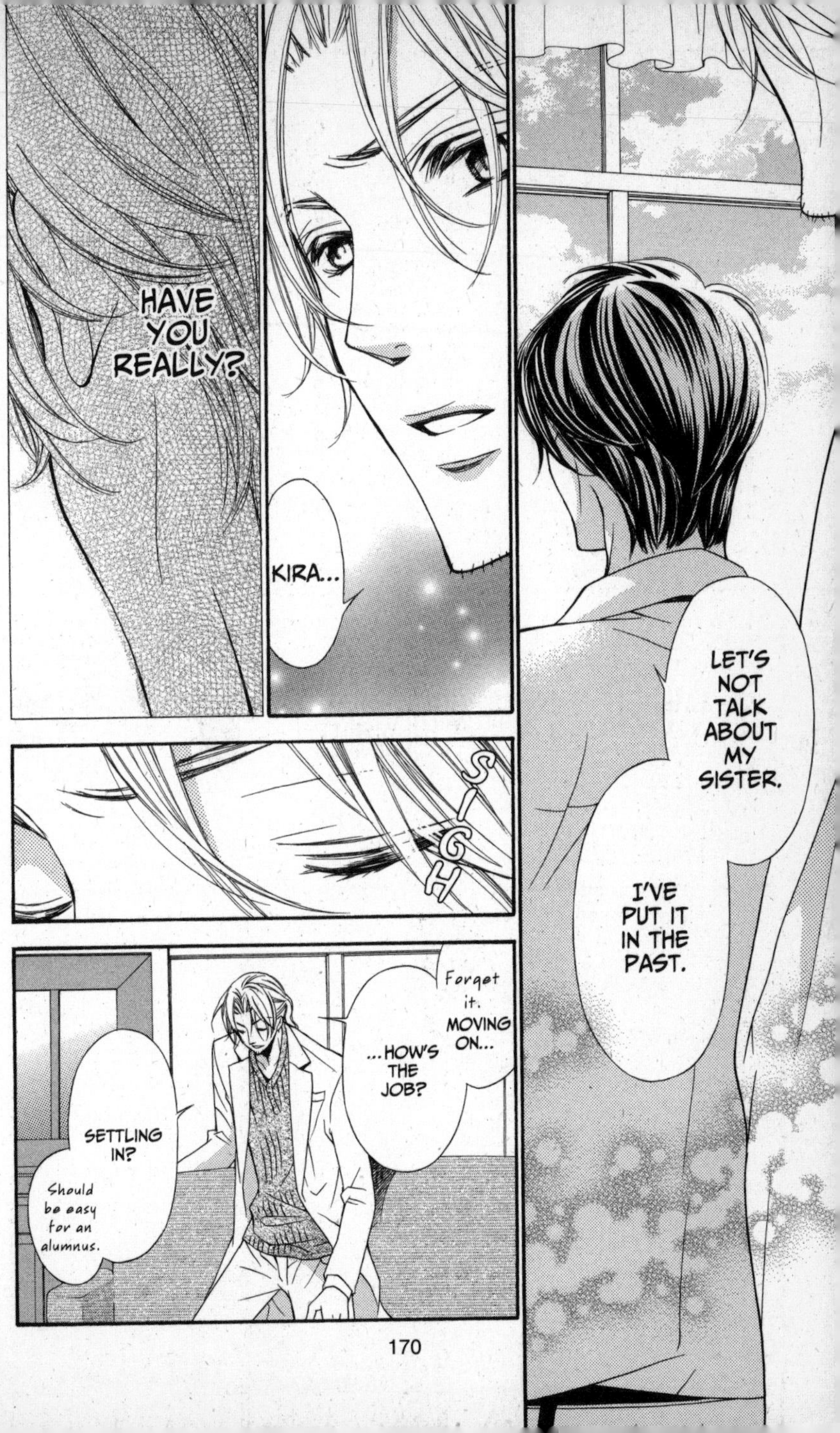
LET'S NOT TALK ABOUT MY SISTER.
I'VE PUT IT IN THE PAST.
KIRA...
HAVE YOU REALLY?
SIGH
Forget it. MOVING ON...
...HOW'S THE JOB?
SETTLING IN?
Should be easy for an alumnus.

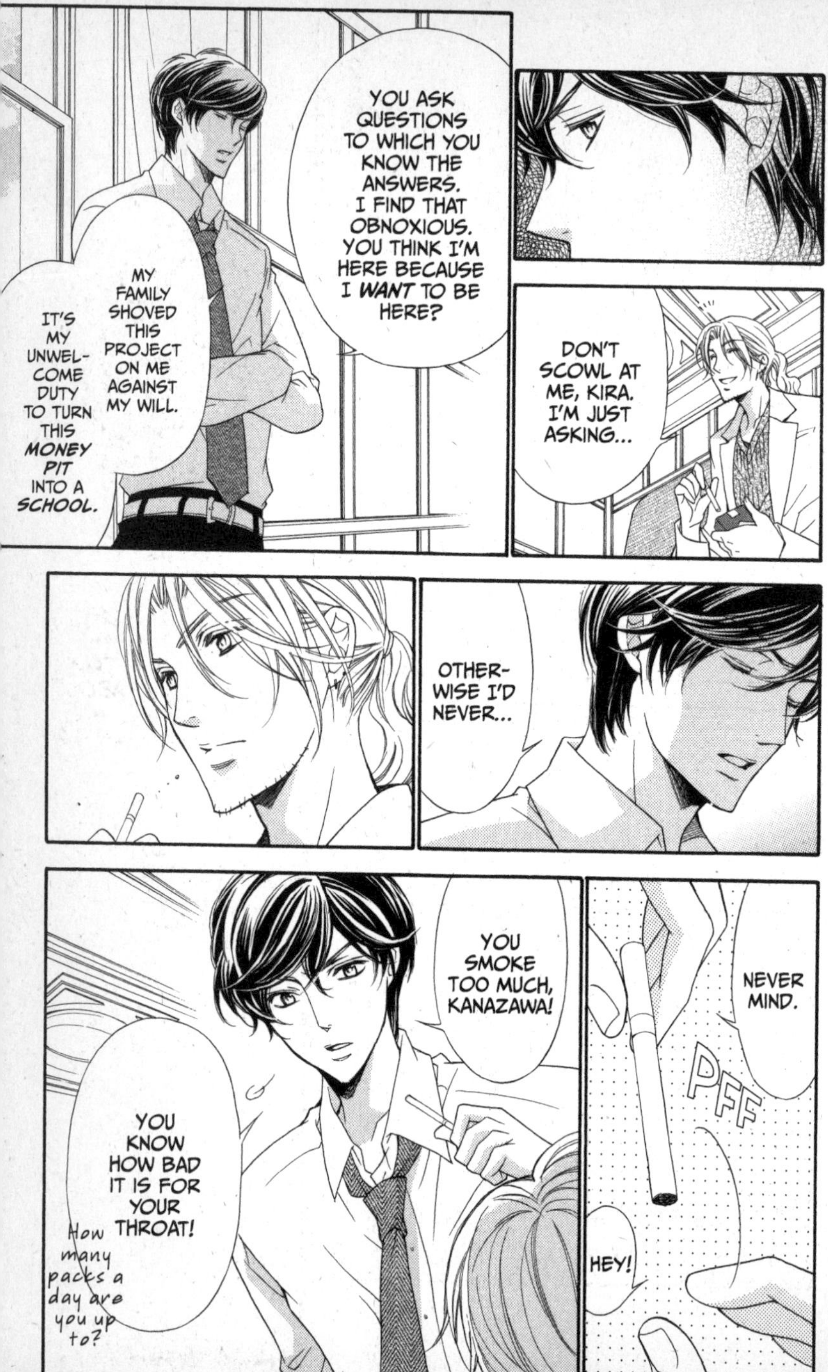
DON'T SCOWL AT ME, KIRA. I'M JUST ASKING...
YOU ASK QUESTIONS TO WHICH YOU KNOW THE ANSWERS. I FIND THAT OBNOXIOUS. YOU THINK I'M HERE BECAUSE I *WANT* TO BE HERE?
MY FAMILY SHOVED THIS PROJECT ON ME AGAINST MY WILL.
IT'S MY UNWELCOME DUTY TO TURN THIS **MONEY PIT** INTO A **SCHOOL**.
OTHERWISE I'D NEVER...
NEVER MIND.
PFF
HEY!
YOU SMOKE TOO MUCH, KANAZAWA!
YOU KNOW HOW BAD IT IS FOR YOUR THROAT!
How many packs a day are you up to?

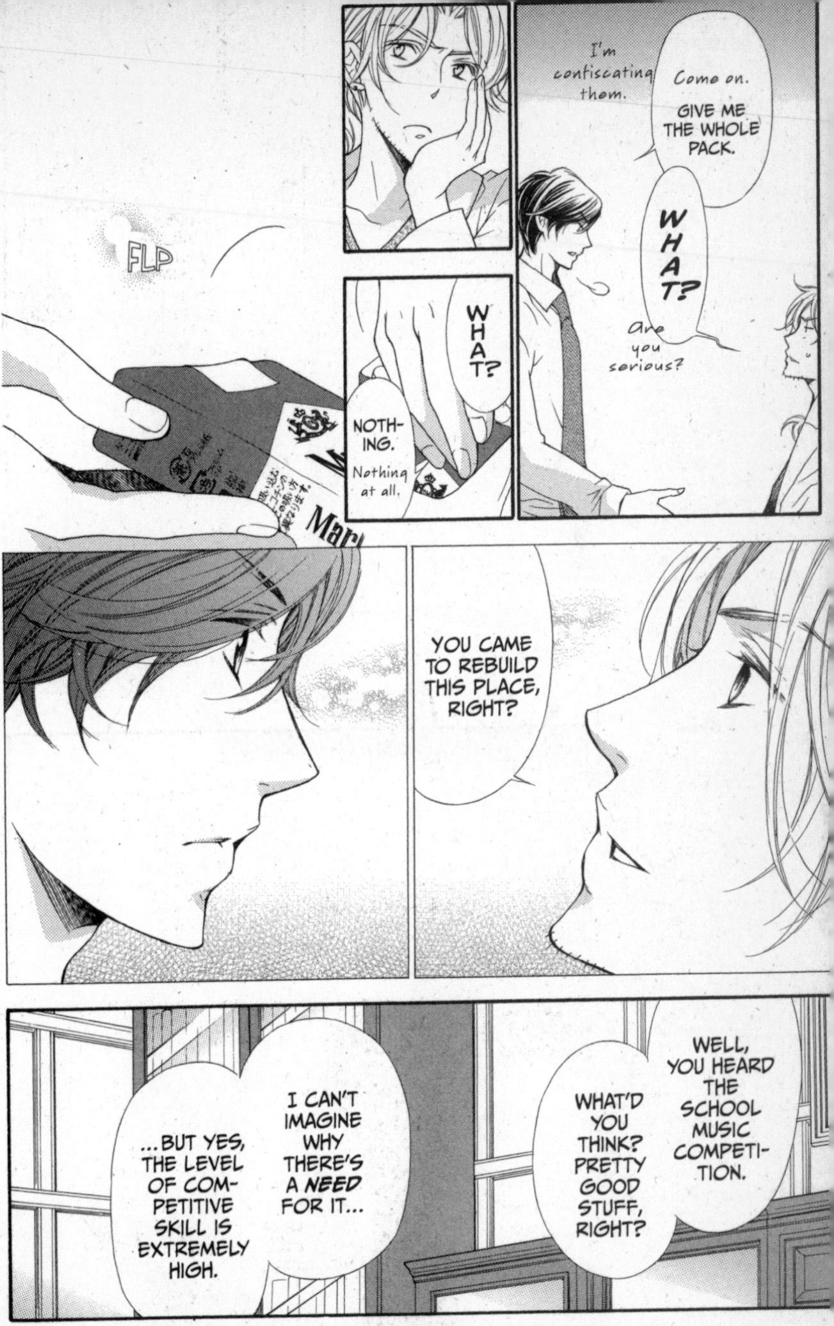
Come on. GIVE ME THE WHOLE PACK.
I'm confiscating them.
WHAT?
Are you serious?
WHAT?
NOTHING.
Nothing at all.
FLP
YOU CAME TO REBUILD THIS PLACE, RIGHT?
WELL, YOU HEARD THE SCHOOL MUSIC COMPETITION.
WHAT'D YOU THINK? PRETTY GOOD STUFF, RIGHT?
I CAN'T IMAGINE WHY THERE'S A ***NEED*** FOR IT...
...BUT YES, THE LEVEL OF COMPETITIVE SKILL IS EXTREMELY HIGH.

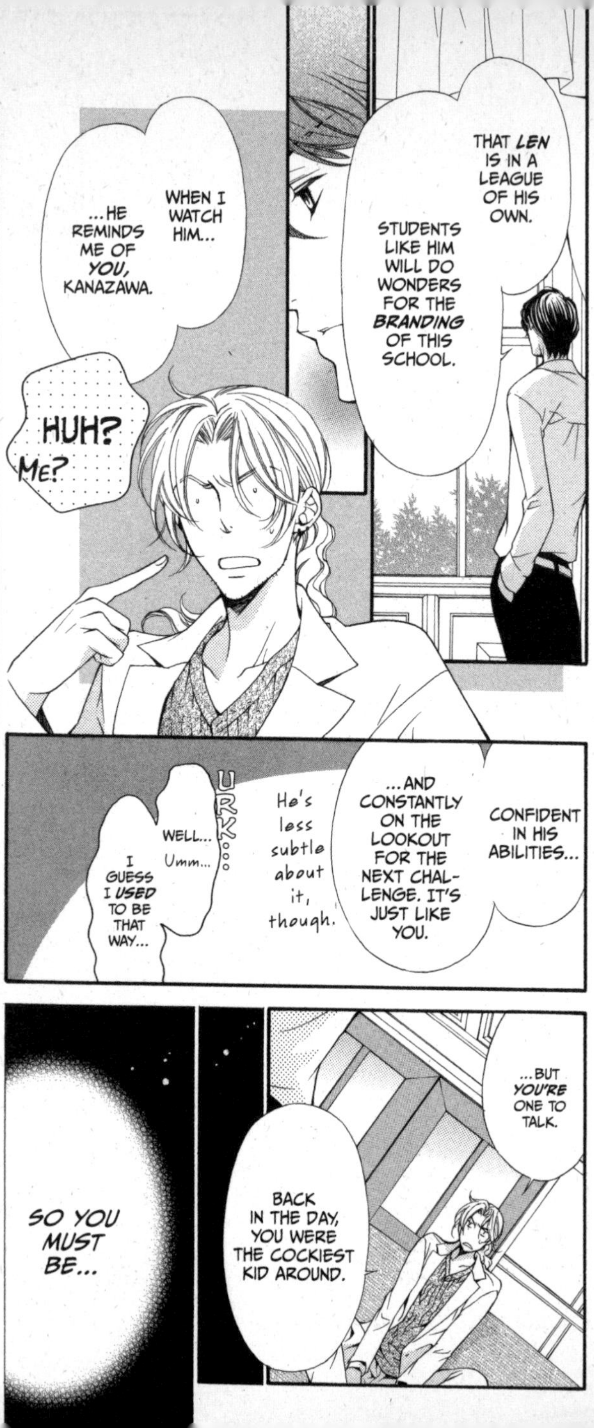
THAT *LEN* IS IN A LEAGUE OF HIS OWN.
STUDENTS LIKE HIM WILL DO WONDERS FOR THE *BRANDING* OF THIS SCHOOL.
WHEN I WATCH HIM...
...HE REMINDS ME OF *YOU*, KANAZAWA.
HUH? ME?
CONFIDENT IN HIS ABILITIES...
...AND CONSTANTLY ON THE LOOKOUT FOR THE NEXT CHAL-LENGE. IT'S JUST LIKE YOU.
He's less subtle about it, though.
URK...
WELL... Umm...
I GUESS I *USED* TO BE THAT WAY...
...BUT *YOU'RE* ONE TO TALK.
BACK IN THE DAY, YOU WERE THE COCKIEST KID AROUND.
SO YOU MUST BE...

Here's Shoko as a little girl. I have a feeling not much has changed about her.

This last story is a short piece about two of the adult characters. It was featured in *LaLa Special*. I think they were the oldest characters in the magazine by a long shot.

I'd always wanted to draw the young Kanazawa, so it was a lot of fun.

Young Shoko

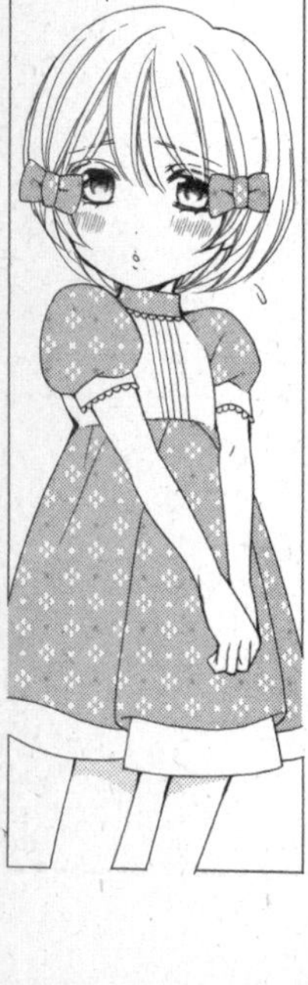

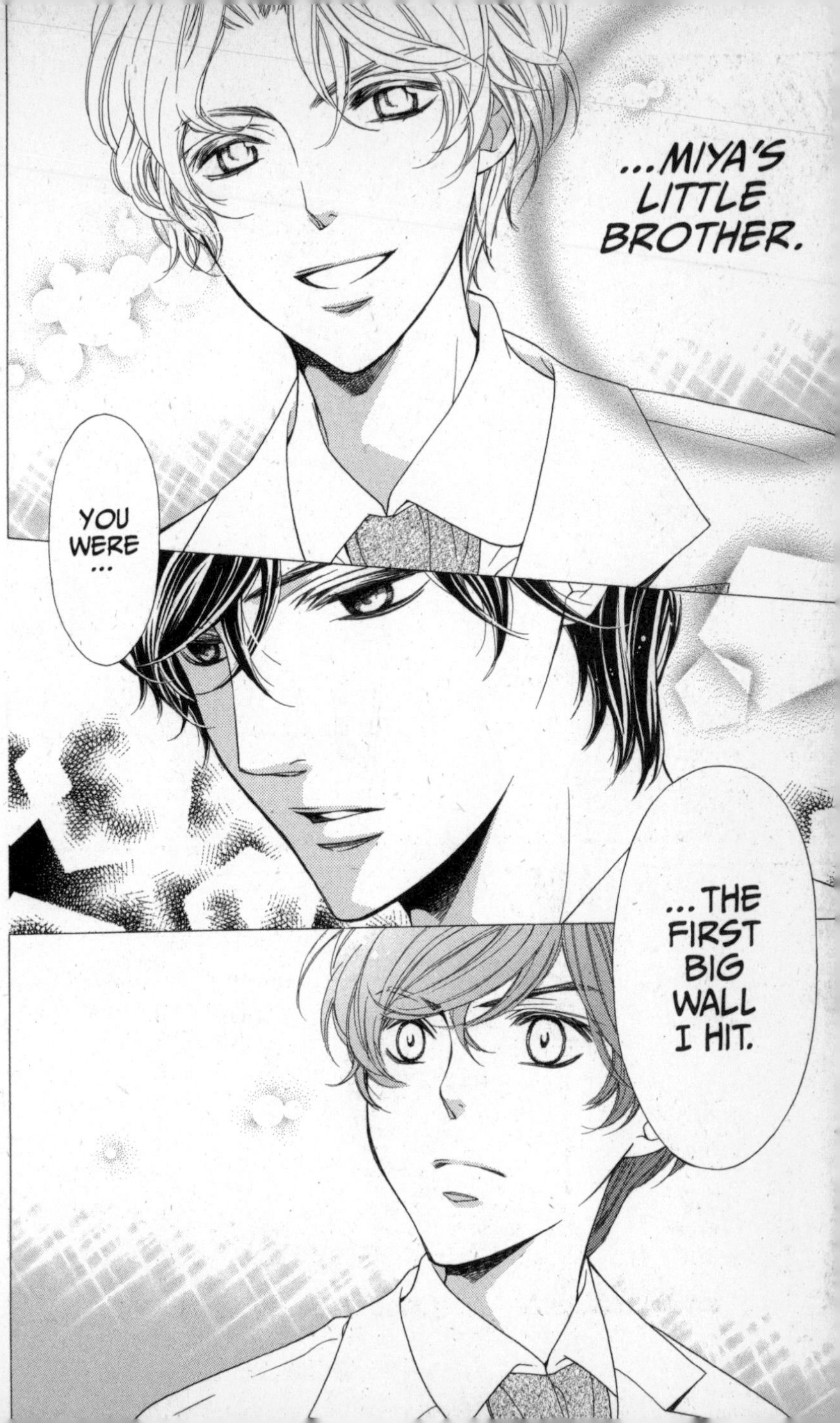
...MIYA'S LITTLE BROTHER.
YOU WERE ...
...THE FIRST BIG WALL I HIT.

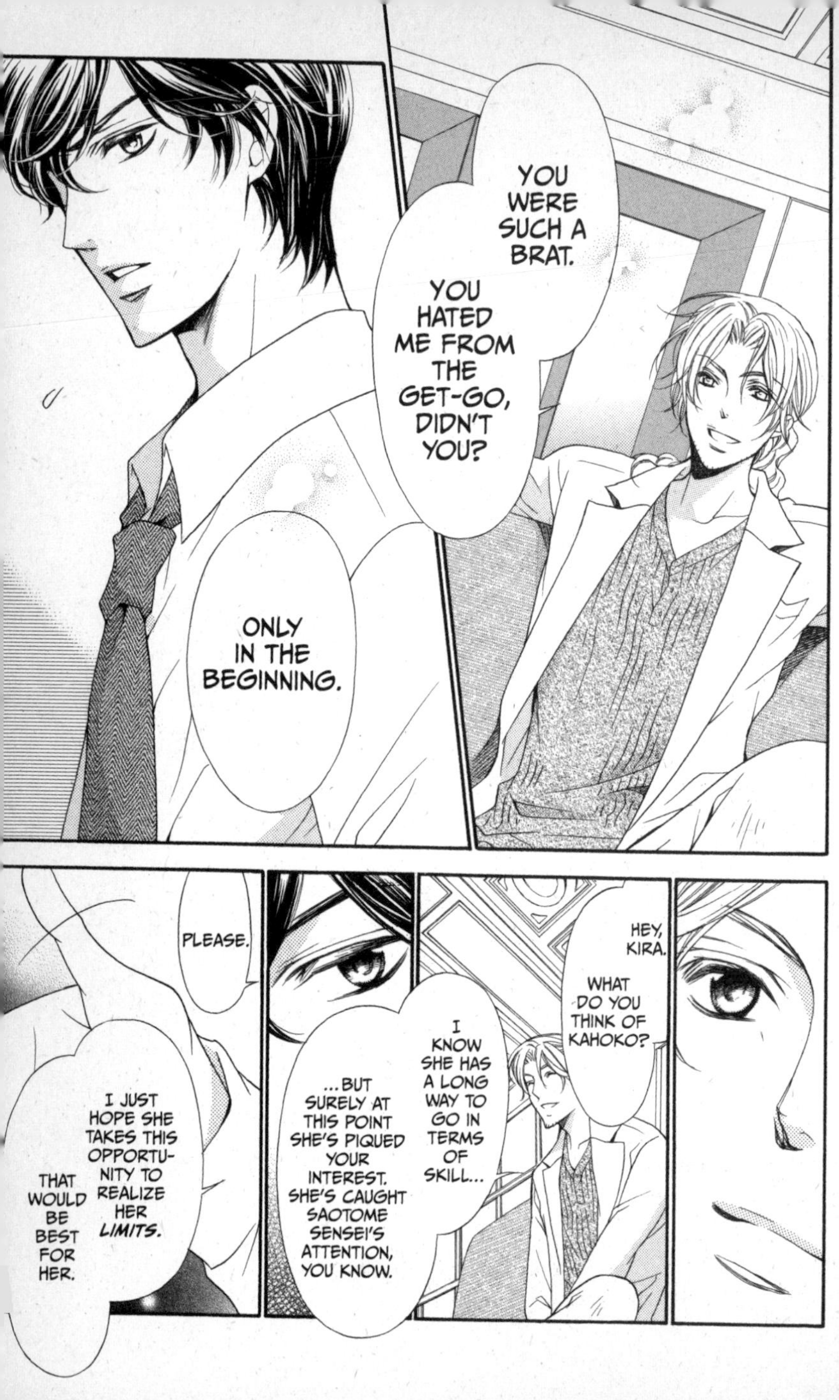
YOU WERE SUCH A BRAT.
YOU HATED ME FROM THE GET-GO, DIDN'T YOU?
ONLY IN THE BEGINNING.
HEY, KIRA.
WHAT DO YOU THINK OF KAHOKO?
I KNOW SHE HAS A LONG WAY TO GO IN TERMS OF SKILL...
...BUT SURELY AT THIS POINT SHE'S PIQUED YOUR INTEREST. SHE'S CAUGHT SAOTOME SENSEI'S ATTENTION, YOU KNOW.
PLEASE.
I JUST HOPE SHE TAKES THIS OPPORTUNITY TO REALIZE HER *LIMITS.*
THAT WOULD BE BEST FOR HER.

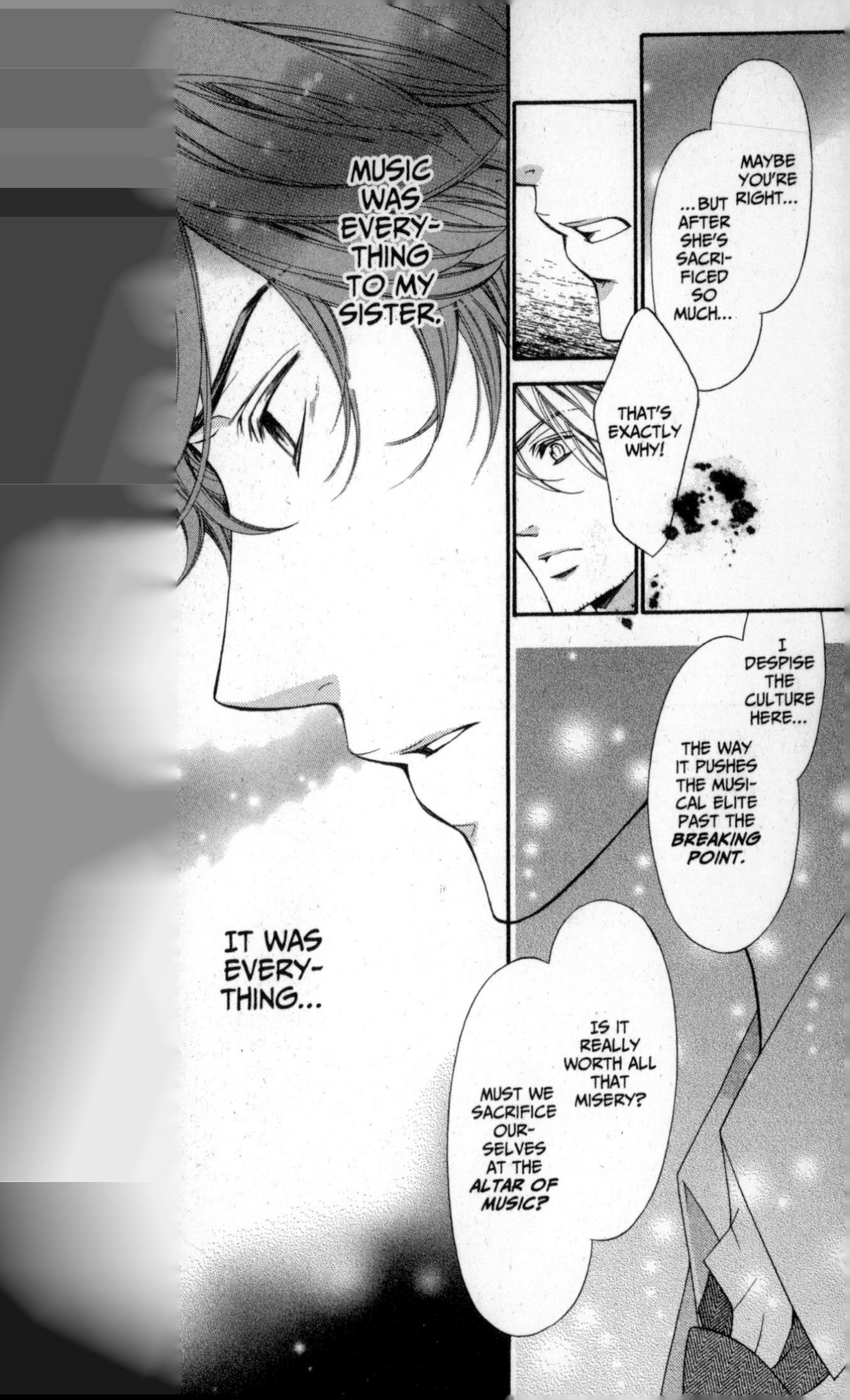

MAYBE YOU'RE RIGHT...
...BUT AFTER SHE'S SACRIFICED SO MUCH...
THAT'S EXACTLY WHY!
I DESPISE THE CULTURE HERE...
THE WAY IT PUSHES THE MUSICAL ELITE PAST THE ***BREAKING POINT.***
IS IT REALLY WORTH ALL THAT MISERY?
MUST WE SACRIFICE OURSELVES AT THE ***ALTAR OF MUSIC?***
MUSIC WAS EVERYTHING TO MY SISTER.
IT WAS EVERYTHING...

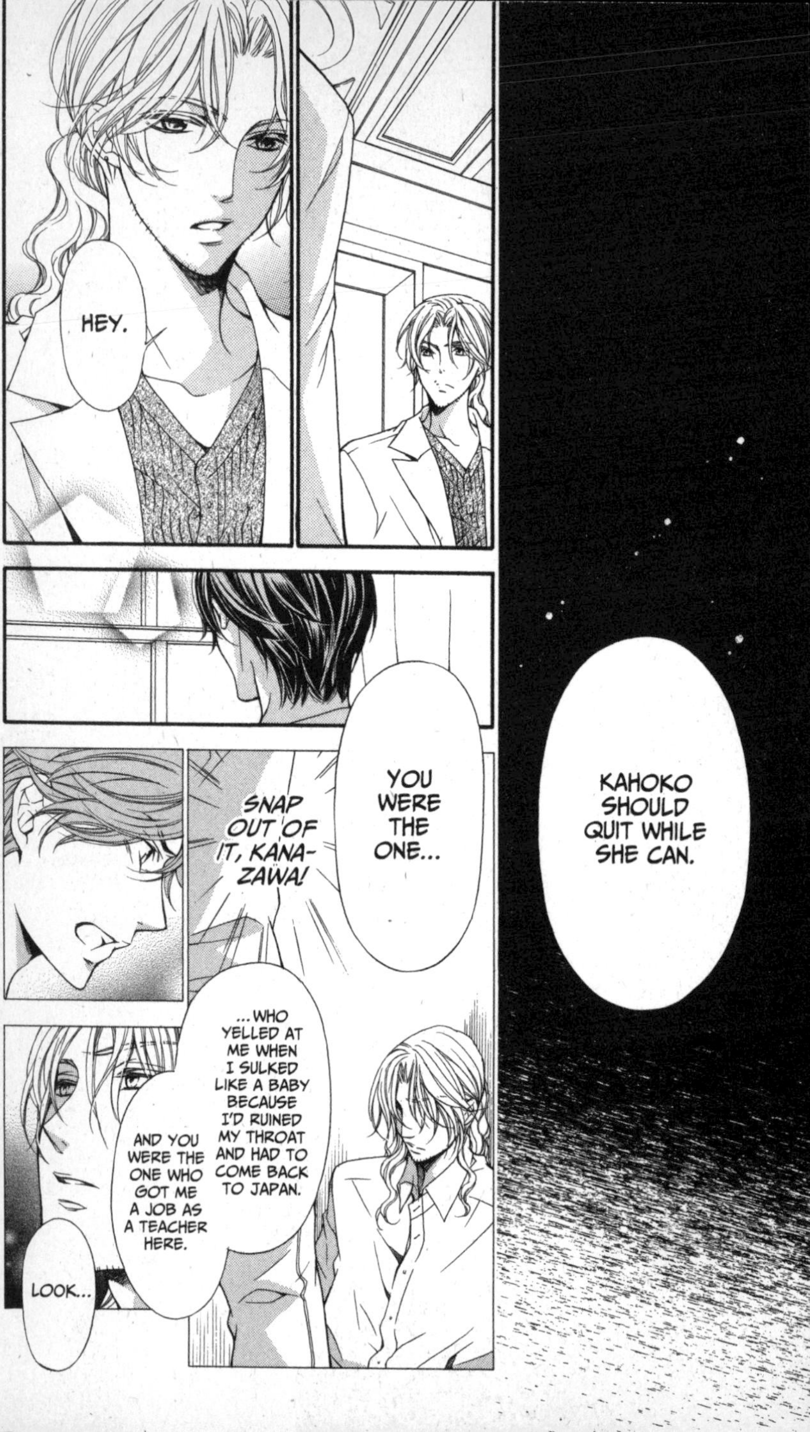
KAHOKO SHOULD QUIT WHILE SHE CAN.
HEY.
YOU WERE THE ONE...
SNAP OUT OF IT, KANA-ZAWA!
...WHO YELLED AT ME WHEN I SULKED LIKE A BABY BECAUSE I'D RUINED MY THROAT AND HAD TO COME BACK TO JAPAN.
AND YOU WERE THE ONE WHO GOT ME A JOB AS A TEACHER HERE.
LOOK...

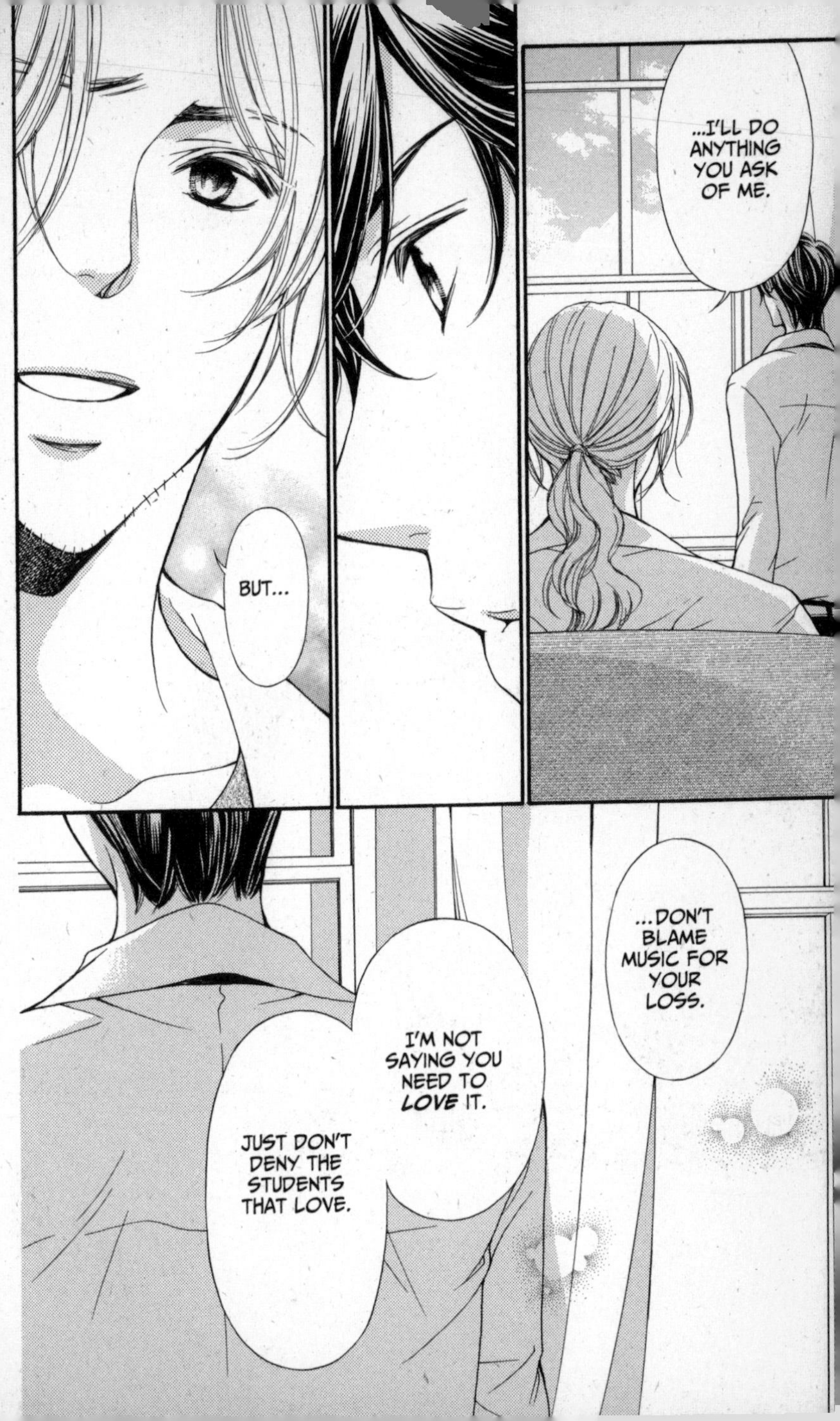
...I'LL DO ANYTHING YOU ASK OF ME.
BUT...
...DON'T BLAME MUSIC FOR YOUR LOSS.
I'M NOT SAYING YOU NEED TO *LOVE* IT.
JUST DON'T DENY THE STUDENTS THAT LOVE.

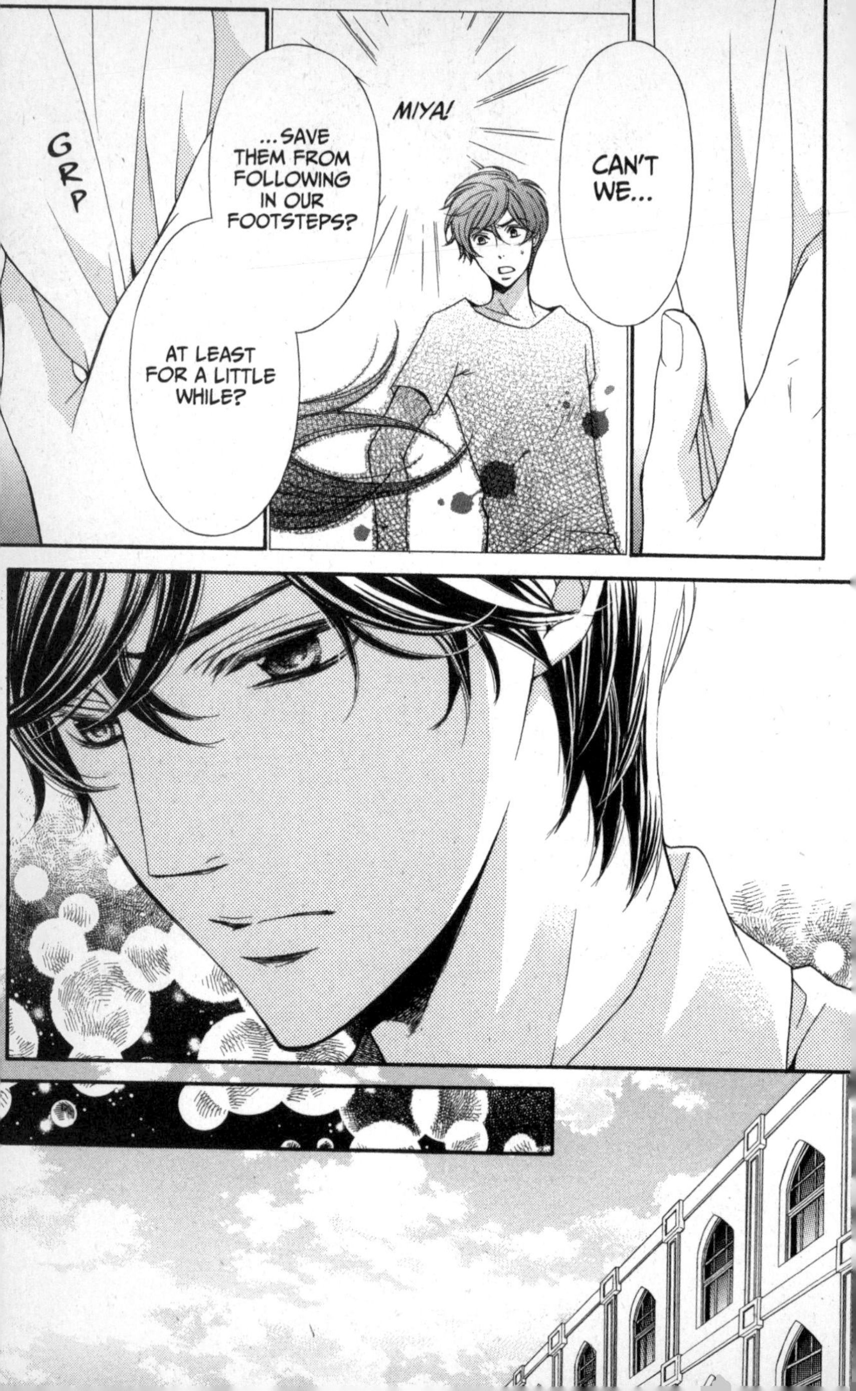
CAN'T WE...
...SAVE THEM FROM FOLLOWING IN OUR FOOTSTEPS?
AT LEAST FOR A LITTLE WHILE?
MIYA!
GRP

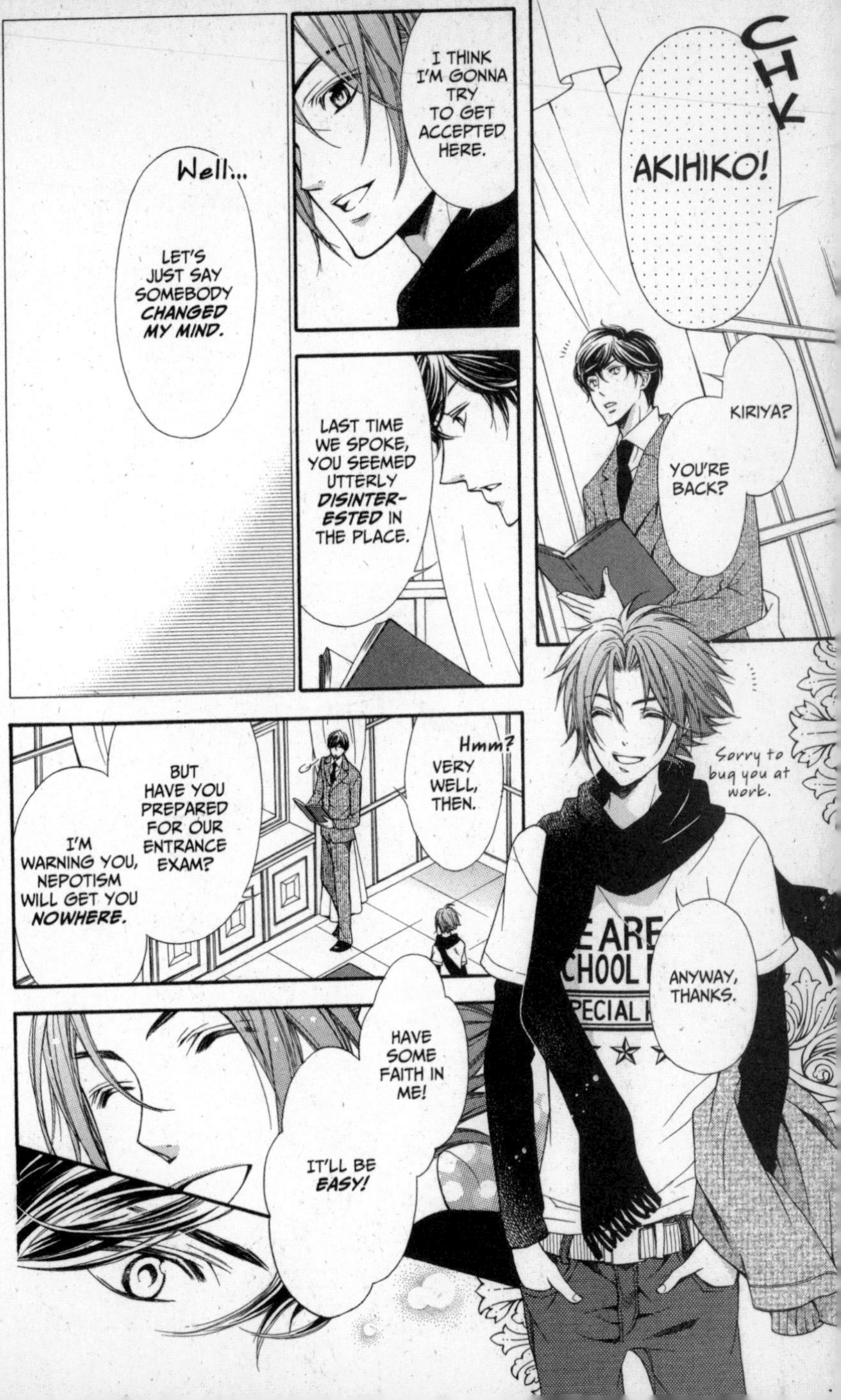
CHK
AKIHIKO!
KIRIYA?
YOU'RE BACK?
Sorry to bug you at work.
ANYWAY, THANKS.
I THINK I'M GONNA TRY TO GET ACCEPTED HERE.
LAST TIME WE SPOKE, YOU SEEMED UTTERLY DISINTER-ESTED IN THE PLACE.
Well...
LET'S JUST SAY SOMEBODY CHANGED MY MIND.
Hmm?
VERY WELL, THEN.
BUT HAVE YOU PREPARED FOR OUR ENTRANCE EXAM?
I'M WARNING YOU, NEPOTISM WILL GET YOU NOWHERE.
HAVE SOME FAITH IN ME!
IT'LL BE EASY!

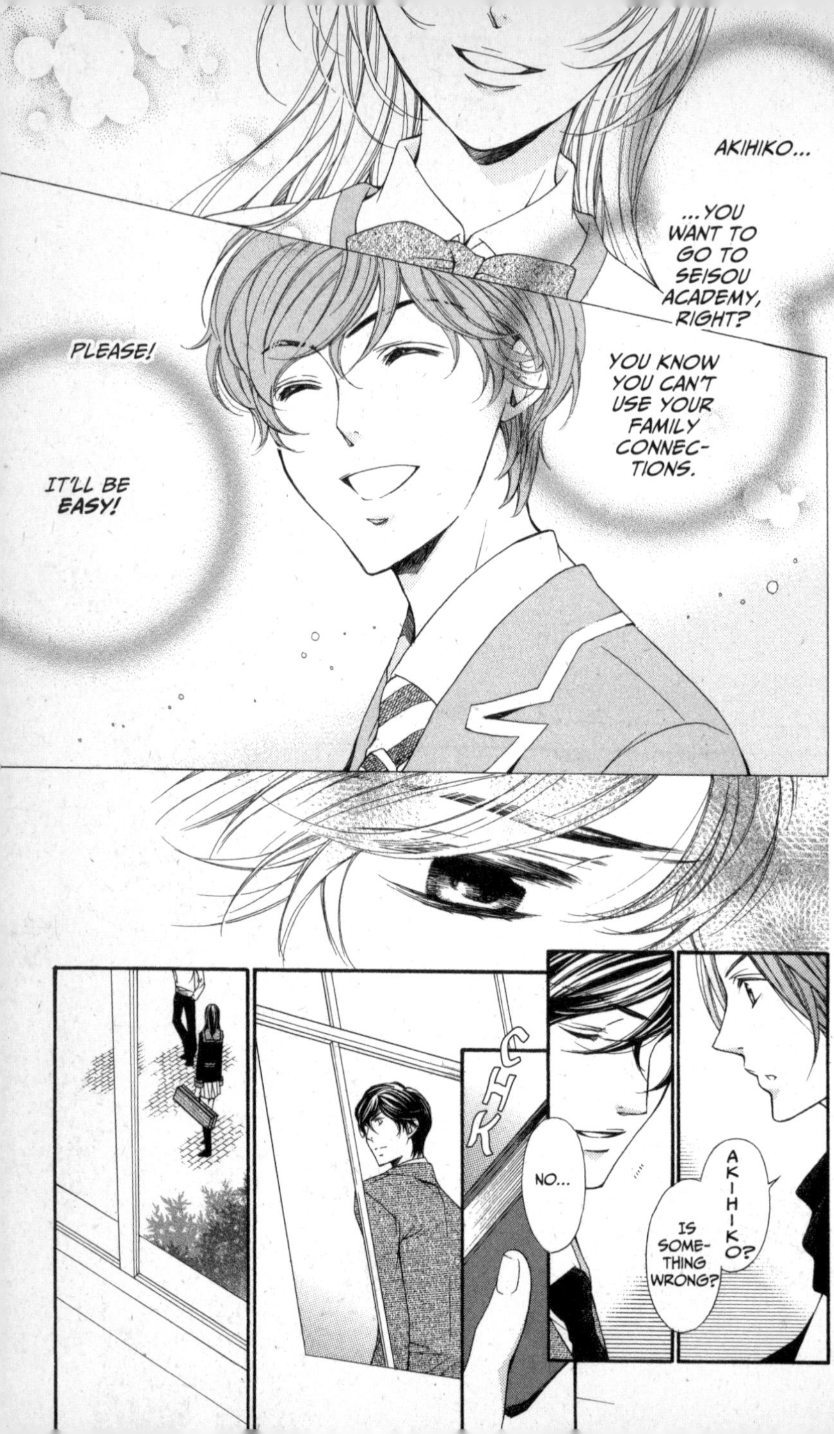
AKIHIKO...
...YOU WANT TO GO TO SEISOU ACADEMY, RIGHT?
YOU KNOW YOU CAN'T USE YOUR FAMILY CONNEC-TIONS.
PLEASE!
IT'LL BE EASY!
AKIHIKO?
IS SOME-THING WRONG?
NO...
CHK

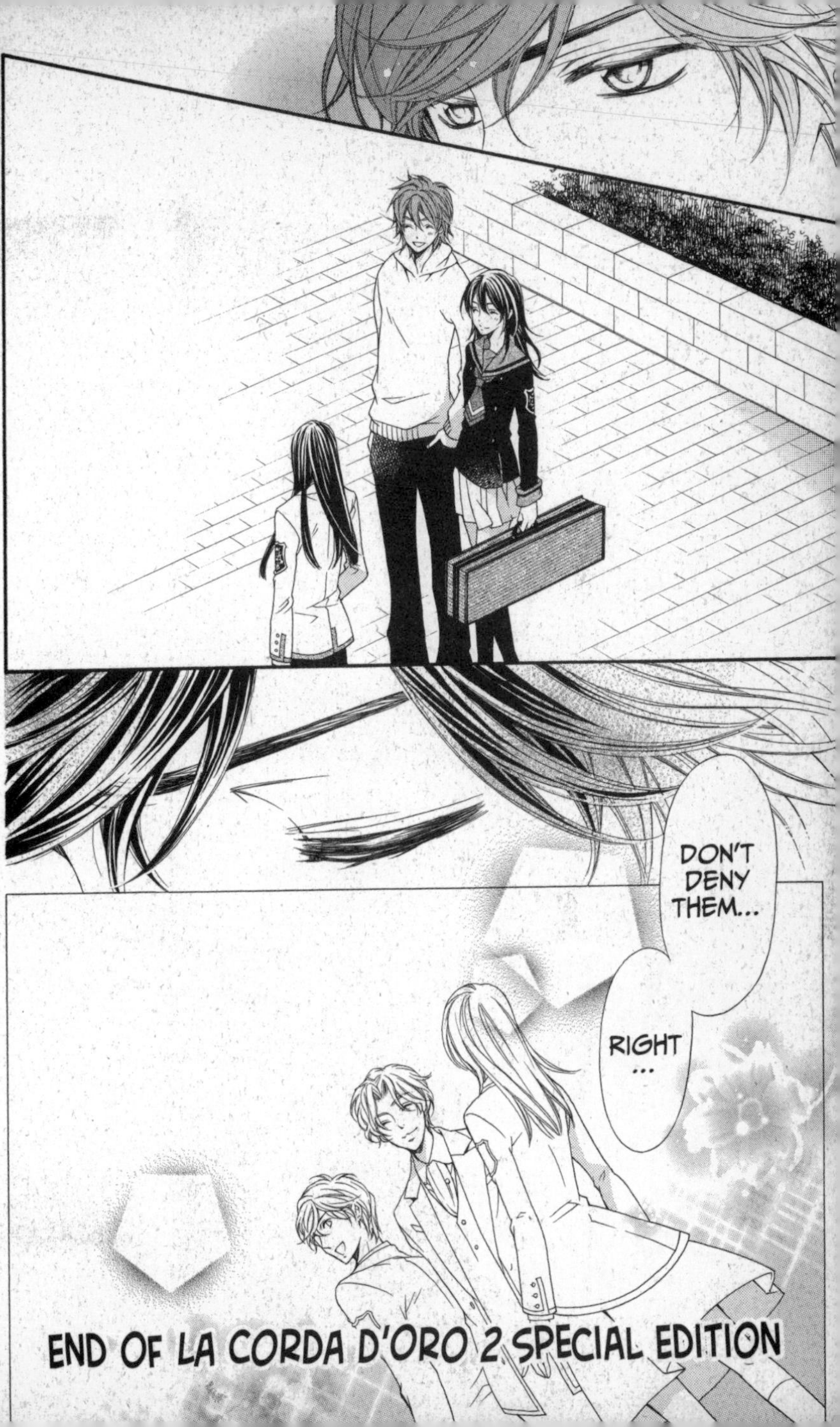
DON'T DENY THEM...
RIGHT ...
END OF LA CORDA D'ORO 2 SPECIAL EDITION

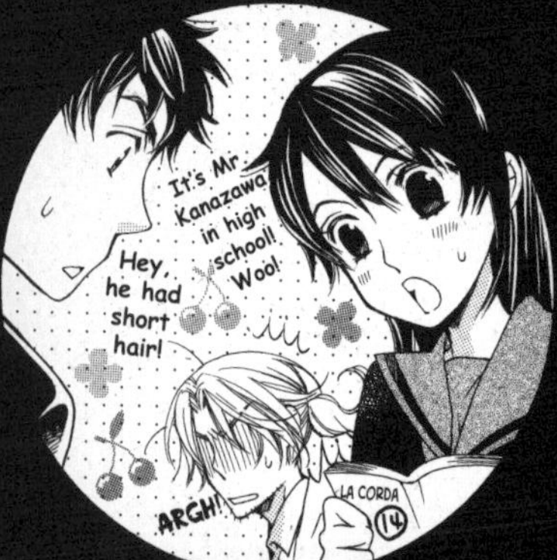

It's Mr. Kanazawa in high school! Wo!
Hey, he had short hair!
ARGH!
LA CORDA 14

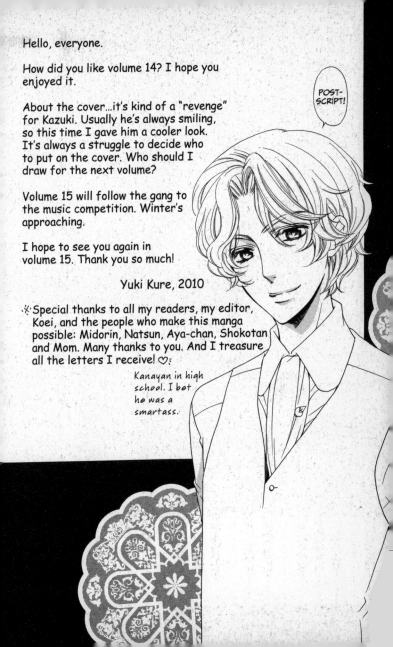

Hello, everyone.

How did you like volume 14? I hope you enjoyed it.

About the cover...it's kind of a "revenge" for Kazuki. Usually he's always smiling, so this time I gave him a cooler look. It's always a struggle to decide who to put on the cover. Who should I draw for the next volume?

Volume 15 will follow the gang to the music competition. Winter's approaching.

I hope to see you again in volume 15. Thank you so much!

Yuki Kure, 2010

❊Special thanks to all my readers, my editor, Koei, and the people who make this manga possible: Midorin, Natsun, Aya-chan, Shokotan and Mom. Many thanks to you. And I treasure all the letters I receive! ♡

POST-SCRIPT!

Kanayan in high school. I bet he was a smartass.

SPECIAL THANKS

M.Shiino
N.Sato
A.Kashima
S.Asahina
C.Nanai
M.Morinaga

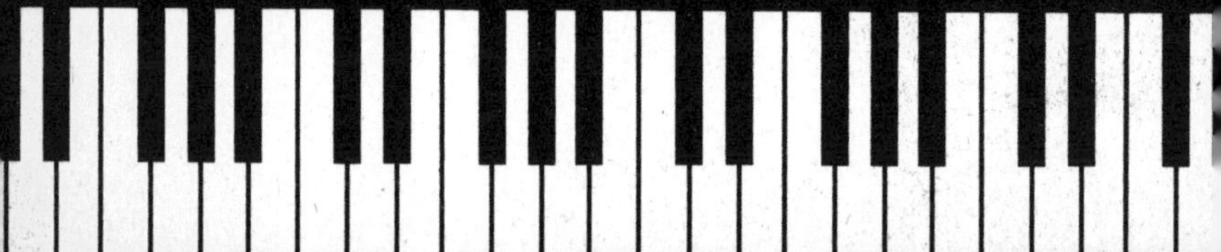

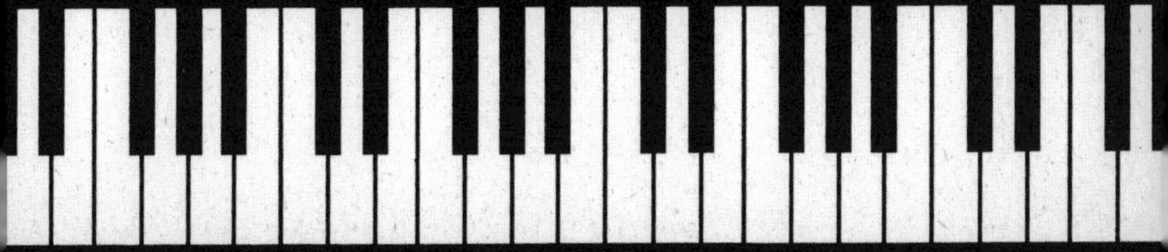

La Corda d'Oro End Notes

You can appreciate music just by listening to it, but knowing the story behind a piece can help enhance your enjoyment. In that spirit, here is background information about some of the topics mentioned in *La Corda d'Oro*. Enjoy!

Page 94, panel 5: *Romeo and Juliet*
Sergei Prokofiev's ballet *Romeo and Juliet*, based on Shakespeare's play, is one of the world's most beloved ballets. At the time it was written, however, it was considered shocking for its *avant garde* style and extremely challenging choreography. Prokofiev struggled for years to bring it to the stage, inspiring ballerina Galina Ulanova, who played Juliet, to comment, "Never was a story of more woe than this of Prokofiev and his Romeo."

Page 95, panel 3: "Montagues and Capulets"
This piece, also known as the "Dance of the Knights," is from Act I, Scene 2 of Prokofiev's *Romeo and Juliet*. The dark, plodding theme is perhaps the best-known piece of music from the ballet and can often be heard in film and TV soundtracks.

Page 122, panel 2: takoyaki
A popular snack food, *takoyaki* are fried dough balls with chunks of octopus, topped with sauce, dried bonito flakes, green seaweed powder and mayonnaise.

Page 143, panel 2: *Scherzo Tarantella*
Henryk Wieniawski's *Scherzo Tarantella* is a fast, technically challenging piece based on a traditional Italian folk dance. In volume 5, Len was prevented from playing *Scherzo Tarantella* in the Second Selection when jealous classmates locked him in a closet, forcing him to miss the performance.

Page 146, panel 2: *Ave Maria*
Although there are many compositions by this name, the piece referred to here is Franz Schubert's *Ellens dritter Gesang*, often called *Ave Maria* because the accompanying chorus opens with those words.

Page 173: *LaLa Special*
LaLa is the magazine in which *La Corda d'Oro* runs in Japan. *LaLa Special* is a supplemental magazine featuring side stories and one-shots by the *LaLa* artists.

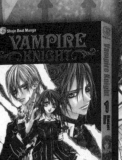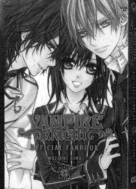

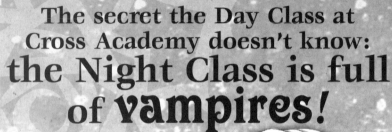
The secret the Day Class at Cross Academy doesn't know: **the Night Class is full of vampires!**

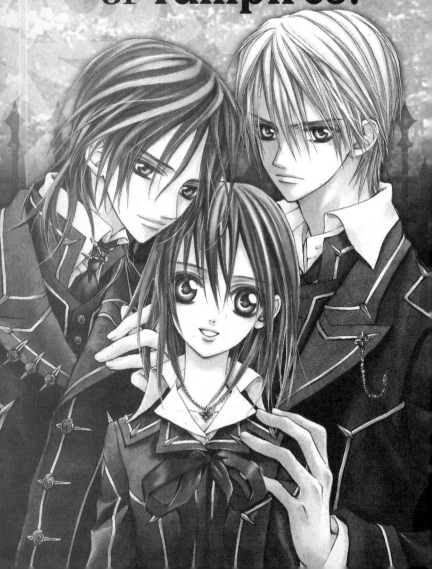

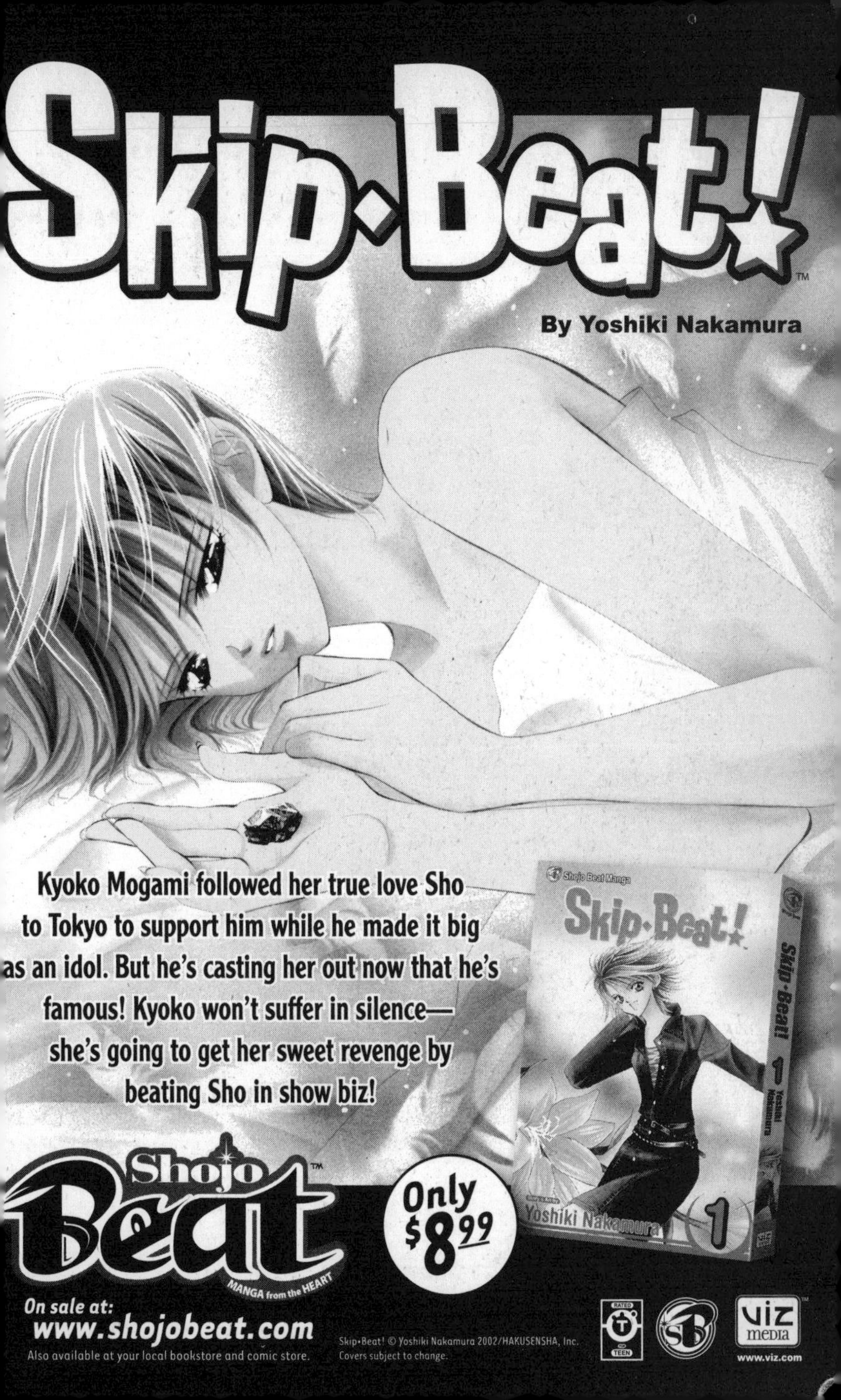
Skip·Beat!
™
By Yoshiki Nakamura
Kyoko Mogami followed her true love Sho to Tokyo to support him while he made it big as an idol. But he's casting her out now that he's famous! Kyoko won't suffer in silence— she's going to get her sweet revenge by beating Sho in show biz!
Shojo Beat Manga
Skip·Beat!
Yoshiki Nakamura
1
Shojo Beat ™
MANGA from the HEART
Only $8.99
On sale at:
www.shojobeat.com
Also available at your local bookstore and comic store.
Skip·Beat! © Yoshiki Nakamura 2002/HAKUSENSHA, Inc.
Covers subject to change.
RATED T TEEN
viz media
www.viz.com

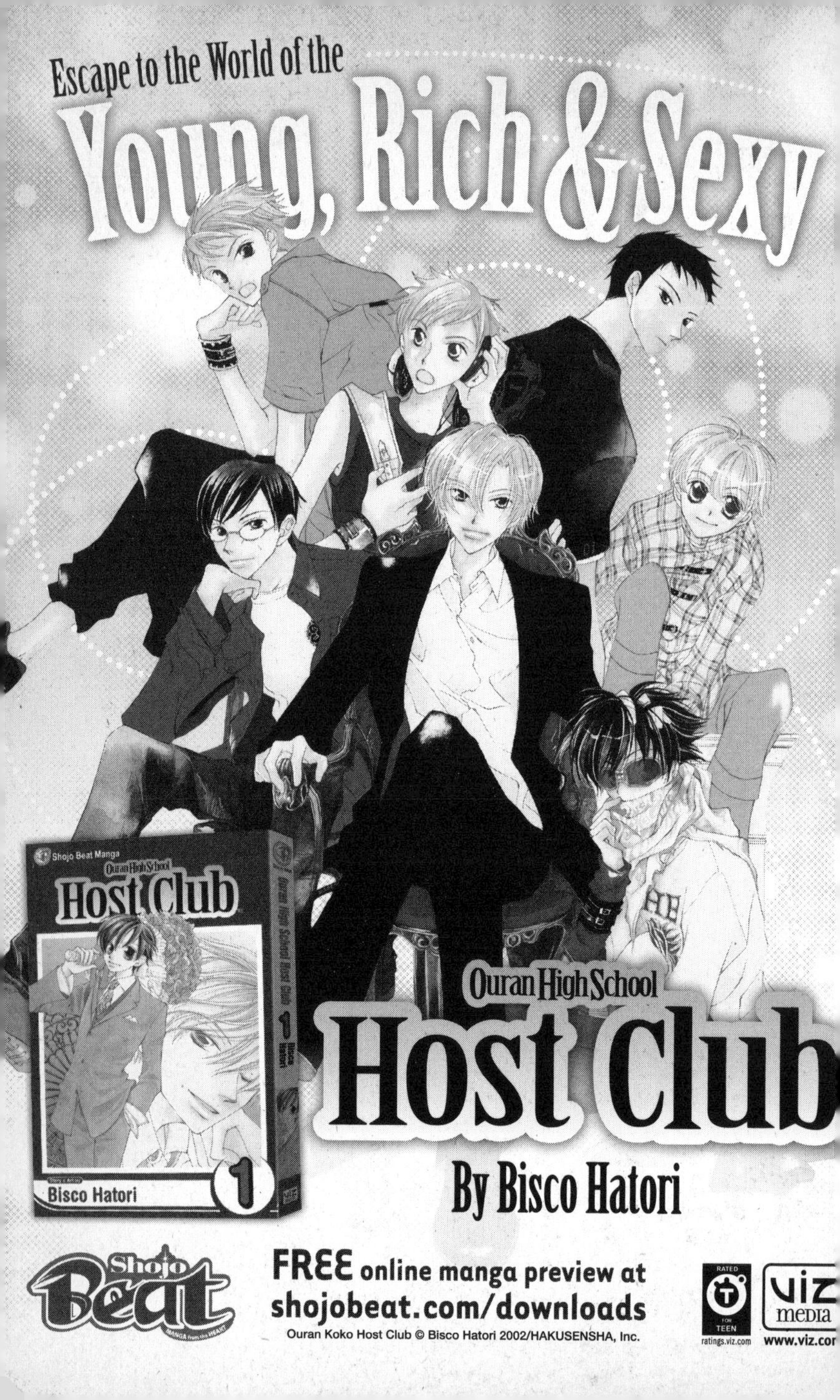
Escape to the World of the
Young, Rich & Sexy
Shojo Beat Manga
Ouran High School
Host Club
Bisco Hatori
1
Ouran High School
Host Club
By Bisco Hatori
Shojo Beat
FREE online manga preview at
shojobeat.com/downloads
Ouran Koko Host Club © Bisco Hatori 2002/HAKUSENSHA, Inc.
RATED T FOR TEEN
ratings.viz.com
VIZ media
www.viz.co

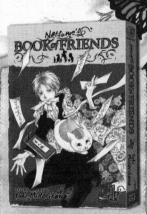